Love's Peril
CHERYL HOLT

Copyright © 2013 Cheryl Holt

All rights reserved. No part of this book may be reproduced or transmitted in any form or by any electronic or mechanical means, including photocopying, recording or by any information storage and retrieval system, without the written permission of the publisher, except where permitted by law.

Cover design by Angela Waters
Interior format by The Killion Group

Praise for New York Times Bestselling Author CHERYL HOLT

"Best storyteller of the year..."
Romantic Times Magazine

"A master writer..."
Fallen Angel Reviews

"The Queen of Erotic Romance..."
Book Cover Reviews

"Cheryl Holt is magnificent..."
Reader to Reader Reviews

"From cover to cover, I was spellbound. Truly outstanding..."
Romance Junkies

"A classic love story with hot, fiery passion dripping from every page. There's nothing better than curling up with a great book and this one totally qualifies."
Fresh Fiction

"This is a masterpiece of storytelling. A sensual delight scattered with rose petals that are divinely arousing. Oh my, yes indeedy!"
Reader to Reader Reviews

Praise for Cheryl Holt's "Lord Trent" trilogy

"A true guilty pleasure!"
Novels Alive TV

"LOVE'S PROMISE can't take the number one spot as my favorite by Ms. Holt—that belongs to her book NICHOLAS—but it's currently running a close second."
Manic Readers

"The book was brilliant...can't wait for Book #2."
Harlie's Book Reviews

"I guarantee you won't want to put this one down. Holt's fast-paced dialogue, paired with the emotional turmoil, will keep you turning the pages all the way to the end."
Susana's Parlour

"...A great love story populated with many flawed characters. Highly recommend it."
Bookworm 2 Bookworm Reviews

BOOKS BY CHERYL HOLT

LOVE'S PERIL
LOVE'S PRICE
LOVE'S PROMISE
SWEET SURRENDER
MUD CREEK
MARRY ME
LOVE ME
KISS ME
SEDUCE ME
KNIGHT OF SEDUCTION
NICHOLAS
DREAMS OF DESIRE
TASTE OF TEMPTATION
PROMISE OF PLEASURE
SLEEPING WITH THE DEVIL
DOUBLE FANTASY
FORBIDDEN FANTASY
SECRET FANTASY
TOO WICKED TO WED
TOO TEMPTING TO TOUCH
TOO HOT TO HANDLE
THE WEDDING NIGHT
FURTHER THAN PASSION
DEEPER THAN DESIRE
MORE THAN SEDUCTION
COMPLETE ABANDON
ABSOLUTE PLEASURE
TOTAL SURRENDER
LOVE LESSONS
MOUNTAIN DREAMS
MY TRUE LOVE
MY ONLY LOVE
MEG'S SECRET ADMIRER
WAY OF THE HEART

CHAPTER ONE

Bramble Bay Estate, English Coast, June 1815...

Sarah Teasdale marched down the rutted lane. She was distracted and furious, so she wasn't paying attention. She tripped on a rock, twisted her ankle and fell, landing in a heap in the dirt.

She'd been shopping in the village and was walking home, so the contents of her basket spilled everywhere. The decanter of expensive brandy she'd specifically gone to purchase cracked open, the amber liquid spilling on the ground.

Luckily, she was alone, so no one had witnessed her humiliating tumble.

"Serves you right," she scolded.

All morning, she'd been in a dither, angry with her stepmother, Mildred, when it was pointless to be upset.

Sarah's mother had died when she was a baby, and her father had remarried shortly after. Sarah had no memories of her mother, and at age twenty-five, it seemed there had been no maternal figure but Mildred. Yet Mildred had never liked Sarah, though Sarah had no idea why.

She glanced about, taking stock of her location, her condition. Her palms were scraped and bleeding, her skirt muddy and torn where her knees had hit the gravel.

The rip in the fabric could be patched without too much trouble, which was a relief. Mildred was very stingy. She refused to spend even the smallest amounts on Sarah, declining to provide the barest necessities such as new undergarments, shoes, or gowns.

Sarah's life was so terrible, and she'd been so horribly abused, that she could have been Cinderella in the fairytale. That's how she felt: lonely and unappreciated and maltreated.

When her father, Bernard, had been alive, she and Mildred had lumped along without too much tension or bickering. Mildred's worst excesses had always occurred when Bernard wasn't looking. But Bernard had been deceased for several years, and Mildred's festering dislike of Sarah had been given free rein.

Still, despite Mildred's snubs and slights, Sarah tried to be helpful and obliging. She had to constantly remind herself that Mildred was simply a very unhappy, miserable person. In Sarah's dealings with her, she had to avoid the protracted arguments that fueled Mildred's temper.

The only other option was for Sarah to leave Bramble Bay, as Mildred often suggested. Yet Bramble Bay had been the Teasdale family home for two centuries, and Sarah was Bernard's only daughter—her sole sibling being her half-brother, Hedley.

Hedley was Mildred's son with Bernard. At Bernard's death, Hedley had inherited everything, with Sarah not receiving a penny of support, and Hedley and Mildred treated Sarah like an interloper. But she shouldn't have to leave and wouldn't let them chase her away.

Tears welled into her eyes, and she swiped them away. Normally, she wasn't ever gloomy, and she never moped or mourned her plight. Yet sometimes, she was just so tired of her meager, unpalatable existence. She'd give anything to change it.

A horse's hooves sounded around the bend in the road, and momentarily, a man trotted into view, mounted on a very fine white stallion. He reined in and stared down from his fancy saddle.

With his golden-blond hair and striking green eyes, he was incredibly handsome. He had a high forehead, sharp cheekbones, and aristocratic nose. He was broad in the shoulders, muscled in his chest and thighs. His skin was bronzed from the sun, as if he worked out-of-doors, but he wasn't dressed as a laborer.

Attired in a flowing white shirt, tan breeches, and a pair of scuffed riding boots, he was actually quite dashing. Clean shaven, but needing to visit his barber, his hair was too long, pulled into a ponytail with a length of black ribbon.

And he had a looped gold earring in his ear.

She'd never seen a man with an earring before and couldn't decide what to make of it. The odd piece of jewelry probably indicated low character—perhaps he was a brigand—and she supposed she should be afraid of him. After all, she was on a deserted stretch of lane. Since she'd departed the village, she hadn't encountered another soul. If he had wicked intentions, there was no defender to rush to her aid.

But she didn't sense any menace. He had a dagger in a sheath at his waist, and a pistol strapped behind his saddle, so he certainly looked as if he could be dangerous, but he was smiling.

"Hello, *chérie*." His voice was tinged with a slight French accent. "Are you all right?"

"I think I am."

"What happened?"

"I tripped and fell."

"Are you injured?"

"Just my pride."

With the agility of a circus performer, he leapt to the ground and walked over. He dropped to his knees and reached for her hand.

"You've cut yourself."

"Yes."

"From your tumble?"

"Yes."

He retrieved a kerchief from his sleeve and gallantly pressed it to the oozing blood on her scraped palm. Then he stood and gathered the items from her spilled basket, placing them back inside it.

He picked up the empty brandy bottle.

"Waste of good liquor," he murmured.

"Yes, it was, and I'll never hear the end of it."

Her comment was petulant and snappish, and she was perplexed as to why she'd uttered it in front of a stranger.

He chuckled. "I take it you have someone impatiently waiting for you to arrive so they can begin imbibing."

"We're having important guests, and my stepmother wants to serve them the very best. There's a renowned vintner in the village, so I went to fetch his most expensive brew."

"Too bad for your guests that they'll miss out."

"They'll have to make do with our typical fare," she grumpily complained. "They're so hoity-toity. How will they bear it?"

"You don't like the company that's coming?"

"I've never met them, but I'm sure I won't care for them a bit."

Mildred was in a veritable flurry about the visit, the house in an uproar of preparation, and Mildred's excitement only dampened Sarah's enthusiasm. The more Mildred fussed, the more Sarah groused. They were like oil and water.

At Sarah's peevishness, the man chuckled again and held up the bottle. Seeing that there was a sip or two in the bottom, he swallowed the dregs, then pitched the decanter into the forest.

"It's delicious," he said. "Your stepmother definitely knows how to impress."

"Yes, she does."

Sarah still hadn't pushed herself to her feet. Her back ached, her knees ached, and her head was pounding. She was feeling inordinately glum, and if he hadn't ridden by, she might have sat there all day.

"Can you stand, *chérie*?" he asked.

"Probably. I haven't tried yet."

"Let me help you."

She should have declined his offer, but she was weary, and he was being very kind. And he was French. His looks, clothes, stallion, and accent provided a foreign flare that was fascinating.

Why not permit him to assist her?

She couldn't remember the last time a handsome fellow had paid her any notice, and she relished his courtesy. Their estate, Bramble Bay, was on the coast and not near any large towns or main thoroughfares, so there were few chances for bachelors to cross her path.

At age eighteen, she'd been engaged to Patrick, but he'd joined the army and promptly gotten himself killed. He'd been a neighbor and childhood friend, and after he'd died, she'd lost interest in matrimony. Her father hadn't pressed her to choose another beau, and she was regretting his lack of foresight.

If he'd urged her to wed, if he'd found her a husband, she'd be established in her own home. Mildred—with her rages and disagreeable temperament—would be naught but an unpleasant memory.

Sarah's gallant companion clasped her arm and lifted her. He was very strong, so the move required very little effort on his part. With a swift tug, she was on her feet, the rapid motion carrying her into him so that, suddenly, their bodies were touching all the way down.

She'd never previously been so close to an adult male, and the abrupt positioning rattled her. She could feel his broad chest, his flat stomach and hard thighs, their proximity so thrilling that butterflies swarmed in her belly.

He was very masculine, very virile, and she was extremely aware of him on a feminine, instinctual level. He smelled so good, like fresh air and horses, and it was all she could do to keep from rubbing herself against him like a contented cat.

He was very tall, six feet at least, and she was only five-foot-five in her shoes, so he towered over her. She gazed up at him, held rapt by the green of his eyes. They were a deep emerald hue, enhanced by the surrounding foliage of the woods. The sky was very blue, puffy clouds floating by overhead, and as she studied him, she was dizzy and unnerved.

She didn't know how to interact with someone like him, didn't know how she should behave.

"Pardon me." Her cheeks blushed bright red, and she stepped away.

As she put weight on her ankle, she winced in pain. He noticed at once and reached out to steady her.

"Ah, *chérie,* it appears you have injured yourself more than you claimed."

"It's just a sprain. I'm fine."

"You're walking home?"

"Yes."

"Let me give you a ride the rest of the way."

"That's not necessary."

"I insist."

Although he seemed cordial and charming, the manner in which he voiced the word *insist* was disconcerting. Beneath his layers of French allure, there was a steely core. He wasn't the type to brook refusal or disobedience, and she wondered who he was.

What purpose had brought him down her rural road? If she declined his assistance, what might he do?

She peered over at his horse, at him, at his horse again.

In her boring, monotonous life, there were very few surprises. It would be quite an adventure to climb onto the large animal and proceed to Bramble Bay. But she couldn't imagine prancing up the drive in such a scandalous fashion. What would Mildred say? What would the servants think?

"I'd better not. Thank you, though."

She bent down to retrieve her basket, and as she spun to go, the turn wrenched her foot even more. She took several hobbling steps, glad her back was to him so he couldn't see her grimace.

"Mademoiselle?" he said from behind her.

She glanced over her shoulder. "Yes?"

"You are not walking."

Before she realized what he intended, he strode over and picked her up. In an instant, she was cradled to his chest. The shocking move jerked the basket from her hands, the contents spilling on the ground again.

"Put me down!" she huffed.

"No."

"Put me down!"

"Don't argue with me, *chérie*. I don't like it."

"You can't just…manhandle me."

"I already have." He grinned, looking like the very devil.

"You're a brute."

"Yes, I am, and I always have been."

"You can't stumble on a strange female and treat her however you please."

"Can't I?" he sarcastically retorted. "*Mon Dieu!* I didn't know."

He whistled to his horse, and the animal pranced over. The man lifted her onto the saddle, her bottom perched on the smooth leather, her legs dangling over the side so she faced him. He scooped up her basket and thrust it at her, then he leapt up behind, settling himself on the horse's rear.

She was confused over what to do with herself. They were crammed together in a very small space, her side resting against his front. With him so near, she felt young and defenseless and out of her element.

"I don't want a ride," she fumed.

"I don't care."

"Would you listen to me?"

"No. I never heed foolish women."

"I'm not being foolish."

"You're not?" He slipped an arm around her waist and snuggled her closer. "Be quiet and be gracious, *chérie*. Accept my ride."

"I don't wish to."

"So? Accept it anyway."

"What if someone sees us? My reputation will be in shreds."

"Why? Because you are injured and I'm helping you?"

"Yes."

"You British have the most peculiar rules. I doubt I will ever figure them out." He frowned. "Where are we headed?"

She pointed down the lane. "This way."

"Is it far?"

"No, not far."

His horse began to walk—though she couldn't discern that he'd given it any visible command—and they continued on in a strained silence. Each clop of the horse's hooves shifted her about so she kept bumping into him. Her shoulder and arm were in intimate contact with his chest. She'd lurch away and stiffen her spine, but immediately be thrown into him again. Separation was impossible.

"Relax, *chérie*," he murmured. "I won't let you fall."

"I didn't imagine you would."

"Are you afraid of me?"

"Yes."

"I don't bite."

"You might."

"You're too pretty," he said. "I would hate to leave any marks."

She was flustered by his flattery.

He's French, she told herself. *He probably spews compliments like candy.* Yet she couldn't stop the rush of delight that swept through her.

Her father had always claimed she was pretty, and her fiancé Patrick had thought so, too. But Mildred insisted she wasn't, and Mildred's cutting insults had been hurled for so many years that it was difficult to discount them.

Secretly, Sarah knew Mildred was wrong, that she was jealous. Mildred was very plain and unexceptional, while Sarah resembled her mother who had been renowned as a great beauty. She'd inherited her mother's lush auburn hair, her bright blue eyes, merry dimples, and curvaceous shape. She looked fetching and smart—at least when she was attired in a halfway decent gown—and she wasn't vain in her assessment.

She had a mirror in her bedchamber and could clearly see herself in it. Her father's opinion had been the correct one. Not Mildred's, and it was refreshing to be reminded of the truth by a very handsome, very dashing stranger—even if he likely said the same to every female he encountered.

"What is your name, *chérie?*" he asked.

"Why should I tell you?"

"Because I am a very friendly person, and I'm making friendly conversation."

For an eternity, she considered his request, trying to decide if she should oblige him. Ultimately, she couldn't think of a reason *not* to reveal her identity.

"I am Miss Sarah Teasdale."

Oddly, her name riveted him so thoroughly that even his horse seemed to freeze in mid-stride.

"Teasdale?"

"Yes."

"Really?"

"Yes, really."

She shifted to peer up at him, which was a mistake. He was very captivating, very mesmerizing, and she was sitting much too close. Quickly, she glanced away.

"You must be related to Bernard and Mildred Teasdale," he mused, more to himself than to her.

"Bernard was my father, and Mildred is my stepmother."

"And Hedley?"

"Hedley is my half-brother." She scowled. "How do you know my family?"

"Oh, I don't," he casually said. "I've just heard of them."

She was positive he was lying but as to what facts?

"Why are you out alone?" His tone was scolding. "Why don't you have a driver and carriage?"

"It's a long story."

"I have time to listen to it."

"It's easier if I walk." She shrugged, acting as if Mildred's refusal to allow her use of the gig wasn't worth mentioning. "I don't like to fuss over trivialities, and it's a lovely day to be outside."

"Yes, it is."

She stared up at him again, and he was evaluating her so meticulously that she bristled with apprehension. He was very shrewd, very astute, and she felt as if he could delve down into the forlorn parts of her being, that he could view all the petty hurts and sad yearnings she kept concealed from the world.

She didn't want him to see so much, didn't want him to understand so much about her.

"Why are you in the area, Mr...?"

She paused, waiting for him to explain, to introduce himself. He hesitated, then said, "My name is John...Sinclair."

It took him forever to settle on a surname, so he had to be lying about that, too.

"What's wrong?" she chided. "Are you suffering from amnesia?

Have you forgotten who you are?"

"No, I have several names. I was simply debating which to provide."

"Well, that certainly sounds sinister."

"I have French relations, but English ones, too. I always have to pick who I'm claiming as my own."

"I bet you have an interesting family tree."

"You have no idea, *chérie*."

They arrived at the gates of Bramble Bay, and she gazed down the orchard-lined drive to the manor house at the end. The afternoon sun shone on the bricks so they were a warm peach shade. The glass in the windows sparkled, the roses adding splashes of color. Beyond the mansion, the manicured lawns sloped to the ocean, the waves lapping on the rocky shore.

She practically sighed with pleasure.

It was such a beautiful spot, like a perfectly painted landscape, and she never grew tired of looking at it. How long would she be permitted to stay? How long would she have the right to call it her own? Would Mildred kick her out someday in a flurry of temper? Would Sarah become too dispirited and leave before she was tossed out?

Mildred was pressuring her to marry their neighbor, Sheldon Fishburn, but he was thirty years older than Sarah, and he was Patrick's father, had been her own father's best friend. Would she eventually be so discouraged that she would agree to the match?

She fought off a shudder. She'd rather sell herself into slavery than marry Patrick's stodgy, boring father. She hadn't had many lucky breaks in her life, but when she wed, it would be for love. If there was a bit of passion thrown into the mix, she'd take that, too.

What she wouldn't accept was a tedious, cold union where both parties were miserable—as Bernard and Mildred had been miserable—and that's what she'd have with Sheldon.

Sarah peered up at Mr. Sinclair.

"You still haven't told me why you're in the neighborhood."

"No, I haven't." He was being deliberately elusive and mysterious.

"Is it a secret?"

"No."

"Then why are you here?"

"You're very nosy."

"I like to think I'm being protective. You appear to know all about my family, but I know nothing about you. Are you a criminal? Are you a robber? Should we be locking the silverware at night?"

"You have silverware that's worth stealing?" He studied the house with a keen eye as if he might rush in and pilfer their valuables.

"Very funny," she snorted.

He urged his horse onward, and they started down the drive.

"I'm scouting…property."

There was another hesitation in his response. Why was she sure he was a complete fraud? But even as the thought unnerved her, she suffered a thrill that he might move to a nearby estate.

"Scouting for yourself? Or for someone else?"

"Maybe for myself. Maybe for someone else," he furtively replied.

"We might be neighbors?" She tried to keep her query light and casual.

"Perhaps."

"So we might cross paths again?"

"We might."

He continued on to the manor, circled the fountain and halted at the grand stairs that led up to the ornate front doors. Fortunately, the butler hadn't noted her approach, and no servants were lurking, so no one witnessed her scandalous return.

Without dismounting, he lifted her down and set her on her feet.

"Can you make it inside on your own?" he asked.

"Yes."

She smiled up at him, his kerchief wadded in her hand so he wouldn't notice it and expect her to give it back. She wondered if she'd ever see him again, and it occurred to her that it would be a very sad thing if she didn't.

His golden hair gleamed in the bright sun, his emerald eyes reflecting the grass and trees. He was charismatic and charming and fascinating, and she would be sorry to have him leave.

There were a thousand questions on the tip of her tongue. She wanted to invite him to keep in touch, to visit whenever he was in the area, to arrive unannounced and cheer her with his captivating presence.

Of course any such comments would be too forward and totally inappropriate, so she swallowed them down.

"Thank you for coming to my aid," she courteously said. "Thank you for the ride."

"You're welcome, my little damsel in distress. Have a care."

"I will."

"Goodbye, *chérie*."

He grinned and cantered off.

She stood frozen in her spot, watching until he vanished from sight. She was positive he'd turn around and wave, but he didn't.

She wrenched away and hobbled up the stairs.

John Harcourt Sinclair—also known as Jean Pierre, *Le Terreur Français*—sat on his horse, staring at Bramble Bay Manor. He was out on the road, the main chimney and slated roof just visible through the woods.

He was the most notorious pirate in the world, the kingdom's most wanted criminal. For years, he'd disrupted British shipping lanes, had attacked and scuttled British ships, had plundered and pillaged and created mayhem wherever he went.

No one could figure out what drove him or how to thwart him, and there were hundreds of bounties on his head, posted in port towns from Rome to Jamaica.

He'd grown up in Paris, so he spoke fluent French and had the air and style of a Frenchman. So it was assumed he was French, and the authorities in particular were searching for a Frenchman, but his mother had been a British countess, his father a British earl, so he was as British as a man could be.

He peered over at his best and only friend, Raven Hook. Raven served as First Mate on his ships and participated in his schemes and anarchy. He was brave and dangerous and loyal to a fault, and John couldn't imagine a finer partner.

From the day they'd met, when John had been a starving street urchin who'd botched his first attempt to steal food, Raven had watched over him.

John had been ten, and Raven a much older and wiser fifteen. He'd been kind and shrewd, had taught John how to survive, how to cheat and fight and win. He'd tamped down John's worst urges, had tempered his worst ideas and plans, had guarded his back when John couldn't be dissuaded from folly.

Their life of crime had left them obscenely rich. As opposed to their difficult beginnings, they could now buy anything, have anything, do anything, but that didn't mean they were ready to halt their mischief. John hadn't yet destroyed all the enemies on his list, and there was still too much revenge to be had. Mildred and Hedley Teasdale were next.

"Was it wise to ride up to the house?" Raven asked.

They conversed in English, practicing it, having to remember that deception was paramount.

"I wasn't noticed by anyone," John insisted, "and if I was, how can it matter? People see what they want to see. I'm merely a passing stranger, assisting Miss Teasdale after she'd twisted her ankle. They'd never connect me with the man who's about to arrive."

"What if that little worm, Hedley, had strolled by? He'd have recognized you."

"But what could he have done?"

"You shouldn't tip your hand."

"I haven't."

John stared at Bramble Bay Manor again.

He'd been waiting so long for this moment, had plotted and conspired and schemed, and he was so close to the end. He was anxious to finish it.

"When the front parlor is mine," he said, "how grand will I look, sitting on the sofa by the fire?"

"You plan to sit on the sofa by the fire? I thought the idea was to take ownership, then let it go to ruin."

John nodded. "It's still the plan, but I certainly intend to wallow in my spoils before I wreck the place."

"What will happen to Mildred and Hedley when you're through with them?"

"Who cares what happens?"

"It's what I like about you, John. You're the most heartless bastard I've ever met, which means I'm not the biggest brute who ever lived. There's always someone worse than me. That would be you."

"I'm happy to be of service."

They scrutinized the house, the grounds, John thinking about the sweetness of vengeance. There was such satisfaction in knowing that Mildred would be sorry, that none of her dreams for Hedley would ever come true.

"What about Miss Teasdale?" Raven asked. "Did you realize Hedley had a sister?"

"No."

"What's she like?"

"She's a tiny sprite. Pretty. Amusing, but foolish—like all women."

"Too bad for her to be caught in all this."

"Yes, too bad."

When he'd stumbled on Sarah Teasdale on the side of the road, he'd been greatly humored by her.

Though she'd been injured and alone, she hadn't been afraid of him, and she'd exhibited an enormous amount of pluck. She was fetching and funny and refreshing, and he'd enjoyed their chat much more than he should have.

His world was a jumble of sailors and ports and perilous, daring sea assaults that often left him physically wounded. He frequently consorted with females, but they were jaded trollops, the only sort available to a man in his position. His current mistress, Annalise, was typical. She was beautiful, but cunning and treacherous, and she never misconstrued her role.

He kept her because she looked stunning on his arm, because she would engage in any decadent, salacious act he requested without grumbling or nagging.

So he never encountered the likes of Sarah Teasdale, and he wondered about her past, her circumstances. She was probably the girl his mother could have been—sheltered, adored, pampered—if Fate had pushed his mother down a wiser, better path.

He was absurdly eager to see Miss Teasdale again. As he waltzed into the foyer at Bramble Bay, like a king on summer progress, she'd likely faint.

"What will become of Miss Teasdale when you're through?" Raven asked. "I know you're not concerned about Hedley or Mildred, but Miss Teasdale is innocent."

John grinned. "I might have mercy on her and take on another mistress."

"Annalise might have a few choice words to say about that."

"No, she won't."

"I can't imagine Miss Teasdale would consent to an indecent arrangement. From your description of her, she seems to be very British. If you mentioned a lewd liaison, you'd drive her into a swoon."

"There are worse things than being attached to a rich man like me."

"Yes, there are: having a reckless brother, losing your home because of him, being tossed out with just the clothes on your back."

"Precisely," John grimly agreed. "Once she's faced with catastrophe, I might be exactly what she needs."

Raven snorted out a laugh. "I wouldn't count on it if I were you."

John laughed, too. It was amusing to think of a relationship with Miss Teasdale, but she wasn't worth the bother. And from his brief meeting with her, he could tell she was quite fond of Bramble Bay. After she learned how he'd ruined Hedley, she wouldn't be kindly inclined to any continuing acquaintance.

"Let's go," John said. "We're due to arrive tomorrow. I want to double check all the details to make sure we haven't forgotten anything."

"We haven't."

"I want to be *sure*," John firmly stated. "I've been preparing for this moment all my life. I'll leave nothing to chance."

They turned their horses and rode away.

CHAPTER TWO

"Can you see anything?"

"No, and be silent. I won't give Mildred the satisfaction of knowing we care enough to spy."

Sarah was hovered on the second floor landing with her friend, Caroline Patterson.

Caroline's parents had died when she was a girl, and Sarah's father had been her guardian. They were the same age—twenty-five—and had been raised together like sisters.

They were peeking down into the foyer, observing the approach of Mildred's mysterious guests. Sarah had watched, agog, as their carriage meandered up the drive. It was large and ornate, with a fancy crest painted on the door. Four liveried footmen were perched on the rails, and it was pulled by six white horses that had clopped in a perfect rhythm.

A horde of servants had rushed outside to unload their massive pile of luggage. How long did they intend to stay?

For the past two weeks, the entire house had been abuzz with preparations for the auspicious visit. Hedley had traveled from town to be present. They were his acquaintances, and he and his mother were huddled below, dressed in their finest clothes and obviously anxious to impress.

Sarah hadn't asked who the people were or why they were so important. Nor had she and Caroline been invited to greet them. If Mildred disliked Sarah, she disliked Caroline even more. Sarah, at least, had been Bernard's daughter and had some claim to food and shelter at Bramble Bay.

In Mildred's eyes, Caroline was an interloper who couldn't so much as boast a blood relationship. She was viewed as a trespasser, and thus, undeserving of sustenance or sanctuary.

Caroline's antipathy toward Mildred was mutual. After Bernard had passed away, Mildred had convinced Caroline to marry Mildred's distant cousin who lived in London. He was a successful barrister with a suitable home and good income, but he was also a violent, drunken fiend.

Caroline had tolerated his ill-treatment for two years, then she'd run away. She was hiding at Bramble Bay, afraid for her life, and terrified that her husband would find her. He'd already come searching twice, and Mildred kept threatening to tell him that Caroline was on the premises.

So far, Sarah had persuaded Mildred to be merciful, but she doubted Mildred would extend charity to Caroline for much longer. If Mildred betrayed Caroline to her brute of a spouse, Sarah wasn't sure what she'd do.

For the moment, she was enjoying Caroline's company. They might have been fourteen again, laughing at bitter Mildred and spoiled Hedley. Neither she nor Caroline was interested in Mildred's guests, except to the extent that they hoped the visit would be brief and uneventful.

Mildred had been very stressed, which made her short-tempered and rude, so the staff was in a frenzied state, snapping and bickering and being generally unpleasant.

There was a flurry of motion out on the stoop. The butler straightened and announced, "Mrs. Teasdale, Master Hedley, may I introduce Mr. Raven Hook."

A man entered. He was a handsome, imposing giant. His name, Raven, fit him. His hair was black, his clothes were black, his boots were black. He had no expression on his face, but he looked positively lethal. He had a dagger in a sheath on one side of his waist and a sword on the other that dropped to the floor.

"Who is he?" Caroline whispered, her brows rising with astonishment.

"I have no idea."

"Why would Hedley even know someone like that?"

"Your guess is as good as mine."

A woman entered next. She was voluptuous and statuesque, like an Amazon warrior goddess, with violet-colored eyes and luxurious blond hair that curled to her bottom. She wore a bright red gown and tons of gold jewelry so she appeared wealthy and foreign and exotic.

She was so striking that it was difficult to glance away. She noticed Hedley staring, and she smirked, aware of her splendor, of her effect on males.

"And who is that?" Caroline whispered again.

"Aphrodite?" Sarah muttered in reply.

"If Hedley isn't careful," Caroline snickered, "he'll drool on himself."

The butler intoned, "Miss Annalise Dubois."

Miss Dubois preened, then walked over to stand by Mr. Hook.

The butler continued. "Finally, may I present Mr. John Sinclair."

To Sarah's stunned surprise, Mr. Sinclair—her dashing savior and champion from the prior afternoon—sauntered into the foyer. His golden-blond hair was still pulled into a ponytail, but it was the only thing about him that was the same.

He was dressed in a lavender coat that had silver embroidery on the hem. The stitching was so exquisite that the thread was probably actual, spun silver. His boots were polished black, with huge silver buckles, and his fingers were weighted down with silver rings.

His shirt was blinding white, his cravat designed from what had to be miles of Belgian lace. There was lace at his cuffs too, dangling across his wrists and hands. Tiny stones sparkled from his coat, cravat, and rings, and she suspected he was covered in diamonds.

He was so spectacularly attired, so rich and elegant and...*beautiful,* that if someone pronounced him to be royalty, she would have believed it.

"Oh, my lord," Caroline murmured, "would you look at him? Have you ever seen the likes?"

"No," Sarah murmured in return.

"Who could he be? Why has he come?"

"I wouldn't dare speculate."

At his arrival, Mildred and Hedley were all aflutter. Hedley rushed over, dragging Mildred with him.

"Mother, this is Mr. Sinclair."

Mildred curtsied. "Hello, Mr. Sinclair. Welcome to our humble home."

Mr. Sinclair didn't respond, but glared down his imperious nose, giving the distinct impression that he possessed an extreme dislike for both of them.

Hedley reached out as if to shake Mr. Sinclair's hand, and Sinclair simply frowned until Hedley, unnerved and embarrassed, stepped back and dropped his arm to his side.

"It's been a long journey," Miss Dubois said, her voice sultry and alluring, her accent very French. "Are our rooms ready?"

"Yes...ah...of course," Mildred stammered, intimidated by the tall, daunting woman. "Would you first join us for some refreshments?"

Mildred gestured to the front parlor. The salon had been prepared for them, a cheery fire burning in the grate even though it was a warm summer day. Trays of food and decanters of wine had been arranged on the tables. The servants had gone to an enormous amount of trouble, but apparently, it had been a wasted effort.

Miss Dubois peeked at Mr. Sinclair, read something in his eyes, then shook her head. "We're tired from our journey."

"I...understand," Mildred stammered again. "How about supper? Will you dine with us?"

"Perhaps."

Mildred bristled with irritation, but quickly tamped it down. She clapped her hands, and two footmen dashed over to escort the trio up the stairs.

Miss Dubois slid a proprietary arm around Mr. Sinclair's waist and asked, "Have you honored my request?"

"As to what?" Mildred said.

"I am Monsieur Sinclair's very special friend"—Miss Dubois purred the word *special*—"and we can't bear to be parted for a single second. We must have adjoining rooms."

"Yes, I've placed you together," Mildred said.

In adjoining rooms? For a couple that wasn't married? What could Mildred be thinking? Was she ill? Was she mad?

She was a stickler for the proprieties. Her diatribes about rituals and reputations were legendary, and Sarah and Caroline had spent years, giggling over Mildred's persnickety etiquette.

Yet she would allow Mr. Sinclair and Miss Dubois to share a bedchamber? It was disgraceful. It was shocking. It was incredible.

Sarah gasped. She didn't mean to; it just slipped out.

No one noticed, except for Mr. Sinclair and Mr. Hook. They seemed vigilantly focused and on alert for hazards. They glanced up, and Mr. Sinclair saw her before she could slither out of sight.

He winked—the ass—then casually looked away, his expression bored and aloof. A footman motioned for him to start up the stairs, and he and Miss Dubois promenaded over and began to climb.

They were such an arresting pair: attractive, stunning, magnificently attired. And they were proceeding directly toward the spot where Sarah and Caroline were lurking.

"Let's get out of here," she urged Caroline, and Caroline didn't have to be told twice.

They scurried away to the servants' stairs, Sarah hobbling on her sore ankle. By the time they were outside on the verandah, Sarah's temper was flaring.

Who was John Sinclair? What game was he playing?

"What's wrong, Sarah?" Caroline inquired. "You're in a state."

"Remember yesterday, when I fell out on the road."

"Yes. A handsome stranger came along, like a prince out of a fairytale, and carried you home. You lucky dog."

"It was him!"

"Who?"

"Mr. Sinclair. My knight in shining armor was Mr. Sinclair."

"I thought you figured him to be a traveling laborer."

"I didn't know what he was. He spoke well and was dressed in fine clothes, but they were ordinary, informal clothes. Not…a suit fit for a king."

"You said he was scouting properties in the area, that he was hoping to purchase a residence."

They frowned, and Sarah cautiously asked, "You don't suppose he's here to…buy Bramble Bay, do you?"

"No, no," Caroline hastily insisted. "Hedley would never sell it. Mildred wouldn't let him." She paused. "Would she?"

Hedley was Mildred's darling, beloved boy. He was five years younger than Sarah, age twenty, but he seemed much younger than that.

He'd been cosseted and spoiled by Mildred, his every whim granted, his follies and foibles ignored, and he was worse off for it. He'd grown to be an arrogant, frivolous wastrel who viewed himself as a dandy. He spent all his time in London, gambling, racing fast carriages, and chasing fast girls.

Mildred had convinced him that he was wonderful, and he believed the whole world owed him whatever he wished to have.

Bernard hadn't been a nobleman, so Bramble Bay wasn't entailed. Hedley could sell it if he wanted to, but it was their home. Sarah would never agree to such a reckless decision, and she refused to accept that Mildred or Hedley would consider it.

But she didn't trust Mildred, and if Hedley chose to pursue a certain path, Mildred would never stop him.

What was Hedley thinking? What about Mr. Sinclair? What was happening?

"I can't predict what Hedley and Mildred might do," Sarah claimed, her heart sinking, because she absolutely knew. Hedley had repeatedly proved himself capable of any negligent conduct, and Mildred would never counter his excesses.

"I didn't like the looks of Mr. Hook or Miss Dubois," Caroline said.

"Neither did I."

"And Mr. Sinclair is definitely plotting mischief."

"I have a very bad feeling about this. I'd best find out what they're up to."

"How would you?"

Sarah analyzed her options. If she confronted Mildred with irksome questions, her stepmother would tell her to mind her own business. Sarah and Hedley were cordial, and he might or might not admit the truth, depending on whether he was in a jam and didn't want her to learn of it.

He'd always been jealous of Sarah. Their father had favored her, and compared to Hedley, she'd been an easy child to raise. She'd never caused trouble or behaved as she shouldn't. Hedley hated that Sarah coasted through life with so few difficulties, while he constantly bounced from disaster to disaster.

Of course his adversities were of his own creation and any consequences thoroughly deserved. Not that he would ever acknowledge it.

"I should talk to Mr. Sinclair," Sarah ultimately said.

"Are you sure?"

"He's affable and approachable. After the uproar from their arrival dies down, I'll seek him out."

"What will you say?"

"I'll simply ask what he's about. I'm positive I can get him to confide in me."

"What if you don't like his answers?"

"Then I'll speak to Mildred so she knows to be wary of him and his friends."

"You're mad to involve yourself with him or with Mildred."

"Do you have a better suggestion?"

"We could just wait until it all crashes down on our heads."

Sarah scoffed. "That's not a plan, Caroline."

"No, I suppose it isn't."

Sarah went inside, her thoughts awhirl as she tried to decide when and how to tackle Mr. Sinclair.

It was late afternoon, the house quiet, the staff settled in for tea. The hallways were deserted, the shadows lengthening.

Sarah neared Mr. Sinclair's suite, and she rolled her eyes at her ridiculousness. Would she knock and demand entrance? Would she meet with him in his private quarters? The outrageous notion didn't bear contemplating, yet she was about to proceed.

Though every instinct screamed her lunacy, she was excited to be with him again. She wanted to grab him by his fancy lapels, to shake him for being so mystifying, for lying to her the previous day, for concealing his identity.

Obviously, he'd been spying on the property and taking note of the surrounding area. To what end?

She tiptoed over and held very still, listening, but heard no voices. The door was ajar, and she peeked in, but didn't see anyone. She pushed it a little wider and moved into the threshold so she had a better view.

The sitting room was empty, the inner bedchamber, too. His beautiful lavender coat was casually tossed on a chair, a sleeve drooping on the floor. His black riding boots were haphazardly thrown in the corner.

He'd sampled the brandy; a decanter had been opened, a glass next to it. She remembered her comment out on the road, where she'd petulantly complained about Mildred's stuffy guests, that they would have to suffer with the Teasdale family's typical fare, and her cheeks reddened with embarrassment.

She hoped he didn't recall her insult, but she was certain he would. She doubted he ever forgot any detail. He was an intriguing enigma, and she was much too fascinated.

A magnet might have been pulling her forward for she strolled into the suite and went over to the lavender coat. She ran her palm over the lush fabric. Up close, the garment was even more magnificent. Where would a person purchase such a thing? How much would it cost?

Clearly, Mr. Sinclair was extremely wealthy, but from what endeavor?

Her brother, Hedley, prided himself on his wardrobe, and he had many expensive coats, but she'd never seen an item remotely similar. Poor Hedley. When he and Mr. Sinclair stood side by side, Hedley looked positively dismal.

She walked into the bedchamber and assessed his scattered belongings, trying to glean some clue about him from his satchels and trunks.

The servants had unpacked and hung some of his shirts in the cupboard. Realizing she was insane, she slinked over and smoothed her fingers across the exotic apparel. She took a sleeve and pressed it to her nose, detecting his masculine scent in the material.

As she studied the various pieces, she was disturbed to discover that the lengthy hems hid many weapons, pistols, daggers, swords.

Men carried weapons when they traveled. The roads were generally safe, but still, an encounter with a brigand could occur. Yet he seemed heavily armed in a fashion that was much more lethal than necessary.

There were no dangers at Bramble Bay. No criminals camping in the park, no highwaymen robbing carriages as they rolled by. Why would he feel the need for so much protection?

She knew she should sneak out, that she'd pushed the limit of what she could explain if she was caught snooping. But she was too curious, and she continued on to his dressing room. She peeked in and, still seeing no one, she brazenly entered.

He'd washed and shaved. A towel had been pitched on the floor, his razor and soap brush balanced on the table by the washstand. Creeping over, she traced her thumb across the ivory handle of the brush, then picked it up, gauging its weight, liking the cool glide of ivory on her skin. She imagined him stroking the bristles over his handsome face, and she was utterly riveted by seductive visions of him unclad and proceeding with his ablutions.

Without warning, the door to the adjacent bedchamber opened, and he stepped through and drew it shut behind him. He turned and, grinning his devil's grin, he sauntered over.

She should have squealed with alarm and raced out, but at his sudden appearance, she was too stunned to move.

He wasn't wearing a shirt, so his chest was bare, his hair unbound and curling over his shoulders. He was simply too striking and remarkable, and she was practically giddy with emotions she didn't understand.

His trousers were loose, the first few buttons undone, his navel visible, as well as a smattering of hair that descended to parts unknown. She'd heard that men and women were built differently in their private areas, and Caroline had told her shocking stories about how those differences were put to use in the marital bed, but Sarah was confused on what exactly was concealed under all that fabric.

He noticed where her attention had been concentrated, and his grin widened.

"Hello, my damsel in distress."

She was still holding his shaving brush, and she dropped it as if it was on fire.

"Mr. Sinclair, I apologize for interrupting. I didn't realize you were here. I brought you some…ah…towels."

"Towels. Really?"

"Yes."

"Are you spying or snooping?"

"Neither."

"So you were dying to be alone with me. Admit it."

He kept coming, approaching until he was so near that the tips of his boots slipped under the hem of her skirt. She could feel his body's heat, could smell his skin, the aroma of the soap with which he'd recently bathed.

"What is it you want?" His voice was low and inviting.

"Nothing. I…I…"

"I'll give you whatever it is. Just tell me."

He leaned in, and she lurched back, but the wall was behind her, blocking any retreat.

"Are you curious, my innocent little maiden?"

"Curious about what?" she asked, then she frowned. "Wait a minute. Where is your French accent?"

"What French accent?"

"When I met you out on the road, you had a French accent."

"When we *met* on the road?" He scowled as if perplexed as to what she referred. "We couldn't have."

"Don't deny it," she snapped. "I fell, and you lifted me up on your horse and brought me home."

"Did I? I don't recall, although how I could forget a girl as pretty as you is quite a mystery."

She studied him, wishing she could read his mind, wishing she could open the top of his head and peer inside to decipher his thoughts.

"Don't lie to me," she firmly said.

"Am I lying?"

"You blasted oaf! You know you are."

The worst gleam of mischief blazed in his mesmerizing green eyes. "I *might* recollect, but if you mention it to anyone, I'll say you're mad."

"What are you doing at Bramble Bay? Tell me the truth."

"The truth? I'm visiting your stepmother and brother. I'm their special *guest*. What would you imagine I'm doing?"

"I have no idea. Why are you here?"

She was determined to get a credible answer from him, but he ignored her and braced his palms on the wall so she was trapped between his arms. She should have shoved him away and stomped out, but to her eternal disgust, she didn't want to leave.

He was completely focused on her, his attention thoroughly captured, and she could think of no finer experience than to have him gazing at her with such heightened interest. He leaned even nearer so his body was pressed to hers all the way down. She could feel the ripple of muscle in his chest and stomach, the hard expanse of his thighs.

"I don't want to talk about Hedley or Mildred," he said.

"What do you want to talk about?"

"You and me."

He dipped down, and to her astonished surprise, he bit her nape. The nip of his teeth, the soft caress of his lips, caused goose bumps to cascade down her spine and legs.

His wicked fingers went to her hair, and with a few flicks of his wrist, he plucked out her combs, and the heavy mass toppled down.

She was so astounded—both by his bold advance and by the tempting sensations being produced—that she stood like an imbecile and let him proceed. But only for a moment.

The man was a sorcerer who overwhelmed her good judgment. She put a hand on his chest and eased him away. He stepped back, but just a tiny distance so she would realize he was moving away because *he* chose to and not because she had insisted.

"Stop that," she scolded.

"Stop what?"

"I can't dawdle in here while you bite my shoulder."

"Why not?"

"I barely know you, and what I've learned so far worries me greatly."

"I could do more than bite you. Where you're concerned, I have all sorts of naughty suggestions."

"You do not," she scoffed.

"Oh, I absolutely do."

He reached down and had the audacity to unbutton the top button on her dress. She gasped and slapped his fingers away.

"You are a menace."

"Ah, *chérie*"—a hint of his French accent slipped into his voice— "you are the one who sneaked into my room. What am I to think? It appears you want something from me, and I'm happy to give it to you."

"I don't want anything."

"Don't you? If I had to guess, I'd say you crave what I'm eager to provide."

He chuckled and set his thumb on her chin, tipping her face toward him as he bent down and touched his lips to hers.

She'd been kissed before—by Patrick, her long ago fiancé—but it had been years since it had happened. She was frozen in place, riveted by him. But quickly, she remembered herself and yanked away, managing only to bang her head on the wall.

"Don't do that," she fumed.

"Or what?"

"Or…I don't know, but I didn't come in here to be kissed by you."

"Perhaps you should ponder the actual reason for your arrival. The house is quiet and supper won't be served for ages. No one will miss you if we spend a few hours together."

"Doing what?"

"If you have to ask, then I am certain you should stay so I can show you."

He dipped down as if he'd kiss her again, and her heart was racing so hard, she thought she might swoon. It dawned on her that she'd love to misbehave in ways she should never allow. She felt bewitched, as if he had magical powers and had cast a spell on her.

She couldn't predict what might have transpired, but the door to the adjoining room was wrenched open again, and Annalise Dubois entered from the other bedchamber.

"Jean Pierre—" On seeing Sarah huddled with Mr. Sinclair, she bristled with affront. "*Mon Dieu,* Jean Pierre! I can't leave you alone for two seconds, and you are trying to tumble the servants."

Sarah moaned with dismay and stumbled away from him as he turned to Miss Dubois.

"You have the worst habit of interrupting," he told her, "when I really wish you wouldn't."

"I traveled with you for your pleasure," Miss Dubois pointed out. "Not mine. If you require intimate company, you don't need to seduce the housemaids."

"I'm not a servant!" Sarah indignantly huffed, but they ignored her.

"I couldn't resist," Mr. Sinclair said. "I came in, and she was in here—with her hair down and her gown unbuttoned. She was practically begging to be ravished."

"I was not!" Sarah seethed as Miss Dubois snapped, "I'm sure she was."

Sarah gazed at Mr. Sinclair, at Miss Dubois. Their long acquaintance was clear, a thousand visual messages flitting between them. They were so closely attuned, they could quarrel without speaking a word.

As to Sarah, she had never been more horrified, and if Miss Dubois mentioned the incident to Mildred, what catastrophe would result?

Before Sarah could scurry out and run to safety, Miss Dubois strutted over. She was very tall, very angry, and she towered over Sarah.

"Be gone, you little harlot," Miss Dubois growled.

"How dare you insult me!"

"If I catch you sniffing after Jean Pierre again, I'll do more than insult you. I'll tell Madame Teasdale. I don't imagine she would like to hear about your low morals."

"I wasn't sniffing after him," Sarah insisted. "I brought him some towels."

"A likely story," Miss Dubois scoffed. "If I find you with him again, I'll have you whipped, then fired. You won't look quite so pretty if you're living in a ditch."

"You are insane," Sarah mumbled.

The imposing woman raised a fist as if she might strike Sarah. Sarah blanched and hurried down the hall, Mr. Sinclair's laughter ringing in her ears.

CHAPTER THREE

It was nearly eleven o'clock. The moon hadn't risen, so darkness provided a fine shield behind which mischief could be perpetrated.

John glanced about, saw no one, and hefted himself onto the small balcony outside Sarah Teasdale's bedroom suite. The French windows were open, the curtains rippling with a gust of balmy sea air.

As he'd hoped, Miss Teasdale was present. She was seated at a table in the corner, eating a late and cold supper from a tray. There was no fire in the grate, and a single candle burned next to her plate. She was a lonely sight, locked away like a naughty child.

Mildred hadn't yet introduced him to Miss Teasdale. And Raven had mentioned that there was another female on the premises too, a buxom blond named Caroline who appeared to be about Sarah's age.

Why would Mildred hide them? Had she refused Miss Teasdale permission to dine with the company? Or had Miss Teasdale declined to socialize? For some inexplicable reason, he was desperate to learn the answer to that question.

Women loved him and always had, starting with his mother and moving on from there. His handsome looks, illicit parentage, and scandalous familial history were titillating. But it was his aura of power and danger that drew them in and spurred them to recklessness.

They swarmed like moths to a flame, but of course, it was impossible to get close. He never let anyone matter, because he was convinced his life expectancy would be very short.

He would never bond with a female, just to have her widowed. From watching his own mother die a slow, miserable death, he was aware of how hard it was for a woman on her own. He would never allow a woman to attach herself, would never allow a woman to count on him. He'd only fail her.

It was his way.

But he was irked by the notion that Miss Teasdale might not have wished to socialize with him. Mildred Teasdale was laboring under the mistaken impression that she could charm him into mercy so she'd hosted a lavish supper. John had scarcely tasted the food because he'd been too busy wondering why Miss Teasdale hadn't joined them.

At the moment, she was ready for bed, wearing a nightgown and robe. The nightgown was a virginal white, with flowers stitched across the bodice and hem. The robe was a lilac hue that set off the blue of her eyes. Her feet were bare, and he grinned, delighted to note that her toenails were painted pink.

Her beautiful hair was down and brushed out, and he'd never previously seen tresses in quite that shade. While most men preferred blond trollops, he considered himself a connoisseur of loose doxies. Red hair always tantalized him, but russet-haired doxies were difficult to find.

He liked auburn hair. He liked *her* auburn hair.

He still didn't know why she'd been in his dressing room earlier in the afternoon. If Annalise hadn't arrived, he wasn't sure what might have happened. He'd kissed her as a lark, as a joke, but the chaste embrace had rattled him in ways he didn't like. He was anxious to kiss her again, but more thoroughly, so he could discover what it was about her that was so alluring.

Tired of lurking like a specter on the balcony, he parted the curtains and walked inside.

"Hello, Sarah."

She jumped a mile, leaping up with such force that her chair toppled over.

"What are you doing?" she hissed. "Are you mad?"

"Yes, I've always been told that I am."

"You can't just…just…come into my bedchamber."

"I can, and I have."

She made a shooing motion with her hand. "Get out of here."

"No."

He took a step toward her, and she took one back. He took another, and she did, too.

Her cheeks flushed with agitation, she was clutching at the lapels of her robe, and he thought she was so pretty, so tempting. He was about to reach out and trace his fingers down her hair, to revel in the lush softness, when she lurched away and dashed to the door that led to the hall.

She opened it and peeked out. Seeing no one, she tried to shoo him away again.

"Will you get out?"

"No."

He marched over, laid a palm on the wood and banged it shut. There was no key in the keyhole, so he retrieved a knife from his pocket and jiggered the lock so it clicked into place, trapping her.

She gaped, aghast. "I knew you were a criminal. I knew it!"

"I'm not a criminal," he lied. "I'm just…handy with tools."

"No, you're a criminal. And a menace. Let me out."

"No."

"I won't stay in here with you, and I can't believe you'd think it appropriate to enter. Let me out. At once!"

"No."

"Is that the only word you know?"

"No, and you can't toss me out. I'm bigger than you."

"Really?" she sarcastically oozed. "I hadn't noticed."

She stomped back to the table, sat, and began eating again. She ignored him, and he was irritated by her disregard.

She jumbled loose all sorts of unusual emotions that he didn't like suffering. Around her, he felt protective and strong, but foolish and out of his element, too. He might have been ten years old and breathless with his first crush. He wanted her to be in awe of him, to fawn and flatter, to be glad he'd arrived.

He was being driven by insane notions. Why had he sneaked in? What, precisely, was he hoping to accomplish? He hadn't a clue.

He went over and pulled up a chair across from her. He slouched and stretched out his legs, enjoying her company, enjoying how nervous he made her. She attempted to proceed with her meal, but a strained silence festered, and she couldn't stand it.

"What are you staring at?" she demanded.

"You."

"Obviously. Why?"

"You fascinate me, but damned if I can figure it out."

"Don't curse. I don't like it."

He supposed he could have apologized for his rough language, but he was extremely arrogant and never apologized about anything. Or he supposed he could have informed her that the house and every item in it now belonged to him—Hedley had gambled it all away—and he could act however he pleased.

But he didn't tell her. Mildred wanted to break the news herself, and he'd given her another day to carry out the distasteful task.

To his consternation, he was troubled over what was about to transpire. The servants were courteous and well-trained, and they would be devastated to lose their positions.

As to Miss Teasdale, what would she think when she found out what Hedley had done? What would she think when she learned that John was the owner of Bramble Bay and that he didn't care about her home or the people in it.

He'd spent so many years plotting vengeance and pursuing his various retaliations that he'd assumed he was immune to shame or guilt. Apparently, a few flickers of conscience still lingered.

He felt sorry for her and wondered where she'd end up. Had she other kin? Was there anyone to provide shelter and assistance?

He'd jokingly told Raven that he might offer to keep her as a mistress, and it occurred to him that it was a proposition he might eventually tender. He doubted she'd be worth the bother, but how could a man guess what benefits a woman could ultimately supply?

"You didn't come down to supper," he said.

"No, I didn't."

He waited, but she didn't explain.

"Why not?"

"It isn't any of your business, is it?"

"Humor me."

"No."

She picked up her fork to start eating again, but he clasped her wrist and took the utensil from her.

They engaged in a visual battle she could never win. She didn't comprehend how tough he was, didn't understand the deeds of which he was capable. She was a poor, unprotected female, with no husband or father to watch over her. She could never best him, and it was pointless to try.

"Fine," she huffed. "I didn't join you, because Mildred asked me not to. You're *such* an important guest"—she batted her lashes in a facetious way that made him grin—"and she was afraid my frivolous presence would upset your digestion."

"She didn't say that."

"She didn't have to. Besides, I don't like you or your friends, and I didn't want to dine with you."

"Not like me?" He gestured down his torso. "What's not to like?"

"You're a bully and a fiend, and I'm not certain why you're here, but I'm positive you're up to no good."

He nodded. "You could be right."

"Where is your mistress?" From her expression, it was clear she was hoping to rattle him by mentioning Annalise. "Won't she be angry if she finds out you're with me?"

His grin widened. "You're jealous."

"Hardly."

He studied her, amused at how she couldn't hold his gaze.

"Yes, you are. You're jealous."

"The woman is a trollop."

"She definitely is. It's the only type of female who interests me."

"I would never be jealous of someone like her."

"You're a very curious person—as you demonstrated when you sneaked into my bedchamber."

"I didn't sneak in."

"Call it what you will. I fascinate you, and I'm happy to regale you with stories. Would you like me to tell you why I keep Annalise? Would you like me to tell you all the ways she entertains me?"

Her eyes flashed daggers. "Oh, stop it. You're embarrassing yourself. And me."

"Are you truly an innocent maiden?"

"How crass of you to inquire."

"I don't meet many innocent women."

"I'm sure you don't. I'm sure you spend all your time rolling in the gutter with slatterns."

"You've summed up my life perfectly. Perhaps I should hire you to write my biography."

"You wouldn't like my tone. Or my ending. I'd have you killed off—by me, because I'm so aggravated by you."

"Women usually love me. How have I earned your disfavor?"

"There's something fishy about you. I can't decide what it is, but I'll figure it out."

He sighed. There were many, many things *fishy* about him. It was such a long list, if he chose to enlighten her as to his proclivities, it would likely take a whole year to confess it all.

"I'm simply visiting in the area," he fibbed.

"Liar."

"Yes, I am a liar. I always have been." He clasped her wrist again and stroked a thumb across the spot where her pulse beat so furiously. "While I'm here, I want you to come down to supper."

"Why?"

"Because it's no fun without you there."

"You don't even know me. Why would you utter such a ridiculous comment? I could be the most boring supper companion who ever lived, and you'd be stuck with me."

"You wouldn't have to talk. You could merely sit and let me stare at you."

"Don't flirt with me. I don't like it."

She yanked away and tucked her hand under her thigh so he couldn't grab for it again.

"Every woman likes a man to flirt."

"Not this woman."

"Now who's lying?"

He leaned forward, his elbows on the table. She didn't like him moving nearer, and she leaned back in her chair, shifting as far away as possible.

Poor girl. She hadn't yet realized that he always got his way. If she tried to avoid him, he'd make her stay by his side just to prove that he could. If she tried to keep her distance, he'd push and push and push until she gave up and behaved as he demanded.

It was his nature, inherited from his father, Charles Sinclair, Earl of Trent, who by all accounts was an arrogant, unyielding ass. John had never met Charles, but he'd heard plenty of stories, and he believed them all. He was possessed of Charles's worst traits and none of his good ones. Actually, Charles didn't have any good ones.

"If a disaster occurred at Bramble Bay," he asked, "would you have anywhere to go?"

"What do you mean? What might happen?"

"I'm just posing a question. You seem fairly miserable with Mildred and Hedley."

"I'm not miserable," she insisted, but her dour glare belied her remark.

"What if you had to leave? Are there any kin who would take you in?"

"No."

"What would you do?"

"I've often wondered myself," she surprised him by admitting. "I'd like to leave Bramble Bay, but I haven't the funds. And my friend Caroline is here. She's in a bit of a...jam. If I left, I'd have to bring her with me. There would be two of us needing shelter, and I have no idea how I'd provide it."

"You don't get along with Mildred."

"No."

"How about Hedley?"

"I get on with Hedley all right. He's too reckless for my tastes."

"How old are you?"

"Twenty-five. How old are you?"

"Thirty. Why aren't you married?"

"Why aren't you?"

He laughed. "What sane woman would have me?"

"That's the truest thing you've said since we met."

"Your father has been dead for several years," he pressed. "Why didn't he select a husband for you before he passed?"

She shrugged. "I was engaged to a neighbor boy when I was younger. He died in the army, and I wasn't much interested after that."

"You have no other prospects?"

"Mildred is pestering me to marry our neighbor Mr. Fishburn, and he's amenable. I suppose I could agree in a pinch."

"Why don't you?"

"Because he's thirty years older than I am, has already outlived three wives, and he was my fiancé's father." She scowled with irritation. "It seems a bit tawdry to me."

John gave a mock shudder. "Mildred certainly knows how to pick a winner."

"Yes, she certainly does."

"Do you have a dowry?"

"Honestly! You're so nosy. My private life is none of your business."

"I'm making it my business. Do you have a dowry?"

"I thought my father had put some money aside, but after the will was read, Mildred learned that he hadn't."

"You trust Mildred's word on it?"

"I don't have much choice."

"It never occurred to you that she might lie?"

"Why would she lie? She'd love to be shed of me. If there was dowry money tucked away somewhere, she'd be first in line to arrange a match for me."

"Would you like to marry? If you could stumble on a husband who would be better than your neighbor?"

"Why? Are you offering?"

"No," he swiftly said, and she snorted with disgust.

She scrutinized him, her derision clear, her impatience blatant. Suddenly, she appeared much more weary than he'd deemed her to be.

"You've barged in to my room when you shouldn't have," she scolded, "and you've peppered me with rude questions—that I've answered when I shouldn't have. I'm tired, and it's been a long day."

"If I asked you to be my mistress, what would you say?"

"Your...*mistress*?" she sputtered.

"I'd send Annalise away, and you could take her place."

She stared and stared, then she shook her head. "My hearing must be affected. I could have sworn you just suggested that I be your mistress."

"I did."

She slapped her hands over her eyes, and for an eternity, she sat there. Her body started to tremble, and for a horrified instant, he presumed she was crying. Then he realized she was laughing.

"Oh, my lord," she mused to herself, "this—*this!!*—is what my life has come to." She pulled her hands away, and her gaze was firm and furious. "No, I won't be your mistress, Mr. Sinclair. I have no idea why you would assume you could make such an indelicate proposal to me."

"I'm handsome and very rich, and I can be extremely generous when the mood strikes me."

"Bully for you."

"You can't predict what might happen in the future. You shouldn't be so hasty."

"In a thousand years, I would never agree."

"You might."

"Not if I was starving on the street."

"I'll ask you later—when your situation might be more dire."

"It will be a waste of time." She stood and gestured to the window by which he'd entered. "Tell me why you're really here. Tell me one true thing, then go."

"You'll find out soon enough."

"That's precisely why I'm worried about you."

"You should be nicer to me."

"I've been plenty *nice*. Now go before I scream for help."

"Who could help you? When I am in the room, who would dare?"

He stood, too, and stepped to her. She didn't move a muscle, didn't reveal any fear by so much as a quiver of her brow. He could do anything to her. He was bigger and stronger and so very fierce in his actions and passions, but she recognized he wouldn't hurt her.

Each moment he spent with her was novel and refreshing, and he was overcome by the most potent need to be connected to her.

He slid an arm around her waist and drew her to him. She was dressed in her nightclothes, and with no corset or undergarments to hide her feminine parts, he could feel her pert breasts, the taut nipples poking into his chest like shards of glass. But it was the scent of her skin and hair that was most arousing.

She smelled like sunshine and flowers, like woman and fertile earth, and the aromas called to him like a siren song that—if he wasn't careful—would lure him to his doom. He'd be crushed to death on a rocky shore.

He might have been balanced on a tightrope, an unusual urge about to sweep him away. Desire was racing in his veins, pounding in his phallus, burning in his mind, and spurring him to take her, to have her.

He—who never lost control—was desperate to proceed to ravishment. He was like a stallion sighting his favorite mare, like a sultan in his harem, espying a new and pretty virgin.

He took a deep breath, calming his nerves, tamping his lust down to a manageable level.

"Close your eyes, Sarah."

"Why?"

"You know why."

"Are you going to kiss me again?"

"I believe I am."

"I wish you wouldn't."

"It's not up to you. With me, it will *never* be up to you."

"I don't want this behavior from you, and I don't understand why it's occurring. If I've done something to make you think that I—"

"Sarah!" he interrupted.

"What?"

"Close your eyes!"

She shook her head, as if to refuse, but her body ignored her. Against her will, her lashes drifted down, and he touched his mouth to hers. It was very brief, very chaste, just a quick brush of his lips to her own, yet he was so disturbed by it that he rapidly pulled away.

He frowned down at her, feeling alarmed and anxious to flee the room immediately.

She actually sighed with pleasure and smiled up at him. To his delight, she didn't try to slip out of his arms. She stayed where she was, her torso pressed to his, giving ample proof that she wasn't quite as resistant as she claimed to be.

"That wasn't so bad," she said.

He snorted. "High praise indeed."

"You've had your kiss. Would you go now?"

"I love it when a woman begs."

"What will it take for me to be shed of you?"

"Maybe if I kissed you again, I might finally have my fill."

He didn't suppose he'd ever have his *fill* of her, which frightened him very much.

His charade in England was about concluded. Hedley was hinting that he'd like another card game, that he'd like a last opportunity to win everything back. John was tempted to humor the foolish boy who was too blind to grasp that he could never best John at any endeavor.

John was one of the world's greatest gamblers—mostly because he had no conscience and cheated with relish. It was another trait he'd inherited from his father who was also a renowned gamester and charlatan.

He'd risked life and limb, arrest and hanging, merely to carry out his reprisal against Mildred. He'd accomplished his goal by ruining Hedley. It had been easy to trick Hedley, but Mildred had always been the target, and she would suffer the most from Hedley's negligence.

John was at the end, a day away from the finale, and he didn't have time to waste with Sarah Teasdale. So what was he doing?

For once, he had no command of himself. He wanted to kiss her forever, and apparently, he wouldn't be able to drag himself away until he was satisfied that he'd made a point with her. The fact that he had no idea what point he was trying to make was irksome and annoying, but if he left Bramble Bay and never saw her again, he was positive he'd regret that he hadn't forged ahead when he'd had the chance.

"Your fill?" She frowned up at him. "Your fill of what?"

"Of you."

"Me! You grow more absurd by the minute."

"I realize it's bizarre, but you've thoroughly captivated me."

"I couldn't have."

"You did."

"You're pestering me because I don't like you."

"Perhaps."

"Women fawn over you. You're used to it—I've seen you with Miss Dubois—and you can't stand that I'm not in awe."

"No, I can't, but you should be."

"Give me one reason why."

"Because I'm wonderful, and you'll never meet a man like me again."

She chuckled. "I'm sure that's true."

"You should take advantage of the situation while you still can. We're drawn to each other; we shouldn't fight it."

"We're not drawn to each other, Mr. Sinclair. I have no interest in you at all, and you're simply a lunatic who is bothering me when you shouldn't be."

"You have no interest in me?"

"No, none."

"Call me John."

"No, and you have to stop calling me Sarah."

"I love your name. It suits you. *Miss Teasdale* is too stuffy." She looked exasperated with him, but a tad charmed, as well. "In another day or two," he told her, "you won't ever see me again."

"You're leaving? And here I thought you were planning an extended visit."

Actually, *she* would be leaving, along with everyone else. But he didn't tell her that.

"Once we're parted, will you miss me?" he asked.

"Always, Mr. Sinclair," she sarcastically said. "I'll pine away for the rest of my life. Are you happy now? You've thoroughly captivated me, too. I'm completely ensnared. I'll never be the same."

At her sassy comment, he laughed and laughed. "You intrigue me beyond measure, Sarah."

"I'm so delighted to hear it."

"You will miss me, and I believe I will miss you, too."

"Of course you will. You'll be absolutely devastated by the loss of me."

"Let's say goodbye—as if it matters."

She studied him, as if committing his face to memory, and she nodded her agreement to have a fond farewell.

"Goodbye, Mr. Sinclair."

"John, remember?"

"Goodbye, John."

"Goodbye, Sarah."

He tightened the arm that still clasped her waist, and he drew her to him so he could dip down and steal another kiss. She didn't protest so he told himself she was amenable.

He kissed her as if he meant it, as if she was special to him and their parting would break his heart. It couldn't—he had no heart—but it was amusing to pretend.

Obviously, she'd been kissed before. She definitely knew how, so her deceased swain must have taught her a few things prior to his perishing. Fleetingly, John wondered if she'd learned any other pertinent lessons, if she wasn't quite as maidenly as she seemed.

He never trifled with innocents. There were too many willing trollops in his world so he didn't have to. But it would be refreshing to avail himself of someone like her, someone who was unsullied and uncorrupted by circumstances.

He riffled through her beautiful hair, stroking her shoulders and back. She fit against him exactly right, as if she'd been created for him alone, and he reveled in the notion that she was his in even this small way.

To have better access, he leaned her across his arm and shoved at the lapels of her robe so he could untie the bow at the front of her nightgown. He slipped a hand inside and covered her breast, his thumb teasing her nipple.

He'd gone farther than he should have, which she instantly made clear. She grabbed his wrist and jerked it away, wrenching her mouth from his.

For the briefest second, he was so overcome by lust that he seriously considered ignoring her. She was petite and defenseless, her suite in a secluded area of the mansion. He could easily pick her up and carry her to the bed in the other room. He could hold her down and ravish her and hardly be winded from the struggle.

Yet he genuinely liked her and didn't want her to have such a horrid opinion of him. Over the next hours and days, she'd have many other reasons to hate him. Let those be the basis for her loathing.

"No, no, no," she scolded as she twisted away. "We're not doing this."

She gazed up at him, appearing rumpled and adorable. He liked that he could fluster her, that he could disconcert her. She wouldn't ever forget him, would stew and recollect.

He smiled. "You can't blame me for trying."

"Yes, I can. I can't stand my ground with you, and I'm annoyed by my weakness. I take one look at you, and my common sense flies out the window."

"You're wild about me."

"I guess I must be. Why else would I allow you such liberties?"

"I wouldn't have any fun if I didn't make an attempt."

"You're really pushing your luck with me."

"Yes, I am, but that's always been my way. You'd be surprised how far a man can go when he's daring and bold."

"No, I wouldn't. The only *daring* man I've ever known is Hedley, and his audacity has constantly led him to ruin."

In light of Hedley's most recent egregious conduct, John couldn't argue.

"When I decided to come here," he said, "I didn't realize Hedley had a sister. I hope you'll remember that."

Completely confused, she frowned. "All right. I'll remember."

He shrugged. "I'm sorry. Not about Hedley, but about you. Remember that too, will you?"

"All right," she said again more slowly.

"I regret that you were caught up in it. I wish there could have been a different ending for you."

"What are you telling me?"

"If you have trouble later on, if you require assistance, my friend Mr. Hook can contact me." It was an offer he'd never intended to extend. But he had. "I'll help you."

"Help me what?"

He touched a finger to her forehead, then traced it down the bridge of her nose, across her lips and chin and throat, to her cleavage.

His body was prodding him to continue, to start in again, but he couldn't. She was about to witness plenty of bad behavior from him. No need to make it worse.

"*Au revoir, chérie.*"

He lifted her hand and placed a very hot kiss on the inside of her wrist. Then he turned and walked away.

"Mr. Sinclair!" He kept on, and she snapped, "John! What is happening? Tell me!"

He glanced back, but couldn't bear to see how pretty she looked, how young and alone.

He couldn't explain the rage that drove him, the revenge that motivated him. He was a burning cauldron of ire and fury, and she had no business standing so close. She'd only be incinerated by the flames.

He whipped away and went to the door, jiggled his knife in the lock. It clicked open easily, and he vanished into the night, not caring a whit if there was anyone in the hall who might notice him as he sneaked out of her room.

CHAPTER FOUR

"He's agreed to play again, Mother. It's wonderful news."

"I don't know, Hedley. You haven't had much success so far."

"I can beat him! I'm sure of it."

That's what you said last time, Mildred nearly snapped, but what was the point?

It was futile to scold. The damage was done, and the only question remaining was how they could maneuver to the end with the least amount of scandal and difficulty.

She and Hedley were sequestered in her sitting room, the morning sun shining in the windows. When she'd initially wed Bernard, the remodel of the pretty parlor had been her first task as a bride.

She'd been devastated by her marriage, furious and bereaved at having plunged to the bottom of society's ladder. In coming to Bramble Bay, a small and unremarkable estate beyond the edge of nowhere, she'd been desperate for a quiet sanctuary where she could retire from her hectic duties and calm herself sufficiently that she could continue on.

She'd had to run Bernard's household, as well as raise his daughter *and* his ward. She'd had to endure his nightly urges. He'd been in his forties and determined to sire a son, so he'd never missed an evening.

Through it all, the sole benefit, her sole joy, had been Hedley.

Bernard had always cautioned that she was spoiling Hedley, that her fussing and cosseting was making him weak and unreliable. It had been the root of all their quarrels. She'd envisioned such a grand future for Hedley that she'd been blind to any flaw or moral failing. Oh, how she hated to admit that Bernard had been correct.

Hedley was the worst sort of profligate and gambler. His habit was an almost uncontrollable madness. He would be overcome by the need to wager, by the certainty that he could win. There was no stopping him, and by the time she'd realized the extent of his obsession, it had been too late.

If she'd been more astute, if she'd paid more attention, could she have seen the disaster approaching? Could she have prevented this dire conclusion?

She didn't think so, and she refused to accept any blame. Hedley had moved to London when he turned eighteen, and he'd insisted on taking charge of the family finances, but he wasn't good with money or numbers.

He complained about their bank accounts, about the income from the estate, how it was never big enough to cover his expenses.

The past year had been a nightmare as creditors had begun to contact her. She hadn't known how to answer their curt messages. As legal judgments had been delivered, she'd ignored them, her fury growing with each humiliating episode.

Her father had been an earl, descended from a long line of aristocrats. No paltry creditor would have dared embarrass him by demanding remuneration for a bill that was overdue. But Mildred had had to marry down due to the outrageous behavior of her older sister Florence. There had been no chance for Mildred to have a husband suitable to her station.

Florence had made a brilliant match, had wed an earl herself and birthed him two sons. Then she'd shocked the entire world when she'd fled to Paris with her lover, Charles Sinclair, Lord Trent.

After that debacle, an aristocratic spouse for Mildred was impossible. In light of her sister's disgrace, what sane man would trust Mildred?

She'd been forced to wed Bernard who was little more than a country farmer, dumped on him at seventeen, after his wife had died. Mildred's father had declared it the best he could do and that she ought to be grateful he'd found her a husband at all.

But she'd never been grateful, and because of Bernard's lowly status, the property wasn't entailed. They weren't protected from predators like John Sinclair.

With the instincts of a vulture, he'd swept in and lured Hedley into a card game he never should have attempted. John Sinclair was very much like Charles Sinclair who'd tantalized idiotic Florence with dreams of the gaiety to be had in France, and Mildred wondered if Mr. Sinclair wasn't related to Charles.

She'd asked him once, but he'd claimed no connection to or knowledge of Lord Trent. But a rogue who would steal a woman's home in a card game would certainly stoop to lying. She'd never met Lord Trent, but she'd heard he was blond and handsome, as was Mr. Sinclair. If she ultimately learned that Mr. Sinclair and Lord Trent were distant kin, she wouldn't be surprised in the least.

"I have to try, Mother." Hedley yanked her from her bitter reverie. "What other choice is there?"

"I suppose there's none."

"I can win it all back. I'm positive." He came over and knelt by her chair, and he clasped her hands. His gaze was so earnest, his demeanor so pleading. "Say you'll help me. Say you'll support me in this."

She'd never been able to deny him anything. That was the whole problem.

She sighed with resignation. "What would you have me do?"

"We'll need one of the rooms, probably the side parlor overlooking the garden, set up for an extended use."

"Extended use? What does that mean?"

"We might continue for several days so servants will have to provide a constant stream of food and cigars and brandy. It could take a bit of maneuvering for me to work him into a corner."

She studied her son. With his brown hair and big blue eyes, he was very attractive, but with his slight build and thin frame, he appeared small and very young. She thought of John Sinclair, of his size and maturity and masculine attributes.

He was thirty, so he was only a decade older than Hedley, but in stature and deportment, he seemed a hundred years older. She didn't expect Hedley could work him into a *corner* or anywhere else. Yet if Hedley didn't wager with Mr. Sinclair again, they'd exhausted their options.

Mildred had always loathed Sarah. She was happy and pleasant— Hedley's exact opposite—and adored by everyone at Bramble Bay. Mildred couldn't imagine telling her of Hedley's shameful conduct, couldn't bear to envision the censure Sarah would level at them both.

Wasn't it best to try every possible alternative? If Hedley gambled, where was the harm? There was nothing left to lose. He'd already bet every item of value, right down to the silverware in the drawers.

She peered out the window, across the sloping lawn to the shimmering ocean in the distance, speculating as to how many more times she'd be able to stare out at the familiar sight.

She could see her reflection in the glass. She was only forty-one, her hair still mostly brown, with a few strands of silver to show her age. Her blue eyes, so much like Hedley's, could sparkle on the rare occasions when she was feeling cheery. But worry over his catastrophe had thinned her torso until she was positively emaciated.

Ire swept through her. She couldn't have anymore children, and she yearned to be a decade younger. If she was, she'd rush next door to visit their neighbor, Sheldon Fishburn.

He was rich and established and planning to wed again, and Mildred could have snagged him if she hadn't been so old. But he was desperate for an heir. Poor, deceased Patrick was the lone child Sheldon had ever sired, and with him being in his sixties, he had to get a boy brewing with a new wife before it was too late.

He was willing to have Sarah despite her advanced age of twenty-five. Yet Sarah—in her typical snobbish fashion—deemed herself too good for him.

Well, Mildred couldn't wait to hear Sarah's opinion in another day or so. As the world came crashing down, and she had nowhere to live and no kin to take her in, she wouldn't think Sheldon quite so elderly or tedious.

"All right, darling," she finally said. "Let me summon the housekeeper. We'll prepare the parlor for your game. When would you like to start?"

"How about tonight after supper?"

"Fine. Everything will be arranged as you've requested."

"Thank you, Mother! Thank you!" He pulled her to her feet, hugged her and danced her around the room. She wished his enthusiasm could be catching, that she could muster some optimism for the outcome, but she was drowning in the worst sense of foreboding.

"Hedley, honestly. Calm yourself."

"I'll save us, Mother. I will!"

"Yes, I'm sure you'll save us all."

"I'll send Mr. Sinclair packing—with his tail tucked between his legs. Just see if I don't."

"You will, Hedley. You will."

She was too weary to be happy, too afraid for the future. She eased away from him, went to her bedchamber, and closed the door.

        ℮ᴅ   ℮ᴅ   ℮ᴅ   ℮ᴅ

"Hello, Mr. Hook."

"Hello, Miss Patterson. Or should I say Mrs. Patterson?"

"Who told you I was married."

"A little bird."

Caroline frowned.

She didn't want the servants chatting about her private business to strangers. When she'd run away from her husband Archibald and slinked to Bramble Bay, Sarah had been very clear with the staff as to the need for secrecy.

Archibald had already come looking for her twice, and he'd stopped in the tavern in the village to mention he would pay a reward for her return.

The ass!

The servants liked Sarah, and Caroline thought they liked her, too. She hoped they'd help to conceal her at Bramble Bay, but the reward was a potent inducement. It unnerved her that people would openly discuss her with an outsider like Mr. Hook.

If they would talk to him, they would eventually talk to Archie.

"Should I call you Miss or Mrs. Patterson?" Mr. Hook asked. "Which is it?"

Caroline wouldn't admit she was married, because he'd follow up with questions as to why she was hiding.

"How about if you call me Caroline?"

"Caroline it is."

They were out on the verandah behind the house. The sun had set, the last twilight having flickered out. She'd been up in her room, avoiding Mr. Sinclair and Mildred and Hedley, when she'd noticed Mr. Hook. He'd been by himself, leaned against the balustrade, drinking a brandy and staring out at the ocean as if he wished he was sailing on it.

He scared her—but in a good and feminine manner. He was dark and dashing and unlike any man she'd ever met. With his black hair and eyes, his black attire and boots, he exuded danger and menace, and he intrigued her in ways he shouldn't.

Archie had always insisted she was mad, and she had to wonder if he wasn't correct. She'd been battered and shamed and abused by him, and she'd kill herself before she'd go back. She was broke and alone and Sarah her only friend.

Yet she was curious as to what Mr. Hook would look like without his clothes.

After being wed to Archie, after learning how disgusting a male body could be, after being taught her wifely duty and failing at it so miserably, why would a salacious thought ever cross her mind?

But Mr. Hook generated that type of rumination. A woman—even one who was as troubled and lost as she was—could start having all sorts of riotous imaginings.

Mr. Hook was the kind of fellow she'd once dreamed about having as a husband. She'd been a wistful romantic who'd read novels and yearned to have a prince carry her away.

By the time Mildred had arranged the match with Archie, Caroline had set her sights quite a bit lower. She'd had no dowry or prospects, and Bernard had passed away, so he hadn't been around to urge caution or select someone more suitable.

As a lure to entice a spouse, there had just been her blond hair, blue eyes, curvaceous figure, and merry personality. Dull, bumbling Archibald Patterson had been eager to have her.

He was Mildred's cousin, and Caroline had been so grateful to Mildred for finding him. But she'd been acquainted with Mildred forever, and she should have remembered to be wary.

Archie was nice enough when he was sober, but he was a heavy drinker, and alcohol changed him into a maniac. Although the bruises had faded, she still had aching bones that were a memento of what could happen if a girl wasn't careful.

So why would she flirt with Mr. Hook? When danger oozed from his every pore, what was she hoping to achieve? Perhaps she was attracted to violence and cruelty. Perhaps she didn't believe she deserved any better.

"Are you married, Mr. Hook?" she asked.

"Gad, no. What woman would have me?"

"Oh, I don't know." Her interested gaze meandered down his torso. "Any number of females might assume you were worth it."

Had those words come out of her own mouth? What was wrong with her?

She'd been sending a message, and he definitely received it. He paused and studied her, his eyes taking their own meander down her body.

"It must get boring out here in the country," he said.

"It does."

"It must be difficult to entertain yourself."

"I used to think so, but lately, my luck has been improving."

She leaned nearer, liking how tall he was, how broad across the shoulders and arms. He leaned in too, so close that his trousers brushed her skirt, the toes of his boots slipping under the hem.

"You want something from me," he murmured. "What is it?"

"What makes you suppose I want something?"

"I've danced around this ballroom a few times before."

"Have you? Then why are you asking? Don't you know?"

He eased away and chuckled. "Yes, I know, but I'm sure if I gave it to you, you'd die from shock."

"You have quite a high impression of yourself."

"It's all deserved."

She laughed and stepped in again. Sparks flew, the air electric with sensation, and she felt wild and free.

"It's very dark down by the beach," she boldly said. "Would you like to take a stroll?"

"Little lady"—he pulled her to him so she was cradled to his chest—"I'd love to *stroll* with you until you were too sore to walk back to the house on your own."

She wasn't certain what he meant by his remark. She understood it was sexual, but had no idea how a woman could become too sore to walk from carnal activity.

"Let's go"—brazenly, she nodded to the sloping lawn—"if you think you're *man* enough."

"I'm man enough. Don't you worry about that." But to her enormous disappointment, he set her away. "I can't tonight."

"Why not?"

"I'm busy."

"With what? It seems to me you're loitering on the verandah and drinking a brandy. You don't look busy."

"John and Hedley are playing cards again."

It was the last comment she'd expected, and she scowled. "They're playing cards?"

"Yes, and I have to watch John's back and keep track of the gold and the chips."

"They'll be wagering?"

"Yes."

"For large stakes?"

"Yes."

Questions raced through Caroline's head. Why would Hedley gamble with Mr. Sinclair? He behaved outrageously in London, but why bring his sordid habits to Bramble Bay? Why would Mildred allow it?

Mildred had never been able to stand up to Hedley, but this conduct had to be beyond the pale.

"Why are they gambling?" she asked.

"The reason all men do: to win."

"To win what?"

"Hedley believes he can recover Bramble Bay."

"Recover Bramble Bay from what?"

He sucked in a sharp breath. "I'm sorry. I thought Mildred was telling everyone today. I thought you knew."

"Knew what?"

"Hedley gambled away the estate."

She gasped. "He what?"

"He played with John several months ago and bet too heavily. So he kept arranging new games, but he couldn't regain any ground."

"What are you saying?" Caroline frantically inquired. "How much has he lost?"

He gestured around. "Everything."

"What do you mean by *everything*? The house? The land? The furniture? The animals and plows and barns?"

"Yes."

"The clothes on our backs?"

His grim expression turned kind. "Yes, but John won't take your clothes. He'll let you have your personal things. Especially you ladies. He's not cruel that way."

She couldn't wrap her mind around the calamity he was revealing. It was common fact that Hedley was spoiled and reckless, but apparently, she'd had no idea. If Bramble Bay was lost, where would she go? Where would Sarah go? What would become of those who depended on the place for their incomes and survival?

Tears welled into her eyes. She wasn't a Teasdale, but Bramble Bay had always been her home. The beautiful spot had been forfeited over a stupid card game? How could Mr. Hook be so cavalier?

"Stop them!" she demanded.

"I can't."

"Make Mr. Sinclair give it back. Make him."

"It's out of my hands, Caroline."

"You're his friend. You could dissuade him if you wanted to."

He shook his head. "I don't want to. I'm determined that Hedley and Mildred get exactly what they deserve."

"Get what they *deserve*? What are you talking about?"

"It's not my story to tell."

"Whose story is it?" He was stoically silent, and she said, "It's Mr. Sinclair's?"

He didn't reply, which told her all she needed to know.

She whipped away and ran into the house, shouting for Sarah.

⌒   ⌒   ⌒   ⌒

"You didn't come down to supper. I was hoping you would."

Sarah smiled at Sheldon who'd been invited to dine as he frequently was. They were chatting in the main parlor. Since she was a baby, he'd been a constant fixture in her life. He was their neighbor, Patrick's father, and her father's friend.

He was sixty, boring, steady and dull, but rich and settled, his estate as fine as Bramble Bay.

He was bald as a ball, short and stout, his body plump from ease and affluence. His round face was covered with a bushy mustache and shaggy muttonchops. As a young man, he'd quickly outlived three wives who'd died from various causes, so he'd declared himself unlucky and gave up wedded bliss.

But age and inheritance issues were spurring him to try again. At Mildred's urging, he'd been pressing the topic with Sarah, but she couldn't make herself consent. Particularly not after Caroline had described marital duty.

Sarah simply couldn't envision removing her clothes, watching as Sheldon removed his, then letting him touch her all over. It sounded tawdry, as if she'd be letting her own father do those things to her.

She kept delaying her answer, kept praying an alternative would present itself, but it was silly to dither. She had no dowry, so there was no handsome suitor who would ride up the drive and rescue her.

Sheldon was the only one who had offered. He was the only one who was willing to have her. Why couldn't she say *yes*? What was wrong with her?

"I've been avoiding the supper table," she explained. "Would you think I was horrid if I confessed that I don't care for Mildred's guests?"

"I didn't much enjoy them either."

"I stay away so I don't embarrass myself by being rude."

"That Sinclair fellow was all right, but Mr. Hook was odd and disconcerting. He looked utterly dangerous. And Miss Dubois, well, the less said about her, the better."

"I agree completely."

"Why are they here?"

"Mr. Sinclair claims he's viewing property in the area."

"With an eye toward buying?"

"I guess."

"They might eventually be our neighbors?"

"I wouldn't want to speculate, but it seems likely."

He chuckled. "The annual Christmas dance at the church would certainly be more lively with those three in attendance."

Sarah chuckled, too. "It certainly would be. If Miss Dubois sauntered in, the vicar would have an apoplexy."

They snickered, then quieted, Sheldon sipping his nightly brandy. He always had precisely one glass after supper, but Sarah didn't join in. He didn't countenance women imbibing of spirits, and even though Sarah rarely drank, his prohibition made her eager to grab the bottle and down the contents—just to spite him.

"Have you thought about our last conversation?" he said, and her heart sank.

She'd hoped to slog through the evening without marriage being mentioned, but he was growing impatient.

"My feelings haven't changed, Sheldon. I wish you'd go to town and interview other candidates. There are so many ladies who would be delighted by your interest. I can't decide, and it's unfair for you to have to wait on me."

"You know I hate London, and at my age, I'm not about to run around, trying to charm some girl whose family I've never met. You and I are well-suited. I'm accustomed to you, and there would be no surprises."

"No, there wouldn't be," which was the main problem.

She really and truly suspected—if she wed him—she'd die of boredom, but she couldn't get him to shift his attention. He expected his constant visits to generate enthusiasm, but with his intractability and her equivocation, each discussion was more unpleasant.

Motion out on the verandah distracted her, and she glanced out to see Mr. Hook lazily balanced on the balustrade. Mr. Sinclair walked up to him, and they whispered like conspirators, their heads close so they wouldn't be overheard.

It was dark outside, a few lamps burning in the garden. The dim light glinted off his blond hair, shrouding him in a golden halo so he was even more striking.

Since he'd sneaked into her bedchamber the previous evening, she hadn't been able to think of anything but him. She was awhirl with memories: how he'd smelled, how he'd felt when he took her in his arms and kissed her.

She shouldn't have let him, but where he was concerned, she was overly attracted and couldn't behave. Like a besotted girl, she'd spent the day trying to cross paths with him, but he'd been conspicuously absent. He'd said he was leaving soon, and she couldn't imagine him going without her furthering their acquaintance.

He appeared to want something from her, but she appeared to want something from him, too. What was it? Flattery? A bone of kindness thrown her way? A few compliments?

He was virile and magnificent, and observing him—while sitting with Sheldon and enduring another tedious chat—was almost painful. Yet it was beneficial, too. It solidified her decision. She'd hold out. She'd marry for love and affection, or she wouldn't marry at all.

Mr. Sinclair whispered a final comment to Mr. Hook, then strolled away, and Sarah rose from her seat, as if hypnotized, as if she'd abandon Sheldon to chase after Mr. Sinclair.

"Honestly, Sarah," Sheldon snapped, "have you listened to a word I've said?"

"I apologize, Sheldon. I'm not myself tonight. Would you like to"—she paused, struggling to devise a means of passing the time before she lost her mind—"would you like to climb to the overlook? The moon is up. The view is probably spectacular. We can take the telescope and see if there are any ships sailing by."

He pursed his lips, his mustache quivering. "You're aware of the trouble I have with my knees. I can't manage the trail."

"Yes, of course. I shouldn't have suggested it. How about a game of cards?"

She was saved by Caroline rushing in. Her friend was agitated, her color high, her cheeks flushed bright red.

"Sarah, there you are! I've been searching everywhere." She frowned at Sheldon. "Sheldon, I'm sorry, but I have to speak with Sarah. Alone."

"What is it?" Sarah asked.

"Can you come?" Caroline gestured to the hall, her eyes flashing an urgent message.

"Sheldon, would you excuse me? I'll be right back."

"I don't think you will be, Sarah," Caroline warned.

Sarah sighed. Mildred had invited Sheldon to supper, then had vanished immediately after the meal. So she wasn't available to entertain him.

"I'll hurry," she told him.

"Don't bother." His aggravation was clear. "Caroline has her petticoat in a wad. I'm sure it will require hours and hours to get it unraveled."

"Sheldon…" Sarah extended a hand in supplication, but he didn't take it.

He pushed himself to his feet. "I should head home. Make my goodbyes to Mildred, will you?"

"I will."

"I'll stop by tomorrow, when things are less hectic."

He huffed out, then Caroline shut the door, assuring their privacy.

"This better be good," Sarah said. "We've annoyed Sheldon, and

I'll never hear the end of it—from him or from Mildred."

"Sheldon can choke on a crow." Caroline had never liked the man. "You won't believe what I just learned."

"What?"

"I was talking to Mr. Hook out on the verandah."

"Really, Caroline, should you socialize with him?"

"Well, we're lucky I was." She led Sarah to the sofa and eased them both down.

"What did he say?"

"Mr. Sinclair is a gambler."

"Oh, no." A sick feeling of dread surged through Sarah's stomach. "Why do I suspect I won't like what you're about to tell me?"

"Hedley gambled with him. He lost and lost and lost, and finally, he bet Bramble Bay."

"Hedley bet...Bramble Bay?"

"Yes. Mr. Sinclair won it—right down to the clothes on our backs."

Sarah's eyes narrowed, and she shook her head, wanting to deny Caroline's words.

"No, it can't be. It just can't be. You must have misheard."

"I didn't, Sarah. He's owned it for months, and he's here to take possession."

"Take...possession? He expects to move in and we are to...what? To leave?"

"Yes."

"With a few bags over our shoulders like a pack of vagrants."

"We won't get to take any bags. Nothing belongs to us anymore."

Sarah recalled her conversation with him the prior night. He'd mentioned leaving, that he'd never see her again, and she'd assumed he meant that *he* was leaving. He'd peppered her with questions about whether she had a dowry, whether she had anywhere to go if disaster struck.

She'd thought he was simply being nosy, but apparently, he'd been concerned as to what would become of her after he tossed her out of her home.

Fury sparked.

Bramble Bay had been in her family for generations. Even though Hedley had inherited it when their father died, Sarah didn't view it as Hedley's. Bramble Bay was *hers,* the Teasdale ancestral seat, and it wasn't his to fritter away. Nor could Mr. Sinclair seize it with a turn of the cards.

It would be nice if such wretched conduct was illegal, but it wasn't. The kingdom was rife with stories of ruination, of squandered fortunes and lost property. She'd never paid much heed to the woeful tales, deeming the participants to have suffered their just desserts for immoral behavior.

But now, they were dealing with *her* home, *her* world, and Hedley's catastrophe would crush all of them—when they'd played no part in the debacle. She refused to accept such a heinous result.

"And guess what?" Caroline continued.

"What?"

"They're gambling tonight. Here in the house."

"Gambling? Why?"

"Hedley wants a chance to win everything back. Mr. Sinclair agreed to let him try."

Sarah pondered foolish, spoiled Hedley, and urbane, sophisticated John Sinclair. Only an imbecile would figure it to be an even match.

"That's insane," Sarah fumed. "Mr. Sinclair will eat him alive."

"I certainly think so."

"You're sure, Caroline? You're not making this up?"

"As if I could invent a tragedy this horrid! I asked Mr. Hook if he'd like to stroll down to the beach, and he can't because he'll be busy keeping track of Mr. Sinclair's gold coins."

"I'm in a state of shock."

"So am I, and listen to this: I pleaded with Mr. Hook to intervene, to dissuade Mr. Sinclair, but he said he wouldn't because Mildred and Hedley are getting exactly what they deserve."

"What they *deserve?* What does that mean? Prior to yesterday, I'd never seen Mr. Sinclair before in my life. How could he know enough about us to hate us?"

"I have no idea, but obviously, there are things transpiring that are beyond our imagining."

A bit earlier, Mr. Sinclair had been out on the verandah with Mr. Hook. They'd looked guilty, like conspirators hatching a scheme, and hadn't she felt from the very beginning that he was a dodgy fellow?

He never gave a straight answer to any question, never admitted his business or even his true name. And he was French—though he pretended not to be.

Hedley had been alone in London, where he liked to be noticed, where he liked to have others presume he was more important than he could ever be.

A fool like Hedley would be bait for a shark like Mr. Sinclair. She was convinced their meeting hadn't been an accident. Had Mr. Sinclair specifically plotted to ruin Hedley? Or had Hedley simply been an easy mark who'd crossed Mr. Sinclair's path at the wrong moment?

Sarah jumped to her feet.

"Where are you going?" Caroline asked.

"To find Mr. Sinclair. I have to put a stop to this."

"How can you?"

"He's fond of me. I'll beg him; he'll be merciful."

"I wouldn't count on it, Sarah. Mr. Hook says they're very determined."

Sarah started for the door just as Mildred entered the room.

"How long have you known about this?" Sarah seethed.

Panic flashed in Mildred's eyes, but she quickly tamped it down.

"Known about what?" she blandly inquired.

"About Hedley's gambling loss. About the fact that Mr. Sinclair owns my home."

"It's my home, too."

"It was my father's home, my ancestors' home. Not yours." Sarah was surprised by the venom in her voice. "You never liked it here."

"It hardly matters now, does it? Not when it's all gone."

"How long have you known?"

Sarah shouted the query, her words ringing off the high ceiling. At witnessing Sarah's rage, Mildred blanched and stepped away, which was a good thing. If she'd been within reach, Sarah might have slapped her.

"Four or five months," Mildred baldly admitted.

"Were you ever planning to tell me?"

"I planned to tomorrow—after it was truly over."

Sarah sagged with defeat. "What am I to do? Couldn't you—for once in your life—have thought of me and that perhaps I could have used some time to make arrangements for myself?"

"Why haven't I *thought* of you?" Mildred scoffed. "Why do you suppose I've been pleading with you to marry Sheldon? Were I you, I'd haul myself over to his house immediately and persuade him to have you while he's still willing—for I'm sure that when the details are generally disseminated, he might not be quite so smitten."

"You witch," Caroline muttered.

"As to you," Mildred said to Caroline, "if you're here in the morning, I'm writing to Archibald to inform him of where you are. He can come fetch you—with my blessing."

She whipped away and stomped out.

CHAPTER FIVE

Feeling as if she was marching to the gallows, Sarah approached the door to Mr. Sinclair's room. She knew she shouldn't have come again, but she had to speak with him immediately.

After Mildred had stormed off, Sarah had flagged down a housemaid and asked about the card game.

It was starting in an hour, in a downstairs parlor. A dozen footmen would spend the night, carting in liquor and cigars and food. The bacchanal would continue until Mr. Sinclair had won everything from Hedley yet again. There would be no stopping him until he'd proved his point—whatever it might be.

Once he'd crushed Hedley beneath his boot, once he'd humiliated Hedley one last time, what would become of her brother? What would become of all of them?

She knocked and knocked, but received no answer, so she pressed her ear to the wood. Inside, she could hear voices. She spun the knob and walked in. The sitting room and bedchamber were empty, and boldly, she kept on, foolishly proceeding to the dressing room where the voices grew more distinct.

She halted in the doorway and studied the sordid scene.

Mr. Sinclair and Miss Dubois were together, preparing as if to attend a fancy party.

Miss Dubois was attired in a dazzling red gown that sparkled when she moved. The neckline was scooped so low, her corset pushing her breasts so high, that Sarah could see the pink rim circling her nipples. If she leaned forward, her breasts would be fully visible.

Was it intentional? Hedley would certainly be distracted by the risqué display.

Dubois's blond hair was elaborately coiffed, with an exotic mix of braids, curls, and red feathers that matched her gown. She was drenched in a tantalizing perfume, an intoxicating scent that would definitely divert a boy of Hedley's limited sophistication.

Mr. Sinclair was standing in the middle of the floor as Miss Dubois fluttered around him, attaching bulky, gaudy rings on his fingers.

He was wearing another magnificent coat, another intricate cravat, lace and embroidery giving evidence of obscenely expensive tailoring. Dubois fussed with his sleeves, the lace, making sure every item was perfectly placed.

Through it all, they were smiling, talking as if they'd been married for years, as if they were intimately connected. And though it was stupid to be hurt, Sarah couldn't prevent a surge of jealousy.

She was so lonely and unappreciated, and when he'd sneaked in the previous evening, when he'd kissed her and pretended concern for her condition, she'd assumed fondness had blossomed. But he was a libertine and could have been kissing her or any woman.

Miss Dubois was finished with her task, and she took an assessing stroll around his person. When she was in front of him again, she sighed with satisfaction.

"You are a sight, *mon ami,*" she whispered.

"Of course I am."

"Poor Hedley. He'll remember this night—and regret it—for as long as he lives."

"Here's hoping."

They laughed, and Miss Dubois rose on tiptoe and kissed him on the mouth.

"Are you ready?" she asked.

"I was born ready."

"Let's go. Hedley will be growing impatient."

"Mr. Sinclair?" Sarah murmured.

They frowned and glanced over to see who had arrived.

"Sarah," he said, "what are you doing here?"

"May I speak with you?" He appeared as if he'd refuse, and she added, "It's important."

"You hussy," Miss Dubois snapped. "Haven't I warned you to stay away? Will you not listen?"

Dubois stepped menacingly, as if she would storm over and assault Sarah, and John stopped her with a wave of his hand.

"Go down without me," he told Miss Dubois. "I'll join you in a few minutes."

"No, Jean Pierre," she pouted. "We must go down together."

He nodded to her door. "Wait in your room then. I'll be in shortly."

She might have argued, but his scowl kept her silent. She tossed her fabulous hair and stomped out, shutting the door with a determined click. Sarah wondered if she was kneeling on the other side, peeking in the keyhole. She couldn't imagine Miss Dubois surrendering Sinclair's attention without a fight.

Sarah stared at him, but couldn't seem to begin. She was desperate to make sense of who he was, of which John was the *real* John Sinclair and which was the illusion. He had so many faces, so many façades.

She thought she was looking at the genuine man. This hardened, imperious stranger was someone she didn't know and didn't like, and the notion left her incredibly weary. How could she reason with a person who had no conscience?

"Is it true?" she finally inquired.

"Is what true?"

He couldn't hold her gaze. He went over to a table, picked up a decanter of whiskey, and poured himself a drink. Sipping it, he turned and leaned against the wall. He watched her, aloof, bored, determined.

"Don't toy with me," she said. "Not about this."

"All right, I won't."

"Do you own Bramble Bay now? Did you steal it from Hedley?"

He bristled with temper. "I didn't steal it from Hedley. He frittered it away. Before you start assigning blame, let's be clear about what happened. He's arrogantly irresponsible and had no business involving himself with me."

"Fine. He frittered it away. Don't keep it. Give it back."

"No."

"It's my home."

"I realize that, and while it will provide scant solace, I am sorry."

"No, you're not."

He shrugged, but didn't comment.

"If you've already won everything," she asked, "what's the point of tonight?"

"There is no point. Hedley wants to try his luck again, but he has no luck."

"Then why wager with him?"

"Why not?"

"How can you be so flippant about this?"

"I'm not being flippant. I'm very, very serious. This property—down to the smallest candle stub—is mine. I'm happy to prove it to your brother again."

"Another loss will kill him. He cares about me and his mother. When he grasps the full ramifications, it will crush him. He'll never recover."

"What becomes of him later is not my affair."

"It will kill *me*," she caustically spat. "Is that any of your affair?"

"I'm sorry, *chérie*. I wasn't aware that Hedley had a sister, and I hate that you were swept up in it."

"Don't go through with it. I'm begging you."

"Don't beg," he said, but she walked over and dropped to her knees. Tears flooded her eyes as she clutched the lapels of his beautiful coat.

"Please, Jean Pierre. Is that your real name? Please John or Jean Pierre or whoever you are. Have mercy on me. Have mercy on my family."

He stared down at her, his expression unmoved. "I have no mercy to share."

"Yes, you do. You can be kind. I'm sure of it. I've witnessed it in you."

"I'm no one's savior, Sarah." He chuckled, but desolately. "I once tried to murder my own brother. I stabbed him with a sword—the blade went completely through his body. We were at sea, and I put him in a lifeboat and set him adrift with no food or water. I wanted him to die. He didn't, but I wanted it so badly."

She shook her head, refusing to believe it. "You couldn't have."

"I did, *chérie*. And if I could act so dastardly toward my own brother, why would you suppose I'd be concerned over a worm like Hedley?"

"Please!" she beseeched, the tears overflowing.

"Get up, Sarah." He pulled her to her feet. "I can't bear to see you so sad." There was a towel on a shelf next to them. He grabbed it to dab at her wet cheeks, but she shoved him away.

"I thought you were fond of me," she said.

"I was. I am."

"How can I sway you?"

"You can't. I have been pursuing my course for too long now, and I can't change it. I don't *wish* to change it."

"Mr. Hook claims that Hedley and Mildred deserve to lose Bramble Bay."

He raised a brow. "I'll have to remind him that it's dangerous to be so indiscreet."

"What has brought on this catastrophe? You feel they deserve it, but the disaster will fall on me. Haven't I the right to know what's driving you?"

For an eternity, he glared down at her, and she presumed he wouldn't speak, but ultimately, he said, "I will tell you a story, but if you repeat it, I'll call you a liar."

"What did they do to you?"

He led her to a nearby chair and eased her down. He gulped the dregs of his glass, poured himself another and gulped that too, giving her the distinct impression that his explanation would be extremely difficult.

"Once upon a time, there was a British woman who married much too young and whose husband was a brute. In a moment of youthful foolishness, she left him and traveled to Paris. She thought she could be happy there, but she never was."

"What happened to her?"

"She died, poor and cold and alone, with no one by her side except her son. She came from a very rich family, and he wrote to them. He begged them to send money for food, for medicine, for a house where they could buy wood and have fires on winter days."

"But they sent no money?"

"No, and her lofty relatives weren't content to simply deny assistance. They had to write back to say that the woman *deserved* her fate, that she had disgraced them and they would never forgive her."

She peered up at him, pondering the tale. "It was you. You were the son."

"Yes, and Florence Harcourt was my mother."

She gasped. "Florence was your mother?"

"Yes."

Sarah actually shuddered with dread. Her entire life, she'd heard about immoral, scandalous Florence who'd fled her husband and two babies to flit off to Paris with a lover.

Florence's shocking behavior had wrecked Mildred's family, had ruined her chance for a magnificent marriage. Mildred still fumed over the debacle even though it had been thirty years since Florence had run away.

"When the mother passed on"—he remained dispassionately composed—"her son was holding her hand. He vowed to avenge her. As she took her dying breath, he vowed to retaliate against all those who had been so cruel."

"Vengeance won't heal you, John."

"I never expected it would."

"It won't make you feel better about what transpired."

"I beg to disagree. So far, I've carried out numerous retaliations, and it's made me feel quite grand."

"Mildred is your *aunt,* John. Hedley is your cousin."

"I have no kin," he firmly stated, "and family means nothing to me."

"Then I am very, very sorry for you."

The door to the adjoining bedchamber opened, and Miss Dubois peeked in.

"Jean Pierre, we must go down."

He sighed. "Yes, we must."

Sarah tried one last time. "Don't do this, John."

"I must finish it." He stroked a thumb across her bottom lip. "It will be over very soon."

"It will never be over," she insisted, "not when you're raging like this."

"Goodbye, *chérie,* and don't be sad. I hate to see tears on your pretty cheeks."

He turned and walked over to Miss Dubois. She took his arm, and they departed without another word.

"That can't be right." Hedley studied the cards John had laid on the table, and he shook his head in bewilderment. "You couldn't have been holding an ace."

John shrugged and sipped his drink. "You don't seem to have much luck at cards, Hedley. Perhaps you should choose a new hobby."

"Let's play again," Hedley demanded.

"No."

"In case you haven't noticed, this is my home we're wagering over." Hedley said it as if the fact was newly revealed.

"We've been betting for months, Hedley, and I've been more than patient. When will you decide you've had enough?"

"We're both gentlemen, Sinclair. You have to give me a chance to recoup my losses. It's only sporting."

"I've given you six chances. I've been extremely accommodating, and there's no reason to continue with this charade."

"You can't have my home!" Hedley shouted the remark. "I refuse to let you steal it from me."

John scrutinized his cousin, struggling to find a resemblance in their features, but didn't see any. And there was certainly no similarity of character.

Upon Hedley entering the room, he'd been pompously egotistical, hurling insults and boasting of his lineage and name. Now, he was drenched in perspiration, gulping down liquor, fretting and mumbling to himself.

John was freshly bathed and barbered, powdered and perfumed, his clothes exquisitely laundered and his expensive outfit not having so much as a wrinkle in the fabric. The task of beating Hedley required little concentration and almost no skill, and he hadn't broken a sweat. He was bored and ready to end it once and for all.

They'd been playing for just three hours, starting at the point where it had all begun the prior winter. They'd rapidly arrived at the finish line—with John winning all.

He hadn't cheated a single time. Hedley was so bad at tracking the cards that he couldn't deduce what was coming, while John was so adept, his mind so shrewdly calculating, that he could predict his cards before he picked them up.

Hedley was also handicapped by his inability to control himself. As his losses mounted, he became frantic, drank too much, grew more animated and less perceptive, so his problems escalated. It didn't help that his face was an open book, his emotions and distress clear as day.

With Hedley, there were no surprises. John could guess his every move before Hedley knew, himself, what step he would take.

John felt as if he was trapped in an odd fable where the same things occurred over and over, where the characters were laboring under a wicked spell and couldn't escape. How was he to break the enchantment and free himself?

"Let's each draw one card," Hedley said. "High card wins."

"Wins what?"

"We'll play for the whole estate! All I've bet in the past. All I've lost. You owe me that, Sinclair!"

The next card in the deck was a deuce, the one after that a king, so John was happy to agree. He tossed the top card to Hedley, the second one to himself.

Hedley stared and stared, then wailed, "This can't be happening!"

"I'm declaring this to be over."

"I want to roll dice. I'll have better luck with dice."

"No."

"You have to let me!"

"No, I don't."

Hedley was growing surly and petulant, and Annalise understood her role. She rose from her chair and came over. She leaned across Hedley, blocking John from view, as she refilled Hedley's glass.

"Calm yourself, Master Hedley," she murmured as if she had his best interests at heart. "You're so distraught."

She was usually a fine distraction, but Hedley was working himself into a full-fledged tantrum, so her effectiveness had collapsed. She flashed John a look of resignation, then sidled back to her chair.

"I don't know how you keep doing it." Hedley leveled his glare at John.

"Doing what?"

"In all these months, I haven't won a single hand." He pounded his fist on the table. "Not a single one!"

"I've told you and told you, Hedley: You're not much of a gambler."

Hedley's cheeks reddened, and he appeared very much like the spoiled, cosseted child he must have been when he was small. John could vividly picture him stamping his foot, demanding a candy from Mildred who would have rushed to the kitchen to find him the largest piece in the house.

For John, there had been no candy, no pleasant store of memories. His childhood was a depressing tale of poverty and tribulation and barely getting by. Envy and malice flared—over the easy life Hedley had had, at how he'd wasted it—but John swiftly tamped down the strident sentiments.

There was no reason to hate Hedley. He was just the vessel to make Mildred sorry, to teach her what it was like to be afraid and poor and alone.

"You have to be cheating," Hedley blurted out.

Annalise gasped, John stiffened, and Raven stepped in. Hedley's words were dangerous and deadly and could get him killed. A man's honor was all he had, and though John possessed little of it, he was very proud, very vain. He wouldn't sit quietly and be insulted in the most hideous way possible.

Raven tried to smooth over the tense moment. "I'm sure we misheard, my friend."

"Did I stutter?" Hedley snidely fumed. "Are you deaf? He cheats. It's the only answer."

Raven glowered at Hedley, his disdain clear. "I would urge caution, Mr. Teasdale. You're upset, and it's typical to blame—"

"I'm calling him a cheat! I'm saying it to his face."

Hedley crossed his arms over his chest and stared at John, daring him to comment, daring him to react.

"You're quick with your allegations," Raven warned, "but we won't listen to nonsense. Apologize, and we'll forget your accusation."

"I won't."

"I'll ask one more time."

Hedley was young and smug and ridiculous. "I'd rather be boiled in oil than apologize to him about anything."

Raven peered over at John. "Shall I handle it for you?"

"No."

"Handle what?" Hedley sneered at John. "I'm calling you a cheat. What will you do about it? Will you have your lackey scold me?"

John smiled malevolently. "I suppose we could try pistols at dawn."

"Pistols!" Hedley snapped, the lethal prospect not having occurred to him.

"Yes, I'd be happy to shoot your worthless ass out in the woods."

Raven leaned in and said, "Or I can carry you out there right now. I'll slit your throat and bury you in a shallow grave. It will save John the trouble of loading his gun and having to get up early."

Hedley blanched. "You're threatening me!"

"I certainly am, you pathetic weasel." Raven slapped a palm on the table. "Apologize to John—or you're dead."

"You can't talk to me like that," Hedley whined. "I'll bring my mother in here. She'll tell you."

Raven rolled his eyes and bit down a guffaw. Annalise shook her head with disgust. John simply studied his cousin, but he was thinking about Sarah, how she'd bravely sought him out, how she'd begged so prettily on Hedley's behalf.

Laws of inheritance were bizarrely concocted. Because John's parents had never married, he'd been spurned and ignored and—to his shame—spat upon as a lad. His father, Charles Sinclair, hadn't even wanted Florence to give John the Sinclair surname.

But she had anyway, after he'd left Paris and returned to England. They'd never seen Charles Sinclair again, and they'd received no support from him.

Charles had never sired any legitimate children with his aging, bitter British wife. He'd only produced bastards, and John was brilliant and tough and shrewd. He would have been an excellent heir to Charles's wealth, an excellent custodian to protect and grow his estates. Yet he couldn't—because of the law and its absurd pronouncements on who was legitimate and who wasn't.

Sarah and Hedley had both been Bernard's children, but because Hedley was male, he'd inherited everything. Hedley had heedlessly proceeded without the smallest worry as to how his actions would affect his sister. Sarah was at Hedley's mercy, at Mildred's mercy.

Where was the equity in that? How much better, how much fairer, the world would be if Bramble Bay had been bequeathed to Sarah. She would have guarded and cherished it.

John had told her that he was sorry, and he truly was. Sorry that she'd been caught in the mess. Sorry that Hedley was her brother. Sorry that she was in such jeopardy, but it didn't change anything.

John wouldn't back down or relent.

"Don't drag your mother into it, Hedley," John chided. "Be a man. Fight your own battles."

"I can't tell her I failed again!"

Hedley was so wretched that John could barely stand to stay in the room. "You should have thought of the consequences last winter before we started."

"I can't figure out how this happened."

"You lose all the time, Hedley. We inquired in town. You're the worst gambler in history."

Hedley gaped at Annalise, at Raven, as if they might help him. When he looked at John again, he actually had tears in his eyes, and he swiped at them with his hand.

"What now?" he asked, his misery plain.

Raven answered for John. "Now, we toss all of you out on the road where you belong."

"But we haven't made any plans. We haven't packed or notified the servants or…or…" His voice trailed off, the ramifications sinking in. "We're not ready to go."

John scoffed. "That's hardly my problem. You've had an eternity to make arrangements."

"Could we have another month?"

"I won't have you loitering."

"The servants and my sister and Caroline…" He swallowed down a sob. "And my mother! This is all my fault. She doesn't deserve this ending."

The moment was incredibly awkward. John felt as if he was kicking a puppy. He considered walking out, having Raven deal with the rest of it, when Hedley begged, "Let's draw cards to see if you'll let us stay. Just thirty days. How can it matter to you?"

"I have no desire to be gracious, and I only bet when my opponent has items of value to wager. I've said you can keep your clothes, so you don't have anything else to stake."

"I'll…I'll…" Hedley stopped, resembling a trapped fox who hears the dogs approaching. "I'll give you my sister."

"Give her *how*?"

"She's pretty and chaste, and she's never been married. You can have her—in exchange for the thirty days."

John bristled with offense. "I can *have* her. Are you saying what I think you're saying?"

Annalise shifted uneasily in her chair. Though she fought to hide it, she was a very jealous person, and she didn't like the direction the conversation was traveling.

"Jean Pierre?" she murmured. "May I speak?"

He didn't so much as glance at her. "Would you excuse us, Annalise?"

"But Jean Pierre!"

"Not now, Annalise," he snapped.

Raven went over, took her arm, and escorted her out. There were two footmen in the corner, observing with wide-eyed fascination. John nodded to Raven, and he escorted them out, too.

When it was just the three of them, John gestured to Hedley.

"Continue."

"My mother must have sufficient opportunity to pack and prepare." More vehemently, he repeated, "She must!"

"So you've claimed."

"You can entertain yourself with Sarah."

"For how long?"

"For…as long as you wish. Until you grow weary of her."

"She's quite fetching. What if I never grow weary? What if I keep her forever? It hardly seems fair that you're pleading for thirty days, while she could be bound for a lifetime."

"You wouldn't keep her that long," Hedley scoffed. "You have sophisticated tastes. You'll quickly tire of her, and she'll move on."

To where? John mused. Where—precisely—did Hedley imagine Sarah would go when John was finished with her? Obviously, Hedley didn't care a whit about her, and John was so incensed that he wondered if he shouldn't kill Hedley then and there.

He had a knife in his boot. He could reach for it and stab Hedley in the heart before the selfish oaf inhaled another breath. John would rid the world of his obnoxious, repulsive presence.

Why let him live? Then again, John liked Sarah very much, and he didn't suppose she'd look too kindly on John slaying Hedley.

John drummed his fingers on the table.

The bet was common enough. Fathers and brothers often wagered their female family members when there was nothing left to barter. Unscrupulous roués constantly trolled for pretty girls, driving bets to absurd amounts that couldn't be paid, then offering to settle for a sister or a daughter who'd caught their licentious eyes.

So Hedley's conduct wasn't unusual. It was shocking, though. And revolting.

How could John leave her at Hedley's mercy? If John didn't take her under his wing, what might happen to her? What other bets might Hedley end up making? What other low sorts of fellows might salivate over the chance to have her? What other disasters might her brother inflict?

John peeked up at Raven, and Raven shrugged, indicating that he had no opinion on what John should do.

"It's a deal," John finally said. "Miss Teasdale is mine, and you have your thirty days."

Hedley was so relieved that he nearly slid to the floor in a heap. "Thank you! Thank you! My mother will be so grateful."

"I'm sure she will be," John seethed. What a despicable child his aunt had raised. What a menace. What an embarrassing lump of clay.

"You're welcome to remain as our guests," Hedley magnanimously stated, "unless you have somewhere else you need to be in the interim?"

Now that Hedley had won a reprieve, he was absurdly eager to push John and Raven out the door. Hedley probably assumed he could be shed of John, then come up with a rescue plan.

The boy was an idiot, and John couldn't understand why he hadn't committed murder when the prospect had first occurred to him.

"No, Hedley," John countered. "Let me be blatantly clear. You and your mother may remain at Bramble Bay as *my* guests—for the next thirty days."

"But...but..."

"Get it through your thick head. The house is mine. The estate is mine. You have a month to vacate. Mr. Hook will stay to guarantee you don't steal the silverware when you go."

Hedley's face contorted in an unbecoming pout. "You're being grossly unfair."

"No, I'm being overly generous." John stood, not able to bear his cousin's company another second. "Will you tell Miss Teasdale or will I?"

For a fleeting moment, Hedley actually looked ashamed. "I'll tell her."

"Should you be the one? She won't be too happy to hear this result from you."

"She can be obstinate, so I'll have to make her see reason."

"You do that," John fumed. "I won't permit her to refuse, and if she tries, you and your mother will depart immediately."

"I can't be responsible for Sarah's behavior!"

"Can't you?"

"No. She's very stubborn."

"She has tonight to come to grips with what you've done."

"I'll need more time with her!"

"You can't have it." John appeared thunderous, like the Angel of Death. "I'll claim her as my prize tomorrow. Be sure she knows. And a bit of advice, Hedley?"

"What?" Hedley sullenly said.

"You never apologized to me for your insult to my honor, and no one gets away with that kind of slight. You should meticulously avoid me, for if I have the misfortune to bump into you when I'm in a bad mood, I'll kill you, and I'll smile while it's happening."

John stormed out, and as he left, Raven muttered, "I couldn't have put it better myself."

CHAPTER SIX

"Will you have a brandy?"

"No."

"How about a late supper? I could have the cook awakened to prepare something for you."

"No."

Annalise glanced at the clock on the mantle. It was just past eleven.

If Hedley had been any kind of gambler, the game might have lasted until dawn or longer. Matters had proceeded so quickly that she and Jean Pierre were already back in their suite. The whole night stretched ahead of them.

She was in the dressing room, brushing her hair, and he was in her bedchamber, stretched out on her bed. He was in an odd mood, and she wasn't sure what had happened with Hedley once he'd had Raven escort her out.

He'd never been an avid talker, and from the beginning of their relationship, he'd instructed her that she shouldn't question him on any topic. If he wanted her to possess certain information, he would tell her. Otherwise, she was kept in the dark.

On the one hand, she was relieved that he hid details from her. If he was ever arrested, there would be very little she could confess about him. On the other hand, she'd been with him for two years.

In nearly every way, she could be considered his wife. She lived with him in his castle in France, and when he was away from home, she managed the residence so he would receive a warm welcome when he dropped anchor in his small harbor. She shared his bed and helped him with some of his schemes and swindles.

She'd grown up in Paris, on the fringe of the royal court where her mother had been a courtesan and had schooled Annalise in deception and plotting. When Annalise had met Jean Pierre, she'd been working at a very private, very expensive brothel.

He'd been instantly smitten and had offered to buy out her contract from the owner. Annalise hadn't hesitated to consent.

She'd abandoned her life in Paris for him, had abandoned her friends and her regular clients. She'd moved to the coast specifically to please him, to make him happy.

Didn't she deserve to know his business?

Hedley had dangled his pretty sister in front of Jean Pierre, and Jean Pierre would gladly take her from Hedley. Annalise had observed Jean Pierre earlier in the evening when Mademoiselle Teasdale had begged him to halt the game.

There had been a chemistry between them that Annalise hadn't liked. He was enthralled by Sarah Teasdale and had plainly been wondering if she could be seduced.

Had Hedley given her to Jean Pierre? Annalise was dying to find out and could barely keep from marching in and demanding answers he would never provide.

He had the morals of a stray dog and would lie down with any woman who tempted him. He didn't believe in monogamy or fidelity, and he'd been clear from the start that he wouldn't be faithful. She was not allowed to pester him about his flirtations, so she spent most of her time swallowing down her fury, but not letting him realize her upset.

Doxies constantly threw themselves at him, and Annalise had to chase them away. She'd wait until he deemed an affair to be ended, then *she* would threaten and bully his lovers to never return.

They could never bear to part with him, but they didn't understand that he bonded with no female. His liaison with Annalise was as close as he would ever come to a connection, and she intended that their arrangement continue for as long as he was content with her, which—if she was lucky—would be forever.

She gazed into the mirror, frowning at a tiny line that had appeared on the side of her mouth. Quickly, she smoothed over it with a cosmetic. Jean Pierre assumed she was twenty-three, but in reality, she was his same age of thirty. She would never give him the slightest hint that she wasn't as young as he presumed her to be.

She stepped out of her petticoat and drawers and slipped into a lace robe that left nothing to the imagination. Then she spun back and forth in front of the mirror, assessing her breasts, her profile.

"Magnifique!" she murmured to herself. She was stunning, like no other woman who'd ever crossed his path.

He'd never been able to resist her—not from the very first—and she was eager to remind him of why he'd bought her, why he kept her. By dawn, Mademoiselle Teasdale would be but a distant memory.

She sashayed into her bedchamber, and he was staring at the ceiling and lost in thought. He heard her approach, and he glanced over, delighting her with how she captured his attention. The entire center of her torso was visible, her shaved mons luring him to misbehave.

She walked in and sat on the edge of the mattress. He was wearing his trousers and boots, but he'd shed his coat and shirt, so his chest was bare. She placed her hand on his shoulder, caressing a recent wound. A few months earlier, he'd been shot, and the injury still plagued him.

His body had been damaged in numerous ways: burns and stabbings and gunshots and broken bones. Many mornings, it was difficult for him to rise and face the day, and she always worked to ease his discomfort.

"Would you like me to massage your shoulder?" she asked.

"Not tonight," he surprised her by saying.

He typically welcomed her ministrations, and a lengthy massage was the starting foray that led to other things.

She climbed onto the bed and straddled his lap. Shucking off her robe, she gave him a good look at her fabulous bosom, her slender waist and rounded hips.

"What shall we do instead?" she flirtatiously inquired.

"My bout with Hedley exhausted me. Let's just rest a bit."

"I can cure your exhaustion."

"You certainly can," he replied, but he didn't sound all that enthused.

He was such a cold, aloof man. She hadn't thought he could be flustered by any circumstance, so she hadn't worried about traveling to Bramble Bay to ruin his cousin and aunt. But ever since they'd arrived, he'd been acting strangely.

The sooner they went back to France the better.

She scooted down, her busy fingers unbuttoning his trousers. He watched her, appearing completely detached as she pulled out his phallus. He was long and hard, and she never grew weary of pleasuring him. He was a precise and skilled lover, and she knew how to satisfy him in every manner he enjoyed.

She dipped down and sucked him into her mouth. He took a few slow, leisurely thrusts, then drew away. She sat up and glared at him, unable to read any emotion in his eyes.

"I'm not in the mood," he said.

The comment was the most frightening one he'd ever uttered. He was *always* in the mood. He was *always* ready to fornicate. There had never been a moment in the prior two years that he had refused to proceed.

"You're joking," she huffed.

"I told you I was weary."

He stood, and she was naked and alone on the bed. She felt stupid and underdressed and unappreciated. She felt like the prostitute she was.

"What is it, *mon ami?*" she asked.

"I hate it here in England."

"Then let's depart. Let's saddle the horses and canter to the ship. We don't have to remain."

"I can't leave yet. The situation with Hedley and Mildred is too unsettled."

"*Merde!* Forget about them. Let Raven stay and toss them out on the road."

"I have to see it through to the end."

"No, you don't. Let's sail to Spain and lounge on the beach for a few weeks. You're happy when you're there."

He scrutinized her, and the worst niggle of concern slithered down her spine. He seemed to be evaluating her for purposes he'd never previously considered, seemed to be taking her measure, deciding if she was worth the bother.

"I'm going for a ride," he suddenly said.

"Now?" she snapped with more ire than she should have displayed.

"I need to clear my head."

"I could clear it for you if you'd just lie back down."

"You can't fix what's wrong with me."

He looked callous and bored, and she couldn't stand to be with him when he was out of sorts.

"Fine, go." She waved to the door.

"And when I return, I want to sleep alone. Don't come in and pester me."

"I won't, I won't."

"In the morning, we have to talk."

He stomped out, and before she could think to say, *About what?,* he was in his own room, the door closed behind him.

She yearned to storm over and start a quarrel, but didn't dare. He simply wouldn't tolerate a show of anger, and she flopped down on the mattress and pounded her fist on the pillow.

Why was he vexed with her? Why now? Was he excited by his new virgin, Mademoiselle Teasdale? Was he planning to train her to take Annalise's place? He had better not be!

She could kill as well as any man, and she'd committed murder once—had stabbed a violent lover to death in Paris—so she'd proved herself capable of homicide.

After all she'd done for Jean Pierre, after all she'd relinquished, if he thought he could put her aside, he would be very, very sorry.

"Sarah, is that you?"

Raven shook his head at his absurdity. It had been many years since he'd trifled with a gently-bred female, and he'd never had any manners.

Earlier, out on the verandah, Caroline Patterson had begun a flirtation. Was she still amenable?

He hoped so, or else he'd just committed the most humiliating blunder ever.

"It's not Sarah," he replied.

She was in her dressing room, and she peeked into her bedchamber to discover him leaned against the doorframe.

"Mr. Hook?"

She was surprised, but didn't scream, which was a relief.

"Yes, hello."

"What are you doing in here?"

He shrugged, feeling stupid and out of his element. "The card game ended sooner than I expected. I figured you might be awake."

"So you barged in?"

"Yes, I'm obnoxious that way. It's easier than waiting to be invited."

"It's very late, and I'm not in any condition to walk in the garden."

"I don't want to walk in the garden."

"What is it then?"

He gestured to her. "Come here, and I'll show you."

"I don't care for the look in your eye. Tell me instead."

"No. Come to me." He gestured again, less patiently.

She'd been preparing for bed, so she was wearing only a robe with nothing on underneath. Her beautiful blond hair was down and brushed out, the lush curls falling to her shapely bottom. Her feet were bare.

She tugged at the lapels on her robe, yanked at the sash to pull it tighter, and he nearly laughed. As if a paltry sash could keep him from doing whatever he pleased. In his habits and actions, he was too much like John. He barked out commands, and people jumped to obey.

He had to calm himself, had to remember he shouldn't scare her. She'd dangled a dalliance, and he was determined to accept what she'd offered. If she'd changed her mind, he'd simply change it back again.

He wouldn't be denied. He never was. Not by anyone.

He went over to her, pushed her hand away and drew her to him. He loosened the sash, exposing her cleavage.

Behind her, there was a large silver bathing tub. It was filled with rose-scented hot water, steam rising. Towels were stacked on a dresser. He'd interrupted at the perfect moment, and he grinned. The prospects were ripe for misbehaving.

"What happened with Hedley and Mr. Sinclair?" she asked.

"Nothing that hasn't already happened several times before."

"Hedley lost?"

"Of course. He had no chance with John. He never had a chance."

"What will become of us?"

"You have thirty days to find somewhere to go."

She snorted with derision. "You make it sound as if it's simple to move on. You act as if we all have a dozen homes and can flit among them at our leisure."

"Aren't you married? Why don't you return to your husband?"

She stared and stared, seeming to be perched on the edge of a confession. Ultimately, she said, "It's a long story."

"Does he live in the area? Or is he in London?"

She nodded to the sitting room. "Did you lock the door when you came in?"

"Yes."

"You're awfully sure of yourself. How could you be certain I wouldn't shout for help?"

"You're a wee mite. If you'd called out, I could have silenced you quickly enough."

"That's quite a…violent statement. Are you in the habit of abusing women?"

"Not lately."

"Well…good. I'm glad to hear it."

He pointed to the tub. "You were about to bathe."

"Yes, I was."

"Go ahead. I'll pull up a chair and watch."

Her eyes widened with shock—but with interest, too.

He wondered about her husband.

Since he and John had arrived at the estate, he'd spent his time lurking and listening, cajoling housemaids and bribing footmen. He knew most of what could be gleaned about the affairs in the house.

Mrs. Patterson had left to marry, but had recently returned and had no plans to leave. The servants were reluctant to mention why. They liked her and were extremely loyal to Sarah Teasdale. Obviously, Caroline Patterson had secrets, but he'd eventually pry them out of her.

"You'll watch me bathe?" Her astonishment was clear.

"Yes, and I'll enjoy myself, too."

"But I usually wash in the nude."

"I certainly hope so."

"I've now spoken to you on exactly two occasions. It seems a tad…*forward* of you to expect to stay."

"I can never predict what John might ask of me. I might be here for a year, or he might have me ride off tomorrow. If I'm ordered away, I'll never have the opportunity to spread your thighs."

"Mr. Hook! Honestly." Her cheeks flamed, and she waved a hand to cool them. "You overwhelm me with your bold talk."

"I don't like to flirt and dawdle. I like to get down to business."

"I'm not a whore in a brothel," she starkly said. "There's no need to hurry. I'm not peeking at the clock so I can tell you when your hour is up."

"You know about whores and brothels, do you? From who? Your husband?"

Her cheeks flushed an even deeper shade of red, which provided a great deal of information about her. No doubt the ass visited whores. No doubt he regaled her with details of his antics. Did he claim she didn't keep him satisfied? Did he claim she'd failed as a woman?

Wouldn't Raven be thrilled to show her that her husband was wrong?

He reached for the belt of her robe and untied it so the lapels were loose, so her center was bared. He slipped his hands inside and rested them on her waist, just at the spot where her tummy flared to her curvaceous hips.

"The water's getting cold," he said. "You'd best climb in."

She peered up at him, her mind awhirl, and he could practically read her thoughts. She was intrigued by his suggestion, but she was a typical British female. Her entire life, she'd have been told to never flaunt herself or engage in a ribald display. But she chafed at those restrictions and was eager to break the chains that bound her to modest conduct.

"I'd have to pin up my hair," she said.

"Then do it."

She twisted the lengthy tresses into a knot and stabbed in a few combs so her blond curls were haphazardly balanced. She looked even more beautiful, even more sexy and alluring.

"Climb in." He pointed to the tub again.

"I don't know if I can."

She was trembling and not able to proceed on her own. He went over to her and spun her so her back was to him. He nibbled at her nape, goose bumps cascading down her arms, as he cupped her breasts and pinched the nipples. She moaned with delight and dismay.

"Let me watch," he murmured. "You want to. You want me to see."

"I don't think I do."

"Trust me: You can't wait."

She moaned again. "I can't seem to tell you *no.*"

"You shouldn't tell me *no.* We're alone and we're attracted to each other. There's no one to complain about what we do."

Except her errant spouse, but who the hell cared about him? If Caroline committed a bit of adultery, the oaf would never learn of it. So where was the harm? Raven would make her feel better about herself as a woman, and he'd relish every minute of their risqué escapade.

He tugged on the robe, and it slid down and pooled in a heap at her feet. He laid a palm on her bottom and urged her toward the tub.

With her suddenly naked, she craved the security of the water.

She dashed over, leapt in and scooted down, trying to conceal herself, but not having much luck. She turned to face him, and she was wary, as if terrified over what he'd demand next and convinced she'd go along with any insane request.

He walked over to the tub, his thighs braced on the edge. The water wasn't very deep and didn't provide much cover. He leaned down and kissed her, his tongue in her mouth, his finger dipping to her breast again. Being very rough, he plucked and pulled on the nipple, giving her more than she probably expected to receive, but then, that had always been his way.

He was a large man, with big appetites. An enormous amount of any sustenance was required for him to decide he'd had his fill.

He drew away, and as she eased down, his cock was hard as stone.

"You, Mr. Hook, are extremely dangerous to my peace of mind."

"Good. Wash yourself."

"Where should I start?"

"Just do what you'd do if I wasn't here."

He grabbed a footstool and sat, his gaze locked on hers. Finally, she shrugged off her anxiety, ignoring him as if he wasn't present. She took a bar of scented soap, swished it and glided it across her arms and chest, between her legs and over her delectable backside.

She reached for a ladle on a nearby table, dunked it and used it to rinse off the soap. Shortly, she was clean and slippery and fragrant. She dropped the ladle on the floor.

"Now what?" she inquired.

"Climb out. Dry yourself."

She complied, her acquiescence titillating him, goading him to recklessness.

He avidly observed as she rubbed a towel over her skin, beginning at her shoulders and slowly working to her toes. She tossed the towel away, then straightened.

"Finished?" he inquired.

"Yes."

"Take your hair down."

She yanked out the combs, and the blond mass swept down in a golden wave.

"Come here."

He was still seated on the stool and eye to eye with her pussy. Several tortured seconds passed before she could move. She took a hesitant step, then another.

"What are you going to do to me?" she asked.

"What do you think I'm going to do?"

"I'm not very experienced at this. I've never had anything like this happen to me, and I'm not sure what you want."

"I'll tell you."

He clutched her ass and brought her close. He sniffed at her, touched her, slid a finger inside. Then he stroked his tongue across her.

She squealed with surprise and attempted to squirm away, but he wouldn't release her.

She frowned. "Why did you do that?"

"Because I was dying to learn how you taste."

"How I taste?"

"Yes."

Her bewildered expression apprised him that she might be married, but she was correct: She wasn't very experienced.

He unbuttoned the flap on his trousers, freed his cock, then guided her down. In a quick instant, he was fully impaled. They were awkwardly positioned, sitting on the low stool with little to balance them. Her legs were spread wide, straddling his lap.

"Ride me," he told her.

"What does that mean?"

He clasped her flanks and shifted her back and forth, teaching her the rhythm, showing her how. At first, it was a bit clumsy, but she rapidly figured out a tempo that satisfied her.

Clearly, she'd never been on top or been in charge, and he let her have fun and explore, delighted with whatever she chose to try.

Their passion escalated, her body tensing. He latched on to a nipple, sucking hard, and with an anguished gasp, she shattered and cried out. He held her through the tumult, elated as she soared to the peak, as she tumbled down. She collapsed against him.

"What was that?" she wheezed when she could speak again.

He smirked. "It was sexual pleasure."

"There's pleasure in this?"

He laughed. "Yes, my dear trollop. There's significant pleasure in this."

She looked perplexed and perturbed. "I didn't know."

"Obviously."

She studied him, confusion rocking her, then she asked, "Can we do it again?"

"We can do it all night if you want."

She grinned. "I think I...*want*. I think I do."

He set her away, stood, and tucked his phallus into his trousers. He nodded to the door. "Get into bed."

"Why?"

"Because it's my turn, and I'd like to lie down where I can be more comfortable."

"Yes, sir, Mr. Hook."

She saluted as if she was a lowly private in the army. Then she scurried away and leapt onto the mattress. He followed more slowly. They had until dawn, and there was no reason to hurry. No reason at

℃℀℃℀℃℀℃℀

"Come in, Sarah."

"What do you want?"

Mildred silently observed as Sarah entered the room. She was sullen and grim, and Mildred had had to send a housemaid three times to request her presence before she'd finally complied with Mildred's demand for a meeting.

If the stupid girl was irate over their squabble, wait until she learned the ramifications of Hedley's latest debacle.

They were in Mildred's suite and locked away from the rest of the house. Hedley paced in the corner. He hadn't slept. His clothes were disheveled, and he reeked of alcohol.

She'd loved him so fervidly that her entire life had been given over to positioning him so he could become a grand gentleman in society. She didn't think that type of potent affection could vanish, but maybe it could.

She swallowed down a wave of rage that was so intense, she worried she might choke to death on it.

"Sit down," she told Sarah, and she motioned to the chair across.

Sarah trudged over and plopped down, and she appeared as awful as Hedley. There were dark circles under her eyes, and she hadn't dressed her hair. It hung down her back and was tied with a single ribbon.

"What do you want?" Sarah asked again. "And please be brief. I'm not feeling very well and—for obvious reasons—I'm not too keen on speaking with you right now."

"I don't need quite so much attitude from you."

Sarah snorted. "I don't need quite so much from you either."

"There are matters we must discuss, and it will be easier if we can remain courteous and cordial."

Sarah sneered at Hedley, "You don't look so good. Rough night?"

"A very rough night," he grumbled.

"How was the card game?"

Hedley diligently ignored her, so Mildred had to respond for him.

"It went as badly as could be expected."

"So everything is still lost?"

"Yes. Everything is lost."

"Is Mr. Sinclair tossing us out immediately? Should I return to my room and pack my bags?" Her hot, furious gaze landed on Hedley. "Or have you gambled away my clothes, too?"

"We don't have to leave immediately," Mildred advised.

"When, then?"

"He's given us a month—with certain conditions attached."

"What conditions?"

"Hedley will explain."

Hedley blanched. "Mother! I can't tell her. Don't make me!"

"It's your fiasco, Hedley. It's your duty to inform her."

"Inform me of what?" Sarah snapped.

Mildred braced, terrified over how Sarah would react to the news. Sarah had to be handled carefully, had to be led in the right direction.

Mr. Sinclair wouldn't allow Sarah to balk, and if she tried, he'd force her to comply *and* he'd evict Mildred. Since Sarah would have to relent, why should Mildred suffer?

There was no option for Sarah except to say *yes,* and it was pointless to wait for Hedley to clarify the details. He'd only make Sarah angrier than she already was, would only make her agreement harder to obtain.

Mildred said, "There has been a bump in the road in our negotiations with Mr. Sinclair."

"What sort of *bump*?"

"We requested thirty days to vacate, and in order for him to permit it, he demanded a surety to guarantee our departure."

"What surety? You just admitted there was nothing left."

Hedley spat, "There was one thing left."

"Be silent, Hedley," Mildred said, as Sarah asked, "What was it?"

"Mr. Sinclair is…smitten by you."

Sarah guffawed. "Smitten? By me? You're joking."

"No, he's very intrigued."

Sarah studied Mildred, then Hedley, then Mildred again. Her distrust was palpable. "So he's intrigued by me," she warily mused. "What are you saying?"

"He'd like to spend some time with you."

"He wants to spend *time* with me?"

"Yes."

"How much time?"

Mildred tamped down her nerves. "The next month."

Sarah frowned, grappling to decipher what was really happening.

"I'm confused," she finally said.

"That's understandable." Mildred was all smiles, all commiseration.

"What exactly is he asking me to do?"

"Well, he thinks you're very pretty, and you've never been married. In cases like this, a man will occasionally suggest a…ah…that is…"

Mildred simply couldn't blurt it out.

She'd never liked Sarah, but she'd never wished her to come to any actual harm. If Sarah succumbed to Mr. Sinclair's advances, there would be no hope for her later on. She'd never be able to wed, and with how their luck was running, she'd likely wind up with a babe in her belly. But her situation wouldn't matter to him. When he was through with her, he'd ride off into the sunset.

For a fleeting moment, Mildred flushed with shame. Bernard had bequeathed a fine dowry to Sarah, but Hedley had squandered it. Mildred had been too shocked to confess the theft to Sarah, so she'd lied and claimed there had been no dowry.

If Mildred had stood up to Hedley, if she'd declined to turn over the bank accounts, she could have used the money as it was intended by Bernard. Sarah would be wed, with a husband and home of her own. Hedley's shenanigans would have had no effect, because Mildred could have prevailed on Sarah to take her in, and Sarah would have. She was kind that way, kind as Mildred had never known how to be.

It was one more sin to lay at Hedley's feet. One more disaster that he'd orchestrated. Would the catastrophes ever end?

"Spit it out, Mildred," Sarah barked.

"I can't say it." Looking bleak, Mildred glared at Hedley. "You have to tell her."

Mildred glowered until Hedley realized she wouldn't yield. He stumbled over and sat next to Sarah. He clasped her hand.

"My dearest sister," he started, and Sarah yanked away.

"What have you done now?" she hissed.

"Mr. Sinclair has agreed to…to…have you as his mistress."

"No!"

"Yes." Hedley nodded as if he could coax her into it.

"No!" She leapt up and lurched to the other side of the room.

"It's for thirty days, Sarah," Hedley cajoled. "He's a handsome fellow. It won't be so bad."

"I won't do it," she fumed. "I don't care what you wagered. I don't care what you arranged with him. I won't do it!"

A hard gleam infused Hedley's gaze. "If you refuse, we have to depart immediately. Can you go upstairs and pack your bag, Sarah? Can you make Mother? Can you make Caroline?"

Sarah was so angry, she was shaking. She pointed a condemning finger at Hedley. "How dare you put me in this predicament! If Father was alive, what would he think of you?"

The mention of Bernard was too much for Hedley. Hedley had yearned to impress Bernard, but never had. Bernard had always complained that Hedley was lazy and spoiled, that he didn't try or apply himself.

They'd often quarreled over what Bernard had viewed as Hedley's hollow traits, and Hedley couldn't bear to have Bernard cited, because they were all aware of what Bernard's opinion would have been.

He stomped to his own corner, and brother and sister scowled like pugilists in opposite sides of the ring.

"Before this goes any farther," Sarah ultimately said, "there's something you should know."

"What?"

"I talked to Mr. Sinclair. I begged him to give the estate back to us."

"Yes, and we can see how well you succeeded," Hedley jeered.

"He told me a secret about his past."

"What is it?" Mildred asked.

"He claims he is Florence's son."

Mildred gasped. "He what?"

"He has an old vendetta against you, and he traveled here deliberately to destroy you. He used Hedley to accomplish it."

Mildred's mind raced. Hadn't she once speculated over Sinclair's surname? Hadn't she wondered if he was related to the despicable rogue, Charles Sinclair?

She struggled to recall Mr. Sinclair's face, tried to decide if he resembled Florence. But it had been three decades since Florence had fled England. It was so difficult to remember her features.

"He had to be jesting," Mildred insisted. "He can't be kin to us."

"He wasn't jesting," Sarah replied. "He was very, very serious. What did you do to him, Mildred? Why is he so angry with you?"

"I did nothing to him!" she insisted, but she had to glance away.

As a boy, he'd written to her, and she vividly recollected the letter. Florence had been gravely ill, and he'd been terrified and alone. He'd pleaded for money, for help. Mildred should have ignored his appeal—Bernard had sternly advised her to—but she'd been so bitter over Florence and the disasters she'd wrought by running off with Charles Sinclair.

Her rash act had wrecked numerous lives. Mildred's parents had died of shame. Florence's husband had died of shame too, but he'd drowned himself with alcohol. Her two young boys had had to be raised without a mother, had had to endure a lifetime of censure, while watching their father waste away. Mildred had had to marry Bernard, had tumbled down society's ladder until she'd arrived at the bottom.

The very least her sister had deserved was a severe scolding for all the damage she'd caused. Mildred had viciously responded to the boy's letter, apprising him of what she thought of his mother, that he should wallow in the filthy trough Florence had dug for both of them.

Could Mr. Sinclair really be Florence's son? Could it be possible? Could a caustic letter still have him raging decades later?

She nearly wailed with dismay.

It wasn't Mildred's fault that Florence had been seduced by Charles Sinclair. It was Florence's fault—and Charles Sinclair's fault. John Sinclair was the very worst sort of illegitimate bastard. If he wanted to blame someone for his troubles, the true culprits were his own selfish, debauched parents.

"You did nothing to Florence's son?" Sarah scoffed. "Why don't I believe you? Mr. Sinclair is positively bent on vengeance. How much will we allow him to take from us? And why must *I* accommodate him? I didn't even know Florence. Why is this calamity landing on me?"

"He's not Florence's boy," Mildred staunchly declared. "The last I heard, and from very reliable sources, the child died of consumption in Paris a year after Florence passed away."

"He *is* her son," Sarah shouted, "and look at the havoc he's wreaking! Tell me how to stop it! Tell me how to stop *him*!"

Mildred couldn't have the discussion descend to bickering and bellowing. They all had to remain calm. "I'm sorry you're upset, but we're all in a state. I need you to compose yourself and give me your answer."

"My answer to what?"

"We must make arrangements as to where we'll be living in another month. I've written to Caroline's husband to come fetch her."

"You what?" Sarah seethed.

"I wrote to Archibald. Where can she go but back to her husband? I haven't the funds to support her. Shall I throw her out on the road?"

"How could you, Mildred? What is wrong with you?"

"I'm trying my best, Sarah, in very difficult circumstances."

"No, you're not. You're being your usual cruel self. You'll never change."

"You're distraught, so I'll ignore your insults."

"Ignore them if you wish, but I won't cease voicing them. I've put up with you my entire life, and I'm certainly beginning to question why I have. What have you ever done for me that was any benefit at all?"

Mildred was determined that Sarah see reason.

"Mr. Sinclair let us speak to you on his behalf," she coolly said. "He was anxious for us to explain the situation."

"I will *not* be his mistress. How dare you ask it of me!"

"Sarah, what is our other option? Shall we leave at once? Think, girl! Think."

"Honestly, Sarah," Hedley interjected, "where would we go? Will you trudge down the lane, with a pillowcase full of clothes balanced on your shoulder?"

"I won't do it," she hotly repeated. "I will *not!*"

She was so adamant in her response, so aggrieved and offended. What did the foolish ninny expect to occur? Did she suppose Mr. Sinclair would simply nod and permit her to renege?

"You can't refuse, Sarah," Mildred tried again. "Mr. Sinclair won't let you."

"Mr. Sinclair can jump off a cliff."

"I gave him my word," Hedley whined.

"I don't care."

"You don't seem to realize the jam you're in," Hedley said.

"The jam *I* am in? I'm in no jam. You caused this, and I suggest you find Mr. Sinclair and have him take his thirty days out of your hide."

"Sarah," Mildred chided, "it's pointless for the three of us to quarrel."

"Why shouldn't we? I may start to say things I've always been dying to say."

"How can I make you understand the facts?"

"You have made me understand, Mildred. I understand every blasted detail. Hedley ruined our lives, you were complicit, and you have the gall to demand that I suffer the consequences for his behavior. My answer is still no, *no*, NO!"

She stormed out, and Mildred and Hedley were frozen in place, listening as her angry strides vanished down the hallway.

"That went well," Hedley sarcastically said.

"Shut up, Hedley. Just shut up."

"What should we do now?"

"I have no idea."

She walked to the window and stared out at the ocean, showing him her back until he had the good grace to slink away.

CHAPTER SEVEN

Sarah stood on the rocky promontory of Bramble Headland and gazed off to the horizon.

Throughout her life, she'd climbed to the spectacular spot to stare at the ocean. She was up above the mortal world, where it was just wind and waves and sky, and she felt she could see to the end of the earth.

From her high perch, the manor looked tiny and perfect, like a doll's house where only good things happened and nothing bad could ever occur.

How could such a tranquil place breed so much sadness and strife?

Off to her left, the trail wound through the grass and over the cliff, a scenic shortcut that led to Sheldon's.

She'd just returned from there, having rushed to speak with him after her quarrel with Mildred and Hedley. Sheldon knew her family better than anyone, was older and wiser and had dealt with numerous tragedies of his own.

Yet to her extreme dismay, he'd been called away to London and would be gone for weeks so she'd received no advice or assistance. She could have asked the housekeeper to let her stay, to hide her. But she'd been too embarrassed to confess the scandal that was raging on the Teasdale side of the hill.

She'd staggered away, feeling like a shipwreck survivor. She had to find Caroline, had to warn her that Archie was coming, that they likely had a few days to prepare before he rolled up the drive.

Once she located Caroline and told her of Mildred's perfidy, how was Sarah to proceed? John Sinclair and his friends were still lodged in her home, and she had no power to dislodge them. Mildred and Hedley were still there too, and Sarah wished she had the right to march down and demand they all leave.

She was the only one who had ever loved Bramble Bay. The estate didn't matter to any of them. It had simply been a token to be bartered over. Why should Sinclair or Mildred or Hedley be allowed to continue living on the property? When they'd caused such trouble, why should they get to remain?

A wave of fury—directed at her father—washed over her. He'd understood what Hedley was like, so why had he put her in such jeopardy?

She hoped he was peering down from Heaven and could see how his poor decisions had endangered her. She hoped he was ashamed and aghast.

She glanced at the manor again and was distressed to note that John Sinclair was on his stallion and trotting toward her. For once, he didn't appear as the rich, pompous overlord he pretended to be. He was dressed as he'd been the first time she'd met him: a flowing white shirt, tan breeches, and black boots. The wind riffled his hair, his shirt flapping against his skin.

He was fixated on her, his determination plainly visible, so he must have spoken to Mildred and Hedley. They'd have painted her in a horrid light, would have apprised him that Sarah had been completely unreasonable.

She watched him approach, and he was practically daring her to run so he could chase her down and demonstrate his superiority over her. But where was there a safe refuge? There was no way to escape, nowhere to hide.

He kept coming until he was beside her, and he reined in and extended his hand.

"Climb up."

"No."

"I'll give you a ride to the house so you don't have to walk."

"No."

"I don't permit people to refuse my commands." His magnificent eyes were flashing daggers.

"So? I just did."

"I'm not in the habit of asking twice."

"Then you'll really hate dealing with me, because I'm not too keen on obeying orders."

He leapt to the ground and stepped to her, and she was immediately and vividly reminded of his size and power. He was very intimidating, and he used his stature and height to overwhelm and confuse.

"I've talked to your brother and stepmother."

"Bully for you."

"They seem to have left you with the impression that you can decline to honor Hedley's bet."

"No, they didn't. They insisted I comply, but I won't. Mildred's days of bossing me are over."

He studied her, then snorted with derision. "You blame me for this."

"Yes, I absolutely blame you."

"I don't suppose it occurred to you that your brother might be at fault."

"That absolutely occurred to me, too. I blame both of you. I *loathe* both of you."

He grabbed her by the shoulders and shook her. "I did it for you."

"Don't make me laugh. You did it for yourself."

"Why would I have?"

"Because you could, because you're bigger and stronger and male. Because you enjoy humiliating others, because you enjoy having the chance to humiliate *me*."

As if she'd burned him, he released her and stomped off to the edge of the cliff to stare out at the ocean. Far off in the distance, the sails of a passing ship were discernible.

They stood, frozen in place, until it faded from sight. Then he whipped around.

"If I hadn't agreed to his proposal," he said, "what do you think might have happened to you?"

"Oh, I don't know," she acerbically mused. "Perhaps I could have stayed with a neighbor. Perhaps I could have remained in my home—where I have always lived until you stole it."

"I didn't steal it!" he bellowed.

He stormed over, an angry finger wagging in her face.

"Your brother wagered you of his own accord."

"I don't believe you. I'm sure it was all your idea."

"No, he brought it up out of the blue—to buy himself more time."

"More time to what?"

"To renege, to change the result, to thwart me."

"As if he could," she scoffed. "He and Mildred are deranged to imagine they could prevent you from behaving however you wish."

"Precisely," he concurred. "And once he suggested I take you off his hands, can you actually assume—if I'd refused—he wouldn't have sold you to someone else?"

She frowned. "What do you mean?"

"Men wager their sisters all the time. It's not illegal. What if he'd ridden to London and offered your chastity in a London gambling hall?"

The notion shocked her, had her reeling. "Be silent."

"I won't be. I've been in those places. I've seen the crazed bets that are tendered. What would your chances have been to avoid a worse ending than the one I arranged for you?"

"Aren't you wonderful! My hero!"

"I saved your pretty behind, you little fool. I wouldn't deem it inappropriate to hear a bit of thanks from you."

She was so irate, she was trembling. "Are you claiming I should be honored that you were haggling over me as if I was a prized cow?"

"No. I'm claiming your brother could have earned a fortune off of you. I'm surprised he hasn't already tried it. You were upset when he announced that he'd lost the estate. What if he'd announced he lost you, too? To some stranger? To some diseased libertine or perverted reprobate?"

She blanched and stumbled away as if he'd slapped her.

Hadn't she endured sufficient agony for one day? Hadn't he done enough? Hadn't Hedley? Was she to spend the rest of her life, laboring under the horrid realization that it could have been much more dire? Hedley was irresponsible and immature, but must she now accept that he was mad, as well?

"He wouldn't have done that to me," she insisted, but without much vigor.

"He wouldn't? I was there, Sarah." With a deadly finality, he repeated, "I was there! Don't tell me what he wouldn't have done. I saw it with my own two eyes. You're nothing to him."

"Stop it," she begged, his words pounding into her like blows. "Give us back our home."

"Give it back? To Hedley? Are you insane?"

"Then let us have our thirty days to leave. Release me from the wager."

"No."

"Show me that you can be kind. Show me that you are a gentleman, that you know how to act like one."

"That's the problem for you, chérie. I am not a gentleman, and I've never acted like one."

"Yes, you have. I've witnessed it. Free me from this wretched folly."

"No." He was growing more obstinate. "I will have what is mine."

"*I* am not yours!" she shouted.

"You're wrong about that. I have won you, and I claim you as my own."

"This isn't Africa, and I am not a slave that can be bought and sold."

"No, but you are an unprotected female who has been bartered away by her brother." He paused, his expression grim. "And if I don't keep you, who might he offer you to next? Are you willing to risk it?"

Tears surged into her eyes; she couldn't stop them.

She felt so helpless, so betrayed. By John Sinclair. By Mildred. By Hedley. By her father who should have protected her, but hadn't.

If her own father hadn't bothered over her, if her own brother would gamble her away, what hope was there for her to stagger on in a decent way? If she didn't yield to Sinclair's demands, what would become of her? Yet if she succumbed to his debauched scheme, what would become of her?

There were no valid choices, no satisfactory conclusions. There was only calamity and chaos and John Sinclair positioned like a brick wall between the life she'd previously had and the life she would have in the future.

"Oh, *chérie,*" he murmured, "don't cry. Hedley isn't worth it."

"But my home is worth it. My life is worth it."

"No, it isn't. You've been trapped here with these despicable people—who never loved you, who will never cherish you. Hedley tossed you away, and though you don't realize it at the moment, this is a good thing. Now you truly know him. Now you're free of him."

"I didn't need to be freed. I was never bound."

"Yes, you were."

He came over and took her in his arms. She didn't fight him, didn't push him away. She was so bereft she could barely stand, and if he hadn't been holding her, she'd have collapsed to the ground in a grief-stricken heap.

"It will be all right, Sarah," he said.

"How can you say that?"

"There are worse fates in this world than being attached to a man like me."

"I can't think of any."

"I've sailed the Seven Seas. I've observed women's lives, women's troubles. You'll always be safe with me."

"I was safe before you arrived."

"You only thought you were."

She sighed, her melancholy increasing. "What now?"

"I will care for you—in my way."

She chuckled glumly. "In your *way?*"

"I will treat you well, and I'll be generous. It's more than most women expect to receive."

She eased back so she could gaze up at him.

"Don't do this to me," she whispered.

"I have to."

"No, you don't. Please go away. Please leave us so we can return to how it used to be before you came."

As if she hadn't spoken, he continued. "I will take you away from here. We'll sail to France—to my home. You'll be shed of Hedley and Mildred. You'll be happy there."

"In France? I could never travel to France with you. Besides, why would we journey so far when it's only for thirty days?"

He frowned, confused. "It's not thirty days."

"Hedley said it was for a month, while he and Mildred packed and made plans."

"No, it's not for a month."

"How long is it then?"

"Until I'm weary of you."

"You own me forever?"

"Yes, forever—if I wish it. Do you see why you must let me take you away? Do you understand why it's not safe for you to remain?"

She shook her head, struggling to absorb this latest news.

Hedley had permanently sold her? It might be forever?

She tried to picture herself in France, residing with Mr. Sinclair and his accursed Annalise Dubois. Would he keep both of them? Would he flit from bed to bed?

She recalled Miss Dubois's jealousy when she'd caught Sarah in his bedchamber. Somehow, Sarah could envision the beautiful harlot agreeing to share him.

"Tell me one true thing about you," she pleaded as she had previously, being desperate to comprehend what drove him. "Tell me one thing that's real."

"My name is John Sinclair."

"But you have other names."

"Yes."

"Tell me all of them."

"It's best if you don't know them."

"Why? Are you a criminal?"

"What if I am? It can make no difference in our relationship."

"Not make a difference? Are you mad?" He stoically regarded her, but didn't answer, and she pressed on. "Were you lying about Florence being your mother?"

He shrugged. "How can it matter if she was or not?"

"Is Mildred your aunt? Is Hedley your cousin?"

"It's not necessary to concern yourself over them anymore. They're not your family. They never were."

"Who will be my family now? You?"

"No." A flash of bleak honestly crossed his face. "I have no need of family."

"Then what do you need?"

"You know what it is. You know what I want from you."

He stared down her body, so she would grasp what he intended she surrender. But she was a maiden who had scant clues as to men and women and their behavior when they were alone. She had no idea how to carry on as he was demanding. "Whatever it is that you're seeking from me," she said, "I can't provide it."

"Yes, you can. I'll show you how, and you'll give it to me—freely and as gladly as you are able. If you try, then I swear that I will always support and protect you."

For the briefest instant, she considered his proposal. After all, what were her options? Why not let him take care of her? How was it any different from marrying a rich husband to obtain security?

Yet as swiftly as the possibility arose, she shoved it away.

She was just an ordinary woman, from a rural village in the country. She'd had a moral upbringing, and she knew right from wrong, virtue from sin. She would never blithely agree to his indecent proposition. Not even to keep a roof over her head. Not even to have food to eat or clothes to wear.

"I can't do it," she insisted.

"You can, *chérie*. You will. You must."

He dipped down and touched his lips to hers, the kiss rattling her. She was so surprised by it that she didn't pull away. Oh, how she wished he was a more honorable sort of man, that they'd met under better circumstances.

She moaned with dismay, her distress acute, her knees finally buckling as she'd worried they might. He merely tightened his grip, cradling her more firmly to his chest.

"Have me, Sarah. Want me. Let me want you in return."

"It's so wrong."

"It's not wrong. It's absolutely right."

He deepened the kiss, his tongue sliding into her mouth, his crafty hand cupping her breast.

The sensations he generated were too overwhelming, too irresistible to be believed. She was frozen—with astonishment and alarm—and she simply held on and allowed him to have his way with her. She hadn't the fortitude to force him to desist. She didn't actually want him to desist.

From the very first moment, she'd been attracted to him. She'd snooped in his bedchamber, had permitted him to enter her own room in the dead of night. She'd told no one of his inappropriate visit and had reveled in the impropriety.

No wonder he presumed her to be interested in a liaison. Since he'd arrived, she'd constantly encouraged him. But she wasn't who he assumed her to be, and she couldn't behave as he was commanding.

He drew away, his gaze so riveting that she couldn't figure out what to make of it. She hadn't realized that a man could stare at a woman as he was, that she could feel unique and cherished and beloved.

He seemed captivated by her, and he was wealthy and handsome and offering himself, claiming to desire all the amorous attention she could give him.

Was she insane to refuse?

She could travel to France, could live in his home, and he would teach her things that—being unmarried—she'd never expected to learn. It could be an exciting adventure.

Many females would have jumped at the chance, but she wasn't one of them. Hedley had narrowed her options, but there had to be other choices she hadn't considered. She simply needed some quiet hours to think of what they might be. She had to escape from Hedley and from John Sinclair, had to hide and regroup and start over.

She knew where Sheldon was staying in London. Perhaps that was the answer. She could sneak to town and seek protection from her father's old friend. Yes, that's what she would do.

"I'm pleased with you," Mr. Sinclair murmured—as if she was a new mare he was purchasing.

She wanted to hit him. "I'm delighted to hear it."

"You've been kissed before."

"I have. I was engaged years ago, remember?"

"Are you still a maid?"

She gnawed on her cheek, the urge to slap him growing by leaps and bounds.

"You insult me by asking."

"Your brother said that you are chaste. I have to be sure I'm getting what I bargained for."

"Shut up, Mr. Sinclair." She whipped away and marched down the hill.

"Our discussion is not finished," he haughtily intoned. "I don't give you leave to depart."

She glared over her shoulder. "So? You don't own me, and I don't have to stand here and be disparaged by you."

He dipped his head in agreement. "My apologies if I offended."

"Obviously, you're used to dealing with whores like Miss Dubois."

"I am. I admit it."

She'd never previously uttered a scandalous word like *whore*, and she felt as if she'd stumbled off a high cliff, that she was falling and falling through the air. Where would she be when she landed at the bottom?

"I'm not like her."

"I'm glad that you are not."

"You can't speak to me as you would to her. You can't treat me as you would treat her."

"You're correct. I have dabbled with trollops for a very long time, and I have forgotten myself and my manners. I have some."

"Marvelous. I hope you'll display them from here on out."

"I will."

"Now if you'll excuse me, I'd like to be alone."

She was shaky from the terrible day, from her race to Sheldon's house, from Mr. Sinclair's kiss, from his domineering ways. Too many awful things had happened, too many challenges had been presented, too many decisions had to be made. If she spent another second with him, she couldn't predict how she might react.

She kept on, and momentarily, she heard him riding up behind her. He extended his hand.

"There's no need for you to walk. I can take you down."

She stared and stared, but didn't reach for him, and he sighed as if she was a puppy he was training and she had difficulty learning the tricks he was teaching.

"It's silly to fight me," he said. "You can't win."

"I can try."

"But you won't succeed. There's no point in exhausting yourself."

He didn't move, but continued to sternly gaze at her, confident that—through sheer force of will—he could pressure her to relent.

He had such an overbearing personality. How had he acquired such arrogant traits? If Florence was his mother, then the Earl of Trent was his father. Was it simply his aristocratic blood showing itself? Or was he naturally imperious? How could anyone defy him and survive to tell the tale?

Finally, she clasped hold, and with ease, he lifted her and settled her in front of him. He was astride, but she was perched sideways, her body crushed to his chest.

The horse started down, its swaying gait shifting her back and forth, and she struggled not to lean against Sinclair, but it was impossible to avoid contact.

He was humored by her paltry attempts to keep some space between them, and he slipped an arm around her waist and snuggled her nearer. She gave up the fight again, quickly recognizing that what he'd said was correct: She couldn't win with him.

They arrived at the house, and he dropped her to her feet.

"That wasn't so bad, was it?" he asked.

"It was pretty bad," she petulantly replied, and he laughed.

"I can't have you wandering unless I know where you are."

She grumbled with frustration. "Mr. Sinclair, I have—"

"Call me John."

"No. Mr. Sinclair, I have lived at Bramble Bay all my life. I am perfectly capable of taking a stroll without your permission."

"I'm afraid I have to insist."

"And I'm afraid I have to insist, too."

He grinned his devil's grin, and she steeled herself against it, refusing to enjoy the sight.

"We'll see who prevails in this battle of ours," he said.

"Yes, we will."

"I'm quite adept at getting what I want."

"So am I," she lied.

In fact, she was a mediator, a conciliator. She didn't like quarreling or arguments, and she tried to make everyone happy. With kin like Mildred and Hedley, she'd had plenty of practice. She was a veritable expert at ensuring that relationships ran smoothly, that there was no discord.

"We leave tomorrow," he advised.

"Leave? Leave for where?"

"For France."

"I'm not going to France with you."

"We sail in the evening, with the tide."

"No, *we* don't."

"We'll depart Bramble Bay at three in order to reach my ship on time."

"Aren't you listening?"

"Aren't you? Don't bring much. A satchel of personal items will be sufficient."

"Won't I need any clothes?" she sarcastically inquired. "Will you have me strutting about in the nude?"

"Yes," he alarmed her by saying. "I don't like your attire. It conceals your beauty."

The compliment flummoxed her. He'd noticed her attire? He didn't like it? It concealed her beauty?

"My clothes are fine," she tersely snapped.

"No, they're not. I'll buy you new when we arrive."

He yanked on the reins and rode off.

She'd hoped to have some time to change his mind, to dissuade him from his folly, but apparently, *time* was the one thing she didn't have. Whatever she planned, however she traveled to London to escape him, it would have to be carried out before three the next afternoon.

CHAPTER EIGHT

"My husband is not at home."

"He is."

"He is not."

Phillip Sinclair sighed with resignation.

It was always difficult to call on his father, Charles Sinclair, Earl of Trent. Charles's wife, Susan, hated Phillip and never wanted him admitted. The servants had specific instructions to let him in over her objection, and they answered to Charles—not Susan—so Phillip's visits were a never-ending source of discord.

Phillip was Charles's oldest and very illegitimate child, so he was the consummate reminder to Susan that her husband was a roué and scoundrel. She loathed Phillip for all he represented as to the state of her awful and pointless marriage to Charles. From the very first day, it had unfolded like a bad carriage accident.

Charles was nearing fifty and had been wed to Susan for three decades. But she'd never bore him any children, and she was beyond the age now where she ever could. To her shame, her errant, salacious husband had bastards around every corner.

She was bitter and aggrieved, and she and Charles rarely spoke, never socialized, and made concerted attempts never to stay in the same residence at the same time.

"I know he's here, Countess," Phillip said. "He sent for me."

"He couldn't have." Her gaze was cold and hard, her lie baldly voiced. "He's not even in London."

"You may discuss it with him after I'm gone."

Phillip stepped around her and marched down the hall to the library at the rear of the house. With each stride, he cursed his father for having Phillip caught in the middle. Again.

He wished Charles would put Susan out of her misery and live separately from her. But Charles wasn't bothered by her rages and tantrums. As with most else in his life, Charles felt no guilt over his horrid treatment of her and had no ability to commiserate. If she pitched a fit, it was a waste of emotional effort, because Charles wouldn't notice.

Phillip had been sired during one of Charles's early seductions. His mother had been a naïve debutante who hadn't understood the dangers posed by a rogue like Charles.

Charles was—and always had been—extremely dashing, extremely charming, extremely magnetic, and women couldn't resist his charismatic pull. They were easily captivated, lifted their skirts when they shouldn't, then stupidly expected a continuing attachment with him.

But Charles never formed attachments. There seemed to be an aspect missing in his personality. He didn't bond or love, was unable to be loyal or faithful, and he was never concerned that he couldn't be the man they were hoping.

He reveled in the flirtation and the chase, but once the prize was won, his interest quickly waned. Yet despite his low reputation, despite the stories and scandals, each female thought that *she* would be the one to ensnare him. Most of them never fell *out* of love, even years and decades later when it was painfully clear that he wasn't coming back and would take no responsibility for any damage he'd caused.

He was that sort of scoundrel, but Phillip liked him anyway.

Due to his profligate philandering, Charles likely had dozens of illicit offspring, and Phillip was determined to locate as many of them as he could. He manipulated Charles in minor ways, forcing him to cough up money for dowries or housing or school. The remunerations were small, and Charles loudly complained about each expenditure, but the financial assistance changed lives, and Phillip wouldn't be deterred from his quest.

The butler was waiting at the library door. He announced Phillip, and Phillip entered to find Charles seated behind his desk, reading through a stack of paperwork. He was having a brandy, a cheroot smoldering in a tray by his hand. He had many vices, liquor and tobacco being just two of them.

He was still very handsome, his golden-blond hair only slightly silvered, his emerald eyes mesmerizing. He was thin and dapper and fit, looking very much as he had when he was twenty and ruining girls from London to Rome.

"I heard you speaking to someone," Charles said. "Were you fighting with Susan?"

"Yes." Phillip went to the sideboard and dispensed a large amount of brandy into his own glass, then settled himself in the chair across. "She walked by when I arrived. She insisted you weren't here."

"Obviously, you didn't believe her."

"I didn't imagine you'd invite me, then leave. You must enjoy making me suffer whenever I visit. She seems to stand in the front foyer, watching for me."

"When I invite you, I never pause to wonder about her opinion.

My desire to see you has nothing to do with her."

"I realize that, but I detest having to quarrel with her. Why don't you move? Why doesn't she? You own several dozen properties in numerous cities and countries. Why don't you separate once and for all?"

It was a question Phillip frequently asked, but the answer was always the same, and this time was no different.

"Susan can reside wherever she chooses," Charles said. "She knows that. I will buy her a home—any home she requests—but she doesn't want me to. She likes being miserable. If she wasn't festering and unhappy, she'd be completely lost."

Phillip suspected it was true. In some bizarre way, Susan reveled in the constant humiliation of being Charles's wife. If she left him, she wouldn't be able to keep track of his many children, wouldn't be able to continually rage at the unfairness.

Charles's offspring occasionally appeared on her stoop, seeking help, seeking money. Phillip had spread word far and wide that they should travel to London to be acknowledged, to be welcomed. Hackney drivers all over the city had been apprised that they should deliver any Sinclair child to Phillip, that their fare would be paid.

They didn't always go to Phillip's, though. Sometimes, they showed up at Charles's by mistake, and it was easy to tell when one of Charles's bastards was knocking.

Charles's bloodlines were strong, his blond hair and green eyes passed on in most instances. And they all had a birthmark on their wrist in the shape of a figure-eight. It was called the 'Mark of Trent', a brand that indicated a paternity Charles couldn't deny.

Susan never had to guess who was loitering on her stoop. The evidence was patently clear.

"You haven't stopped by in weeks," Charles said. "How have you been?"

"Busy. Fanny is planning a supper party." Fanny was Phillip's half-sister, Charles's daughter, the first sibling Phillip had found. "She wants you to come."

Charles wrinkled his nose with distaste. "You know I don't like these family…gatherings."

"Humor me. Come anyway." Phillip stared him down, their identical green eyes locked in stubborn combat.

"I'll think about it."

"She's sending you an invitation, and it matters to her to have you there. I'd better hear that you've accepted."

"I suppose Helen and Harriet will be there, too."

"Of course." They were twins, two more sisters Phillip had located.

"So their husbands will be there."

Helen and Harriet were married to brothers, James and Tristan

Harcourt. There was bad blood between the men and Charles. When they were tiny boys, their mother, Florence, had run away to Paris where she'd engaged in a torrid affair with Charles.

She'd fallen in love, birthed a child named Jean Pierre, then been abandoned by Charles in the foreign country. She'd died years later, poverty-stricken and alone and unmourned by anyone except her illicit son.

James and Tristan blamed Charles and had loathed him for decades. Now, they'd wed Charles's daughters. These days, their family get-togethers were never dull.

"If you attend," Phillip said, "James and Tristan have promised to be on their best behavior."

"What does that mean? They won't take a stick to me when I arrive?"

"They will be courteous and civil."

"And if they're not? What if Fanny's party is ruined with a bunch of sniping and bickering?"

"Then Fanny will take a stick to all three of you. She won't tolerate any nonsense."

Charles grumbled with irritation. "Why do I put up with you, Phillip?"

"I have no idea. Why do you?"

"It's a great mystery of the universe."

"Unknowable by mere mortals?"

"Yes."

Charles flashed one of his rare smiles, giving Phillip a glimpse of what many women saw when they met him. He had a way of looking at a person, as if he was intrigued, as if he was smitten, as if he was concerned, but it was a charade. He was callous and detached and not interested in anything but himself and his own pleasure.

He lit another cheroot and pushed his empty glass across the desk for Phillip to refill. They sipped companionably, enjoying each other's company.

Charles liked to complain about Phillip, liked to insist that Phillip goaded him into actions he didn't wish to take. But beneath his veneer of boredom and apathy, Charles had permitted Phillip to establish a genuine friendship. Phillip had gotten as close as anyone ever could, and he was grateful for the connection his father had allowed.

"What is the purpose of my visit?" Phillip said. "What did you need?"

"I received the strangest letter."

"A letter?"

"Yes, and I wanted to show it to you." Charles unlocked a desk drawer and retrieved it. He unfolded it and scowled at the words that had been penned. "It's from a woman named Mildred Teasdale. Are you acquainted with her?"

"No. Are you?"

"No. She's a widow. Her husband was Bernard Teasdale"—Charles raised a questioning brow, but Phillip shook his head, not recognizing the man's name either—"and their estate is out on the coast near Dover."

"Why did she write to you?"

"Well, it seems her son, Hedley, has gambled away the property, and she's begging for my help."

"For *your* help? If she would contact you for assistance, she obviously hasn't heard any stories about you."

Charles ignored the insult, but he paused, actually looking disconcerted. "Apparently, the man who won their estate is Jean Pierre."

Phillip bit down a gasp of surprise. "Jean Pierre?"

"Yes, and he's there now, ready to take possession."

"He's in England?"

Charles shrugged. "So she claims."

Jean Pierre was the boy Charles had sired with Florence Harcourt. He was Phillip's half-brother, Fanny's and Helen's and Harriet's half-brother. Tristan and James Harcourt's half-brother.

Florence had had a difficult life in France. She'd flitted on the edge of the community of British expatriates, mooching and ingratiating herself, a ruse that had worked until people had gotten weary of supporting her.

She'd died when Jean Pierre was ten, and they'd assumed he'd perished too, ragged and forsaken on the streets of Paris.

The prior year, they'd learned differently. Tristan and Harriet had been at sea when Tristan's ship was attacked by the vicious pirate, *Le Terreur Français*. The brutal criminal had tried his best to kill Tristan, then Tristan and Harriet had been set adrift to perish in a lifeboat. They'd survived, but only because Fate had intervened.

As Tristan lay near death, the pirate had announced that he was Jean Pierre, Tristan's brother. It was a secret Charles and Phillip had kept buried, so Jean Pierre's identity had never been revealed. Everyone—particularly members of the Royal Navy who were searching for him—thought they were hunting for a Frenchman.

But he was very, very English.

Somehow, he'd figured out how to sail and fight and rampage. No one was safe from his dangerous mayhem. He was a menace on the high seas, with his meticulous brand of vengeance reserved for those British citizens who'd been stupid enough to scorn Florence Harcourt when she'd been desperate and ailing in Paris.

He hadn't come after Charles, though, and Phillip wasn't sure why. Charles owned plantations in the West Indies, and his ships regularly sailed back and forth bringing cotton, rum, and sugar to London.

Perhaps Charles had merely been lucky, but it was probably just a matter of time before Charles's fleet was scuttled, too. An attack would cause enormous financial losses, losses that Phillip hated to see.

Each farthing of Charles's money that was wasted by Jean Pierre was a farthing Phillip couldn't use for a dowry for a long-lost sister.

Jean Pierre was a fugitive, with the Crown offering a huge bounty for his capture. If he was ever seized, he would be promptly tried and hanged in a very public, very shocking fashion, and Charles and Phillip were determined that it not occur.

Charles was hardly a devoted father, but he refused to have one of his children executed. Jean Pierre was the son of a British countess and a British earl, so a death sentence would be an outrageous ending. Charles wanted Jean Pierre safely away, or if he could not be convinced to halt his crime spree, Charles wanted mercy extended so he didn't hang.

Phillip had been investigating Jean Pierre for months, hoping to glean information as to where he lived or how he carried on when he wasn't wreaking havoc.

So far, Phillip had made no headway. Could Jean Pierre be in England? Was it possible? Could he be that reckless? Could he be that brazen?

There were few witnesses who could identify him. When he boarded a vessel, his victims were so terrified that they couldn't give good descriptions later on. There were wildly varied reports and no accurate sketches. He could be anyone, except that he had Tristan's same height and build, and the Sinclair golden-blond hair and expressive green eyes.

Jean Pierre was the spitting image of his father, of Phillip. If Phillip and Jean Pierre stood side by side, they would look like, well, *brothers.*

"He's going by the name of John Sinclair," Charles said.

"How very British of him," Phillip scoffed. "Why would Mrs. Teasdale assume he's your son?"

"Evidently, he told someone."

"He's not hiding the relationship?"

"No."

"What is she asking you to do specifically?"

"She wants me to travel to their estate—it's called Bramble Bay—and persuade Jean Pierre to leave them alone and let them keep their property."

"As if you would."

Charles was a consummate gambler who played for the highest stakes. He would never expect a man to relinquish what he'd won with a shuffle of the cards.

Phillip considered for a moment, then scowled. "Has she

mentioned any other pertinent details?"

"Like what?"

"Jean Pierre revenges himself against those who wronged his mother."

"He hasn't come after me."

"I suspect your turn is approaching," Phillip snidely said. "If he's at this estate, this Bramble Bay, he must have a strong reason for being there. He's risking life and limb by showing his face in England."

"Only if he's caught."

"Still, though," Phillip pressed, "Mrs. Teasdale and her son must have some connection to Florence, and Jean Pierre plans to destroy them because of it."

"I suppose."

"Could Mrs. Teasdale be correct? Could it be him?"

"I can't think it's likely."

"Yet you're worried it might be."

"Yes, except that I read a newspaper report the other day that his ship had recently been sighted in the Mediterranean, that he was anchored off the coast of Italy. The Navy is sending some ships to see if he's there."

"Perhaps it's a ruse. Perhaps he spread the rumors himself so they're looking for him in Italy, while he's in Dover, playing cards."

"Could he be that devious?" Charles inquired.

Phillip snorted. "He's your son, Charles. Yes, he could be that devious. He's a chip off the old block."

"Like father, like son?" Charles caustically mused.

They stared and stared. Finally, Phillip said, "Are you asking me to ride to Bramble Bay?"

"Would you? If it's him, maybe you could talk some sense into him. You're probably the only one who could."

Phillip studied his father, wanting to refuse, wanting to insist it would be a waste of time, that it was ludicrous to imagine Jean Pierre casually gambling in Dover. But Charles rarely requested any favor from Phillip. Though Phillip loathed Charles for much of what he'd done with his sorry life, Phillip adored him, too.

In that regard, Phillip was no different than any of the girls Charles had seduced over the years. It was impossible to deflect Charles's charm and allure, and Phillip was idiotically anxious to make Charles proud.

"I'll go," Phillip ultimately said, "but I doubt he's there."

"Humor me."

"I will. If he *is* there, why would he listen to me on any topic?"

"It's worth a try."

"Yes, it is."

"Better than him swinging from the hangman's tree."

"I couldn't bear it," Phillip concurred, "and I know Harriet couldn't either."

Harriet was particularly disturbed by Jean Pierre's plight. She thought he was too alone, that if he discovered he had siblings who cared about him, he'd stop lashing out and the whole world would be safer.

Phillip downed his drink and stood.

"When will you leave?" Charles inquired.

"In a day or two."

"Send me a message the minute you learn what's happening."

"Should I invite him to travel to London with me? Should I ask him to meet you? Would you grant him an introduction?"

"I'm guessing he wouldn't be impressed by the offer." Charles considered, then said, "You could bring him to meet his sisters. They'd like it if he would."

"All right, and if he *is* the man who won Hedley Teasdale's estate, should I attempt to convince him to give it back?"

"Let's not get crazy," Charles scoffed. "A gambling debt has to be honored."

"He's a *pirate,* Charles. Honor doesn't factor into the equation."

"Honor among thieves, Phillip. Honor among thieves."

Phillip sighed and left. He'd meant to head home, but his conversation with Charles had him unnerved and excited.

Jean Pierre was a mysterious character, a notorious character, a dangerous character. And he was Phillip's brother. What would it be like to meet him face to face? What would he think of Phillip? What would Phillip think of him?

The Crown wanted Jean Pierre dead, but that was because he'd put so many affluent men's noses out of joint. He'd scuttled their ships and stole their cargo, causing untold financial losses to numerous aristocratic families.

But the common people were agog over his bold attacks and thrilled by his bravery and daring. They cheered his antics as if he was a modern-day Robin Hood. He took from the rich, but didn't give to the poor, and they didn't mind. He was very deliberate in relieving the wealthy of what they had, so he was a hero to many.

Could he be persuaded to stop before he was caught and hanged? Or before his luck ran out and he was killed in a mêlée? How could Phillip dissuade him?

He rode to Fanny's house, figuring she'd be busy with planning her party. She and Michael had been married for two years, and she never missed a chance to celebrate.

He predicted that Helen and Harriet would be with her. The half-sisters were the same age—twenty-three—and born the same year, providing stark evidence that Charles had the morals of a dog. They were fast friends and closer than any full-blooded sisters could ever be.

He entered without knocking, and as he'd suspected, the trio was in Fanny's front parlor. They were lounged on the sofas, drinking tea and debating supper menus and entertainment. Whenever he walked into a room, they chirped with delight, which always had him smiling. They made him nostalgic for the decades they'd lost as children, when they hadn't known of one another, when they hadn't realized they had family.

"Weren't you off to visit Charles?" Fanny inquired once they'd calmed and settled.

"Can't a man have any secrets from you three?"

"No," they replied in unison.

"Anne stopped by," Helen admitted. Anne was Phillip's wife. "She spilled the beans."

"I must remember to tell her to be more discreet about my business."

They laughed at his foolishness. No one could tell Anne anything—especially Phillip.

"What did Charles want?" Helen asked.

Phillip had known Charles his entire life, so he was used to Charles's odd proclivities. Fanny, Helen, and Harriet had been acquainted with him for a year or two, and they were fascinated and perplexed.

In light of Charles's title and reputation, it was an incredible shock and burden to learn that you were his child. It was the sort of parentage that caused people to stare and whisper when you went by on the street.

"He told me the strangest story," Phillip said.

"About what?" Fanny asked.

"Brace yourselves—particularly you, Harriet—but it appears Jean Pierre might be in England."

There was a collective gasp, then Helen asked, "What makes you think so?"

"A woman at a country estate out near Dover wrote to Charles. She claims Jean Pierre won their property in a card game. Supposedly, he's on the premises and threatening to foreclose."

"Why would she write to Charles about that?"

"The man confessed to being Charles's son, and she wants Charles to intervene and force him to give the property back."

"Good luck with that," Harriet muttered. "Jean Pierre is insane. It's not easy to reason with him."

Harriet had had an up close and personal violent encounter with Jean Pierre—when he was at his most lethal, his most vindictive.

When he'd wrecked Tristan's ship and set Tristan and Harriet adrift, he hadn't known that Harriet was his sister. But he'd definitely known that Tristan was his brother, and he'd tried his best to murder

Tristan.

Harriet still had occasional nightmares.

Phillip moved over to sit next to her. He took her hand.

"Charles has asked me to ride there to see if it is Jean Pierre."

Harriet frowned. "You believe it's true?"

Phillip shrugged. "He's going by the name John Sinclair, and he seems to be an Englishman."

"The Jean Pierre I met was very, very French."

"Perhaps he's a skilled actor," Fanny mused.

"Perhaps," Harriet murmured. "He's capable of any nefarious conduct. Why not acting, too?"

"I need your opinion, Harriet," Phillip said. "If he really is our brother, Charles wants me to persuade him to come to London."

"Why?"

"He wants Jean Pierre to meet all of you. He agrees with you that if Jean Pierre discovers he has a family, it might make a difference. He might stop being so angry."

Fanny chuckled miserably. "You give us an enormous amount of credit that's probably not deserved."

"It might eventually save him from the hangman's noose." Phillip studied each sister, letting the ramifications sink in. "That would be beneficial, wouldn't it? If we could keep him from being executed? And if we could convince him to cease his rampaging, we could keep others from being harmed in the future."

"It's worth considering," Helen said, and Fanny nodded.

He gazed at Harriet again. "If I locate him, should I invite him to return to London with me? Would you meet him?"

Harriet shook her head. "You're asking an awful lot, Phillip."

"I realize I am."

"He meant to kill Tristan. He meant to kill me, too."

"Yes, but you were just talking about him the other day. You were saying that you were worried about him."

"It was idle banter, Phillip. It never occurred to me that you might bring him to supper, that I might have to look him in the eye and chat. He's very dangerous—in a way you could never understand unless you'd seen him leap over that ship's rail. He slew several of Tristan's sailors, then he toppled the mast and left the others to starve and die."

Her voice trailed off, and she stared at the floor, lost in painful memories. Phillip doubted she and Tristan would ever fully recover from what had happened to them at Jean Pierre's hands.

Could a person forgive such despicable conduct? Could a person ever move past it? Could a sister find it in her heart to have mercy when her own brother had tried to murder her?

"If you don't want me to invite him, I won't," Phillip said.

Harriet was silent, pondering, and they watched her, hating to have the anguish of that horrid episode revived.

Helen rested a palm on her twin's shoulder and asked, "Are you all right?"

"Yes," Harriet replied, "but...ah...I should go home and speak to Tristan about this."

"I'll go with you," Helen said.

"There's no need," Harriet insisted.

She stood and staggered out. As a maid fetched her cloak and bonnet, as she headed for the door, Helen whispered, "She'll be fine. Don't fret over her."

"I won't."

"And as to me, I'd love to meet Jean Pierre."

"So would I," Fanny added. "Bring him to us if you can."

Helen hurried out to join Harriet, and Phillip and Fanny were left alone in the ornate parlor.

Fanny grinned. "You sure know how to ruin a party."

"It's my most endearing trait," Phillip sarcastically retorted.

"Can you really suppose Jean Pierre would risk setting foot in England?"

"The man is insanely daring so anything is possible."

"Would you like me to ride with you to the coast?"

"To locate the world's most wanted pirate? Are you mad? Michael would skin me alive."

"We wouldn't have to tell him."

"Yes, we would, and *no,* you can't come."

"Spoilsport."

"In this matter? Yes, I admit it. I'm an absolute spoilsport."

"To make it up to me, you'll have to stay and write out invitations. You chased off my helpers."

He could have refused, could have pled pressing business and departed. But Fanny was the first sibling he had found, the first sibling he'd rescued. Their bond was deeper than he would ever have with any of the others.

"I would be delighted to stay," he told her.

He picked up the guest list and began to read the names.

CHAPTER NINE

"I was thinking."

John glared over at Raven. "Don't injure yourself."

"Very funny."

"What were you thinking about?"

"Bramble Bay."

They were in John's bedchamber, which had been Bernard Teasdale's. Hedley hadn't ever claimed it after his father died, so John had figured he might as well have it. His occupancy only underscored his new ownership.

His decision had caused an enormous stir, with Mildred furious about the change and the servants caught between John's orders and Mildred's handwringing. Once it was over, John had moved in.

Mildred's room had been in the adjoining chamber, so she'd been relegated to a lesser suite in another part of the house. She'd refused to go and had bellowed that he couldn't boss her, but in the end, she'd glumly observed as her possessions were carted away.

Clearly, the ramifications were finally settling in for Mildred, the results of Hedley's rash conduct crashing down with stunning effect.

John had been waiting so long to seize Bramble Bay that he'd thought he'd revel in the moment. But she and Hedley were both so unpleasant that he couldn't enjoy himself. He was glad he was leaving, glad he was taking Sarah to France.

By the time he returned, a month would have passed, and Mildred and Hedley would be ejected. He'd never see them again.

"This is a beautiful spot," Raven said.

"It is."

"And there's a deep-water inlet around the north headland." Raven raised a brow. "It would make a fine harbor for certain sailors needing a port in a storm."

John nodded. "It would."

"So...I realize you wanted to scuttle the property and let it fall to ruin, but maybe we shouldn't."

"What should we do with it instead?"

"Keep it? Live in it?"

"Live in it?" John scowled as if they were talking about a filthy, rat-ridden alley rather than a well-tended estate on the English coast. "Why would I?"

"It would be a good haven on this side of the Channel. If circumstances required it, we could rest and nurse our wounds."

"We could."

"The place usually has an excellent income. It's dropped a lot, what with Hedley's mismanagement, but we could hire a competent overseer and get the farm producing. It would mean more money for your already fat bank account."

John was an avid saver. He'd spent too many years watching his mother suffer, watching how poverty ate away at her. The lack of wealth signified the lack of all that mattered. He never intended to be hungry or cold ever again. The bulk of the motive driving him was his determination to be so rich that he could never be poor.

"We'd have to put in our own man to run things," John said. "We couldn't hire just anybody—not if we had to hide here when we were having difficulties."

"Bring Reggie over from France when you come back."

Reginald—Reggie—Thompson was John's clerk and accountant, an annoyingly vain Brit who'd been a trial to his parents. After finishing school, his exasperated father had banished him to Europe. But left to his own devices, Reggie had been drawn to the seedier underbelly of the continent.

He'd been drugged and kidnapped from a disreputable brothel in Paris. The kidnappers had been slavers, and they'd been taking him to Tripoli to sell him on the sexual market where perverted Arabian libertines liked to dabble in pretty boys.

John had stumbled on him when he'd boarded the slave ship. Reggie had begged rescue, and when John agreed, Reggie had been so grateful that he'd sworn eternal loyalty.

He humored John with his fussy ways, but John kept him because he was an absolute wizard with numbers. He also had the heart of a criminal, so he was the perfect employee for John.

"Yes, I could bring Reggie," John said, "if I can convince him to set foot in England again." Reggie's family believed him deceased, and he was in no hurry to enlighten them as to his true condition.

"He could administer the property for you. You wouldn't have to wreck it."

John went over to the window and stared at the sloping lawn that led to the rocky beach. Raven was correct: It was a beautiful spot. Yet John had wanted to destroy it for so long. How could he persuade himself to change course?

He glanced back at his old friend.

"This matters to you?" he asked.

Raven shrugged. "I like it here."

"You'd stay on?"

"I'll stay with you, John. You know that. Wherever you go, that's where I will be. But I'd enjoy living here occasionally, too."

John had met Raven when he was ten and Raven fifteen. Florence had moved them to a village on the coast in Normandy where the costs were much cheaper than Paris. She'd foolishly hoped she might bump into someone heading for England who would pay their fare so they could go, too.

But Florence had never had any kind of luck.

Raven was British, too, and had been in France for years. His father had been a sailor, his mother a vicar's daughter who'd been disowned when they'd eloped. Both his parents had died in France, leaving Raven an orphan.

He'd grown up sailing with his father, and he was the one who'd taught John about wind and waves and water. He'd also taught John to lie and steal and cheat and fight, providing most of the skills that were valuable to their current situation. John was a fast learner and had absorbed and improved on every lesson Raven had imparted.

They were a deadly duo, of like mind and purpose. There could never be two better friends. There could never be two more loyal partners.

"Tell me the real reason you wish to stay," John pressed. "You're not a farmer, and my home in France is much grander. Why are you enthralled by Bramble Bay? It can't be for the scenery."

"I'm smitten by Caroline Patterson, and I'm not ready to be finished with her."

"You've seduced her?"

Raven hemmed and hawed. "I'd say *she* seduced me."

"You like her enough to risk visiting in the future?"

"It's not a risk. Who knows our identity? Who could tattle?"

John smiled grimly. "You might be surprised. Never trust anyone, remember? You taught me that."

"I did."

"We should come back so you can fornicate with an Englishwoman?"

"Yes."

"French women are prettier."

"I'm broadening my horizons. I'm trying new things."

John snorted at that. "Let me think on it."

"Think hard, would you?"

"I will."

Annalise strolled in. She was ensconced in the adjoining suite, in what had been Mildred's bedchamber. It was the worst insult John could have leveled at Mildred, and Annalise was the sort of bad sport to rub Mildred's nose in it every chance she had.

Annalise's vanity and Mildred's irritation were stirring trouble, and he was definitely irked that he'd given Mildred an extra thirty days to vacate. The entire affair would have been much easier if she'd left when he'd originally planned.

John hated discord and quarreling, and he especially detested women's hysterical moods, so Annalise was the ideal mistress. She knew better than to nag, which would inflame his temper.

"Must you leave, Jean Pierre?" she asked.

"Yes, I must."

He was departing shortly—with Sarah. He was sailing with her to France, to shield her from her despicable kin, but to seduce her, too. To claim his prize. He had no intention of ignoring what he had won.

At the moment, she was resistant, but he would charm her into changing her attitude. There would be no force involved. She was all alone in the world, without funds or friends. She needed his protection, and they enjoyed a strident physical attraction. Most relationships started with much less.

Eventually, she'd grasp the reality she faced, and he was happy to help her financially. They would get on fine.

"I'm weary of England," Annalise said. "May I return to France with you?"

"You and Raven must keep an eye on things for me. I can't rest until Mildred and Hedley are evicted. You serve me best by remaining behind."

"Please?" she persisted. "I should go with you. My place is by your side."

She snuggled herself to him, making sure he felt her breasts, her enticing hand firmly planted on his backside. Her goal was clear. She was vehemently opposed to him taking Sarah to France, because she'd begun to view his house as her own.

It was the true reason he was leaving without her. He was eager to be shed of her, though he hadn't fully realized it until he'd considered his pending liaison with Sarah. He wanted Sarah and no longer wanted Annalise.

When he was in France, he would devise a new situation for Annalise. He would buy her an apartment in Paris, would settle an income on her. She wouldn't like the ending, but she'd walk away as a propertied female. It was much more than she could ever have expected to receive from him, and ultimately, she'd be grateful.

"No, Annalise," he told her. "You're staying."

"I won't stay!" she venomously hurled.

"And I won't argue about it."

"But I don't understand this." Her temper flaring, she tossed her magnificent hair, looking aggrieved and livid. "It's your English virgin, isn't it? You'll welcome her into my home. You'll seduce her in my bed—while I'm not there to stop you."

Raven calmly scolded, "It's not your home, Annalise. Remember yourself."

"It's as much mine as anyone's," she fumed. She peered at John, her eyes pleading. "Haven't I given you everything, *mon ami?* Haven't I been the woman you desired? Every single second, haven't I been all that you wished me to be?"

"I'll see you in a month," was John's reply. "Help Raven with Hedley and Mildred. That is what I need from you right now."

He set her away and went to the door, and she stamped her foot.

"Jean Pierre!"

He whipped around. "What?"

"You may not take her!"

John reined in his own burst of fury. "Don't command me, Annalise. You can't."

If he was to make the tide, he couldn't bicker with her. He was meeting Sarah in the foyer—she was probably already there—and they had to ride hard and fast.

He spun and left, and when Annalise called to him again, he kept on as Raven chided, "Let it go, girl. You're being a nuisance."

"How can he shame me like this? Am I to relinquish my spot for a pale, sniveling English virgin? Am I not allowed to protest this outrage?"

"Let it go!" Raven stated more sternly.

Momentarily, John heard Raven coming up from behind.

"Don't mind her," Raven said

"I don't."

"I'll handle her."

"I appreciate it."

"You'll be back in a month?"

"Yes. You know how to contact me if there's trouble?"

"Always. While you're away, will you consider my request about Bramble Bay?"

"Yes, I'll laugh about how your cock is dragging you to England."

"There are worse reasons to return."

"I can't think of any."

They rushed down the stairs, and John was actually excited at the prospect of having Sarah all to himself. There was a hidden, silly elation at the notion of showing her his castle, of letting her see how he'd prospered. He wanted her to be proud. He wanted her to be awed.

But as he marched into the foyer, he was stunned to find that she wasn't there. He gaped around as if he was blind. There was no Sarah. There were no packed bags.

The butler loitered by the door, distinctly avoiding John's incensed gaze. John stormed over, intimidating him with his size and presence.

"Miss Teasdale was to meet me here at three," he snapped.

"Where is she?"

"I have no idea, sir."

"Don't you?"

The man was obviously lying, and John stepped even nearer.

"You can tell me where she is or I will have Mr. Hook take you down to the cellar for a *chat*. You can tell him."

The man gulped in terror. "I don't believe I'd like to accompany him, sir."

"I don't believe you would either," John agreed.

He wouldn't torture an old man, but the butler didn't know that. The threat worked like a charm.

"Mrs. Teasdale may have pertinent information."

"Where is she?"

"In her room, awaiting your arrival."

John stomped up the stairs, Raven dogging his heels, as they proceeded to Mildred's bedroom suite. Her door was closed, and he slammed it open, acting as if he owned the bloody place, which he did.

Mildred was in a chair by the window, staring out at the road as if she was seriously wishing she was on it and heading somewhere far from Bramble Bay.

"Your stepdaughter was to meet me in the foyer at three," John said, "but she's not there."

"I just heard," Mildred glumly responded. She held out a piece of paper. "She gave a note to the housekeeper, with instructions to deliver it to me a few minutes ago." Mildred grimaced with offense. "Can you read, Mr. Sinclair? Or must I read it to you?"

"Don't be smart, Mrs. Teasdale," Raven fumed. "If you'd care to match wits with John, I'm sure he's amenable. Trust me: You'd lose."

John ignored Mildred's insult and Raven's reply.

Over the years, he and his mother had lived with various artists and writers, many of whom had been kind to John. He'd been tutored by some great geniuses, including a stint with an Italian count and inventor who'd taught him several languages.

John absorbed details like a sponge. He was brilliantly analytical, able to calculate complex problems and solve intricate tasks as no other person could. He never boasted of his intellect and certainly wouldn't bother with a dunce like Mildred.

He snatched the letter from her, quickly reading the words penned in a tidy script. There was no salutation, but evidently, it was intended for Mildred.

I can't behave as you and Mr. Sinclair are demanding. You shouldn't have let Hedley harm me this way. I can only wonder what my father would think if he were alive to discover the fate you arranged for me. Shame on you, Mildred. Since I can receive no help from my family, I will find it elsewhere.

She'd signed it as *Miss Sarah Teasdale,* as if she and Mildred weren't acquainted, as if Mildred needed to be reminded of who Sarah was.

"What does she say?" Raven asked.

"She's left," John seethed.

"I didn't know about this," Mildred hurriedly said. "I thought she was up in her room. I'm as surprised as you are."

"Where would she go?" John tersely inquired. His rage was flaring so blatantly that Mildred eased back in her chair, anxious to be out of striking range in case he lashed out.

"If I had to guess, I'd suppose she's off to speak with Mr. Fishburn."

"Who is Mr. Fishburn?"

"He's our neighbor—he was her father's friend—but he was called away to London on business."

"Would she go to London to locate him?"

"You could check with Mrs. Patterson. They've always been thick as thieves. She might have better answers."

John's irate glare fell on Raven, and Raven shrugged, having no idea what Caroline Patterson might confess.

John stormed out, bellowing for Mrs. Patterson, until a servant mentioned that she was on the verandah.

"She has to tell me what she knows," John spat at Raven. "I won't brook any nonsense."

"She'll tell you. I won't permit her to refuse."

They marched outside, and she was sitting at a table, sipping a glass of wine. As they approached, she glanced up, and she looked horridly guilty, as if she'd done wrong and had been expecting to be caught.

No doubt she and Sarah had concocted an escape. But no woman could defy John, especially not when Raven was with him. They were a formidable pair, and Mrs. Patterson didn't stand a chance.

"Where is she?" John inquired without preamble.

"Where is who?"

She tried to sound innocent, but failed, and John slammed a fist on the table, cracking it, spilling her wine, making her jump.

"Don't play games with me," he hissed.

Raven rested a palm on her shoulder, and he leaned down so he was directly in her face.

"You can't keep her secrets," he murmured.

"I have to. I promised."

"This is beyond you and her. You must tell me."

She frowned, trembling. "I can't."

"You can. You must."

She stared at her skirt, her mind working it over.

John glowered at Raven, not having the patience to wait as she dithered.

"Caroline," Raven said, "look at me."

She peeked up. "What?"

"Has Miss Teasdale gone to London?" Raven asked, and she gave an imperceptible nod.

"How did she travel?"

"On the mail coach," Mrs. Patterson whispered. "I had a few pounds in my purse, and she used them to purchase a ticket."

With the admission, she flinched, as if terrified John would hit her.

"Is she hoping to find Mr. Fishburn?" Raven pressed.

"Yes. He's her friend, and she thought he might protect her from…ah…well…"

"Good girl." Raven patted her on the knee.

Mrs. Patterson peered up at John, then at Raven again. She was shaking so badly she could barely stay in her seat.

"Will she…be all right?" she asked Raven. "He won't hurt her, will he?"

"No, he won't hurt her. I swear it."

Raven faced John and inquired, "Should I ride with you?"

"No, remain here and keep things under control."

"Are you sure?"

"Very sure. I'll be back in a month. When I arrive, the house should be empty of the current occupants."

"It will be."

"Be ready to sail."

"What about Bramble Bay? What about the plans we discussed?"

"I have business with my father. That's what is next for us. We'll deal with Bramble Bay later."

John whipped away and hurried to the stables to saddle his horse and race to London like the wind. Sarah could never escape him—no matter how hard she tried.

The sooner she realized that fact, the better off she would be.

Sarah sat at a table in the corner of the dining room. They'd stopped at a roadside inn for exactly thirty minutes, and the driver had warned that he had a strict schedule. There were six passengers, and if any of them were missing when he clicked the reins, they'd be left behind.

She'd ordered a cup of tea and a slice of bread and jam, being too anxious to eat much else.

Before dawn, she'd sneaked from Bramble Bay and hidden away in the village. The mail coach had lumbered by at eleven, and she'd climbed aboard.

They'd been traveling for seven hours, the coach slow as a snail, and she was a nervous wreck. She'd constantly peeked out the window, certain Mr. Sinclair would have learned that she'd fled, that he'd come roaring after her like a rampaging highwayman.

But there'd been no sign of him.

Three o'clock had passed without incident. She wanted to relax, to persuade herself that he didn't care enough to chase after her, but she wouldn't feel safe until she was locked in Sheldon's London house.

Suddenly, she noticed someone was standing by her table. She glanced up and blanched with dismay.

"Hello, Sarah," Mr. Sinclair said. "Fancy meeting you here."

It took her a moment to recover from the shock. "Oh, no."

"Don't make a fuss. Just rise and walk out with me."

She gaped around the room. It was filled with farmers and weary travelers. If she begged for help, would they assist her?

"Go away," she warned, "or I'll scream."

"I really wish you wouldn't make a scene."

He put his hands on his hips in a manner that showed her he had a pistol in a holster at his waist, the weapon shielded by the hem of his coat. He was very calm, his green eyes flashing with temper so he looked capable of any murderous deed.

"What will you do if I refuse?" she asked with disgust. "Will you shoot everyone in the place?"

"Would you like to try me? Go ahead and scream. You'll see my reaction. You won't have to wonder about it."

He appeared different again, like a wealthy brigand: black coat, black trousers, black boots, and a very white shirt that emphasized the ominous effect of the black clothes. The fabric was very fine, perfectly tailored. He was wearing gold jewelry, gold rings, the gold earring dangling from his ear.

He adjusted his coat again, furtively displaying a large knife and the butt of a small dagger shoved up his sleeve.

He was armed to the teeth, equipped for any type of battle. How could she not worry over his true intentions?

He planned that she vanish from England. Would she ever actually make it to France? Was he an insane killer who preyed on young women? Would she be chopped into little pieces and her body never found?

Those sorts of gruesome stories circulated occasionally, but they came from London. The calamities happened to street urchins and trollops who were out in the dark. They didn't happen to gently-reared females of good breeding and good family who'd grown up at quiet country estates.

The image of him as a brutal felon was so at odds with the man he seemed to be. He exuded menace, but not so she was afraid of him. It was merely that he didn't like to be thwarted and was livid when his orders weren't followed.

He was determined that she obey, and she was determined not to, but he was so much more stubborn than she was. How could she fight him? How could anyone?

"How did you find me?"

"Mrs. Patterson tattled."

"She did not," Sarah scoffed.

"She did—with no coaxing at all. It was simple to track you." He nodded to the door. "Let's go. We've missed today's tide, but that's the great thing about the ocean. There's always another tide tomorrow."

They engaged in a staring match she couldn't win. Finally, she asked, "You don't really care about me. Why pursue this?"

"You know why."

"Because in the absurd fantasy world where you reside, you believe you own me?"

"Precisely."

"I don't agree to this. I never have."

"So? You're a woman, Sarah, and your eldest male relative gave you to me. I'm keeping you."

"You. Are. Mad."

"Your brother is too, but at least I'm offering to support you and to be kind. He bartered you away without a moment's hesitation. After that little fiasco, you should be a tad more grateful to me."

"Grateful!" she snorted, and she shook her head. "I won't meekly comply. If you want me to leave, you'll have to drag me out."

"All right."

He pulled back her chair and drew her to her feet. He was very strong, and she was very petite, so he lifted her with ease. No one who observed them would have noticed anything out of the ordinary.

An arm gripping her waist, he carried her out, her toes brushing the floor, but it looked as if she was walking of her own accord.

In the foyer, the proprietor went by, and she reached out to him.

"Would you help me?" she begged.

"With what, miss?"

"I'm being kidnapped." At the strange comment, he frowned, and she swiftly added, "I have no idea who this man is. He accosted me inside, and he's taking me away against my will."

The proprietor's frown deepened, and for the briefest instant, she thought he might intervene, but Mr. Sinclair flashed a rueful smile full of apology and regret.

"This is my wife, sir," he lied.

"Your wife? She's not wearing a ring."

"I'm embarrassed to admit that she removes it." He leaned in and—as if enormously shamed—murmured, "She runs away, and I'm constantly having to chase after her."

"Runs away!" Sarah huffed. "I have no husband, and he's a

lunatic."

"It's a terrible business, sir," Mr. Sinclair falsely confessed. "Her parents and I are at a loss as to how we can control her."

He made a twirling motion by his ear, indicating that Sarah was deranged. The proprietor's gaze softened, and he patted Sarah on the shoulder. "You should listen to your husband, dear."

"He's not my husband!" she insisted more loudly, which only made her sound as crazed as Sinclair had described her to be.

"I'm sorry she bothered you." Mr. Sinclair slipped the proprietor a handful of bills. "I hope this will reimburse you for any trouble she caused."

"She was no trouble," the proprietor claimed, but he pocketed the money.

"Let's go, darling," Mr. Sinclair softly crooned. "If we hurry, we can be home in time for supper."

He flashed another smile at the proprietor, one of masculine exasperation and commiseration, and he lifted Sarah again and strolled out with her. She was so stunned by the exchange that she didn't protest.

His magnificent white stallion was waiting for him. He tossed her up, leapt up behind her, and they trotted away.

He was grinning, preening, delighted with how he'd bested her.

"I hate you," she peevishly said.

"You do not."

"I do."

"You're glad I found you. You're glad I came."

"I repeat: You are insane."

"Yes, I am. I always have been. It's what drives me. You shouldn't forget it."

With a whoop, he kicked the horse into a canter, and she grabbed onto its mane and held tight as they raced away.

CHAPTER TEN

"Tell me, how is London?"

"I don't know. I'm not from London."

"But you must have had occasional news."

"Some."

Sarah glanced over at the man who'd introduced himself as Mr. Reginald Thompson. In his early twenties, he was punctual, fussy, and verbose. Small in stature, tidy in his clothes and habits, he was accountant and factotum to Jean Pierre Sinclair—or whatever his name was. Sarah still wasn't sure what she believed.

Mr. Thompson sighed. "I miss England every so often. Not enough to go back, mind you. And I would never leave Jean Pierre."

They were in Mr. Sinclair's castle—not a house, but a castle—on the French coast, so he was referred to by his French name rather than his English one. He was two different people, with two different personas, and she couldn't decide which was the real one and which the façade.

"You're very loyal to him," Sarah said.

"Yes, absolutely. If he hadn't rescued me"—Mr. Thompson fought down a shudder—"I can't predict what would have happened."

"Why were you in need of rescue?"

"I was kidnapped by slavers—"

"Slavers!"

"Yes, slavers, and with his being a...well..." His sentence trailed off, as if he realized he was about to divulge more than he should. "Let's just say that when he jumped aboard the ship I was on, and I begged him to save me, he didn't hesitate. I owe him my life."

"It certainly sounds like it."

"I would do anything for him," Mr. Thompson passionately gushed.

His gaze could only be described as worshipful, as if Mr. Sinclair was a god who walked on water. At Bramble Bay, Miss Dubois and Mr. Hook had gazed at him the same way. Apparently, he attracted followers as faithfully as honey attracted a bee, and Sarah, herself, hadn't been immune to his many charms.

Of course that was before she'd been forcibly removed from England and whisked to France against her will.

Mr. Thompson was escorting her to a private supper with Mr. Sinclair. The castle had been remodeled with modern comforts, but it had originally been a fortress meant to propel invaders, so there were odd twists and turns in the halls and on the stairs that made it easy to get lost.

So far, she hadn't had a chance to explore, and even though she was furious with Mr. Sinclair for his high-handed behavior, she couldn't deny her fascination—both with him and with the adventure that had been thrust upon her.

She'd never previously been on a ship, and as they'd crossed the Channel, she'd intended to be snippy and rude. But she'd been too intrigued by the maneuvering of the sails, by the sailors going about their duties.

Furtively, she'd watched Mr. Sinclair as he issued orders, as his crew worked together like a well-oiled machine.

He'd been busy with a thousand tasks and had ignored her for the entire trip, which had been irksome. She was angry and aggrieved and feeling incredibly abused, and it was galling that he didn't seem to notice or care.

It had been dark when they'd docked, so she hadn't been able to view his residence. She'd entered through the gates, the walls towering over her, so she hadn't grasped its ancient design, hadn't understood its magnificence.

During their arrival, Mr. Sinclair had been conspicuously absent, and his competent staff had immediately rushed to tend her. A gaggle of pretty housemaids had escorted her to a lovely suite, complete with writing desk and balcony. The furniture was elegant and understated, the feather mattress on the bed too plush for words.

She'd crawled onto it and had instantly fallen into a deep and wonderful sleep. When she'd awakened the next day, the maids were hovering with the news that Mr. Sinclair was still occupied, but that she would meet him for supper.

To the staff, this was an important and significant invitation that required significant preparation. Despite her reticence, despite her insistence that they didn't need to fuss over her, she'd spent the afternoon in her room, being bathed and perfumed and lotioned and massaged.

They'd styled her hair in an intricate coif, attired her in a fabulous green gown that was sewn from a soft, flowing fabric she'd never seen previously. She had an expensive string of diamonds—that she assumed were real—hanging around her neck, diamond earrings dangling from her ears.

As they'd finally declared her ready, when she'd been allowed to look at herself in the mirror, she'd nearly fainted with surprise. The alteration was stunning. She appeared wealthy and beautiful and nothing like the ordinary, boring Miss Sarah Teasdale she'd been all her life.

"You're not the only one who adores Mr. Sinclair," she said to Mr. Thompson. "The servants seem particularly loyal."

"That's because he's saved all of them from dire fates."

"He inspires an enormous amount of devotion."

"He does, he does." Mr. Thompson nodded. "But then, considering everyone's circumstances when rescued, it makes sense."

"He must be very tough, very brave."

"He is."

"What, exactly, is his line of employment? How is it that he's constantly sailing the seas and saving so many strangers?"

Mr. Thompson's brows raised, his mind working, as if his response was a puzzle that had to be deciphered. They were at the top of a curving staircase, and he avoided answering her question by motioning to the closed door in front of them.

"Ah, here we are." He knocked once to announce them and spun the knob. "Enjoy your supper, Miss Teasdale."

"I'm sure I will," she lied.

"I'll catch up with you in the morning. We'll reminisce about England."

"I can't wait," she lied again.

He urged her over the threshold, shut the door behind her, and— she was certain—locked it so she couldn't leave.

She didn't check to find out if he had for she couldn't bear to know. If she'd been locked in, what could she do about it? Pound and bang and shout until her hand was sore and her throat raw?

Evidently, she was in Mr. Sinclair's private quarters, and the place was obviously arranged to provide maximum tranquility. The sitting room was done in soothing shades, the décor and furnishings generating an ambiance of ease and comfort. A cheery fire burned in the grate.

In the adjoining room, she could see his bedchamber, could see his large bed. It had a canopy over the top and a carved headboard fit for a king. She yanked away, refusing to gape, refusing to admit what it indicated.

What was the true reason she'd been brought to him? Was her ruination about to commence?

There was an open archway that led out onto a balcony. A brown-skinned man stood there, wearing a turban and flowing trousers. The house was full of peculiar characters, of all nationalities and colors, many of whom did not speak English or French. It was as if Mr. Sinclair had sailed the world and plucked up a collection of novel, foreign people to serve him.

The man grinned and bowed, gesturing for her to approach, to follow him onto the balcony. She walked over, and he pulled on a curtain and ushered her outside.

Finally, she was face to face with Mr. Sinclair. He was seated at a small table set for two. The linen was blindingly white, the silver polished until it gleamed. Red wine had been poured.

Liveried footmen hovered off to the side. Behind him, over the balcony railing, she could see the bay, the village curved around it, his ship and many others anchored in the harbor.

With the sun dropping in the west, the vista was spectacular, the scenery quaint and picturesque. It could have been a painting, an artist's rendering of a perfect spot on the French coast.

Mr. Sinclair stared at her, and she stared back. The moment was very odd, very dreamlike. She was overcome by an impression of familiarity, as if she'd always known him, as if they'd shared intimate suppers a thousand times previous.

The dashing Frenchman had returned. His white shirt was meticulously embroidered, tons of lace on his cravat and sleeves. He was wearing another expensive coat, but in a green hue that matched her gown. The hem was stitched in gold flowers, and in light of the opulence of his home, she suspected it was real gold thread.

His blond hair was loose, curled on his shoulders, the green of his coat enhancing his striking emerald eyes.

He was such a feast for her female senses, and she felt herself softening toward him. She couldn't wait to dine, merely so she could ogle him all evening. She warned herself to buck up, to be wary, but couldn't muster any genuine affront.

At the sight of her, his hot gaze was inflamed. He studied her carefully, as if eager to ensure his servants had put her in the right costume.

The gown fit like a glove, as if it had been specifically designed for her, and she took some comfort from the fact that it couldn't possibly have belonged to Miss Dubois. His mistress was much taller and broader across the hips and chest, so thankfully, Sarah hadn't been attired in his whore's clothes.

His assessment complete, he pushed back his chair and stood.

"*Chérie,* you are so beautiful." He motioned to her. "Come."

The pretty compliment was too much for her. She'd received so few of them in her life, and she could have dawdled all night, listening to his flattery. How was it that he managed to simultaneously terrorize and awe?

When she didn't move, he repeated, "Come to me, *chérie.*"

She hesitated, suddenly shy, but he simply drew out the other chair and held it for her like the most gallant gentleman. She should have spun away and huffed out, but instead, she stumbled over, unable to ignore his allure, unable to behave as rudely as she ought.

Once she was seated, he shifted nearer so his legs were touching hers, their feet tangled together. He shoved on the sleeve of her dress and kissed the inside of her wrist, his lips lingering on her skin, sending goose bumps down her arm.

She pulled away, hoping to look scolding, but the effect was lost on him. He was fully aware of how thoroughly he overwhelmed her, and he enjoyed it.

"Thank you for joining me," he said.

"Did I have a choice?"

He considered for a moment, then claimed, "You could have refused, but then you would have missed the splendid meal my chef has prepared for us."

"Could I have demanded that a tray be delivered to my room? Would you have allowed me to dine alone?"

"Yes, but you would have missed my charming company. And I would have missed yours. There's no point to our quarreling, is there?"

She thought there was an enormous *point* to it, but she'd already blistered his ears a dozen times over. Talking to him was like talking to a log. He only listened to comments he felt like hearing.

Needing to distract herself, she tried a sip of wine. It was lush and fruity, better than anything she'd ever tasted and a further example of how wealthy he was, how he surrounded himself with pleasures.

"You're French again," she said, the remark sounding like an accusation.

"I always have been French."

"But you can seem as English as I am—when you wish to be."

"I can."

"Why is that?"

"Why do you ask? Are you dying to know more about me?"

"No."

"Liar."

A footman brought a plate of several kinds of food, fish in buttery sauces, mushrooms and other vegetables she didn't recognize.

Mr. Sinclair took a fork, speared a bite of fish and held it out to her. She could have declined, but she was starving and everything smelled delicious.

"Oh, my," she murmured as flavors exploded on her tongue.

"Good, *non?*" he inquired.

"Good, yes."

He chuckled and fed her again, offering her different configurations until she pushed him away.

"Is this the first course?" she asked.

"Yes."

"I have to pace myself, or I'll never keep up with you."

"We'll eat slowly. We can take all night—unless we decide we'd like to amuse ourselves in other ways."

There was no question as to what he referred, and his gaze was so open and inviting that her feminine parts seemed to be melting. How was she supposed to resist him? She felt like Eve in the Garden, being tempted by the snake.

"I've heard," she said, "that the French are adamant about their food."

"They are, but I am especially interested."

"Why is that?"

"I was often hungry when I was young. I constantly told myself that I would grow up to be very, very rich so I could eat whatever I liked whenever I liked."

"You were poor as a boy?"

"Extremely poor. It wasn't so bad while my mother was still alive, but after she died, well, it was a bit dire."

It was very possibly the only true thing he'd ever said to her. A bleak expression crossed his face, but it was quickly masked. Would she ever be allowed another glimpse at his genuine self?

"How old were you when she passed away?"

"Ten."

"Where was your father?"

"Back in England."

"Your father was British?"

"Yes."

"And your mother was French?"

"No, she was British, too."

"So your parents were British, but you were raised in France."

"Mostly in Paris."

"That's why you're a chameleon. You can change nationalities to suit your mood or situation."

He shrugged and smiled. "Perhaps."

She observed him, baffled by his statements. He was an expert at fabrication, and he threw out facts, but she had no ability to judge his veracity.

He'd once claimed his mother was Florence Harcourt, but then he'd denied it. Were his parents British? Was his mother deceased? Had he even *had* parents? He seemed so exotic. Maybe he'd been reared by wolves.

"After your mother died, your father provided no support?"

"He was…busy."

"Too busy to support his son?"

"It was no matter." He shrugged again. "My friend, Raven, helped me to survive. I was fine."

His use of the word *survive* rattled her, and she didn't like the images it conjured. It made her worry over his past, made her feel sorry for him when he deserved no sympathy.

Her father had never been wealthy, but Bramble Bay had been

prosperous, and they'd always had plenty. What would it be like to be alone in the world, to be orphaned and fretting over your next meal?

She envisioned him as he must have been at ten, with no mother or father, and Mr. Hook his savior. With that history, was it any wonder he was mysterious and mystifying?

"You've definitely thrived." She gestured to the balcony, indicating his servants, his castle, his life.

"I have."

"How have you grown so affluent? It must be a fascinating tale."

The servants froze, and an eerie silence fell, as if the Earth had stopped spinning so everyone could listen to his reply.

He grinned. "I might tell you someday."

"Tell me now. Are you in…shipping?"

"You could say that. And salvage. I occasionally retrieve cargo from vessels that are sinking."

A footman bit down a snort, which Mr. Sinclair ignored. "Are you a smuggler?" she baldly inquired.

"Me? Do I look like a criminal to you?"

"No, but you act like one."

He laughed. "How could a brigand accumulate so much wealth?"

"I don't know. How could he?"

He didn't respond, but motioned to the footmen, and they bustled into action, clearing plates, pouring more wine. She was already sated, and she had to remember to restrain herself, to moderate her intake of alcohol. She wasn't a drinker and could rapidly find her inhibitions lowered to a dangerous level.

"Where were you today?" She was much too curious about him and still irked that he'd brought her to his home only to disregard her presence entirely.

"Why? Did you miss me?"

"No."

He laughed again. "Oh, *chérie,* I am so charmed by you."

"I'm glad to be of service."

He pointed to the harbor, to where his ship sat at anchor. "When I travel, even for a short time, many tasks await me when I return."

"You were working?"

"Always. If I didn't, I wouldn't be so rich, would I?"

"No, I suppose you wouldn't."

"I apologize for leaving you alone. I thought you'd enjoy being pampered."

"I enjoyed it very much," she admitted. The experience had been relaxing and soothing. She wouldn't pretend otherwise.

"I'll behave better toward you tomorrow," he stated like a threat. "You can have all my attention."

"*All* your attention?" she hastily said. "I don't believe I'll need quite that much."

"How much of it would you like then? I can spare whatever amount you feel you require."

There was heat in his gaze and innuendo in his words. He was much too sophisticated for her, and she had no idea how to spar with him. She was desperate to change the subject, to focus him on topics other than her pending ruination.

"Tell me why you came to Bramble Bay," she said.

"You know why. To gamble with Hedley."

"Why him specifically? What did he do to you?"

"Hedley? He did nothing."

"So…it was Mildred? I realize she can be exasperating, but how has she spurred your animosity? I'm twenty-five, and I've been living with her for twenty-three years—all of them unpleasant. Yet I'm hardly seething with malice."

"You should be."

"Because she let Hedley give me away?"

"Yes. She was fully complicit and happy to be shed of you."

"All right, she was hideous to me, and I'm livid. Now what's your excuse?"

He took her hand again, and he started rubbing his thumb across her wrist, over and over on the spot where her pulse pounded under her skin.

"You ask so many questions, *chérie*."

"You never answer any of them. Is Mildred your aunt? Was Florence your mother?"

"What if she was?"

"You're surrounded by people, but you seem to be a very solitary person. Why shun your family? Why torment your aunt?"

"Why not?"

"Don't be flip. This quarrel you have with Mildred has wrecked my life, and I think I deserve to know what's driving you."

"My *quarrel* wrecked your life? I beg to differ. Your life wasn't so grand as you recall. There wasn't much to wreck."

"It was *my* life. It was *mine*. Can I go home?"

As was typical when he didn't want to supply information, he nodded to the footmen. Quickly, the table was cleared, just the wine glasses remaining. When she glanced up, the servants had slipped away. The balcony was empty except for the two of them.

"You can't keep me prisoner, Mr. Sinclair."

"You're not a prisoner."

"What am I then?"

"My very special guest, and you're to call me John when we're alone."

"Not Jean Pierre as your mistress does?"

At her crude reference, he didn't bat an eye. "I'll be British for you. You may call me by my British name."

Her temper flared, and she pushed her chair away and went to the balcony railing. She yearned to stomp out, but she couldn't forget the locked door. It would be too humiliating to make a huffed exit, only to find herself trapped. He'd get too much enjoyment out of watching her yank on the knob.

She stared out at the harbor. The sky was a deep indigo, the last vestiges of twilight flickering on the horizon.

Candles were being lit down in the village. Lamps on the ships were lit too, their flames twinkling on the water. She was dressed like a queen, being cosseted like a rich heiress and fawned over by the most handsome, most compelling man she would ever meet.

A perception flashed—that she was a princess in a fairytale, that an evil prince had her imprisoned in his tower. But in fairytales, the evil princes turned out to be heroes in the end.

Who would Mr. Sinclair be at their conclusion?

He came up behind her, his large, warm body pressing into hers. She could feel his chest and stomach, his hard thighs against her bottom and legs. It was so intimately decadent, and she should have elbowed him in the ribs to force him to step away so there was space between them, but to her eternal disgust, she didn't.

When he touched her, he ignited the wildest swings of sensation. Sparks seemed to crackle, the air charged with a new and vibrant energy.

He was so masculine, so strong and powerful, and she relished the feelings he generated. Back at Bramble Bay, when Mildred had pestered her to wed Sheldon, Sarah had ultimately decided she couldn't because she had a romantic heart.

She'd *wanted* a man like John Sinclair to sweep her away. She'd wanted passion and amour and all those silly, feminine things that women craved. Yet he had naught but illicit intentions toward her.

What would it be like to give herself to John Sinclair? Women ruined themselves all the time for love—without the promise of marriage. Why should she be any different? If she seized an immoral solution for herself, she had no family who cared. Who would notice or protest?

He rested his hands on her waist and drew her nearer. The naughty positioning rattled her, sent butterflies careening in her stomach.

He bent down and nibbled at her nape, and she groaned with pleasure, but with dismay, too. She twisted around and looked up at him—and it was a mistake. He was observing her, his attention so fixed that he literally took her breath away.

"Welcome to my home, Sarah," he murmured.

"You can't keep me here, John."

"I can, Sarah. I will."

"It's not right."

"You belong with me," he insisted. "Can't you feel it? Can't you feel that it was meant to be?"

"There's no destiny at work."

"There *is*."

"You're wrong."

He scoffed as if she was a fool.

"You must learn one very important detail about me."

"What is it?" she asked.

"I am never wrong."

"Never?"

"No. Most especially not about this. Not about you."

He dipped down and captured her lips in a torrid kiss.

As had transpired every other moment she'd spent with him, she should have shoved him away, should have refused to participate, but she couldn't pretend to hate his advances.

It was impossible to decline what he offered, and she didn't want to decline. He mesmerized and enticed, steadily wearing down her defenses until there was nothing left of her temper and outrage.

The embrace was all she'd ever dreamed kissing could be. His tongue was in her mouth, his hands in her hair. She was trapped between him and the balcony railing, every inch of his muscular torso crushed to her own.

He roamed freely, caressing her everywhere. With each stroke of his fingers, each glide of his palms, daggers of titillation flitted through her. Desire swirled in her belly, then rampaged out to her extremities.

She was inundated, goaded beyond any manageable place where she could tell him *no* about anything. They'd sailed into a tempest, and the storm was tossing her in every direction. She couldn't fight it or swim to shore. She could only hold on and hope for the best.

Gradually, the onslaught abated. He loosened his grip and drew away, his lips separating from hers.

He peered down at her as if he'd realized secrets about himself that he hadn't fathomed, his concentration potently unnerving. She felt beautiful and unique and beloved, and she had no ability to deflect such a deliberate, calculated assault.

He was too much for her, too capable and shrewd, too skilled at artifice and seduction. How would she ever save herself? Why would she *want* to save herself?

"It's late," he said, "and I'm sure you're tired. Let's get you back to your room."

"My...room?" She frowned.

She'd been certain he'd demand she stay, and she'd been braced to repel any suggestion that they take their affair to the next level. The fact that he didn't wish to, that he wasn't interested, was surprising and annoying.

Had she upset him? Had he changed his mind about her? If so, she should have been celebrating, but she wasn't. She was so confused!

"Why did we stop?"

"You've had a long few days," he kindly advised. "You must be weary."

"I am."

He studied her, looking like the cat that had spotted the canary.

"When I finally make you mine," he said, "it will be because you want it to happen."

"I'll never want it to happen."

"We'll see, *chérie*. We'll find out what you truly want—and what you don't."

He led her to the door in his private quarters. If it had been locked previously by Mr. Thompson, it wasn't locked now. Mr. Sinclair opened it, and his turbaned servant was there.

"Escort Miss Teasdale to her bedchamber," Mr. Sinclair commanded.

The man bowed, but didn't reply. He gestured for Sarah to proceed down the stairs.

She should have started off, but she was ragged with emotion. She'd been kidnapped from all that was familiar, whisked across the ocean to a foreign land where she didn't speak the language. Alone and afraid and completely at his mercy, she was totally flustered by what they'd just done.

Yet he was very calm, very composed, as if their strident kissing had had no effect on him at all. How could he be so unmoved? How could he be so indifferent?

"Goodnight, Sarah."

"Goodnight, John. Will I...see you tomorrow?"

"Absolutely."

She nodded, anxious to say more, to explain that she was distressed and perplexed and scared, that she needed things from him she didn't understand.

If she could clarify what she needed, would he give it to her? She thought he might, and the notion was terrifying and thrilling.

She spun and hurried away.

CHAPTER ELEVEN

"Leave me be."

John glowered at Akmed, his turbaned valet, but the man wouldn't be deterred. He'd arrived to help John prepare for bed, but John wasn't in the mood to be pampered.

It was always the same when he returned from a journey. His servants fell all over themselves, trying to please him.

"Go," he said, motioning to the door.

Akmed shot a fierce glare of disapproval, then huffed out. He had no tongue—it had been cut out by his slave master when he was a boy—so he couldn't verbally complain. But he was very good at getting his point across nonetheless.

The silence settled, John's sense of isolation feeling particularly extreme.

He poured a glass of wine and went out onto the balcony to stare at the harbor. The sight usually soothed him, usually reminded him of how lucky he was, how far he'd come, how successful he'd been.

When he'd first taken ownership of the castle, it had been rundown and decrepit, but he'd eagerly spent the money to make it his home. He'd acquired the property after a rigged card game from a very bad gambler who shouldn't have been playing, but then, most men shouldn't ever have bet against John.

He didn't lose. He won fair and square or he cheated. Either way, he got what he wanted.

He hadn't cared about the castle until he'd seen it. It was a real fortress, built to withstand attack, the ocean acting as a natural moat during high tide and a muddy bog during low tide. The harbor was easily accessible by his ships, the village filled with capable craftsmen who kept him fed and supplied. Considering his line of work, it was a perfect location.

Typically, he enjoyed tarrying on the ramparts like a petty king, gazing over his domain. Yet for once, the vista brought no solace.

His trip to England, where he'd been forced to mingle with his aunt and his cousin, had been incredibly draining. The encounter had stirred old hurts and slights. He was adept at pretending the past didn't bother him, that he'd moved on, but it wasn't true. The past still had the power to wound, to cripple with fury and rage.

The visit had him reflecting on his mother. She'd been so imprudent and stupidly naïve. She'd believed she could desert her aristocratic husband and there would be no consequences. She'd believed that she could involve herself with Charles Sinclair and make him love her when, by all accounts, Charles had never loved anyone.

In that, John and his father were very much alike.

Florence had been exasperatingly sure that Charles would abandon his wife and come back to them, that they'd be a family and live happily ever after.

Then, as her health had begun to deteriorate, she'd started to imagine her husband, the Earl of Westwood, would forgive her. He'd never divorced her, and she'd convinced herself that she could show up in England—with her bastard son by her side—and resume her prior life.

In the decade John had known her, she'd embraced a series of awful decisions that had catapulted them to the bottom of society's ladder until, when she'd died, John had been standing all by himself.

He couldn't figure out if his mother had been a fool or if she'd simply been mad. Perhaps it was a combination of the two: She'd been foolishly mad. Of course he was viewing their experiences through the eyes of a child.

Who could guess why Florence had made so many ridiculous choices? Who could guess at the pressures that had weighed her down? Her husband had been a violent drunkard, and she'd been wed to him at sixteen. As she'd fled to Paris three years later, who could comprehend what she'd endured? Who could blame her for leaving?

The one constant had been her love for John. She'd repeatedly advised him that he'd be a leader of men, that he would take the world by storm and rise to the position his high ancestry demanded. He smiled a grim smile. For all her faults and foibles, she had been very moralistic and decent, teaching him to never lie or cheat or steal.

He scoffed with disgust. When she'd sworn he'd rise in the world, he didn't suppose she meant what had actually occurred.

Memories were eating at him, and he couldn't bear to be alone. Most nights, when he was assailed by doubts or ugly reminiscence, Raven was around to chase off the demons. But Raven was in England, and the only other person on the premises who could distract or entertain him was Sarah. Hours earlier, he'd sent her away because, during their brief supper, he'd been too fascinated, too curious as to what she'd look like without her clothes.

He'd told her that he would deflower her when *she* agreed, when *she* was ready, but he didn't think he was patient enough to wait for her to acquiesce. So what were his options?

He could walk down a short flight of stairs and be in her room. It was his castle, and he was lord and master. She couldn't deny him entrance. Yet if he visited her, what was his plan?

Seduction, yes. But more than that? How much more?

She was hardly prepared for a rough copulation. She was still too angry to grasp that an alliance with John was the best ending for her. But apparently, he couldn't allow her time to come to terms with her new situation.

He wanted to physically bond with her, but it seemed he wanted something else, as well. For reasons he didn't understand and couldn't explain, he needed her to care about him, to like him, to soothe him. He was desperate to know that he could go to her, that she would say just the right comment, that she would smile or scold, and he would feel better merely from being with her.

It was a strange and frightening insight. He consorted with trollops like Annalise so he could have raw, raucous sex, and he'd never seen any other purpose for feminine fraternization.

Evidently, with Sarah, he craved things other women couldn't supply, things he hadn't *wanted* them to supply.

He downed his wine, poured a second glass and downed that, too. Without giving himself opportunity to reflect, he hurried across the balcony and down the stairs. They led to a lower balcony, to the French windows in her suite.

He stepped inside—without announcing his arrival, without asking permission.

The space was dark, illuminated only by the moonlight flooding in. In her bedchamber, a single candle burned on the table by the bed, but she wasn't in it. The blankets and pillows were tidy, the covers not yet pulled back.

In the room beyond—her dressing room—another candle burned, and he could smell warm water and bath salts.

As he realized she must be bathing, that she must be naked and lounged in one of his pretty silver tubs, he was overcome by such a powerful rush of lust that he was dizzy and had to lean against the doorframe to steady himself.

Though he was behaving like the worst bully, like the worst boor, he marched over and entered.

She saw him immediately, and for a moment, she froze. Then she squealed with alarm and dipped down so just her face was visible.

"Go away," she commanded.

"No."

"You can't be in here."

"I can."

Her hair was piled high, combs jammed in various spots to keep the auburn mass balanced. A few wayward strands caressed her shoulders. Her cheeks were rosy, her eyes very, very blue.

He approached the tub, his thighs pressed to the edge, her slender torso barely visible under the soap's bubbles.

"Are you here to ravish me?"

"Yes. No. Maybe. I'm debating."

She blanched with dismay. "I thought an affair was up to *me*. You said so at supper."

"I changed my mind. I never let women decide anything, and I'm not about to start with you."

"John! Listen to how you're talking. You're scaring me."

Not half as much as he was scaring himself.

She was so delectable, so compelling, and he was drawn to her like a moth to a flame. He was crazed with his need for her, which had him wondering if he hadn't inherited some of his mother's lunacy. He'd often suspected that he had.

That was likely the true reason Charles Sinclair had left them in Paris. He'd probably noticed that Florence and John were mad as hatters.

"You have to get out of the water," he said. "You have to get out!"

"Why?"

"Just get out!"

If she didn't dry and cover herself he couldn't predict what he might do.

He grabbed a towel and laid it over the tub. Then he wrapped her in it and dragged her to her feet, lifting her over the rim, her weight throwing him off balance. They staggered awkwardly as he tried to maintain his hold and she tried to keep the towel firmly in place.

"You are insane," she fumed.

"Yes, yes, I already told you I was."

"I should be safe in your home," she ridiculously stated.

"Safe? In my home? Now who's insane?"

"What is wrong with you?"

"Nothing. Everything."

"Aren't there rules about how you have to treat me?"

"No."

"Don't you have to at least pretend to be a gentleman?"

"No."

He gaped about, saw her robe flung over a nearby chair. He draped it over her shoulders and shoved her arms in the sleeves, the wet towel falling away as she yanked at the lapels and furiously tied the belt in a tight knot.

She glared up at him, her ire on a slow boil. She was so lovely and aggrieved. His heart raced faster than it ever had during a sea battle. He was flustered and out of control, desperate to receive boons from her he couldn't begin to name.

Struggling for calm, he took a deep breath, then another. When he could speak in an even tone, he murmured, "Ah, *chérie,* I've made you angry."

"Of course you've made me angry, you arrogant oaf."

"You're so beautiful, Sarah. I can't resist you."

"Don't think you can earn forgiveness by tossing around a few compliments."

"I don't want forgiveness."

"What do you want?"

"Just you. Only you."

His fingertips brushing her cheeks, he leaned down and kissed her.

She was always surprised by his advances so she never protested. She tasted so good and smelled so good, and she intrigued him as no other female ever had. She was innocent and defenseless and all alone in the world. Her vulnerability called to him and ignited his masculine instincts so he was eager to protect and cherish and revere.

Where would it lead? Where would it end?

He picked her up and carried her into the bedchamber. He dropped her on her bed and followed her down, his body pressing her into the soft mattress. He could feel her breasts and thighs, her mons crushed to his phallus. The sole barrier between them was the paltry fabric of her robe and the flap on his trousers, which was no barrier at all.

He gentled the kiss and drew away to find her studying him as if he was a strange scientific specimen. She was taking his measure, trying to figure out what drove him, what made him tick.

Normally, he would have shielded himself from such an avid inspection, but apparently, he was more troubled than he'd realized.

"You're upset," she said.

"No, I'm not," he lied.

"You are. You can tell me what it is."

Her voice was a balm that had him anxious to talk about details he never talked about. He yearned to tell her of his past so she would comprehend his motives, so she would commiserate and empathize.

But it could never happen. He wouldn't let it happen.

"Nothing is wrong." His mask fell into place, his emotions once again controlled and concealed.

She frowned. "How did you do that?"

"Do what?"

"You were so distraught—it was clearly written on your face—but you hid it."

"You're imagining things."

"No, I'm not. It's like a magician's trick. You can take your feelings and stuff them in your pocket where no one can see them."

A slither of disquiet slid down his spine. She was too astute, and he didn't like her heightened perception. It was important that he be an enigma. If she could so easily sense his moods, what else might she sense that she oughtn't to know?

When he was with her, he had to be more careful, but caution was difficult. She rattled loose sentiments he typically kept at bay. Why was she so adept at flustering him? Why was he so on edge?

It had to be that he was simply disturbed by his trip to England, by his being parted from Raven. He needed to reassert himself, to bring himself back to the spot where he could focus on what mattered, on what he required from her.

"If I seem upset," he claimed, "it's because I am so enamored of you, and I can't decide what to do about it."

"You're not enamored of me."

"I am, *chérie*. I can't deny it."

He rolled onto his back and rolled her with him, so she was on top and straddling his lap. She was on her knees, a palm on the mattress to steady herself.

She glowered at him, her wariness evident, but there was a curiosity, as well. He fascinated her, and she couldn't completely shield her interest.

He rested his hands on her flanks and drew her down so their privates connected. Her eyes widened with surprise.

Several combs had fallen from her hair, so he reached up and plucked out the remaining ones, the entire mass swirling down over her shoulders.

Had she any idea how magnificent she was? Had she any idea how enticing?

How was a man—especially one such as himself who had no moral character and no ability to practice restraint—to behave when she was temptation incarnate?

"Let me see you, *chérie*," he murmured.

"What do you mean?"

"You're so beautiful."

"Stop saying that."

"Why should I stop? Why?"

"Because it confuses me. It makes me like you."

"You *should* like me. I've told you a dozen times over."

He pulled on the lapels of her robe to reveal some cleavage, while she tried to tug the fabric together, but he wouldn't permit it. He clasped her hands and held them in his.

"Let me see you," he repeated.

He loosened the belt, the cloth sliding away so her breasts were bared. They were the perfect size, full and rounded, the tips a pretty pink.

He caressed one, then the other as she moaned with dismay and attempted to cover herself again, but he continued to prevent her.

"You're embarrassing me," she said, her cheeks aflame.

"How?"

"I hardly know you. We shouldn't be here like this. We shouldn't—"

He laid a finger on her lips, silencing her.

"Everything between us is right, Sarah. There's no reason to be frightened or ashamed."

"I don't understand you."

"What's to understand?"

"You could have any woman you want, and I'm so opposed to an affair. Why harass me? Why bother with me?"

"You're not opposed to an affair. Let me show you something."

"I wish you wouldn't."

"You'll like it. I promise."

A taut nipple dangled over his mouth, goading him to an insane degree. He sucked at it, laved it, bit and played until she was writhing with pleasure, but also to escape the stimulation he was providing.

He nibbled to the other breast, to the other nipple, and he gave it the same fierce attention. Quickly, he was perched on a perilous ledge where he might perpetrate any reckless deed. She had that capacity to arouse and provoke. If she ever learned the true state of her power over him, how might she use it to coerce him?

The prospects didn't bear contemplating.

He eased her away and snuggled her to his chest, so she was sprawled across him. He frowned at the ceiling, wondering what he'd set in motion. He was fretting over her, over his plans for her, and he couldn't guess what she was thinking.

Eventually, she looked up at him. She was scowling, her expression concerned and aggravated, with a touch of trepidation thrown into the mix.

"Why did you stop?" She was clutching her lapels again.

"I just didn't suppose we should go any farther."

She exhaled a relieved breath. "Good."

He snorted with amusement. "Have you any idea what men and women do when they're alone?"

"Yes, my friend, Caroline, is married, and her description of marital behavior doesn't make me in any hurry to try it. She said it is extremely vile."

"Vile? Really?"

"Yes."

"I wouldn't necessarily take her word for it."

"Why wouldn't I?"

"Have you considered that her husband might not be very skilled at amour? With another sort of fellow, it might actually be pleasant."

Her scowl deepened. "Different men do it differently?"

"Yes. It can be very fun and fulfilling—depending on the expertise of your partner. And if you *like* him or not. That helps. Does she like her husband?"

"No. He's a violent ass."

He shrugged. "I rest my case."

She grumbled but didn't slither away, and he was in no rush to depart either, which was odd. He was still so titillated, his cock begging to be assuaged, but for once, he didn't listen to it.

An unusual intimacy had blossomed, and he felt so much better merely from holding her, merely from being close. Demons had chased him to her room, but they seemed to have been vanquished.

He was content. He was...happy.

He stroked a lazy hand up and down her back, investigating her shape, imprinting it in his memory.

Suddenly, she popped up again, her blue eyes intent and searching.

"You wouldn't hurt me, would you?" she asked.

"You mean *physically* hurt you?"

"Yes. You're so angry sometimes. Caroline's husband used to hit her and do...other things. You wouldn't lash out at me like that, would you?"

"Don't be ridiculous."

"And you wouldn't force me to...well...consort with you against my will?"

"I don't ravish women," he huffed. He didn't have to. There were too many who were available and eager.

"Good," she said again.

She slid off him, and he shifted so he could watch her. He never grew weary of looking at her. He was smitten as a young swain with his first girl.

"You don't have to be afraid of me," he said.

"I'm not. You pretend to be vicious and tough—"

"I am vicious and tough."

"—but beneath the bluster, you're quite kind."

"*I* am kind?" he scoffed.

"Yes. Your clerk, Mr. Thompson, told me that all of your servants are people you rescued from dire straits."

He smiled a tight smile. "Perhaps Mr. Thompson should keep his mouth shut."

"You continued your heroic streak by feeling you rescued me from Hedley."

"I *did* rescue you from Hedley."

"See? You're kind. I just have to figure out how to bend you to my way of thinking so you'll agree to let me go home."

"You have no home."

"Why don't you give Bramble Bay to me?"

"Give you Bramble Bay?"

"Yes. It would solve both our problems."

"How?"

"You can be shed of a property you never wanted."

"I wanted it."

"You did not. For whatever obscure reason, you enjoy punishing

Mildred. But now, you own it, so it will always be a burden to you. Give it to me, and you are free of it."

"No."

"Why not?"

"No," he said more firmly, irked that she had the right of it.

He didn't want Bramble Bay, but he liked the notion that it was his. She was very bright in realizing that he should sign it over to her, but he never would.

If she had someplace where she could be safe from her family, there'd be no need to keep her, but he wouldn't let her go. Not when he was still lusting after her. Not when they shared a destiny he didn't yet understand.

"You can be kind to others," she pressed. "Be kind to *me*."

"Don't pester me, *chérie*. The more you ask, the more I will refuse simply so you know who's in charge."

"You're being a bully."

"Yes, and it's my true tendency. Not kindness. You shouldn't forget it."

He didn't like that she'd moved away, that she was no longer draped across him. He pulled her to him, and she tensed, trying to maintain the space between them.

He was annoyed by her paltry attempt. It was pointless to fight the inevitable, and he tightened his grip. Swiftly, she relented, beginning to grasp that she couldn't win against him. The sooner she accepted that fact, the better off she would be.

He snuggled her to him and swallowed down a sigh of contentment.

"I'm all...jumbled inside," she murmured. "What's wrong with me? It's as if my skin and veins have been scraped raw."

"That's your desire talking. We didn't finish so you're on edge."

"What didn't we finish?"

"There's quite a bit more to it so you'll be unsettled until you let me have my way with you."

"You've already had plenty of your *way*. You don't need more."

"We'll see. By tomorrow, I bet you'll be begging me to sneak back up here so I can give you some relief from your physical misery."

"In your dreams, Mr. Sinclair."

"Yes, in my very vivid, very indecent dreams."

She glanced up. "How about you? Are you on edge?"

"Oh, yes, I'm definitely on edge."

She studied him, her shrewd assessment probing to the center of his cold, black heart. He couldn't abide her detailed scrutiny. She believed he was kind. It was a hilarious opinion, but it tugged at old wounds, making him wish he'd grown up to be the man his mother had intended.

Instead, he was the sort who would toss his aunt out on the road—penniless—with nary a ripple in his conscience. He was the sort who would kill his own brother. His next plan was to start attacking his father's ships, to cripple his father financially, and he'd laugh while doing it.

It was a despicable commentary on his character, and for once, he yearned to be someone else. Sarah looked at him and saw a different man, a misguided but salvageable man. What would it be like if he could be that man for her?

He nestled her down, and she yawned and mumbled, "It's nice to be here with you like this."

"It is."

"I've never slept with anyone before."

"Neither have I."

She snorted with mirth. "Liar."

"When I am in bed with a woman, I don't *sleep* with her. I'm busy with other activities."

"Spoken like a genuine libertine."

The word *libertine* hardly described his sexual proclivities. He dabbled with whores for carnal pleasure, for carnal release. There was no seduction or wooing involved.

He was intrigued that Sarah wasn't a doxy. Her chaste presence shined refreshingly on his sordid existence. She made him feel cleaner, less sullied and despoiled.

She yawned again. "You can't stay in here."

"Yes, I can. In case you didn't notice, this is a castle, and I am its king."

He could sense her smile.

"You're so vain," she said.

"I certainly am."

"I don't want the servants to find you."

"They won't, *chérie*."

And if the servants discovered him in her bed, they wouldn't give it a second thought. They came from rough backgrounds where lechery wasn't surprising and practically expected.

"Close your eyes," he told her.

"I might. I'm so tired."

"I'll wait until you doze off. Then I'll leave."

"Promise?"

"Yes, I promise."

With their passion ebbing, the temperature had cooled. He yanked the blankets over her, and he listened as her breathing slowed, as her body relaxed.

She liked him more than she cared to admit, and it was possible, too, that she was lonely—as he was lonely. It was a quiet night, and it was comforting not to spend it by himself.

She fell into a deep slumber, her cheek on his chest, her arm on his waist. She was so gullible and trusting, but people trusted him at their peril—as she would eventually learn.

Yet for the moment, he wouldn't focus on the negative, wouldn't focus on his low character or evil nature.

He remained much longer than he should have. She was so small and slender, and he felt manly and protective in a fashion he never had the chance to exhibit, but definitely enjoyed.

Dawn broke out on the water, the first hint of light changing the sky from black to indigo.

He slid to the floor and dawdled by the bed, studying her, missing her already. He was suffering from the strongest urge to climb back in, to be next to her when her pretty blue eyes fluttered open later in the morning. But the notion was terrifying and bizarre.

He couldn't be smitten and wouldn't allow himself to be infatuated. Bonds only made a man vulnerable, only distracted him and exposed him to jeopardy.

He turned and tiptoed away—while he had the fortitude to go.

CHAPTER TWELVE

"How dare you show your face in here."

"You can't hide from me forever."

"If you don't think so, then you don't know me very well."

Caroline glared at Raven, wishing she was bigger and stronger so she could push him out of her room. She was furious with him, but even more furious with herself.

Sarah was her only friend, her true sister, the one constant through thick and thin. Sarah—and Bramble Bay—had been Caroline's beacon of safety when she'd run away from her husband.

But when Sarah had needed to flee, Caroline had failed her.

Once Mr. Sinclair had realized Sarah was gone, he and Mr. Hook had come to Caroline for answers. Caroline had expected them to question her, and she'd been positive she could keep Sarah's secrets. Yet Mr. Hook had simply stared at her, Mr. Sinclair had bluffed and barked, and she'd tattled like a frightened ninny.

She was ashamed and embarrassed, and from the moment she'd demonstrated her pathetic lack of loyalty, she'd avoided Mr. Hook like the plague.

She still wasn't sure why she'd participated in the carnal incident he'd previously instigated, but clearly, he was dangerous to her equilibrium and her moral character. If she spent any significant amount of time with him, what else might she try? Who else might she betray?

The prospects were too upsetting to consider.

For all intents and purposes, she was married. A woman with a husband—even a violent, drunken husband—couldn't have sexual relations with strangers.

"Go away," she firmly said.

"No."

"If you don't, I'll scream."

He rolled his eyes. "Don't be melodramatic."

"I will. I mean it."

He shrugged. "So scream. Who will rescue you? Hedley? Mildred?"

He closed her door, spun the key in the lock, and marched across the floor.

At his determined approach, she shrieked with dismay and raced from her sitting room, through her bedchamber and into the dressing room beyond. It was the scene of their prior indiscretion, so she was heading to the precise spot where she shouldn't be.

"I hate you," she fumed as she whirled around.

"You do not."

"You made me tell on Sarah. You made me betray her."

"*I* made you?"

"Yes."

He frowned, then admitted, "I suppose I did."

"I didn't want Mr. Sinclair to take her to France."

Tears surged into her eyes, and she swiped them away, but her distress didn't deter him. He pressed her to the wall, grabbed her thighs and lifted her so her legs were wrapped around his waist. He shoved at the hem of her skirt, his privates crushed to hers.

"What will Mr. Sinclair do to her?" she asked.

"What do you think he'll do?"

"He'll ruin her."

"Yes, but I imagine she'll like it."

"Spoken like a typical, vain male."

"She's too old to still be a virgin. She'll be happy to have her chastity surrendered."

"Not to him! It should be for her husband!"

"Why? So some bumbling oaf like *your* husband can make her miserable?"

She could hardly argue the point, and she muttered, "She's too good for him."

"Of course she is."

"He'll hurt her, he'll—"

"He won't hurt her. He'll seduce her and use her kindly."

"And then what?"

"I have no idea."

"Will I ever see her again?"

"I have no idea about that either."

"She was my friend. I can't bear it that he's taken her away."

"Then I guess I'll have to distract you so you're not quite so lonely."

He cupped her with his palm, ripping her drawers, shredding the fabric so he could slip two fingers inside her. He was rough and crude, as Archie had always been, but with Mr. Hook, she didn't mind. His callous handling was exciting.

He was very strong, holding her to him as he pushed at the bodice of her dress, as he exposed her breasts. He dipped down and sucked on one, biting it, as his thumb flicked over the sensitive spot at the vee of her legs.

In an instant, she shattered with pleasure, but he didn't let up. As she spiraled down, as she regained her composure, he'd somehow unbuttoned his trousers and impaled himself.

His rod was thick and solid, and he began to flex his hips. He was very aroused, the wildness of their coupling quickly spurring him to the end. He growled with satisfaction and emptied himself, spewing his seed into her womb, and for a brief second, she was anxious over the conclusion.

He didn't appear to care if he got her into a jam. Nor had she counseled caution or urged restraint. He goaded her to recklessness. What if he'd impregnated her? How would she explain it?

But then, she remembered that she was barren. It was Archie's interminable complaint over her failing as a wife. They had been wed for two grueling years, yet his seed had never caught. When no babe was created, everyone insisted it was the woman's fault, and Caroline never ceased to fume over the indictment.

Why blame the wife? Why couldn't people consider that it might have been Archie's lack?

Mr. Hook smirked, delighted with how easy she was, how thoroughly corruptible. He drew away and guided her feet to the floor. They stood awkwardly, straightening their clothes.

"I won't be at Bramble Bay for long," he said, "so when I'm in the mood to fornicate, you shouldn't refuse me."

"I'm married."

"Just barely."

"I can't be committing adultery whenever you walk by."

"Why can't you? Your husband hasn't rushed to claim you. The man's an idiot, and I won't let him spoil our fun."

"You're putting me in so much danger."

"How? I won't tell anybody what we're doing. Will you?"

"No."

"You need a few good rides so you can learn what it's like to fuck a real man."

The vulgar term was like a slap in the face. It sounded sordid, driving home how little she knew about him, how wrong her conduct.

Her knees were weak, from the sexual act but also from nerves. She collapsed against the wall, using it as a crutch, using it for balance. She was ashamed, unable to look him in the eye.

"Would you go now?" she asked. "I'm just…just…"

She couldn't describe what she was. He had an ability to inflame rash tendencies she hadn't realized she possessed, and she wasn't sorry for what they'd done. She *wanted* to feel guilty, but didn't. Maybe that was the problem. She was suffering no remorse and was eager to misbehave again.

What sort of woman acted that way? What did it say about her true character?

"I should have sailed to France with John," he told her.

"Why didn't you?"

"I stayed because of you."

"You can't mean that." Feebly, she repeated, "I'm married."

"I don't care. I'll probably depart in a month, and I can't say if I'll ever return."

"I might not see you again?" The notion was alarming.

"No, you might not. My line of work is hectic, and I never know my schedule or where I'll be. So while I'm here, you will *not* hide from me."

"No, I don't suppose I will."

"Would you be willing to move yourself into my bedchamber?"

She gasped with shock. "To live there openly?"

"Yes. We could be together all the time."

The prospect was outrageous and scandalous, but riveting, too. "Mildred would never permit it."

"It's not Mildred's house. It's John's, and he wouldn't give two figs over how we carry on."

She huffed out an astonished breath. "You make me forget myself, Mr. Hook."

"Life is short, Caroline, and my employment hazardous. Who can guess what will happen? I try to seize the day whenever I can."

"I never seize the day."

"Perhaps you should." He spun and strolled out.

She staggered to the sitting room and eased down in a chair. For a long while, she stared at the empty fireplace, reflecting on their budding affair, on what the future held.

In a month, Caroline had to leave Bramble Bay, as everyone else had to leave. Mildred claimed she would write to Archie, to send Caroline home where she belonged. But Caroline wouldn't accept that ending.

If she confessed her dilemma with Archie, would Mr. Hook help her? Would he rescue her? And if she cast her lot with him, what new path would unfold? Could she bear to find out?

She pondered and fretted until a maid's knock interrupted.

"What is it?" she called.

The girl peeked in. "Mrs. Teasdale needs you down in the front parlor."

In light of Caroline's disordered state—and the fact that she could smell Mr. Hook on her skin and clothes—Mildred was the very last person she wanted to see.

"Did she say why?"

"No—just that it's important."

Caroline knew Mildred well. The older woman wouldn't be denied, so it was pointless to refuse.

She sighed. "Tell her I'll be right down."

      ℮〇   ℮〇   ℮〇   ℮〇

Raven stood in an unused bedchamber on the second floor. He was with two of the footmen, completing an inventory of the furnishings. When Hedley and Mildred left for good, he had to be certain he could account for all of John's possessions.

He peered out the window and frowned. There was a small carriage in the drive, a single horse pulling it.

He didn't like anyone to arrive without his being apprised, and the butler had strict instructions to inform him immediately as to any visitors. The idiotic man must have gone straight to Mildred—as if Mildred was still in charge—and it was an indicator of how he wouldn't have a job much longer.

Raven motioned to one of the footmen, and the boy came over.

"Whose carriage is that?"

The boy studied it, scowled, then tentatively ventured, "Ah...I probably know."

"Well?"

"It belongs to Mr. Patterson."

"Caroline Patterson's husband?"

"Yes."

"Why would he be here?"

The boy glanced away. "I really couldn't say, Mr. Hook."

Raven stepped in, meaning to intimidate with his size, with his authority. "Why not?"

The other footman answered, "It's a bad business, Mr. Hook. The housekeeper ordered the staff to stay out of it."

Raven nodded, considering the disturbing comment.

"You two can go to the kitchen for tea. We'll finish later."

He walked out and went to the stairs, and he tiptoed to the landing, where he could see the foyer down below. The servants were conspicuously absent as if—whatever was occurring—they didn't want to witness it.

Shortly, the parlor door opened. Mildred emerged, a man with her who had to be Mr. Patterson. He was forty or so, dressed in a fussy suit and carrying a cane. He was tall and lanky and balding, and Raven loathed him on sight.

"Thank you, Mildred," Mr. Patterson said. "I appreciate your help."

"You're welcome," Mildred replied. "She put me in such an awkward position."

"I'll make sure it doesn't happen again." He barked, "Caroline, come!"

There was a lengthy delay, and finally, Caroline appeared. She'd been crying. Her cheeks were red, her eyes moist. She nearly passed by Mildred without a word, but she thought better of it and halted.

"I can't believe you betrayed me to him."

"You belong with your husband, Caroline."

"You tricked me into marrying him. You were aware of what he was like, and you talked me into it anyway. If he kills me, you won't even care."

Mr. Patterson was irked by the insult. "You will apologize to Mildred for imposing on her," he scolded. "You're lucky she took you in."

"Sarah took me in, not *her*." Caroline glowered at Mildred. "You always hated me. I wish Bernard was alive so he could see how you've ruined us."

Mildred ignored her outrage. "Goodbye, Caroline. Please don't come back. There's no place for you here."

"I'll tell Sarah that you sent for him," Caroline fumed, but Mildred recognized it was an empty threat.

"Archie is your husband. Sarah has no say in the matter."

Mr. Patterson puffed himself up. "My wife will never bother you again, Mildred. I guarantee it."

The remark was chilling. It rang off the rafters with ominous intent. He clutched Caroline's arm, and though she dragged her feet, he simply hauled her off, his grip tight enough to bruise.

"Witch!" Caroline hurled at Mildred before her husband pulled her outside and she vanished from view.

Mildred stoically watched until the butler closed the door after them. Raven marched down the stairs, his boots pounding in an angry rhythm.

"Why is that man on the premises?" he demanded.

"Caroline is being evicted with the rest of us," Mildred explained, "and I'm weary of her foolishness. It's time for her to return home, and with the way she's behaved, she's fortunate her husband will take her back."

She whipped away in a snit, and he stepped in her path to stop her.

"What?" she asked, glaring.

"Go up to your private quarters. Stay there until I permit you to come down again."

"You have no authority over me."

"In John Sinclair's absence, I'm in charge." He leaned in, letting his fury waft over her like a cloud. "Refuse to obey me at your peril, Mrs. Teasdale. Refuse to obey and see what happens."

She hesitated, yearning to defy him, but she prudently relented.

"Barbarian," she spat.

"Yes, I am," he agreed, and he bellowed, "Now go!"

She flinched and scurried off like a scared rabbit. Then he stormed over to the butler, approaching until they were toe to toe.

"What were your instructions about visitors?" he hissed.

"Ah…that you were to be immediately informed."

"Was I not clear? Were you confused by my edict?"

The man gulped with dismay, but didn't respond.

"Wait for me in the library," Raven seethed. "You'll have to make a case as to why you shouldn't be flogged, then fired."

Raven hurried out and tromped down the grand stairs to the drive, where the horse's ass, Archie Patterson, had actually bound Caroline's wrists with a rope.

"How dare you shame me!" Patterson had the audacity to whack her with his cane. "How dare you hide yourself!"

He hit her a second time and a third. Caroline didn't react. She appeared defeated, resigned to her fate.

"Haven't I lectured you?" Patterson complained. "Haven't I warned you where your stubborn attitude will lead?" He shouted, "Get in the carriage!"

Raven sauntered over, and Mr. Patterson was so incensed, he didn't notice Raven. Raven tapped him on the shoulder.

"What is it?" Patterson whirled around. On observing Raven—a foot taller, a yard wider, all dressed in black—he blanched and weakly inquired, "May I help you?"

"Mr. Patterson, I presume?" Raven casually said.

"Yes." He clicked his heels. "Archibald Patterson at your service."

Raven looked at Caroline and asked, "Do you want to leave with him?"

She voiced the word *no*, but couldn't speak it aloud.

Raven gestured to the house. "Go inside."

Patterson stuck out his chest. "Now see here, I am her husband, and I've put up with enough of her nonsense. I won't—"

Raven drew a pistol from his coat and stuck the barrel directly in the center of Patterson's forehead. Patterson froze with stunned surprise. The whole world went still. Not a bird flew. Not a tree swayed in the wind.

"If you open your mouth again," Raven murmured, "I will blow your head off."

Patterson swallowed, his Adam's apple bobbing, but he wisely kept silent.

"Caroline, go!" Raven said.

She ran to the stairs, and once she was out of Patterson's reach, Raven moved the gun away.

"You're getting in your carriage," Raven tightly stated, "and you'll pick up the reins and point your horse toward London. You are never—I repeat, never!—coming back to Bramble Bay. Do you understand me?"

"You can't just—"

"Do you understand!" Raven roared at full volume, and Patterson lurched away.

"I don't know who you think you are, but I don't have to tolerate this treatment. A husband has rights."

"You can choke on your rights," Raven spat.

Patterson glared over at Caroline, where she hovered on the bottom step. "Caroline, I command you to accompany me."

Raven sighed with exasperation. "Are you deaf, Mr. Patterson? Or are you stupid?"

He raised the butt of the pistol and cold-cocked Patterson. Patterson dropped to the dirt, a frantic hand rubbing the spot where the clout had landed. Blood spurted and dripped down his cheek.

"You hit me! You hit me!" he shrieked over and over.

"Yes, and if you don't shut up, I'll hit you again." Raven bent down and pulled Patterson to him until they were nose to nose. "This property doesn't belong to Mildred and Hedley anymore."

"You're lying."

"I'm not lying. My employer owns it, and you're not welcome. If you ride up the drive ever again, I will shoot you as a trespasser." He yanked Patterson to his feet. "Consider yourself warned."

Patterson was dizzy, swaying. Raven lifted him and tossed him into the carriage. He grabbed the reins and wrapped them around Patterson's shaking fingers.

"Caroline is never coming back to you, Patterson," Raven advised.

"We'll see about that!" he huffed, but he didn't sound menacing.

"Go to London and divorce her. Feel free to cite adultery or desertion. Or use them both. I don't care what you choose."

"Adultery!" Patterson wheezed.

"But know this: If I ever see you again, I'll kill you. That's a promise, and I *always* keep my promises."

He walked over and swatted Patterson's horse on the rump. The animal jumped and raced away, Patterson clutching at the reins so he wasn't thrown off. The carriage careened down the lane and out onto the road, and as Patterson disappeared from view, Raven spun to the house.

Caroline was still there, her expression unreadable. What must she think? Since arriving at Bramble Bay, he'd concealed his penchant for violence. He hoped she wasn't frightened or disgusted.

He went over and stopped in front of her. With her on the step, and him on the ground, they were eye to eye.

"How did you do that?" she asked.

"It was easy." Raven waved a hand as if Patterson was a bothersome gnat. "He's a bully, and bullies crumble when threatened."

"You told him to go, and he…left! He was afraid of you."

"As he should be. I can be quite vicious when the situation requires brutality."

"You swore you'd kill him if he returned. Would you?"

"Absolutely."

She studied him forever, and he waited on tenterhooks, terrified over what her opinion might be and whether it would bode ill as to his chances with her.

"Mr. Hook," she eventually said, "you and I are going to be very, very good friends."

"I believe we are. And you should call me Raven. Since I'm happy to murder your husband for you, we don't need to be so formal."

"No, we don't."

He untied her wrists and led her inside.

"May I speak with Mr. John Sinclair?"

"He's not here."

Annalise sat on a sofa by the fire, listening as Raven replied to Phillip Sinclair. It was shocking to have Sinclair pop in and start inquiring about Jean Pierre. He hadn't yet said why he'd traveled to Bramble Bay, but it wasn't difficult to discern the reason.

He and Jean Pierre were definitely brothers. There could be no question as to their close blood relationship. Tall and handsome and imperious. Golden-blond hair. The typical Sinclair green eyes.

If she could push back his sleeve and scrutinize his wrist, she was sure she would see the distinctive birthmark, the 'Mark of Trent' that would indicate Charles Sinclair's paternity.

They had always heard that Lord Trent had sired many illegitimate children, but it was a tad disconcerting to bump into one of them. How had Mr. Sinclair discovered that Jean Pierre was in residence? What else did he know that he shouldn't?

"When will he return?" he asked Raven.

"He won't," Raven lied.

"He's left England?"

"I really can't say."

"May I talk to Mrs. Teasdale instead?"

"That won't be possible. She's indisposed and not having visitors."

Raven had her locked in her room, and she could only venture out when he was around and available to watch her every move.

Mr. Sinclair was very bright and obviously grasped that Raven wasn't being candid. But Sinclair was a stranger and unannounced caller, so he could hardly bluster and demand answers that Raven wasn't inclined to furnish.

"May I inquire," Mr. Sinclair said to Raven, "as to your relationship with John Sinclair?"

"I am his partner."

"Are you allowed to conduct business on his behalf?"

"If I feel like it."

"My father is Charles Sinclair, Earl of Trent."

Raven snidely muttered, "Give him my regards when you get back to London."

Annalise recognized the statement to be a sort of threat. Raven and Jean Pierre had been whispering about Charles Sinclair, and she presumed the exalted man had trouble coming his way.

Mr. Sinclair let the remark pass. He kept assessing Raven, peeking at Annalise, as if trying to figure out their game. But she and Raven had lived lives filled with swindles and deceits. Mr. Sinclair would never learn what they didn't wish him to know.

"My father received a letter from Mrs. Teasdale," Mr. Sinclair explained, "which is why I've traveled to Bramble Bay."

"If the earl would send you on such a long journey," Raven said, "the issue she addressed must have been quite riveting. What was it?"

"She claims John Sinclair is my father's son—and my half-brother. We thought him deceased years ago in Paris, so we were surprised to discover that he was hale and hearty and engaged in mischief in England."

"In mischief? What makes you think so?"

"Mrs. Teasdale tells us that her son, Hedley, gambled away their estate to John. She asked my father to intervene on her behalf."

"To intervene in what fashion?" Raven scoffed.

"To convince John Sinclair to give the property back to the Teasdales."

"Isn't your father a gambler?"

"Well, yes, he is."

"Then he should understand that a gambling debt has to be honored."

"He does understand."

"Yet you came to Bramble Bay anyway," Raven mused. "I'm curious as to why you'd accept Mrs. Teasdale's tale that you're kin to John. You share a surname, but there are many families in the kingdom who can say the same."

"Your Mr. Sinclair confided to someone at Bramble Bay that the earl is his father and his mother was Florence Harcourt, Countess of Westwood."

Annalise swallowed a gasp. He had to have confessed to that pasty-faced witch, Sarah Teasdale, and the notion that Jean Pierre had revealed such a personal detail was infuriating. What else had he told the annoying, indiscreet girl?

Mr. Sinclair paused, expecting the disclosure would loosen Raven's tongue, but it didn't.

"Monsieur Sinclair," Annalise asked, "what are you hoping to achieve by coming here?"

"I simply wanted to see if the rumor is true, to see if he actually is my brother."

"And if he is?"

"I'd like to invite him to visit our family in London. He has several half-sisters there. They would love to meet him."

Raven scowled, and he and Annalise exchanged a significant look.

Family meant nothing to Jean Pierre. The fact that he had a father, that he had siblings, was irrelevant. He would never meet them. He would never allow himself to be claimed by them.

"I'm sorry, Mr. Sinclair," Raven ultimately said, "but you've been misinformed as to John's identity."

"Have I?" Mr. Sinclair's skepticism was overt.

"John has no kin in London," Raven insisted, "and the Earl of Trent is not his father."

"What about Mrs. Teasdale's letter?" Mr. Sinclair asked.

"She must have been confused by what she was told."

Mr. Sinclair studied Raven, then he tried a different tactic. "Is Mrs. Teasdale related to Florence Harcourt?"

"I believe they were sisters," Raven admitted, just to stir the pot.

"Sisters…" Mr. Sinclair murmured to himself. "That explains it."

He waited, but Raven supplied naught more. Finally, Raven rose and motioned to the door. "If you'll excuse us, Mr. Sinclair? We're busy today. It's a pity Mrs. Teasdale wasted your time."

"I appreciate your seeing me." Mr. Sinclair pushed himself to his feet. "Would you give Jean Pierre a message for me?"

Raven and Annalise held perfectly still, not providing any hint that John was also called Jean Pierre.

"As I do not know anyone named Jean Pierre," Raven said, "I can't pass on any message."

Mr. Sinclair gnawed on his cheek, his perplexity obvious.

He was so much like Jean Pierre. Clearly, he yearned to stomp over to Raven, to force him to spill secrets that Raven would never divulge. But Mr. Sinclair was very smart, and he sensed that Raven couldn't be intimidated.

Instead, he kept speaking. "Tell him that our father is worried about him. He's growing too reckless, and we're afraid he'll be caught and hanged. Tell him we'll help him to change his path, and if he ever comes to London, he'll be welcome in my home."

He laid his card on a nearby table and left.

Raven and Annalise stood quietly until the front door was shut behind him. Then they went over to the window to watch as he mounted his horse and trotted away.

"What do you make of that?" Annalise asked.

"Odd."

"He and Jean Pierre are so much alike."

"That old reprobate, Charles Sinclair, has strong bloodlines. I've heard that all his children look exactly the same. Apparently, the stories are true."

"Poor Mildred," Annalise crooned. "The earl won't be riding to her rescue."

Mr. Sinclair rounded the bend and was swallowed up by the trees, and Annalise swung to face Raven.

"When will Jean Pierre be back?"

"He said a month, but how can I guess with any certainty? He'll return when he's ready and not a moment before."

"Is he setting me aside? What did he tell you?"

"I realize you imagine yourself to be extremely important in his life, but you were not mentioned between us when he departed."

Raven couldn't bear to suppose that someone else might get close to Jean Pierre. So Raven had always hated Annalise, and she had always hated him.

He deemed her to be inconsequential and disposable, and he was adept at rattling her. She wished she could rattle him too, but he was incredibly self-possessed. It was impossible to make him feel anything at all.

"What of Sarah Teasdale?" she pressed. "What are his plans for her?"

"Again, I have no idea."

"Will he replace me with her? Will he keep both of us? I won't share him with her!"

"You'll obey his commands," Raven tersely replied, "and you'll obey them gladly or you'll be sent back to Paris."

"You'd like that, wouldn't you?"

"I'd *like* whatever makes Jean Pierre happy. You don't factor into the equation."

"*I* make him happy."

"Do you?" he casually mused.

She studied his eyes, wondering what he meant. What had they discussed? What had they arranged?

Raven could deny all he wanted, but he and Jean Pierre were so attuned, they could read each other's minds. They were one man in two bodies. If she was to be tossed aside, Raven would already have the separation terms drafted.

Ooh, how she detested being a woman. Because she was female, he and Jean Pierre had never trusted her. They never allowed her into their private circle. They viewed her merely as Jean Pierre's concubine, and her reduced role was galling.

Well, if they thought she could be shuffled off to Paris, they were in for a surprise. She would not be discounted!

"You spew lies about me to him," she seethed.

"As I said, Annalise, we *never* discuss you."

"He won't let me go."

"He lets everyone go—eventually. You have to be prepared for it."

"If he tries with me, I'll know you were the cause. You'll be sorry."

He snorted with disgust. "Don't threaten me, Annalise. You sound ridiculous."

"I'll make you pay. I swear it!"

She stormed out, fuming that she couldn't garner the respect she deserved. Raven was so obstinately ignorant over how she could assist Jean Pierre, how she could propel him to ever higher achievements.

She trudged to the stairs and climbed, eager to sulk in her bedchamber. She was bored and on edge, and she loathed Bramble Bay. The food was awful, the servants slothful and rude. With Jean Pierre away, there wasn't a single interesting person with whom she could occupy her time.

But as she reached the landing, she noticed Hedley on the floor above. He hadn't returned to London, but had stayed in the country, purportedly to help his mother pack, but he was actually a hindrance for Mildred.

Annalise suspected that the true reason he hadn't gone to London was because—in the city—he was hounded by creditors. Jean Pierre had spread word that Hedley was destitute, so his lines of credit had been revoked. Debt collectors showed up wherever he went. It was easier to hide at Bramble Bay.

Usually, she avoided him. He was young and imprudent and pathetic, but he was used to the entertainments in town, and he had to be chafing as she was chafing. Plus he was fascinated by her, which was soothing to her bruised ego.

He considered her sophisticated and worldly, and she fueled each of his impressions. He envisioned himself to be an appealing rogue who could win her from Jean Pierre. She wouldn't tamp down his idiotic expectations.

"Miss Dubois," he beamed, "how lovely to see you."

"And you, as well, Monsieur Hedley."

"Are you busy?"

"No."

She joined him, standing so close that her breasts brushed his arm. He grinned, thinking she was smitten, that he could steal her from Jean Pierre.

"A friend sent me a gift from London," he said.

"Really? What is it?"

"A dozen pictures of people indecently posed." He raised a brow as if he'd just mentioned the most sordid sin imaginable.

"You like naughty pictures?" she breathlessly asked, pretending to be shocked.

"Oh, yes. Very much."

She snuggled nearer, giving him a spectacular glimpse of her cleavage.

"May I look at them with you?" she inquired.

"I figured you for the type who would enjoy it." His lips at her ear, he whispered, "He sent me some opium, too. We could smoke it in my room."

"I never have before," she fibbed. "I would be afraid to try it. I might forget myself—and I'd be alone with you. Anything could happen."

He bit down a smirk, assuming he'd tricked her, that she would become intoxicated and he could ravish her.

Mon dieu! Stupid boy.

"You'll be safe with me, Miss Dubois."

She frowned, feigning concern. "If you're sure, Monsieur Hedley."

"You'll be fine."

As he escorted her down the hall to his suite, she rippled with triumph. At least one man in the blasted house thought she was beautiful. At least one man thought she was worth seducing.

Hedley might be a dunce and a fool, but he could prove to be useful, too.

She had warned Raven as to the position owed her by Jean Pierre. If push came to shove, if Sarah Teasdale returned with Jean Pierre and they seemed too intimately connected, Hedley was her brother and had the authority to split them apart.

Hedley was so malleable. He would behave as Annalise demanded.

She entered his room, shut the door, and spun the key in the lock.

CHAPTER THIRTEEN

Sarah climbed the stairs to John's private quarters. While she wanted to pretend she was forced to dine with him, she would be lying. She couldn't wait to be with him again.

He was a sorcerer, and with each passing minute, she was more completely under his command and control. He treated her like royalty, spoiled and cosseted her in ways that she could never have imagined to be seductive, but they were.

His tantalizing assault was meant to wear her down, to win her over, and she was disgusted to admit that it was working. He was grace personified, the consummate gentleman—worldly, sophisticated, able to converse on any topic—and she had no defense against the onslaught.

What was she going to do?

Her French hiatus had quickly fallen into a regular routine.

She was a lazy, pampered guest, who slept in and who, upon waking, had her every wish immediately granted. She had only to mention a certain food, and it would be presented to her. She had only to mention a horse ride or a walk on the beach, and a footman arrived to accompany her.

During the day, John was busy, and if she saw him at all, it was through the window of her room. He'd be down on the wharf, chatting with sailors and merchants, or out on his ship, loading it for what appeared to be a long journey.

She never grew tired of spying on him. He was so baffling, so dangerous to her equilibrium. Her mind was relentlessly awhirl as she wondered where he was, what he was doing, and if he ever thought of her—as she constantly thought of him.

Their suppers had become a ritual she relished. In the late afternoon, her maids would hurry in with a magnificent new gown, with new jewels and shoes. They would spend hours primping her so she looked like a princess.

Then she would proceed to John's suite, to the lovely balcony with the pretty view over the harbor. They would enjoy delicious food and wine, then she'd return to her bedchamber and slumber blissfully until the next morning when it would all begin again.

After that first night, she kept watching the French windows, expecting him to step through. But he hadn't, and she didn't understand why.

She should have been glad he stayed away, that his desire had fled, but she wasn't glad. She was irked and confused and even a tad jealous.

Obviously, his taste ran to trollops like Miss Dubois who knew things about passion that Sarah had never had the chance to learn. She was disgusted to find herself in a competition with Annalise Dubois, and she'd lost. It was humiliating and galling.

She was such a mess! Fretting and envious and detesting women she'd never sought to emulate.

She reached the top of the winding stairs. To her surprise, Akmed wasn't there to escort her inside.

The door was closed, and she knocked and knocked, but no one answered.

For a moment, she worried that she'd gotten the time wrong or that the meal had been canceled, but no. The maids had prepared her as though it was a typical evening.

She dithered, figuring she should go back to her room, but she couldn't bear to. Jean Pierre had ensnared her so thoroughly that their nocturnal repast was the highlight of her existence. It would be too cruel to miss it.

She pressed her ear to the wood, but heard no noises on the other side. She spun the knob and peeked in. The place was empty, but a fire burned in the grate. There was no sign of Akmed or John, no appetizing aromas wafting from the balcony.

She could see the table where they usually sat to eat. There was no white linen or fine silver, no crystal goblets or decanter of wine. What could have happened?

Her pulse pounded with dread. Was he delayed? Was he ill? Had there been an accident?

She knew so little about him. A mishap could have occurred and she wouldn't have been informed. It dawned on her that—should she discover he'd suffered a misfortune—she'd be extremely distressed.

"John, are you here?" she called, but there was no reply.

Suddenly, he appeared in the doorway to his bedchamber. He leaned against the frame, sipping on a glass of liquor and studying her as if he couldn't remember who she was.

For once, he was disheveled, and the sight actually alarmed her. In all the weeks they'd been acquainted, he'd been impeccably dressed and barbered—even when he was out riding the roads in casual attire.

His hair was loose, and he hadn't shaved, so dark stubble shadowed his cheeks. His emerald eyes were haunted and bleak.

He was wearing trousers, but his feet were bare, his shirt

unbuttoned, the hem untucked, the front dangling open to reveal his smooth, intriguing chest.

The changes were unnerving. He—more than anyone she'd ever met—seemed to glide through life with an uncanny ability to shuck off upset or misery. Nothing bothered him. Nothing daunted him. He was always the same: polite, driven, stubborn, intractable. But never sad. Never despairing.

"There you are." She forced a smile. "When I couldn't locate you, I was worried. Are you all right?"

"What time is it?"

"Eight o'clock." She gestured to the balcony, feeling foolish and at a loss. "I guess we're not having supper. No one told me…"

Her voice trailed off.

She wanted to hold him in her arms, to comfort him—as a friend would do, as a wife would do. But she didn't precisely grasp her position in the household. Would he allow her to console him? Should she try?

"Well, I should probably be going," she mumbled.

"You're especially beautiful tonight."

"Thank you."

"You went to so much trouble."

"Your servants did. I just stood and let them pamper me."

"They're excellent at that."

He downed his drink, then flung the glass at the fireplace. It was a soft throw, so it hit the marble, but didn't break. If he'd been hoping for a satisfying crack, he didn't receive it.

"What's wrong?" she asked, taking a hesitant step toward him.

"The afternoon got away from me," he said, which wasn't really an answer. "I didn't realize it was so late."

"You're upset."

"No, I'm not," he claimed, but she didn't believe him.

"You can tell me. I'm a good listener, and if it's private, I can keep a secret."

"Not as good as I can, I'll bet."

"You could be right about that. You're very mysterious."

"You don't know the half of it, Miss Teasdale."

Without a word, he vanished into his bedchamber. She ordered herself to leave, but couldn't make herself depart.

She tiptoed over and saw him by the window, staring out at the sky. He'd poured himself another drink and was gulping it down. His heavy imbibing was another odd change.

When she dined with him, he would have two servings of wine—one before the meal and one during—but no more than that. It was disconcerting to watch him swilling hard liquor.

She felt as if she was perched at a fork in the road that led to two divergent paths. She could follow one back to the hall and return to her room. Or she could go to him, could be the companion and confidante he definitely needed.

If she did that, she would be crossing a line from which she could never rescue herself. She'd be abandoning the life that represented morality and innocence and spinsterhood where she thought she was content to wallow.

She'd be pitching herself onto a more reckless course that would ally her with him in licentious ways she didn't comprehend. No doubt it would bring her an enormous amount of happiness, but also an enormous amount of anguish.

She paused, as if saying goodbye to the person she used to be. Then she walked over to him. He heard her come, and he draped an arm over her shoulder and snuggled her to him.

"I'm sorry I forgot about supper," he told her.

"I forgive you—even though I'm starving and I spent hours getting ready."

"Poor thing," he sarcastically murmured. "All dressed up and nowhere to go."

He dipped down and kissed her, and it was so sweet that she sighed with pleasure.

"You've become the highlight of my day," she said. "You can't just expect me to *not* eat with you."

"I am quite intoxicating, aren't I?" Some of his typical cockiness poked through. "How could you stay away?"

"Vain beast."

"I am." He heaved out a weighty breath, laden with what sounded like sorrow.

"I hate to see you so sad."

"I'm not sad."

"Yes, you are. What happened?"

He was silent for so long that she was convinced he wouldn't confide in her. When they chatted over their evening meals, she did all the talking—about England and her childhood at Bramble Bay.

He'd talk too, but later she'd realize that he hadn't actually revealed a single fact about his past. She really knew no more about him than she had in the beginning.

She was certain this time would be no different, but apparently, his low mood was spurring him to babble in a way he normally never would.

"It's a pretty scene, isn't it?" He nodded to the bay, the village hugging the shore.

"Yes, very pretty."

"Guess how I've managed to accumulate so much wealth." Without waiting for her reply, he baldly announced, "I lied and cheated and pillaged and killed."

"Pillaged and killed?" she scoffed. "You did not."

"I did." He peered down at her. "Imagine every vile deed a man could commit, imagine every evil endeavor, and that has been my life."

She studied his eyes, but he didn't flinch from her thorough assessment.

He could spin such outrageous stories. He enjoyed being an enigma, and she'd never been able to judge his veracity. Was he being candid? Was he fibbing to high heaven?

Finally, she said, "I can't ever decide what I should believe about you."

"Believe me now. It's all true."

"Are you regretting your crimes? Is that why you're brooding?"

"No, I don't regret anything. I'd do it all again—in a heartbeat." His shoulders drooped, and he sighed. "Mildred is my aunt. Hedley is my cousin."

"You're so angry with her. Why?"

"Because of my mother."

"Florence?"

"Yes. Do you know about her?"

"Mildred's disgraced sister?" she mockingly retorted. "The most scandalous woman in the kingdom?"

"I don't care what Mildred told you, but my mother was young and foolish, and her husband was a brute. She ran away. She shouldn't have, but she did."

"She ruined many lives, John," she gently said.

"Including her own."

He eased away and went to sit in a chair. There was a table next to it, a full decanter of liquor. He filled another glass and took a long swallow.

"Why are you drinking so much?" She scolded him as if she had the right to chastise. "I don't like seeing you like this."

She grabbed for the glass, and they engaged in a brief tugging match. But he hadn't the energy to fight, and he relented and let her have it. She placed it out of reach.

"Go back to your room, *chérie*," he wearily said. "Perhaps we'll have our supper tomorrow when I'm feeling more myself."

"I don't want to return to my room."

"Well, you can't stay in here." His hot gaze roamed down her body. "With the mood I'm in, there's no telling how I might behave."

"I'm not afraid of you. Don't act as if you can scare me. You can't."

"Can't I?"

He pushed himself to his feet so he towered over her, reminding her of his greater size, of his position of authority, of how there was no one to save her from him. But she stood her ground and refused to move away as he was obviously hoping she would. He was trying to frighten her, but couldn't. Not anymore.

"Haven't you wondered who I am, *chérie*? Haven't you guessed?"

"Of course I've wondered, and you've been positively furtive in sharing relevant information, so what do you mean? You're John Sinclair, and your French friends call you Jean Pierre. What should I know beyond that?"

"Think, Sarah. Figure it out."

"You're speaking in riddles."

"If you're aware of my mother's situation, then you must have heard of her other sons—my brothers—Tristan and James Harcourt."

"I've heard of them, but I haven't ever met them."

"Even out in the country, there must have been stories about what happened to Tristan two years ago. The entire kingdom was buzzing over it."

She scowled, pondering, the incident ultimately remembered. "He was attacked by pirates. People claimed it was The French Terror. Tristan was set adrift, and he washed up on a deserted island."

"He was left for dead, but he didn't perish."

"And there was a woman named Harriet with him. She survived, too. They fell in love and married after they came home."

"A heartwarming tale, *non*?"

"Yes, it was quite heartwarming. She's become a notorious character in London—because of the experience."

"What else did you hear, Sarah? Did you hear what the pirate told Tristan as he stabbed him through with his sword? As he laughed and watched Tristan's small boat fade into the dark night?"

"I don't know about any words being exchanged between them."

"The pirate said, 'I am Jean Pierre, *Le Terreur Français*'. The pirate said, 'You are my brother, and our mother is finally avenged'. *"

She stared and stared, then swallowed down the lump in her throat. "What are you telling me?"

"I'm *telling* you that I am The French Terror, that I am the man who attacked Tristan Harcourt." He shoved her away and motioned to the door. "You're very fine, *chérie*, and I have cherished our acquaintance, but I am the very last person with whom you should have any contact. Now please go away and leave me be."

But she couldn't depart until she was sure, until she was convinced that it wasn't another of his fabrications.

"Is it true? You're not lying or jesting. You're The French Terror?"

"Yes. I have murdered and stolen and rampaged across the oceans, and I'm not finished."

"There are arrest warrants out everywhere for you. You're to be caught and hanged."

"I am."

"You're lashing out like a lunatic. Why? Be honest for once."

"Because they killed my mother." He shouted the statement, his fury alarming to witness.

"How did they kill her?"

"She was poor and alone and desperate—and she was dying. I was only ten. I wrote to Mildred, I wrote to my father, to my mother's husband and his rich, snobbish friends. I was just a boy, and I begged them to help her, but they laughed in my face."

"I'm so sorry, John."

He seemed shocked by his outburst, and he reined in his temper. "There's no need to be sorry, *chérie.* I swore I would eventually make them pay, and they all are—one by one."

"That's why you took Bramble Bay from Mildred."

"Yes."

"Because she wouldn't help your mother."

"No, not because she wouldn't *help* my mother, but because she's so hateful and vindictive. Mildred needs to understand what it's like to lose everything she loves, to realize that she has no friends."

"You'll die if you're captured."

"Yes, I will."

"Aren't you worried? Aren't you afraid?"

"What is it to me if I am killed? Who would care?"

"Mr. Hook would care. *I* would care."

"And who are you? Why would your concern matter to me?"

He was being deliberately cruel so she'd think he wasn't fond of her, but he couldn't have treated her so well unless he possessed some genuine affection.

"I want you to stop," she insisted.

"Stop what?"

"Your mayhem. I'm begging you."

"I don't wish to stop."

"I'm begging you," she repeated. "I couldn't bear to have you hanged."

"They'll have to find me first."

"You can murder every person in the world who wronged your mother, but it won't make you happy."

"I'm not doing it to be happy."

"Then why are you doing it?"

"Because I can. Because when I seize their precious money and cargo, I feel like a god!"

"Stop it," she said again.

"No."

"Do something else with your life. You're so bright and remarkable. Choose another path. Choose a path that would have made Florence proud."

The mention of his mother seemed to resonate. He calmed, his ire fading.

"I'm taking you back to England tomorrow," he said.

It was the last comment she'd expected. "To...Bramble Bay?"

"Yes."

"But why?"

"Because—as you so poignantly stated—I should make my mother proud. She would hate to know that I had ruined you, so I won't. I'll take you home instead." He shrugged. "I never should have brought you here in the first place, so I'll rectify the damage. I'll give you Bramble Bay as you requested of me earlier."

From the moment she'd initially been apprised of his bet with Hedley, it was the precise information she'd yearned to receive. But now, she wasn't sure it was the conclusion she sought.

If he took her to England, she'd never see him again. Was that what she wanted?

The resounding answer was *no*.

He would dock in Dover, would hire a carriage and deliver her to Bramble Bay. She'd return to the quiet existence she'd always enjoyed before he'd burst into her world and ripped it apart.

She'd farm and garden and visit the neighbors, and some day in the distant future, she'd stumble on an old newspaper from London, and she'd read that Jean Pierre—the famous French pirate—had been arrested and executed. Or perhaps that he'd been slain in a battle, shot in a fight, drowned in a sea accident.

Could she bear it?

Again, the resounding answer was *no*.

Though he'd wagered over her when he shouldn't have, though he'd spirited her to France over her vehement objection, he'd acted with the best of intentions. He'd truly believed he should rescue her from Hedley, that she'd be safer with him than with her treacherous family.

While she'd been sequestered with him, he'd been charming and gracious and wonderful. He made her feel beautiful and prized and unique, and she'd treasured every second of her odd, thrilling sojourn.

"I don't want to go back," she said. "I want to stay with you."

"No. It's time for us to say goodbye."

"I can't."

"You can. I've learned over the years that it's easy to move on, that it's easy to say *adieu*. You'll learn this, too."

"John"—her tone was scolding again—"don't do this to me. Don't do this to us."

"There is no *us*, Sarah. Now please go away. I have loved your company, but I can't stand to hear you beg."

He gripped her arm and led her out. She tried to drag her feet, tried to protest and refuse, but as always happened between them, he was bigger and stronger and he got his way.

He opened the door and, as if by magic, Akmed was there. On

seeing John, he bowed low, but didn't speak.

"Escort Miss Teasdale to her room," John commanded.

Akmed bowed again.

"Will we leave tomorrow?" Sarah asked.

"About one o'clock. I'll have the maids pack all your pretty gowns. You can take them with you. And the jewels too, if you like."

"I don't want any of it," she petulantly said.

"You must take them. When I am far from England, I'd like to picture you walking out on the cliffs at Bramble Bay, wearing the clothes I bought for you."

She stared at him, desperate to figure out how to change his mind.

He'd won her in a card game, had planned to ravish and ruin, then toss her away when he was through. But for reasons she couldn't fathom, he'd suddenly grown very noble. What had it all been about? Was there any purpose at all?

"*Au revoir, chérie,*" he murmured. He stroked his fingers down her cheek. "I'll see you in the morning. We'll have you home so quickly, you won't remember that you were ever gone."

He stepped inside and closed the door.

She dawdled for a moment, and she seriously considered marching in after him. She'd argue and insist that he was wrong for once, that he would *not* have his way.

Yet gradually, it dawned on her that she probably should return to Bramble Bay, that it would be for the best. Especially now that she knew his true identity. Nothing good could come from a liaison. No good ending could ever occur.

Currently, he was alive and free to sail the seas, to practice his particular brand of mayhem, but he wouldn't always enjoy such anonymity and liberty. If she remained with him and the power of the Crown crashed down, she'd be swept up in the chaos, might be crushed along with him.

It was better to leave. It was better to pretend they'd never met.

Akmed gestured to the stairs, and Sarah spun and started down.

CHAPTER FOURTEEN

John paced in his bedchamber, feeling like a lion trapped in a cage.

He'd spent two decades plotting his revenge, and he was at the height of his power, at the apex of his ability to terrorize and offend. He'd believed himself eager to continue, but recently, he'd been distracted by people and events, by old memories rising to the surface.

He was half-mad with second guessing and rumination.

He kept thinking of his mother, wondering what she would say if she could see the brigand he'd become. He kept thinking of Mildred and Hedley and all they had foolishly surrendered to John.

Most of all, he pondered Charles Sinclair, the man who had blithely sired John as he'd sired so many bastard children. John hadn't supposed he cared about Charles, hadn't thought he was interested in meeting him, but suddenly, he was riveted by the prospect that he could.

What was wrong with him? He was no longer a lost boy, surviving on the streets and praying his idiotic orphan's prayer that his father would magically appear and rescue him. He'd have had better luck asking an angel to fly down from Heaven than to expect Charles Sinclair to play the part of hero.

Earlier in the afternoon, a letter had arrived from Bramble Bay, with Raven apprising John of the surprising visit by Phillip Sinclair. John had always been aware of Phillip, but had never crossed paths with him. He hadn't *wanted* to cross paths.

Apparently, Phillip Sinclair knew John's identity and had traveled to the country specifically to speak with John. He claimed John had sisters in London who were worried about John. He claimed Charles was worried, too.

Charles was demanding that John cease his rampages so he wasn't captured and hanged. It was the strangest news ever, and John should have discounted it. But the notion that Charles was concerned had rattled John as nothing had in years.

He'd convinced himself that he didn't need a family, that he was fine on his own with his solitary existence and Raven as his one true friend. Yet evidently, he was craving acceptance as desperately as he had when he was ten and watching his mother—the exalted Countess of Westwood—be lowered into a pauper's grave.

He hurled his empty liquor glass at the fireplace. Finally, the piece of heavy crystal smashed as he intended, but the loud shatter didn't soothe his distress.

His work was deadly and dangerous, and he could only carry out his attacks if he was totally focused, if he was paying attention to the smallest detail. His father was next. The plans were drafted, the ships to be destroyed already chosen. John had to prepare—both mentally and physically—for the sea assaults that were approaching.

He couldn't be distracted, couldn't be moping and obsessing over his brother Phillip, over his sisters and whether they were pretty and kind.

Sarah was just down the stairs, and he was dying to go to her, dying to tell her about Raven's letter.

The message had upset him so much that he'd forgotten their supper. That's how preoccupied he was! He couldn't remember to cancel a measly supper party. If he couldn't manage such an elementary task, how could he complete a vicious ocean raid with any aplomb?

He hadn't meant to reveal his identity to Sarah, but in a moment of pique, he'd told her who he was. He'd done it to frighten her. Over the past few nights, he'd realized that his sly seduction was succeeding, that she was growing fond of him. He was becoming enamored, too.

She had him considering a normal connection, and he'd actually begun to imagine he could attach himself to her, perhaps even marry her and make her his own forever. He'd been trapped in a fantasy, in his fantasy castle, in his fantasy life, as if he wasn't a brutal criminal, as if he wasn't a heartless, murdering bandit.

His burgeoning affection had been so extraordinary and so out of character that he'd confessed some of his many sins, wanting her to have no illusions, wanting to kill any sentiment that had festered. He had to sever the ties he'd created, had to cut her loose so that she was simply a female he'd left behind.

Then he had to get down to business, had to finish what he'd started with Charles Sinclair.

But oh, how he yearned to have her just one time. He could practically taste temptation on his tongue.

He had to leave her be! What good could come from a hasty deflowering? What good could come from a casual, hurried farewell? There was no purpose to ruining her, and it would be cruel to proceed.

He'd agreed to give her Bramble Bay, so she'd return to England, a wealthy, propertied woman. Suitors would beat down her door, and she'd be able to have her pick of husbands. Yet if he stole her chastity, he'd destroy her chance for a happy future.

Despite her sudden affluence, no gentleman would have her if she'd played the whore for Jean Pierre—the most notorious felon in the kingdom.

He liked her too much to hurt her, but he was an arrogant ass too, and it was so difficult for him to deny himself. And...he was so bitterly *lonely*. There! He'd admitted it. He was lonely and regretting and brimming with remorse in a way he couldn't bear.

He didn't know how to vanquish his current demons. Raven knew how, but Raven was on the other side of the Channel.

Sarah was close by, and she was extremely malleable. He could persuade her into any conduct.

Not certain what he planned, he staggered to the sitting room. As a sailor, he believed in portents and signs, so he wouldn't decide what to do. He would descend to the next floor and let circumstances decide for him.

He pulled open the door, and he had to blink and blink, not sure of what he was seeing. Sarah was standing there—like an apparition. He felt as if he'd conjured her just from pondering her so intently.

She was wearing a green negligee and robe he'd bought her. The fabric was soft and silky, and it hugged her shapely torso like a glove. He'd once observed the type of sleepwear she preferred—stuffy, virginal gowns that concealed every inch of skin—so she was exposing much more than was comfortable for her.

Nervously, she clutched at the lapels of the robe, but there wasn't sufficient material to give her the protection she sought.

"Sarah?" he murmured, not positive she was real, if he was hallucinating.

"I've been thinking about what you told me."

"I shouldn't have burdened you. I'm sorry."

"Don't be sorry. I'm glad I finally learned the truth."

"It doesn't change anything."

"Yes, it does. It changes everything."

"I don't see how."

"Don't send me away, Jean Pierre. Please don't."

Her use of his French name solidified a profound bond between them. She seemed to be offering her acceptance of who and what he was, seemed to be saying she'd discovered his worst faults and cared about him anyway.

He'd wanted a sign and here it was. He would never discount or ignore it.

At the same instant, he reached for her and she stepped to him and leapt into his arms. He swept her up, her legs circling his waist, and he was kissing her and kissing her.

Whirling them around, he kicked the door shut and carried her to his bedchamber. He marched straight to the bed and dropped her onto the mattress, tumbling down with her.

Like a madman, he swooped in. He couldn't hold her tightly enough, couldn't attach himself completely enough. For once, he was desperate to connect so thoroughly that he didn't know where his body ended and hers began.

The robe was an impediment, and he yanked it off her shoulders. Then he drew down the straps on her negligee to reveal her beautiful breasts. He caressed the shapely mounds, plucking at the nipples, and quickly, she responded, her hips moving with his own.

He nibbled a trail down her neck, her chest, and sucked a taut nipple into his mouth. He bit and played with it until she was writhing with desire.

Gradually, he worked her negligee down and off so she was naked beneath him. He might have paused to feast on her glorious anatomy, but he wouldn't let her realize how far they had traveled down the carnal road.

He tormented her breasts as his fingers drifted down her tummy and into her sheath. The strange touch rattled her, and she froze.

"It's all right," he whispered.

"You can do whatever you want to me," she hastily said. "I don't mind."

He smiled. "That's probably the very last thing you should say to a cad like me."

"I was just surprised. I've never been…well…"

Her cheeks flushed with embarrassment, providing stark evidence of how awfully he was behaving. She was so innocent that she didn't have the vocabulary to discuss salacious conduct. He had to recall that she was a maiden, had to slow down, had to praise and tempt and arouse. But he was quite sure he hadn't the finesse to make it as wonderful as she deserved.

No matter what transpired in the future, he would never marry her. If she got too close, it would endanger her, so a sexual encounter was all he could offer. She would never have a real wedding night, with a loving, devoted husband.

He couldn't give her a matrimonial bond, but he could give her passion so in the coming months and years, she would have fond memories of the event. Hopefully, she'd remember *him* fondly, too, and would recollect only the good parts and none of the bad.

"Have you any idea of what's about to happen?" he asked.

"Just what my friend Caroline told me."

"It's very physical."

"That's what she said."

"Would you like me to explain?"

"No. You do what you want. I'm happy to let you."

"What brought about this change of heart?"

"I was alone in my room, and it dawned on me that I couldn't bear to leave you."

"Of course you can."

"No, you're wrong. If you took me to England and sailed away, I couldn't survive it." She laid a hand on his cheek. "I guess you've started to be important to me."

"Me? The man you hate? The man you loathe?"

"I don't hate you." Her expression was so open, so trusting and absurdly naïve. She wasn't the sort of woman who would fabricate sentiment, wasn't a doxy like Annalise who'd been taught at an early age to say what a man longed to hear. If Sarah professed affection, it was genuine.

In his entire life, no female had looked at him as she was, as if he was magnificent and amazing. She flustered him, had him eager to admit his own heightened sentiment.

There were words on the tip of his tongue that couldn't be voiced aloud. He was anxious to declare himself, but if he uttered a single comment, she would believe him. She'd expect him to follow through, but he never would. She was too fine, and he was too corrupt, and they could never go forward in any sane way.

The physical realm was where he thrived, where he knew the rules, where he understood the consequences.

He fell to her breasts again, his fingers down below, stroking her until she tensed and cried out. He laughed, delighted with her, with her sexual ease, with her willingness to accept him and what he could give her.

He held her through the tumult, and as she tumbled down, he was preening, thrilled with what he'd done. She'd needed a man in her bed; she'd be better off for it.

"What was that?" she gasped when she could speak again.

"*That* was sexual pleasure."

"Oh, my."

"It was only the first part, though. Let me show you the rest."

With any other lover, he could have paced himself, could have remained detached and indifferent. But with her, he couldn't delay. He rose onto his knees and tugged off his shirt. As he undid the buttons on his trousers, she watched with an avid feminine interest.

He stretched out on top of her, and as his bare chest connected with hers, the air seemed to spark and sizzle. She drew him near to initiate a kiss of her own.

"Are we going to...?"

"Yes."

"Caroline said it will hurt."

"For a minute. Then it will always feel grand."

She was so serious, so solemn. "Promise me something."

"Anything," he stated, but it was a lie. He never made promises because he never kept them.

"Promise we'll be together forever."

"We'll be together. I promise."

"And it will be just me—from now on. No more trollops. You have to cease your womanizing. Especially with Miss Dubois."

"Absolutely. I've already sent her away."

"We can still go to England, but you can't leave me there."

"I won't, *chérie*."

"Or if you want me to live with you in France, I will. Just ask me."

"I want it all with you, Sarah."

He didn't have enough fingers to count all the falsehoods he'd just spewed.

He was never monogamous, and while he'd decided to split with Annalise, he'd replace her as soon as another doxy caught his fancy.

As to Sarah, he would take her to England, then sneak away—so she'd be safe from him, so she could rightly claim to authorities later on that she had no idea where he was or what he was doing.

She truly believed he could be a better man. She had such faith in him, and he would always cherish her for that. In the future, he would have Reggie and Raven check on her occasionally to ensure that she was thriving, that Hedley and Mildred weren't imposing on her and had no ability to harm her.

But once he returned her to Bramble Bay, he would never see her again.

The fact that he wouldn't, that they were nearing a final goodbye, was extremely disconcerting. A wave of anguish bubbled up, and he shoved it down. They were about to engage in the only enduring tie they would ever have, and he was tired of waiting for it to occur.

He began kissing her again, his hands roaming over her body until she was moaning and squirming beneath him. This time, she knew what was coming, and she embraced the onslaught. He continued until she was at the edge, until he could toss her over with ease.

He widened her thighs, his torso dropping between them. He pulled his trousers to his flanks, freeing his cock to center the tip in her sheath. At the odd positioning, she tensed, and he kissed her sweetly, tenderly.

"Don't be afraid," he told her.

"I'm not."

"It will be over in a moment."

"And it will be all right afterwards, won't it?"

"Yes."

But as he gazed down at her, he felt horrid. He had no honorable intentions toward her—he never had honorable intentions—as she would learn after it was too late to undo the damage.

"Now I need you to promise *me* something," he said.

"What is it?"

"Promise me you'll never be sorry we did this."

"I never will be."

"No matter what happens, you have to always be glad it was me."

"I'll always be glad, Jean Pierre. 'Til my dying day."

He flexed, wedging himself in, wedging in a bit more.

She tensed again, and he murmured, "Try to relax."

"I'm trying. It just seems...strange."

"It will be wonderful. Trust me."

"I do trust you. I always will."

Her remark was too dear, too foolish, and he yanked away and dipped to her breasts as he touched her between her legs. In a thrice, she cried out as he pushed with his hips. With very little effort, he glided inside, his cock buried to the hilt.

She huffed out a breath of surprise.

"Is it finished?" she asked.

"Almost."

A tear formed at the corner of her eye, and he kissed it away.

"I'm not a virgin anymore, am I?"

"No."

"I'm so delighted it was you."

"I am, too." She was hot and tight, her virgin's blood luring him to his doom. "Put your arms around me."

"Like this?"

"Yes, just like that. Hold me."

"I will."

He tried to restrain himself, tried to keep from ramming into her like a rampaging bull, but he couldn't maintain any dignity or decorum. He was too overwhelmed by her and always had been. Finally, they were at the spot where Fate had led them from the very start.

After a few hearty thrusts, his lust surged, his seed burning through his loins, and he spilled himself against her womb. He probably shouldn't have, but he'd never sired a child, not in all his years of philandering, and there was no reason to expect it would end any differently with her.

He drove himself into her over and over, the pleasure continuing for an eternity, until eventually, he reached the apex and ground to a halt. He drew away and slid to the side as she rolled to face him. They were nose to nose, and he was relieved to see that she was smiling.

"You survived." He was smiling, too.

"All in one piece."

"You're mine now. Mine forever."

"Yes, yours forever."

"No one can ever take away what we did. No one can ever change it."

"No, and I'm so happy."

"So am I, *chérie*." And he really and truly was. About that one thing, he wasn't lying at all.

"What do we do now?" she asked.

"We rest for a few minutes, then we do it again." He raised a brow. "Unless you're too sore?"

"It didn't hurt very much." Her cheeks flushed a pretty pink color. "I think I could try it again."

He sighed with contentment, and for a long while, they were quiet, lost in thought, with her draped across his chest.

"I found out some interesting news today," he said when he hadn't intended to speak.

"What was it?"

"I have a brother."

"A brother? How wonderful."

"I've never met him, but somehow, he discovered that I'd been at Bramble Bay. He came there to introduce himself."

She popped up and looked at him. "He came to Bramble Bay?"

"Yes. Raven wrote me a letter. It's why I was upset earlier."

"What's his name?"

"Phillip Sinclair. My father wasn't the most circumspect man. He has many illegitimate children besides me."

"I'd heard that."

"Phillip is the oldest." He snuggled her down. "Charles sent word with Phillip."

"A message for you? From your father?"

"Yes. He knows about my line of…work. I suppose from Tristan Harcourt. He warned me to be careful, to stop my attacks so I don't end up killed or hanged."

"Thank the Lord." She rose up again. "Will you listen to him any better than you've listened to me?"

"I wouldn't count on it."

"He's your *father*, Jean Pierre. You have to listen to him." She frowned. "Have you ever had any previous contact with him?"

"No. Never."

"My goodness."

They stared and stared, and she eased down, a lazy hand rubbing over his heart as if she could sense how much it was aching.

"This must be quite a shock," she mused.

"It is."

"It must be distressing, too, to hear from him after all this time."

"That's putting it mildly." He chuckled miserably. "Guess what else?"

"What?"

"I have sisters."

"Sisters! An entire family!"

"Yes. They want me to come to London. They want to meet me." He still couldn't believe it. "Phillip invited me to stay with him in his home."

"You'll visit them, won't you?"

"No," he scoffed.

She lifted up and scowled. "What do you mean, *no*?"

"I would never meet them."

"Why not? You've always been on your own and had to make your own way. You'd have some relatives. You wouldn't be so lonely."

"I'm not lonely," he lied.

She scrutinized his expression, then snorted with disgust. "You're afraid to go."

"I'm not afraid."

"You are! You're scared they might not like you, that they might not be kind."

"You're being absurd," he mumbled and glanced away.

She kissed him on the mouth.

"You don't have to be frightened," she insisted. "I'll accompany you. I'll help you get through it."

"I'm not going."

"Of course you are." She appeared shrewd, wise beyond her years. "It will be fine, Jean Pierre. It will be grand. You'll see."

He couldn't fathom how it would be, and he nestled her down.

They were silent, and he allowed himself a short fantasy where he was welcomed into a room of blond-haired, green-eyed men and women who looked and acted exactly like him. The notion was so enthralling that he yearned for it with a peculiar intensity. Yet as quickly as the vision tantalized, he pushed it away.

He wouldn't ponder Charles or Phillip Sinclair, wouldn't mope over the fact that he'd never met his sisters.

Where the Sinclairs were concerned, he had one goal: Charles's financial ruination. As he began the assaults on Charles's ships, his objectives would be realized. His half-siblings would suffer when Charles suffered. They'd lose when Charles lost.

John refused to feel sorry for any of them.

He was alone, but happy with his life. He wouldn't change anything—except perhaps to have a way of keeping Sarah by his side for a time. But a relationship between them wasn't meant to be.

"Are you tired?" he asked.

"No." She peeked up, grinning with mischief. "Are you?"

"Definitely not."

"You said we could do it again."

"We can, *chérie*. We certainly can."

He pulled her to him and started in once more.

CHAPTER FIFTEEN

"I have a letter from Jean Pierre."

"Is he on his way back?"

"Yes."

Annalise stared at Raven, her pulse racing.

Jean Pierre was supposed to have been gone for a month, but it had been six weeks. With each day that passed, she was more furious.

When he'd sailed away with his pale English virgin, she'd told herself that such a weak, ridiculous female could never hold his interest. What could Mademoiselle Teasdale possibly provide that Jean Pierre would consider valuable?

Annalise hadn't reconciled herself to his seduction of Sarah Teasdale. She'd tried to convince herself that Mademoiselle Teasdale was simply a skirt he could lift when the mood struck him. She'd tried not to be wrathfully jealous, but she was.

If Jean Pierre had merely lusted after Mademoiselle Teasdale, if he'd fornicated a few times, then grown bored, Annalise could forgive him for his indiscretion. But if he'd become smitten, if he'd developed an attachment with the stupid girl, Annalise felt she might react quite violently.

"Has he a message for me?" she asked.

"Yes, actually. He has an extensive message for you."

Raven's face gave nothing away. He was adept at hiding his thoughts, which was why he was so dangerous. He could slay a man, and the poor idiot would be dead on the ground before he realized Raven was upset.

"Sit down, Annalise," he rattled her by saying.

"I'll stand."

"No, you need to sit."

They were in the estate office at Bramble Bay where Raven spent a good portion of every morning reviewing the ledgers. It was a tedious chore for a seafaring man, but he was skilled with numbers and would do whatever Jean Pierre requested. Even mathematics.

He was seated behind the desk, and he gestured to the chair across. She wanted to refuse, just on general principle, but it was pointless to fight Raven—as it was pointless to fight Jean Pierre. It was best not to argue with either of them.

"Fine, I'll sit."

"Thank you. I'd rather not quarrel with you today."

She was desperate to delay the pending conversation, so she took an inordinate amount of time settling down, straightening her skirt. Once she felt sufficiently braced, she looked him in the eye.

"What's happening?" she snapped.

"He's asked me to make some arrangements for you."

"What sort of arrangements?"

"He's sending you to Paris."

Her heart literally skipped a beat, but to conceal her rage and disgust, she kept her expression blank.

"I don't wish to go to Paris."

"It's not up to you."

"I've been away from home for months. I'm weary and would like to return to the castle."

"You won't be returning."

She understood what he was telling her, but she was determined to feign confusion. "I'm sick of England. Will Jean Pierre travel to France with me?"

Raven's annoyance flared. "You're being deliberately obtuse. You know how these things work. Don't be difficult."

"I have no idea how these things *work*. My place is with Jean Pierre. I'll not languish in Paris and leave him without the female comfort he's retained me to supply."

Raven sighed, appearing as if Jean Pierre had finally dumped a task on him that was too loathsome to assume.

"Let me be blunt, Annalise. He's putting you aside."

"He is not."

"He is. Now you can fuss and complain and waste energy battling the inevitable, or you can be grateful for the time you had with him and be happy with the parting gifts he's prepared to bestow."

"I want no gifts," she spat. "I want my spot with him."

"It's over, Annalise."

They engaged in a staring match, but Raven was unflappable and impossible to fluster, while Annalise was hotheaded and irate and eager to lash out.

"Two years!" She slapped her palm on the desktop, the loud smack ringing off the ceiling. "I gave him two years of my life!"

"That's much more than any other woman can claim. Be glad of it."

"He made promises to me."

"He never did."

"He said we'd always be together. He said he would always keep me."

"You're being absurd," he scoffed. "Lie to yourself if you choose, but don't lie to me."

"I won't let him go! I won't!"

Raven sighed again. "He's being extremely generous and granting you much more than I feel you deserve."

"Rude dog! Don't speak to me as if I am a servant."

He ignored her insult. "I tried to talk him out of it, but he wouldn't listen. If it had been up to me, you'd have gotten much less."

Raven pulled out a piece of paper and laid it on the desktop, which was galling. He was aware that Annalise couldn't read, couldn't decipher for herself the true provisions.

Luckily, he saved her any embarrassment by verbally explaining the terms. But she scarcely paid attention as he listed an apartment in a wealthy neighborhood, an allowance, money for servants.

Her mother had been a courtesan, had raised Annalise to be a courtesan. Annalise had slithered through the Paris underworld with similar women, all using their bodies to obtain the support they needed.

They'd secretly dreamed that their keepers would fall in love and marry them, but that never occurred. The men were usually already married, so the next biggest hope was for a lengthy relationship, followed by a pension at the end.

Only a very tiny handful were ever fortunate enough to receive what Jean Pierre was offering, but she was too incensed to accept with any grace.

She'd always recognized that her situation with him was temporary, but she'd persuaded herself that it would continue forever with no changes. Yet Jean Pierre snapped his fingers, and it was wiped away as if it had never been.

Her temper had always been her downfall, and this occasion was no different.

"How can I be positive he will give me what you've mentioned?"

"He said he would, and his word is law."

She pointed to the document. "That paper could say anything and I wouldn't know."

"I've told you the terms, Annalise. Don't call me a liar."

"If I refuse or if I want more, what then?"

"Then you'll get nothing. You'll return to France as a pauper with only the clothes on your back."

She grabbed the document and ripped it to shreds.

"I demand to speak with him."

"You can't."

"I can and I will," she hissed. "I demand to hear it from his own treacherous lips. I demand he tell me to my face that he no longer needs me."

"He'll be here on Friday. You have to depart before then."

"I won't!"

"I've booked passage for you, sailing out of Dover on Thursday afternoon."

"It is wasted money for I won't use the ticket you have purchased."

His expression grew steely, his eyes cold. "If you don't go on your own, I will personally tie you onto a horse and drag your ass to Dover. I will personally carry you on board and have the captain bind you to the bulkhead for the trip across the Channel."

"You always hated me," she fumed.

"No. I always loved Jean Pierre. His wishes come first with me."

"Why is he doing this? Tell me the truth."

"I have no idea."

"Guess then."

"I suppose he's tired of you."

"Has he told you he's tired?"

"Yes, Annalise, he's told me for months."

"How could it be? I've given him everything."

"You're a difficult woman, Annalise." When she would have argued, he held up a hand, stopping her protest. "You are. Don't deny it. You're bossy and jealous and overbearing, and he's no longer in the mood for your antics."

"I've caused no trouble! He has paramours around every corner, and I've never complained a single time."

"At the moment, with his pending business ventures, he's under an enormous amount of pressure. He needs peace and quiet. He needs friendship and comfort. You bring too much drama into his life."

"All of a sudden, he's decided this?" She tossed her hair, wanting Raven to look, wanting him to remember how beautiful she was. "Why now?"

He didn't reply, and her gaze became surly and cruel.

"It's Mademoiselle Teasdale, isn't it? He's keeping her instead."

He shrugged. "I don't know."

"Has she asked him to split with me? Was it her price for spreading her legs?"

"Don't be vulgar, Annalise. I don't like it when you are."

"Is she coming with him? Is that why I must leave on Thursday? Her marvelous presence can't be sullied by me. Is she insisting I depart before she arrives?"

"You're giving me a headache."

"If you send me to France against my will, I'll simply go to the castle and wait for him there."

"The servants have their orders. They won't let you in."

The remark was a slap in the face. The castle was the most exotic residence in the world, and though she'd understood that she shouldn't feel attached to it, she'd begun to think of it as her own.

She wasn't some glorified hostess and housekeeper. She was mistress to Jean Pierre—the most fascinating, most dashing man who'd ever lived. If she wasn't his mistress anymore, who was she? What facet remained about which she could preen and brag?

No other man could ever match up to him. From here on out, it was a slide downhill until she landed at the bottom, squashed beneath some bald, boring dolt who smelled of bodily odor and talked about his wife while sawing away between Annalise's shapely thighs.

"I'll get even with him," she furiously warned. "I'll make him sorry."

"You're being ridiculous. Please go before I get angry."

"I will get even, Raven Hook. I swear it."

"Goodbye, Annalise. I'll have a carriage ready at dawn on Thursday. Be prepared to leave so I don't have to haul you out like a bag of flour."

Feeling murderous and aggrieved, she pushed back her chair and rose to her feet. "Tell him for me. Tell him he'll be sorry."

"We've said everything that needs to be said. Go away!"

She glared at him, anxious for him to grasp that she could be dangerous too, that she could terrorize as he and Jean Pierre could terrorize.

But she couldn't garner a reaction. He stared at her and saw a silly, impotent woman. He didn't realize that she could fight back, that she could cause her own brand of mayhem.

Didn't he recollect that she knew many of Jean Pierre's secrets? To whom might she tattle? What might she reveal? Wasn't he worried?

"My name is Annalise Dubois," she said. "Don't ever forget it. Don't let Jean Pierre forget it either."

She whipped away and left, and she was visibly distraught, shaking and muttering to herself in a fashion that was humiliating.

She hurried to the stairs so she could climb to her room and fume in private, but as she glanced up, Hedley was coming down again. Instantly, she masked her expression, hiding any trace of upset.

He was a fool and a child, but he was captivated by her. He constantly regaled her with his exaggerated plans as to how he would eventually retrieve Bramble Bay from Jean Pierre.

With Hedley being penniless, his boasting was humorous. He didn't stand a chance against Jean Pierre, but he was so pathetically confident.

Well, if Jean Pierre suffered a mishap, if he was arrested and hanged, wouldn't Hedley be first in line to claim ownership of Bramble Bay? Jean Pierre was a criminal. If he was convicted of piracy, he couldn't bequeath property to anyone. Wouldn't it revert to Hedley?

He'd be a landowner again, with a steady income and thriving estate. It wasn't close to what Jean Pierre had possessed, but it was prosperous. And Hedley was an immature dunce who could be easily manipulated.

If Annalise allied herself with him, *she* would control him. *She* would be in charge and able to make him behave as she intended. She wouldn't have to put up with an arrogant ass like Jean Pierre who always thought he knew best.

Hedley would be putty in her hands.

"Hedley, darling," she cooed, "how lovely to see you."

"Annalise! Hello."

"I must speak with you," she said.

She led him into a nearby salon. He was like a happy puppy, and he eagerly followed her in and shut the door.

"What is it?" he asked.

"I need you to take me to London tomorrow morning. At dawn."

"London. I hadn't considered going."

"I have to meet with some important people, but I've never been to the city, and I'm nervous about traveling alone. I'd like you to escort me. Can you?"

"Ah…yes, I suppose."

"And we have to sneak away unnoticed. It has to be our secret."

"All right. Why?"

"I'll tell you once we're on the road."

"Tell me now."

"I can't, except to say that I might have figured out how to have Bramble Bay returned to you."

He grinned. "Really? What about Jean Pierre?"

"I think something bad is about to happen to him."

"What's about to happen?"

"When we're on the road, Hedley, and far away from here. You can find out then."

She went to the door and crept into the hall. As she glanced back, he was slack-jawed with surprise, his mouth hanging open.

He was such an unreliable, juvenile bungler. She could only hope that he would be silent for a few hours—until she could be certain Raven didn't know where she was, when she'd left, or where she might be headed.

For she was positive if he found out, she and Hedley would never make it to London alive.

CHAPTER SIXTEEN

"Raven?"

"I'm here. Don't be frightened."

Caroline rose up on an elbow to see him over by the window. He was leaned against the sill and gazing out toward the ocean. Dawn was approaching, but it was still dark, so he didn't have much of a view.

She'd been sleeping, but once she realized he'd left the bed, she'd immediately awakened.

Since the day Archie had shown up at Bramble Bay, she'd been glued to Raven's side. She was terrified Archie might sneak back, that he might catch her while Raven was looking the other way.

Raven knew she worried over it, and he'd scold her—as if her distress was an insult to his ability to protect her—but she couldn't stop fretting. Even though he swore she was safe, she'd written her London address on a piece of paper and slipped it into the pocket of one of his coats so he could find her if she vanished.

They were carrying on like a married couple, as if Raven was her husband instead of Archie. She openly shared his room, not caring a whit what the servants thought about it.

He suffered from insomnia, always vexed by important issues that weighed him down. He never confided in her, though, and she didn't pry, for she was scared of what his explanations might be.

She was living a life that only trollops were ever allowed. She drank and flirted and fornicated with a wild abandon, and she was having so much fun that she was definitely questioning why she'd spent so many years in moral drudgery.

Mr. Sinclair was returning, and Caroline couldn't guess what would transpire when he arrived. Everyone was supposed to be gone, but no one had departed—Mildred and Hedley included. Raven had informed the servants that they might be kept at their positions, so they were all waiting to learn their fates.

As to Mildred and Hedley, he wasn't concerned about their lack of planning and would be thrilled to set them out on the road at Mr. Sinclair's order.

Caroline hadn't made plans either. She wanted to stay with Raven, but she was afraid to ask if she could. He seemed fond of her, but she had no idea if he would welcome a continuing connection. And really, it was risky to consider allying herself with him.

She hadn't discovered much about him or his family or even where he resided other than Mr. Sinclair's home in France, the precise location of said home never being mentioned. She hadn't a clue how he earned his income, except that he assisted Mr. Sinclair with his gambling.

In light of all the ships they owned, she suspected he was a smuggler. How could a woman attach herself to such an enigmatic, dodgy fellow? Then again, when she'd wed Archie, he'd been a pillar of the community and look how that had ended.

"Are you all right?" she inquired.

"I couldn't sleep."

She chuckled. "You *never* sleep. I don't know how you keep going."

"Old habits. My mind is always racing, so I can't calm myself enough to lie still."

He'd pulled on a pair of trousers, the front flap unbuttoned so they hung loosely from his hips. His chest was bare, his feet and calves bare. His forearm was pressed to the wood of the sill, his muscles outlined in the moonlight.

Butterflies swarmed in her belly. Prior to meeting him, she hadn't understood that a man's body could be so beautiful, so stirring.

"I have to leave in a bit," he said, glancing over at her.

"Leave?" She sat up, the blankets pressed to her breasts. Did he mean forever? With no warning or notice?

She must have appeared panicked, because he hastily added, "Just for a few hours. I have to take Annalise to Dover."

"Oh." Her shoulders slumped with relief.

"I'll be back late."

"But you will come back?"

"It'll just be one day, Caroline. You'll be fine."

"Of course I will be," she firmly agreed. "Why are you taking Miss Dubois to Dover?"

"John is sending her to France."

"Good. I don't like her."

"Neither do I."

They shared a conspiratorial smile. Miss Dubois was rude and arrogant. She insulted the servants, issued frivolous demands, and complained constantly. She couldn't go soon enough to suit Caroline.

"He should be here tomorrow," Raven said.

"Mr. Sinclair?"

"Yes. He's on his way to England even as we speak."

"Will he bring Sarah with him?"

"That's the plan."

"Will he have ruined her?"

"I wouldn't view it as a ruination. She'll have been swept off her feet. There'd be no *ruining* involved."

"You men. So vain. So set on yourselves."

"With valid reason. Some of us are wonderful."

"Please spare me your egotistical drivel," she scoffed, and they smiled again. "Then what? Once he arrives, what will happen to Sarah and me?" He didn't reply, so she said, "I haven't made any arrangements for myself."

"I realize that."

"Will I be tossed out of Bramble Bay?"

"I'm not sure what John has decided."

"I thought you could read his mind."

"Usually, but not always."

He spun to peer outside, and he gazed toward the sea so longingly that she could sense his urge to be out on the water, to sail away and never come back to England, to her.

She climbed from the bed, slipped on her robe, and walked up behind him. She wrapped her arms around him and draped herself across his back.

He had terrible scars marring his skin. They appeared to be stab and gunshot wounds. Whatever his occupation, it was obviously perilous and filled with misfortune.

She laid her cheek on the worst scar, a puckered line that ran from his shoulder to his waist. She'd never asked how it had occurred or what had become of the man who'd inflicted it. She couldn't imagine Raven blithely enduring such an injury without reacting, and she doubted his assailant was still alive.

Had Raven killed in battle? Was he that violent? She'd seen him with Archie, had witnessed his calm ability to terrorize and maim. Did she care?

The resounding answer was *no*. She didn't care.

From the day her parents had died when she was a tiny girl, she'd never felt safe. Not at Bramble Bay, where she'd been a poor orphan, hated by Mildred. Not in her horrid marriage to Archie where he'd been drunk and spiteful.

With Raven, she felt safe. With Raven by her side, nothing bad could transpire. When her life had been a long string of fear and worry, how could she begrudge him any fault? How could she not love him?

He snuggled her close so he could nuzzle her hair, inhaling her scent as if he wanted to be certain he never forgot it.

"What if Mr. Sinclair tells me to leave?" she inquired. "The only place I have to go is to my husband."

"I'm hoping John will allow you to remain at Bramble Bay."

"But you don't know."

"No. He had intended to let it rot—"

"Bramble Bay? Why take it from Hedley merely to destroy it?"

"It's complicated."

"It definitely must be."

"Before he left, though, I asked him if we could keep it, if we could visit occasionally."

"What did he say?"

"He didn't. I'm supposing I'll hear more once he rides into the yard."

"Sarah might have prevailed on him to be kind."

He snorted. "I wouldn't count on it. He never listens to women, and he never grows fond. He'll have had just one use for her."

"That being sexual relations."

"Yes."

"So he'll dump her here—wrecked and ruined—then he'll sail off into the sunset?"

"Most likely."

She studied his dark eyes. "What about you? Will you sail off with him?"

"I go where John goes."

"Like a faithful dog?"

"Like a loyal and trusted friend. I guard his back."

"Why are you so devoted?"

"Because he rescued me. He claims *I* rescued him, but it was the other way around. He made me who I am today—instead of who I might have been."

"And who was that?"

"No one good, that's for sure. I was headed for a dreadful end, but he saved me. I'll always be grateful. I'll always follow him and do as he bids me."

He announced it like a threat, like a warning, so she would understand that—no matter what—Mr. Sinclair was most important to him. He was telling her that she could never compete, could never be put above Sinclair in his esteem. But if she couldn't be first in his heart, could she be second? Would that be so bad?

They were quiet, staring out, a hint of dawn lightening the eastern horizon. He sighed and said, "I have to leave."

"To take Miss Dubois to Dover?"

"Yes. I don't imagine she'll depart without an enormous fuss. I need to eat a big breakfast so I have the energy to bicker with her."

"Why doesn't she want to go?"

"Why do you think? John's finished with her, and she's irked."

"Really? Why is he finished?"

He shrugged. "In his personal affairs, I don't try to guess."

She scrutinized him and decided he was lying, being too

circumspect to confess Dubois's transgression.

"What did she do to get herself sent away?" Caroline was eager to have some clue as to Dubois's lapse so she didn't make the same mistake.

"Nothing. John just doesn't bond with women, and he's easily bored in his amorous pursuits."

"He's ready to move on?"

"Yes."

"To Sarah?"

"Like I said, I hate to guess, but she's a tad...tame for his tastes."

"What about you? Do you bond with women?"

"Not usually—especially married women. That's a bit tricky."

"It certainly is. How about *your* amorous pursuits? Are you easily bored, too?"

"I'm not quite as exacting as John, but yes."

"I see..."

She peered out toward the water, feeling adrift and invisible. She'd never been loved by anyone. Why was life so hard? Why did women have so few options?

She wished she was a man so she could work and travel. She'd purchase a ship, then sail off to the edge of the world and start over. She'd have a grand house and host fabulous parties. She'd have a thousand friends, and people would gush about how witty she was, how charming.

She slid away from him, anxious to be alone so she could mope and lick her wounds in private.

"You'd better be going," she muttered. "You shouldn't keep Miss Dubois waiting. She might pitch a fit—which you shouldn't have to endure this early in the morning."

She tried to walk away, but he clasped hold of her wrist.

"Would you come to France with me?" he suddenly asked.

It was the last question she'd expected. "To France?"

"Yes."

"As your what?"

He grinned. "My mistress? My personal trollop? My passion slave?"

"We'd live there? Together?"

"Yes. At John's. He has a huge home or we could build our own."

"We'd carry on openly? With me committing adultery every day?"

"It hasn't seemed to bother you the past month."

"You're mad."

She tried to pull away again, but he only tightened his grip.

"Seriously, Caroline. Would you come?"

"I don't know. I've never been anywhere. And to *France*. I don't even speak the language."

"Your other choice is to stay in England. Perhaps at Bramble Bay. Perhaps out on the road—depending on John's mood when he arrives."

"I realize that."

"I can't stay with you."

"Why not?"

"I told you: I go where John goes."

"He won't remain in England?"

"No longer than is required to return Miss Teasdale and clear up some business. If your husband learned that I'd left, I wouldn't be around to protect you."

For an eternity, they were frozen in their spots, her mind awhirl with possibilities.

She loved and trusted him, but was scared to cast her lot with him. If he grew *bored* with her—as he claimed he frequently did—she'd be stranded in France with no friends or funds.

A few minutes prior, she'd bemoaned the fact that, as a female, she had no options. Now she had so many that she felt dizzy with sorting through them all.

Finally, he flashed a rueful smile. "Forget about it. It was a silly idea."

"No, it wasn't."

But apparently, she'd lost her chance.

He laid a gentle hand on her shoulder. "I couldn't take you to France."

"Why not?"

"I'm never there, and my line of work is…hazardous. If I met with foul play, you'd be alone and far from all that was familiar."

She'd just been lamenting the very same problem, but when he voiced his misgivings, she had to protest.

"I could live there with you. I wouldn't worry about the future."

"No." He shook his head. "It's better if you stay in England. I'll make plans for you so you're safe without me."

"I could do it!" she insisted. "I simply need some time to consider my choices."

"Well, with me, you'd never have the benefit of *time*. Things happen fast with me. And I have to tell you, Caroline, I'm not a man you should count on."

"I could count on you. I'm not afraid to try."

"I'm an unreliable bounder, and whenever I traipsed off to attend to John's affairs, you'd never know if I'd return. No woman should be resigned to such a fate."

With that, he went to the dressing room, and she staggered to the bed and climbed under the covers. The conversation had chilled her, and she curled into a ball, listening as he moved around, as he put on his clothes.

She should have helped him dress, but she felt slighted and snubbed and foolish. She had tears in her eyes, but couldn't figure out why. She hadn't really wanted to go to France, so why be upset that he wouldn't take her? It was just so sad to think that he would sail away with Mr. Sinclair and she'd never see him again.

How would she bear it?

Several minutes later, he emerged, attired for traveling. He proceeded to his wardrobe and opened it, pulling out knives and pistols, arming himself, stuffing weapons into every nook and cranny where they would fit.

"Are you expecting trouble?" she asked.

"Always."

"I wouldn't suppose Miss Dubois to be that dangerous."

"You have no idea," he said, and he chuckled.

He walked over and kissed her.

"Gad, but I've enjoyed knowing you." It sounded like goodbye, as if he already suspected they'd never have another chance to be together.

"Why would you say something like that? You act as if you're leaving forever, as if this is farewell."

"Every parting could be the last with me."

A shiver ran down her spine. "Don't talk that way. You'll court bad luck."

"I was born under a black star, Caroline, but it hasn't caught up with me yet."

"Will you come back tonight? Swear that you will."

"Of course I'll come back. Don't fret so much."

"What about when Mr. Sinclair arrives? Will you leave me then?"

He was quiet, ponderous, then he admitted, "It's possible."

He whipped away and left.

"Raven!" she called.

He glanced over his shoulder. "What?"

"Be careful."

"I always am. I'll be home soon. Keep my spot warm."

Then he was gone, an ominous silence settling in.

She lay very still, trying to calm her racing pulse, trying to chase away her perception of gloom, but she couldn't dispel it.

She crawled out of bed and hastened to the window, hoping she might see him riding off, that she might hear his horse clattering away, but he was nowhere to be found.

John slipped into the cabin on his ship. Sarah was asleep on his bunk, and he liked having her there. Her presence made it seem as if she belonged with him.

They were crossing the Channel, and she'd wanted to stay on

deck, to watch as the sailors carried out their duties. But the seas had been rough, the temperature frigid, and he'd insisted she remain below.

The closing of the door roused her.

"John, is that you?"

"Yes."

She extended her hand, and he hurried over and clasped hold.

He rested a hip on the mattress, leaned over and kissed her. It was sweet and delicious, and as he drew away, he sighed with pleasure. He nestled her to his chest, her cheek directly over his heart.

There was a small window over by his desk. Moonlight streamed in, casting the walls in an eerie blue color. Her auburn hair looked indigo, her sapphire eyes glittering like diamonds.

"When will we arrive?" she asked.

"In a few hours."

"So I have you all to myself?"

"For a bit."

"Lucky me."

She tugged him nearer, thinking he would stretch out with her, but he didn't. The notion of returning her to England had him extremely maudlin in a fashion he hadn't previously allowed her to observe.

"What's wrong?" she said.

"Nothing. I just don't have much time. I can't relax."

"Are you sad?"

"Me? No."

She was so attuned to him now; she could tell he was lying.

"It's hard for you to visit Bramble Bay, isn't it?"

"I wouldn't say *hard*."

"Disconcerting, then."

"Perhaps."

"You haven't changed your mind about Mildred, have you?"

"No, I haven't changed my mind."

The topic disturbed him, and he slid away and went over to stare out the window at the rolling waves.

Over the past few days, she'd been able to extract many promises that he was regretting. He couldn't deny her any request, and he thought he might be in love with her. Yet he'd never been in love before, so he had no guide to explain what was happening. He could barely look at her, because when he did, he was overcome by such a rush of affection that it almost knocked him to his knees.

If that wasn't love, what was it?

She seemed smitten too, and he was flirting with the idea of marrying her.

Should he? If he coerced her into it, he'd have to make some major concessions, and he was greatly torn. He'd have to abandon his pirating. Bandits lived short lives, filled with injury and early death, and he was running on borrowed time.

It wouldn't be fair to wed her, then promptly get himself killed. If he truly wanted her, he'd have to renounce his rampaging, his vendettas and revenge. He'd have to shift his illegal enterprises to legal ones, finally mourn his mother, forgive his father, stop lashing out.

He'd walked on the criminal side of the law for too many decades, and the prospect of completely reinventing himself was annoying and daunting.

He'd already begun to accept small compromises that didn't sit comfortably on his shoulders. She wasn't a vindictive person, and she was determined that Mildred and Hedley not be punished.

She was also determined that John and Mildred reconcile as much as possible, that aunt and nephew come to terms, but the concept was galling and wouldn't occur.

She'd wanted Mildred and Hedley to remain at Bramble Bay, which he wouldn't permit. So he'd agreed to give Mildred six months to leave, plus he'd furnish her with funds so she could establish herself in London.

But he'd drawn the line on Hedley. Hedley had to depart immediately, and John wouldn't provide him with money he'd simply gamble away. Hedley was an adult who needed to take the lumps life threw at him, who needed to cut the apron strings and stand on his own two feet.

John didn't care what transpired, except that Sarah be safe from her relatives. He'd considered giving her title to the property, but he couldn't now. If she owned it, Hedley and Mildred would run roughshod over her. She'd never be free to manage the place.

Reggie Thompson, John's clerk, had accompanied them from France, and he would stay at Bramble Bay to watch over Sarah and enforce her wishes.

"I'll never understand your kindness and ability to forgive." He was still staring out at the endless water.

"And I'll never understand your bitterness and anger, but I'll help you move beyond them."

"You'll make me into a better man, will you?"

"I'm very stubborn, so you can't win against me. Not in this."

He peered over at her. "Why would you bother?"

"Why bother? Are you joking?"

"No."

"I'm mad for you, you thick oaf."

He scoffed. "You shouldn't be."

"That's fine talk from the cad who ruined me. You wore me down until I can't bear to be separated from you, so you're stuck with me. You'll need a crowbar to pry me out of your life."

"Why do I feel as if nothing will ever be the same?"

"Because it won't be—now that I'm interfering and bossing you."
"I didn't think I'd like it, but it's not so bad to have you around."
"If you keep flattering me like that, I'll get a big head."
"Perish the thought."

He smiled, but it was an odd smile. He was dying to share the issues that were roiling him, but he couldn't. He was too used to being alone, to having secrets. He wondered if he'd ever fully trust her, if she'd ever be a friend and confidante.

He didn't like that he was so far away from her, but he was too overwhelmed by her, and he had to put some space between them so he could clearly evaluate all the changes he was mulling.

Was she worth it? Did he actually intend to relinquish everything just for her? When she gazed at him with those pretty blue eyes of hers, he believed he absolutely should, so he had to go somewhere quiet—away from her—where he could make more prudent decisions.

She had this absurd idea that they could travel to London to meet his siblings, to meet his father, and like magic, they'd be one big, happy family. It was an intriguing picture to ponder, but he'd seen too much of humanity and recognized that many things simply couldn't be done—no matter how fervidly you yearned for them to occur.

"Come here, Jean Pierre." She patted the empty spot next to her on the mattress.

"I have to be up on deck very soon."

"Rest with me until then." He didn't take a step toward her, and she added, "You seem troubled. Let me soothe you."

"I'm not troubled," he lied.

Still though, he pushed away from the window and went over to her. He stretched out, and for a minute, they fumbled around, trying to get comfortable. The bunk was narrow, designed for one person, not two, but the confined area guaranteed that they had to snuggle closely.

He rolled on top of her, and he kissed her. He was gentle, tender in a way that was worrying. He felt as if he was saying goodbye. Was he?

"What's vexing you so much?" she inquired.

"I'm glad we met."

"Well…I'm glad we met, too."

"That first day—when you'd sprained your ankle out on the road—you were so fetching."

"You silver-tongued devil. With all these compliments, I'll become annoyingly vain. You'll turn me into a female version of yourself."

"I never thought a woman like you could care about a man like me."

"A woman like *me*? What about me?"

"You're so…different from the women in my world."

"I should hope so."

"You're so fresh and innocent."

"I'm not so innocent anymore." She grinned, trying for levity.

"I hate that I've corrupted you. When I think of Bramble Bay in the future, I want to remember you just as you were that afternoon on the lane."

The comment sounded too final, and she definitely noticed. She frowned. "Why are you talking like this? You act as if we're parting, as if I'll never see you again once I'm home."

He studied her eyes, his expression affectionate and warm. "I'm sorry. I didn't mean to make you feel that way."

He started kissing her again, and quickly, they were swept into a pool of desire.

There wasn't time for disrobing or a slow sizzle of passion that could build and build. At any moment, a crew member could knock on the door and request his assistance up on the deck.

He didn't unbutton her dress, and she didn't tug off his shirt. He didn't suckle her breasts, and she didn't caress his body as he loved her to do.

He opened his trousers, widened her thighs and slipped into her, the hem of her skirt bunched between them. He filled her completely, but still, he could never get near enough, could never hold her as tightly as he needed to, and this occasion was the same.

Though he tried, he couldn't conceal his despair, and she perceived his anguish. She wrapped her arms and legs around him and gripped him fiercely, as if—should she release him—he might float off into the sky.

He thrust into her over and over, his movements almost desperate. With a moan of distress, he spilled himself and collapsed onto her.

For a lengthy interval, they lay like two marble statues, frozen in place. Eventually, he slid onto his side, spooning himself to her. She reached up to find his cheek, to stroke it, and he clasped her palm and kissed the center.

He sighed, his chest rising and falling as he exhaled a heavy breath.

"Tell me what you're thinking," she said.

"I'm just tired."

She elbowed him in the ribs. "You're awfully maudlin tonight. It's not like you."

"I apologize."

"We'll always be together, John. We'll be fine."

"Yes, we will be," he agreed. "Why don't you get some more sleep?"

She yawned. "Will you stay until I doze off?"

"Of course."

He waited, feeling her relax, her respiration slow, then he crept away and tiptoed out. He lurched over to the ladder and plopped down on the bottom rung, his head in his hands.

Could he leave her? Could he deliver her to Bramble Bay, then ride away?

He didn't know, but how could he travel the other path?

It led to marriage and commitment and a tedious existence as a country gentleman and farmer. He'd go mad the first week. He'd drive her mad shortly after, and she'd wind up hating him. There was no route to happiness for them.

It was only a matter of time before he met a bad end, and she deserved a husband who would love her and be with her forever.

What to do? What to do?

The question pounded through him like a blacksmith's hammer striking an anvil. Sick with regret, with confusion, he was frantic to return to his cabin, but in his current state, there was no predicting how foolishly he might behave.

He pushed himself to his feet, clambered up the ladder, and walked to the helm. He had to focus on England, on docking the ship safe and sound.

What would happen after that—how he would proceed, what he would choose—he couldn't begin to guess.

CHAPTER SEVENTEEN

"Am I doing the right thing?"

"Absolutely."

Mildred looked over at Sheldon. They were in the front parlor, enjoying a pot of tea, which they were both having trouble drinking. They chatted like the friends they were, as if there was no chaos looming on the horizon.

With all that was approaching, she'd needed his steady presence, and she was so glad she'd asked him to stop by, that he'd agreed to assist her.

Sarah didn't want him as a spouse, but Mildred wondered what Sarah's opinion would be when she returned from France and was faced with the reality of her situation.

No doubt she'd surrendered the only item a single female had that was of any genuine value—her chastity—and her home was lost. Hedley had squandered her dowry, so she had no money. Her prospects were quite reduced from what they'd been earlier in the summer.

She might conclude that Sheldon wasn't such a bad option, but Mildred was determined to beat Sarah to the prize. Sarah was too stupid to save herself, but Mildred could clearly see the best path. Her husband, Bernard, had been much older than she was, and she wasn't too proud to pick an elderly man the second time around.

Sheldon hadn't yet realized that Mildred should be his wife, but there were ways to force his hand, and she didn't mind using any trick at her disposal to garner what she required.

"I hate all this drama," she said. "I wish it was over."

"I understand," Sheldon sagely concurred. "There's a reason we call it the *quiet* life in the country. We shouldn't have to have our routines disrupted with discord and disputes."

"My thoughts exactly."

Caroline entered the room, and she was extremely preoccupied, so she didn't glance back to notice the disaster looming behind her.

Foolish girl.

"You wanted to speak with me, Mildred?" she asked.

"Yes. Mr. Hook is off the property, chasing after Miss Dubois."

Caroline scowled. "He's not chasing her. He's riding to Dover with her. She's sailing to France today."

"No, I had a note from Hedley. She refused to go to France, and Hedley is escorting her to London. Mr. Hook was particularly aggrieved by her decision and went after her to put her on the ship as was arranged."

"Thank you for telling me," Caroline slowly replied, confused as to why she'd been summoned.

"I sought Sheldon's advice about what should be done with you."

"What should be *done* with me?" Caroline snapped. She'd never liked Sheldon, and he'd never liked her. "I'm an adult, Mildred. You don't need to fret over me as if I was a child. I'm perfectly capable of taking care of myself."

"Really? Are you aware that the entire staff is gossiping about your liaison with Mr. Hook?"

"I fail to see how my relationship with him is any of your business."

"Until Mr. Sinclair comes back, it's still my house, and the people in it are still my servants. If matters resolve as I'm expecting, Bramble Bay will remain my property, so I'm informing you that your immorality has shamed us and it's over."

"Oh, for pity's sake," Caroline grumbled. "Will that be all?"

"Sheldon agrees with me that this is for the best."

"What is for the *best*?"

"Hello, Caroline," Archie said from over by the door.

He was Mildred's distant cousin, and she didn't know him very well, but she'd never observed any outward displays of aggression or even discourtesy. So she hadn't believed Caroline's tales of vicious rages and abuse.

Yet at the moment, with a flush on his cheeks and fire in his eyes, Mildred suspected there might have been some truth to Caroline's stories. But so what? Archie was her husband, and Caroline had always been difficult. If Archie had punished her, Mildred was positive Caroline deserved it.

Caroline whipped around. "Archie! What are you doing here?"

"He never left the village," Mildred explained. "We've been waiting for Mr. Hook to absent himself so Archie could retrieve you."

"She sent for me," Archie added, "the minute Mr. Hook rode down the drive."

He took a step toward Caroline, and she took a step back.

"I won't leave with you." Her stubbornness only ignited his temper.

"You don't think you will?" Archie seethed.

"I'll fight you. You'll have to drag me out."

"I'm happy to drag you."

Archie lunged and grabbed her, and though she tried to wrestle away, he was bigger and stronger and he'd brought a rope. Very quickly, he'd tied her with it, her arms secured at her sides.

Even with her bound, she pulled and tussled, but couldn't escape.

"Caroline," Sheldon chided, "stop resisting."

"Shut up, you stupid fool!" Caroline spat.

"A woman belongs with her husband," Sheldon calmly stated. "You had to go home sooner or later."

"I'll kill myself first!" she insisted.

"You will not," Sheldon evenly replied. "It would be a terrible sin."

Archie felt compelled to interject, "No more terrible than the adultery she's been committing."

Sheldon ignored the crude comment and unfalteringly continued. "Now please leave with your husband. You're disgracing yourself with this wild behavior."

Archie taunted, "Where is your fancy lover, Caroline? Where is he when you need him the most?"

"He'll murder you when he finds out what you've done."

"I wouldn't be too sure—were I you."

Archie was bolstered by the fact that Mr. Sinclair and Mr. Hook would—hopefully—not be pestering them much longer. But if the situation didn't conclude as Mildred anticipated, she feared for Archie.

She'd been living with Mr. Hook for over a month. He wasn't a man to discount or disregard.

"I'm certain of Mr. Hook," Caroline said to Archie. "I'm certain he'll murder you for me."

"Whore!" Archie shouted, and he slapped her.

The scene was incredibly distasteful, and Sheldon stood and scolded, "Mr. Patterson, there's no need for violence. I realize you and your wife have had some problems, but you have custody of her now. Take her away. You're upsetting Mildred."

Archie seized Caroline and, as he'd threatened, dragged her to the door as she hissed and fought like a rabid cat. But he was determined, and she couldn't slow him.

"I'll ask Mr. Hook to kill you too, Mildred," Caroline hurled. "He'll attack when you least expect it, so you'd best keep peeking over your shoulder."

Then she was gone, and Mildred shuddered with relief.

She and Sheldon sat—stunned and affronted—as they listened to Archie haul her out. Shortly, his carriage wheels crunched across the gravel in the drive, his horse's hooves clopping away.

"That was vile," Mildred muttered, and she noticed she was trembling.

"Yes, but it was the only possible ending," Sheldon assured her. "I don't know what Caroline was thinking by coming here and putting you in such an untenable position."

"I would have sent her home immediately, but Sarah wouldn't let me."

"I wish you'd spoken to me weeks ago. I'd have talked sense to both girls."

Mildred flashed him a hot, adoring look. "Yes, I should have confided in you. You've always been such an enormous help to me."

"I try," the annoying, pompous man said.

Mildred sighed. "One down, one to go."

"I pray the encounter with Mr. Sinclair won't be as awful as that."

"It won't be calm or dull. You just met him once, so you don't understand how fierce he can be. I don't imagine he'll surrender quietly."

They tarried, glum and disconcerted, the lone sound the ticking of the clock on the mantle. The servants had been transported to the village so no one walked by in the hall. Time ground to a halt. Occasionally, when Mildred's nerves got the better of her, she'd stroll to the window and stare out at the road.

Eventually, two riders turned in the gate. As they neared, she saw that it was Sarah and John Sinclair.

"It's them," she murmured to Sheldon.

He tiptoed to the foyer and softly called up the stairs, "He's here."

There was no response, but up above her head, she heard a shifting of boots.

She went to the door that led into the adjoining dining room and opened it a crack. Miss Dubois was seated at the table, appearing bored and dangerous, while Hedley was pacing and more nervous than Mildred—if that was possible.

"They're here," Mildred said.

"Are you certain it's them?" Hedley asked.

"Yes. They're approaching the house."

Hedley was rippling with anxiety, but with excitement, too. There was a huge reward for Mr. Sinclair's capture, and he was convinced he would receive it.

Mildred thought Miss Dubois might have a different opinion. Dubois wasn't the type to share, but was more like a poisonous viper, holding very still, hidden from view, ready to strike when no one was watching.

Hedley was completely enamored of Dubois, but he was a horrid judge of character. By involving himself with her, there was no way he'd emerge from the relationship with any benefit.

Mildred glared at Miss Dubois. "I hope you're sure about this."

"I am."

"If you're wrong, or if you've lured my son into a new quagmire with Mr. Sinclair, then I will—"

"You'll what?" Miss Dubois scoffed, cutting Mildred off.

"I won't let Hedley suffer because of you."

"Go away, Madame Teasdale," Dubois snottily retorted. "I don't like you, and I'd really rather you mind your own business instead of mine."

"Will you allow her to treat me like this, Hedley?" Mildred heard the whine in her voice.

"Don't fuss, Mother," Hedley replied. "We'll figure it all out later on. Let's not quarrel at our moment of triumph."

"We mustn't give ourselves away," Dubois added. "Jean Pierre is extremely dangerous, Madame Teasdale. You shouldn't forget it. I haven't."

Mildred wanted to snipe and argue, wanted to grab the woman by her expensive gown and throw her out. Yet Dubois was correct about one pertinent fact: If Mr. Sinclair was the notorious pirate, Jean Pierre—which Mildred couldn't fathom—then they were all at great risk until he was under control.

She pulled the door shut and spun to find Sheldon seated on the sofa. She was too flustered to join him, so she remained by the window, furtively observing as Mr. Sinclair and Sarah reined in, as Mr. Sinclair leapt down and tied the horses.

He helped Sarah down, and they stood very close together. Mr. Sinclair spoke intently to Sarah, rested his fingers on her cheek, and she wistfully studied his eyes.

From the position of their bodies and their poignant expressions, Sarah's infatuation was blatantly clear. But to Mildred's surprise, Mr. Sinclair seemed to possess some genuine fondness of his own. When he looked at Sarah, his gaze was brimming with desire and longing.

Mildred scowled, wishing the blasted man had never met Hedley, wishing he'd been in residence the day Phillip Sinclair had visited from London. Perhaps Phillip Sinclair could have spirited him away, and all this unpleasantness could have been avoided.

She glanced over at Sheldon. "They've dismounted. They're headed inside."

"Buck up, dear," Sheldon murmured. "It will be over in a minute."

He was blithely sipping his tea, but Mildred couldn't bear to act so nonchalant. She went to the hall and peered down to the foyer.

Sarah entered first, then Mr. Sinclair.

"Home sweet home," Sarah said.

"Are you glad to be back?" Sinclair asked her.

"I have mixed feelings." She gaped around, then smiled at him. "I'm so different, but everything here is exactly the same."

As if a signal had been given, a dozen doors slammed open, and soldiers—red coats blazing—raced to surround them.

"Jean Pierre!" the captain of the unit barked, stomping up. "I arrest you on behalf of the Crown."

"Arrest me?" Mr. Sinclair frowned. "How very odd. On what charge?"

But Mildred noticed that he'd surreptitiously shoved Sarah away. A soldier yanked on her arm, separating her from Sinclair.

"John!" Sarah called. "What is it? What's happening?"

"Stay back, Sarah," he called in return.

"Watch his hands! Watch his hands!" a soldier warned.

Before anyone could move, Mr. Sinclair—as if by magic—was holding a pistol. He fired a quick shot, hitting a soldier who collapsed to the floor.

"John!" Sarah shrieked with alarm. She was straining and stretching, trying to reach for him, but she was too short and couldn't push through the wall of soldiers.

They bravely rushed him, and somehow, he managed to steal a saber. He started slashing with it, fighting like a whirlwind, like a tempest, one against thirty.

Someone was yelling, begging for mercy, shouting for Mr. Hook to intervene. It was Sarah, screaming and screaming. The sound rattled Mildred, shamed and agitated her.

The captain muscled his way into the circle, raised his own pistol and clouted Mr. Sinclair on the side of the head. He staggered and fell to his knees, but he continued to brawl, inflicting more and more damage, until Mildred grew frightened, thinking he might win the battle, that he might slay every single soldier, and she'd be left alone to face his fury.

Finally, the captain bellowed, "Sinclair! Jean Pierre!"

Mr. Sinclair whipped about, his glare murderous, when he saw the captain had an arm around Sarah's waist, his gun pressed to her temple.

"Stop now," the captain ordered, "or I'll arrest her as an accomplice. She'll hang along with you."

"Don't listen to him," Sarah told Mr. Sinclair. "I've done nothing wrong, and he can't harm me."

"She'll hang, Sinclair," the captain insisted. "I'll personally see to it."

"Swear to me that you'll let her go," Mr. Sinclair said to the captain. "Give me your word as a gentleman."

"I give you my word—both as a gentleman and as an officer in the king's army."

Mr. Sinclair straightened and dropped his saber, and the captain lowered his pistol and shoved Sarah behind him. A soldier restrained her so she couldn't race over to Mr. Sinclair. Several others wrapped Sinclair with numerous ropes so he was fully secured and couldn't lash out again.

Sarah had once claimed that Mr. Sinclair was Florence's son, that he was Mildred's nephew. What if he was and Mildred had orchestrated this end for him? If Florence was staring down from Heaven, what would she think of Mildred and how she'd treated Florence's beloved boy?

Even though he'd been thoroughly pummeled, he looked magnificent and imperious. He was bleeding from many wounds, his cheekbones, nose, and chin. His knuckles were bruised, his skin scraped raw from throwing fierce punches.

It appeared as if he'd been run through with a sword, too. Blood gushed from a wound at his side. Set against the white of his shirt, the stain was very dark, very severe, yet he stood like a statue, as if he didn't feel any of his injuries.

His gaze was locked on Sarah and filled with such yearning and regret that Mildred had to glance away. Sarah had a hand over her mouth, as if she was choking down more screams or as if she might be ill.

"John," she moaned, "you're hurt."

"I'm fine, *chérie*," he said. "Don't worry about me."

"Where are you taking him?" Sarah demanded of the captain.

"To London. For trial."

"Goodbye, *chérie*," Mr. Sinclair murmured to her. "*Adieu, mi amour.* I will always be yours. Forever."

The captain stepped in so he and Sinclair were toe to toe. He was an older, hardened veteran who'd most likely participated in many battles, but when news went out of who he'd caught, he'd have no more brilliant episode in his career.

"Jean Pierre," the captain announced, "*Le Terreur Français,* I accuse you of piracy on the high seas, murder, robbery, and mayhem. You are a menace to the entire world, and we all rejoice in your capture. Your punishment shall fit your many crimes: death by hanging."

Mr. Sinclair didn't reply, but merely dipped his head, neither admitting nor denying anything. Sarah's knees gave out, and the soldier next to her grabbed her so she didn't collapse in a stunned heap.

"You have the wrong man," she declared. "You've arrested the wrong person."

"We haven't, Miss Teasdale." The captain motioned to one of his men. "Bring the witness to identify him."

The man hurried past Mildred and returned with Miss Dubois. She sauntered into the hall and glared toward the foyer. If she had any opinion on seeing Mr. Sinclair beaten and maimed and bound, it was carefully concealed.

"Mademoiselle Dubois," the captain asked, "is this the pirate known to you as Jean Pierre, *Le Terreur Français?*"

"Yes, that's him," she blandly answered, seeming bored by the whole affair.

"You're sure?"

"Absolutely sure."

The captain nodded to his men. "Take him away."

But Miss Dubois was eager to speak, to be the center of attention. "You shouldn't have betrayed me, Jean Pierre."

"I did nothing to you, Annalise."

"You shouldn't have set me aside. And for a pale, trembling Englishwoman." She spat on the rug like a common fishwife. "I warned Raven that I would have my revenge, and now I have."

"Raven will kill you when he finds you," Mr. Sinclair said.

Everyone gasped.

"Be quiet, you!" the captain sternly commanded.

Mr. Sinclair ignored him, his eyes lethal, his tone deadly. "Beware, Annalise. We'll see who is avenged in the end."

"I told you to be quiet!" the captain fumed, and he hit Mr. Sinclair, delivering a violent blow that rendered Sinclair unconscious. He crumpled to the floor, and the captain kicked him several times, then his men lifted Sinclair and carried him out. Others helped the soldier that Sinclair had shot at the beginning of the fight.

Within seconds, they had all marched out, and a poisonous silence descended. Sheldon came over to Mildred and rested a comforting hand on her shoulder, but Mildred wasn't eased by the gesture.

Miss Dubois and Sarah faced each other, and Dubois was smirking, preening. The old Sarah the one Mildred had known for over two decades—wouldn't have bothered with Dubois, would never have raised a fuss.

But this was a new Sarah, a changed Sarah, who was ferocious and loyal and more resolved than Dubois could ever have hoped to be. Dubois had acted out of jealousy and spite, but Sarah was acting out of love and devotion. Although Dubois hadn't realized it yet, Sarah would win any battles between them.

Sarah stormed down the hall, approaching Dubois.

"Harlot!" Sarah seethed.

"I won't be insulted by you," Miss Dubois huffed.

"Witch! Harlot!" Sarah said again, and she slapped Dubois as hard as she could.

Mildred thought Dubois might strike Sarah in retaliation, but she was caught off guard by Sarah's fury. Sarah looked like an ancient warrior goddess, capable of destroying worlds, and her visible wrath was alarming to witness.

"How dare you!" Miss Dubois raged.

"Who let you into my home so you could mingle with decent people?"

"Spoken from one whore to another," Dubois simpered. "At least I was well paid for my efforts. What did you receive for yours?"

"There is a musket in my father's library," was Sarah's response, "and I know how to use it. I'm going to fetch it. When I return, Miss Dubois, if you are still here, I will shoot you right through the middle of your cold, black heart."

"You don't have the nerve to shoot me."

"You don't think so? Keep standing here until I get back. Keep standing here so you can learn for yourself what I am willing to do."

Sarah spun away and raced to the library.

Sheldon—always the peacemaker—said to Miss Dubois, "Ah...perhaps you should leave?"

Miss Dubois tossed her mane of hair. "I'll only depart if Hedley says I must."

"You should probably go," Sheldon insisted. "We don't want any more trouble." He glanced at Mildred. "Do we, Mildred?"

"No, we definitely don't want more trouble."

"Start walking down the lane," Sheldon told Dubois. "I'll hitch my carriage and pick you up. There's a boarding house in the village. We'll take you to it, and while you settle in, I'll come back for your belongings."

Miss Dubois was ready to refuse, and she glowered toward the dining room, where Hedley had finally slithered out.

"They're demanding I leave," she complained to him. "Must I?"

"She can't stay," Mildred fumed.

"Mother! Of course she can."

Mildred stood up to him for the first time ever. "No, Hedley, she can't."

He hemmed and hawed, then ultimately agreed. "Just for tonight. Just until Sarah has calmed."

Mildred had seen how Mr. Sinclair and Sarah gazed into each other's eyes. She didn't think Sarah would ever calm, but she didn't say so aloud.

Sheldon led Miss Dubois to the door. She bitterly protested, but he was very determined. He pushed her out bodily, slammed the door behind her, and turned the key in the lock.

For a shameful interval, she dawdled on the stoop, banging and screeching to be readmitted. The three of them were frozen in place, pretending she wasn't creating a disturbance, Mildred feeling incredibly distressed by the horrid scene.

Angry footsteps pounded, and Sarah marched up. She was holding Bernard's weapon, and she appeared very lethal.

"Is she gone?" Sarah asked.

"Yes," Sheldon answered, "so let's put the gun away." He tried for a smile. "I wouldn't want it to go off by accident. I wouldn't want you to hurt anyone."

"If it goes off," Sarah caustically snarled, "it won't be by accident."

"Now, now," Sheldon soothed, "let's not be that way. Your father, rest his soul, would hate to have you so upset."

"Who in this house betrayed Mr. Sinclair?" she hissed. "Who betrayed my great friend and love?" She spun on Hedley. "Was it you?"

Sarah seemed so frighteningly dangerous that Mildred was terrified she'd shoot Hedley without pausing to consider.

"Sarah!" she sharply barked.

Sarah whirled to Mildred and bellowed, "Or was it you?"

"Not I," Mildred claimed, but her avowal sounded shifty and untrue.

"He is your nephew!" Sarah shouted. "He is Florence's son! He was coming to make amends, to give us back the estate, to reconcile with you. And you had him arrested on the word of a whore. He'll probably be hanged on the word of a whore!"

Suddenly, she began to weep, her shoulders drooping, and Sheldon grabbed the musket. He attempted to maneuver her into the parlor, but she shook him away.

"Do me a favor, Sheldon," she beseeched.

"I'll assist you however I can."

"If you ever possessed any genuine affection for my father, take Mildred and Hedley away with you. Go home and take them, too."

"Well...all right. I suppose I can."

"For if they remain in my sight another second, I can't predict how I will behave."

She was staring at Sheldon, being too irate to look at Mildred or Hedley.

Sheldon scowled at Mildred and gestured to the door. She didn't move, and he said, "Mildred, please! Let's humor her for a bit."

She sighed with exasperation. "If you insist. Come, Hedley."

At first, he refused, but Mildred clasped his arm and guided him out.

Behind her, Sheldon told Sarah, "I'll stop by later to check on you."

"Where are the servants?" she asked.

"In the village, but they should be back very soon."

"And Mr. Hook?"

"I believe he's in London. I'm not clear on the reason, but I guess he assumed Miss Dubois had gone to the city, and he's searching for her there."

"All the while, she was here, destroying his best friend. He *will* kill her when he finds out."

"Sarah, Sarah," Sheldon clucked, "let's not talk like that."

"Go, Sheldon. Go away and leave me be."

Mildred started down the stairs, dragging a recalcitrant Hedley with her. Miss Dubois was in the drive, appearing vastly amused, as if what they'd done to Mr. Sinclair was a big joke. If Mildred had been a violent sort of person, she'd have whipped Dubois bloody.

When Dubois had initially mentioned John Sinclair's identity to Mildred, when Hedley had gushed that they'd summoned soldiers to catch him, that they intended to collect the reward, it had sounded so easy, so thrilling.

Mildred hadn't considered how awful the event would actually be. Oh, if only she could travel back in time and arrange a different ending!

Sheldon rushed up, and they headed for the stables to fetch his carriage.

"Where are we going?" Miss Dubois demanded.

"*We* are going to Mr. Fishburn's," Mildred said.

"Am I coming with you?"

Sheldon flashed Mildred a telling frown, and Mildred said, "I'm sorry, Miss Dubois, but you're not welcome to join us."

"But...but..." Dubois stammered, "where am I to go?"

"I don't know," Mildred advised, "but I wouldn't loiter in the driveway. Sarah retrieved my husband's gun—as she threatened she would. I'm quite sure if she sees you, she'll shoot you with it."

"She wouldn't!"

"She would." Mildred turned to Sheldon. "Let's hurry. I'm feeling ill."

"As am I." Sheldon looked as miserable as she felt.

"I want to stay with Miss Dubois," Hedley whined.

"Absolutely not," Mildred snapped.

"I'm a grown man, Mother. You can't force me to leave with you."

Mildred was so weary, so aggravated, both by them and the ghastly debacle they'd engineered. They were a pair of fools who'd painted a pretty picture about how simple the arrest would be, but Mildred was certain that nothing they'd hoped to attain would ever be achieved by it.

The entire sordid affair was merely another disaster Hedley had stirred, the ramifications of which would all fall on Mildred.

Sheldon escorted her away, and as they hurried off, Hedley asked Dubois, "Will we get the reward? They have to give it to us, don't they?"

Mildred covered her ears so she couldn't hear Dubois's response.

CHAPTER EIGHTEEN

"There's a visitor for you, Jean Pierre."

"I told you: no visitors except my attorney, Mr. Thompson."

John glared at the guard standing outside his cell. John wished Raven could come, but it was too dangerous. They weren't certain if Annalise had implicated Raven, so Raven couldn't show his face at the prison lest he be seized, too.

If John could do one valiant deed before he was hanged, he would save Raven from suffering the same fate.

Reggie Thompson—John's criminal accountant—was a good alternative to Raven. He was a bland, unobtrusive man who could easily pass as a lawyer. He slipped in and out without generating much notice.

A prisoner of John's wealth and status wasn't expected to rub elbows with the general rabble. He could purchase all the lavish incarceration money could buy, so he was housed in a wing with other affluent citizens, and his fat purse had paid for many bribes to ensure he was suitably cosseted.

Reggie had arranged delivery of every comfort, from Persian rugs to Venetian glassware. A French chef had been hired to prepare his meals.

When John met his Maker, he would be happy to report that he'd spent his last few weeks, surrounded by the opulence and splendor he relished.

"It's not another woman, is it?" John asked.

"No."

The prison had been besieged by females trying to sneak in, and of course, Sarah had stopped by several times, but they'd all been turned away. John wouldn't see anyone except Reggie, and he most especially wouldn't see Sarah. She needed to head home to Bramble Bay and forget about him.

"Who is it then?" he inquired.

"I don't know," the guard responded, "but the warden says you can't refuse this one. He's a rich nob who can go wherever he wants. We have no authority to keep him out."

John rolled his eyes with exasperation. It was probably some aristocrat's son who'd bet at his club that he could bluster his way in to see the notorious French Terror.

It might be amusing to speak with the foolish dandy. It would remind John of how much he loathed the British aristocracy, how glad he was that he'd wreaked so much havoc on them.

A gate clanged, and the guard murmured, "Here he is now."

"Lucky me," John muttered.

The guard bowed deferentially to the visitor, then gestured to John's open door and walked away. John stood in the middle of the cell, oozing boredom, anxious for the horrid moment to be over as quickly as possible.

But when the man stepped over the threshold, John blanched with shock. He'd meant to show no emotion. Otherwise, his reaction would be bandied in the newspapers later on, but gad! What was he to think?

"John Sinclair, I presume?" the man asked.

"Yes."

"And obviously, you know who I am. May I sit?"

John was too astonished to reply and had to shake himself out of his stupor. He pointed to a chair by the stove where a toasty fire crackled in the grate.

Charles Sinclair—his nemesis, his enemy, his father—sauntered in as if he owned the bloody place and settled in the chair John had indicated.

"I have to admit," Charles said, "that I'm a bit undone. May I have a brandy?"

"Certainly."

"I hope you pour French."

"I do."

"They're so much better at everything."

John whipped away, struggling to control his racing pulse, his visceral dislike. But there were other sentiments roaring through him, too: amazement, confusion, distress. His curiosity was flaring, roiling him so thoroughly that, as he reached for the decanter, his hands were trembling.

He poured Charles a glass, but poured his own, too. Desperate to calm himself, he inhaled a deep breath, and another, then spun and delivered the man's brandy. He plopped into the chair opposite.

He was a few inches taller than his father, broader across the shoulders and arms, but other than those slight differences, they looked exactly alike. Charles's blond hair had silvered with age, and John felt as if he'd somehow been transported twenty years into the future, as if he was staring at a vision of himself and how he'd appear when he was older. Not that he would live to be older.

His days were numbered.

John viewed himself as being very intimidating, able to awe and daunt with a glare, but apparently, it was an inherited trait. He glowered at Charles, determined to rattle him, but Charles placidly gazed back, not disturbed in the least.

John took his father's measure, greatly bothered to find that Charles was gracious, handsome, and charming. Over the decades, John had burned with notions of Charles being a wretched lout, the images so virulent that John often described him as an ogre, the type of grotesque monster that lurked under bridges and gobbled up unsuspecting travelers.

Yet his mother had claimed that Charles was wonderful, and her friends in Paris had agreed. John hadn't believed them. He'd pictured Charles as ugly and twisted and horrid. But he wasn't.

There was an aura about him—of composure and assurance—that made you want to wallow in his presence, that made you want to get closer and become a confidante. John could see why a foolish girl like his mother would be smitten by Charles Sinclair, why she'd ruined her life for no good reason.

John was conflicted and perplexed. He'd always told himself that if he ever met Charles, he'd feel nothing, but to his disgust, he was churning with agitation.

He might have been ten again, alone and scared and praying that Charles would rush to France and save him. He could barely stop himself from jumping up and turning in joyous circles as he cried, *He came for me! He came for me!*

"Shall we chat in English," Charles asked, "or is it easier for you in French?"

"Pick your language. It matters not to me."

"I'll stick with French, then. It will keep the guards from eavesdropping." Charles switched as effortlessly as John could, speaking with no accent, as if he'd been born and raised in Paris rather than London.

"It's always unnerving to meet one of my children," Charles said.

"Maybe if you weren't such an unrepentant rogue, you wouldn't have that problem."

"I should probably check to be sure you are who you say you are. I assume you bear my mark?"

He referred to the birthmark on John's wrist, the one in the shape of a figure-eight that was carried by so many of Charles's bastards.

"Unfortunately, yes." John tugged at his sleeve to reveal the evidence. "I wear your mark like a bad stain."

"There's no need to be surly, is there?"

John sighed. "Why are you here, Lord Trent?"

"You may call me Charles if you like. It seems silly to be on formal terms."

"Let's not pretend we're cordial."

"Why can't we be? I don't care for bickering. If we can be civil, we'll come out of this with a much better ending."

"I repeat: Why are you here?"

Charles sipped his drink, very set on himself and not inclined to allow John to control the tenor or topics of conversation. He studied John, as if checking for flaws, then said, "I see all my best traits in you, but I don't see much of Florence. You don't look like her at all."

John straightened as if he'd been poked with a pin. "You don't get to talk to me about my mother."

"Why shouldn't we discuss her? It appears that my relationship with her has been vexing you for ages."

"We're *not* talking about her."

"I'd like you to know that—when I took up with her—I was little more than a boy myself. Back then, I made many bad decisions."

"My *mother* was a bad decision?"

"No, she was actually quite incredible, but I shouldn't have involved myself with her. I was too young and vain to temper my conduct. I thought I was omnipotent and could have whatever I wanted."

John hadn't intended to comment, but his fury had been percolating for thirty years. Before he could remember to be silent, he spat, "When she was dying, I wrote to you. I begged you to help us."

"I never received any letter from you."

"If you had, would you have assisted me?"

Charles lifted his shoulder in an elegant shrug. "Probably not."

"Asshole."

"Would you rather I lied?"

John felt as if he was choking, and it occurred to him that if Charles mentioned Florence again, he might leap over and pummel him to the floor.

Still, Charles persisted. "Your mother was very beautiful."

"Lord Trent, are you aware of the types of criminal behavior for which I'm renowned?"

"Very aware."

"I'd be happy to murder you, right here, right now. I'll strangle you with my bare hands, and I won't break a sweat."

"Don't be melodramatic," Charles scolded as if John was a toddler throwing a tantrum.

"If I say that I won't discuss my mother with you, I expect you to heed my request. I give a command exactly one time, and if I'm forced to give it a second time, there are consequences."

"Honestly, Jean Pierre, you really can be annoying." Charles fussed with the lace on his cravat, smoothed his lapel. "You remind me so much of Phillip. You haven't met him, but if you ever have the chance, you'll find the experience fascinating."

Charles downed the last of his brandy, then held out the glass so John would refill it. John hesitated, then grabbed it and trotted over to the sideboard like a pet dog. As he finished and sat again, Charles was coolly serene, while John was a mess of jumbled emotions.

He'd insisted he wouldn't talk about his mother, but he was awash with questions and yearned to shout: Why did you seduce her? Why did you leave her? Why are you so callous and cold? Why am I so much like you?

Charles was notorious for his high-stakes wagering, and John could see why he was so successful. He was in a cell in Newgate Prison, chatting with a bastard son who was charged with heinous crimes and facing execution. Yet they might have been having tea in a fancy London drawing room.

He was unflappable and unflustered, and John should have been too, but he couldn't match his father in unruffled aplomb.

"I'm told you're an avid gambler," John said.

"I've placed a few bets in my day."

"Can you track the cards? Can you guess which card is coming before it's dealt?"

"Absolutely."

"Do you cheat?"

"Do you?"

"If I have to."

"A chip off the old block," Charles murmured.

John seethed. He wanted to hurt Charles, wanted him to be sorry or at least feign regret, but it seemed impossible to disconcert him.

"You've been married for decades."

"To my wife Susan. Yes."

"What's her opinion of your philandering? I don't imagine your foul habits are conducive to happy banter around the family supper table."

Charles flashed a tight smile. "I don't get to talk about Florence, and you don't get to talk about Susan."

"How many illicit children have you sired anyway?"

"I have no idea. Phillip has found several of them." More to himself than to John, he grumbled, "I sire so many blasted girls."

"You poor thing," John sarcastically cooed. "All those ruined maidens and nothing to show for it but a crop of daughters."

"And two strapping sons," Charles sharply said, "both of whom vex me enormously."

"How does Phillip vex you?"

"He tries to make me a better man—when I don't wish to be."

"Up until this moment, I've never met you. How could *I* be vexing you?"

"You're determined to be hanged, and believe what you will about me, but I won't permit you to be killed in such a pointless way."

"It's always been my fate. There's no reason to deny it."

"What a stupidly ridiculous comment."

"It's true." John shrugged. "From the day I stole my first purse from a man's pocket, I've been heading to the scaffold. I'm amazed I've lasted this long."

"So am I."

"If I'd known I'd arrive at this paltry conclusion, though, I'd have let some oaf shoot me years ago. I hate to give the Crown the pleasure of executing me. I should have arranged my own grand finale. I'd have orchestrated an ending that was much more creative than a noose and a rope."

To John's surprise, fury flared in Charles's eyes. It was there and gone in an instant, but John was positive he'd observed it.

Why would Charles fret over John's predicament? Charles had never previously evinced any concern, not through any of John's lengthy trials and tribulations. Why had he suddenly tripped over his paternal instincts? It made no sense.

"Stop it, Jean Pierre," Charles fervidly said.

"Stop what?"

"Stop bragging about how you want to die, about how they'll kill you."

"Well, they will. Why pretend it won't happen?"

"Fight, dammit! Fight for your life!"

"But that's the problem, Charles. I don't give two figs for my life, and I have no desire to fight for it."

"I won't let you do this."

"I don't see how you can prevent me."

"I'm hiring a lawyer for you."

"I neither want nor need one."

"I won't argue about it. He'll visit you later this afternoon, and I expect you to fully cooperate with whatever he advises."

"Fine," John muttered. "It's your money. Waste it if you choose."

"Then I'm announcing to the entire world that you're my son. I'll provide you with an alibi."

John had just swallowed a mouthful of brandy, and at Charles's absurd remark, the liquor slid down wrong. He coughed and coughed and pounded on his chest.

"You're going to what?" he wheezed when he could speak again.

"I'm publically claiming you. I'll say we've always been close, and we were together on any date they allege an attack to have occurred."

"No, but thank you."

Charles continued as if John hadn't replied. "In return, you'll abandon your life of crime. In a few months, we'll spread stories that the real French Terror's ship sank in a storm, that he and his crew drowned. You'll fade from memory, and the Crown can find other enemies to chase."

"No, Lord Trent."

"Yes, Jean Pierre. You will not dissuade me."

"I'll deny your paternity. I'll deny kinship."

"You hate me that much that you're willing to die over it?"

"I don't hate you. Don't flatter yourself. You're nothing to me, and whether I perish or don't, it's naught to do with you."

Charles snorted with derision. "Gad, you're as stubborn as Phillip."

"I'm not acquainted with the man, but I'll take it as a compliment."

Charles relaxed in his chair, trying to figure out another tactic that might sway John.

What a pretentious ass!

How dare he suppose he could waltz in and tell John how to behave! How dare he suppose he could flaunt his fatherhood and that John would listen because of it! How dare he assume John would be thrilled by his sudden, unwanted interest!

"Your recent whore, Miss Dubois, seems an odd choice for an amorous entanglement."

John scoffed. "As if you'd know my preferences."

"Why involve yourself with someone so unsavory?"

"If you'd ever been in a bed with her, you'd understand."

"She's definitely a woman *scorned*. She's bent on having you hanged."

"So I've been told."

"She's the new belle of London's risqué society, the new darling of the newspapers. She's given a dozen interviews about her experiences as your mistress."

"Don't worry about her. She won't give many more."

"If you have her murdered, it will only go worse for you."

John laughed. "How could it be *worse*? In case you haven't noticed, I'm on death row and merely awaiting my official sentence so it can be carried out with a minimum of fuss and bother."

"Wouldn't it be nice to stay alive simply to thwart her? Wouldn't it be satisfying to call her bluff, to beat her at her game?"

"It doesn't matter what Annalise says about me."

"Yes, it does! She's skewing public opinion against you."

John frowned in confusion. "Why do you care about Annalise Dubois or any of it? Why do you care what happens to me?"

"I don't know," Charles baldly admitted, and they shared a moment of shocked silence. John suspected it was the first true comment Charles had ever uttered.

"If you don't know, Charles, then why don't you leave it be?"

"It's so wrong for you to perish this way. Look at what you've accomplished in your life! Think of what you could become if you put your talents to legitimate ventures. It's such a waste for it to end like this."

John suffered the most annoying spurt of delight. His father thought he was extraordinary! His father was proud! It would have been funny if it wasn't so pathetic.

He sighed with aggravation and regret. "Why don't you go?"

Charles replied with, "Sarah Teasdale came to see me."

On hearing Sarah's name, John felt as if he'd been stabbed in the heart. He was desperate for information about her. Like a smitten boy, he yearned to ask how she was holding up, what she'd said, how she'd acted.

But he'd never reveal his deep and abiding affection, for he was sure that—should others learn the level of his infatuation—they would use it to her detriment. She might be arrested too, might be pressured to disclose details about him. Ultimately, she might be incarcerated, might spend years in prison, unable to gain her release.

So he would never divulge a bond with her. He would never—by the slightest word or deed—allow anyone to realize he had a connection to her at all.

"Miss Teasdale came to see you?" he blandly said. "So?"

"She's very upset that you won't let her visit you."

"Why would I have her visit? She and I are scarcely acquainted."

The lie was so hideous that John wondered if he might be struck by lightning.

"She's such a fine young lady. I can't believe you ruined her."

"That's certainly the pot calling the kettle black."

"I detest that you aren't making better choices in your affairs."

"Despite what she claimed, I had no amorous relationship with her."

"She's such a sweet girl, and she is so pointlessly fond of you."

"I barely know her. I can't imagine why she would be."

"I'm a good judge of character, Jean Pierre. She wasn't lying about your liaison, so I must suppose you're denigrating her in some misguided attempt to protect her."

"If I am, or if I'm not, you don't get to play the role of *father* in this drama. None of this is any of your concern."

"Let me help you, Jean Pierre." Charles was practically begging. "Let me work to have you freed. I'm a peer of the realm. If I give you an alibi, they can't kill you."

"I've already explained: I don't care if they kill me. There's no reason to fight against Fate."

"You could marry Miss Teasdale," Charles passionately urged. "You could start a life with her, sire some children, have a family of your own. You could be happy."

"I'm plenty happy," John insisted, but he was secretly raging.

There could be no greater ending than to be a different man, from a different world. There could be no greater ending than to wed Sarah. But as quickly as the notion arose, he tamped it down.

Sarah deserved to have a grand future. What she *didn't* deserve
was to have a murdering thug for a husband. The genie was out of that
bottle, and there was no way to shove it back inside.

Everyone in the kingdom knew John's identity. Everyone knew
the stories, knew the truth. If he was Sarah's husband, people would
constantly whisper and gossip and accuse. She'd never have a
moment's peace.

It was better if there was no evidence of an association between
them. It was better if he died.

Charles must have realized it was futile to argue. He stared at
John, and John stared back. John felt raw and ragged, as if they'd
been physically brawling, as if he'd been cut and beaten and stabbed
all over again as he had been that day at Bramble Bay when the
soldiers caught him unaware.

"You should probably be going," John murmured.

"What should I tell Miss Teasdale?"

"Don't tell her anything."

"You have no parting words for her?"

"No, none."

Charles scowled. "Oh, John, that seems particularly cruel."

"She'll get over it."

Charles pushed himself to his feet, and he appeared much older
than he had when he'd entered. Some of his urbane charm had
vanished. He looked weary and tired.

"I'll keep fighting for you," he said. "Even if you refuse to help
yourself, I'll help you."

"I told you, Lord Trent: I'll deny any kinship. You'll be wasting
your time."

"I'll do it for Sarah Teasdale, you stupid ass. I'll think of her and
how she lights up when she talks about you."

Charles started out, and John thought he was glad to have his
father leave. Instead, he was swamped by loneliness and doubt.
Should he let Charles walk away? Was he mad to decline Charles's
offer of assistance?

He rippled with disgust. The questions were ridiculous.

Charles had never spent a single minute worrying about John, and
at this late date, it was absurd to consider Charles as some sort of
savior. He'd never been of any use or value to John, and it was silly to
permit a flicker of hope to flare.

John had always known he'd meet a bad end. It had finally
arrived, and he felt half-dead already, as if he had one foot in the
grave. Very soon, it would be over. Who would miss him?

Raven. And Sarah. They'd both grieve for a bit, then they'd move
on.

Yet as Charles reached the door, he said, "Charles…"

His father turned. "What?"

"Let me give you something."

John went to his desk and retrieved the deed to Bramble Bay. He'd planned to have Reggie take it to her, but Charles could deliver it. Though John hadn't deemed himself anxious for his father's good opinion, apparently he was. The gesture might make John seem less of a cad in Charles's eyes.

He hurried over and handed the document to Charles.

"What's this?" Charles asked.

"It's the deed to Bramble Bay. I've signed it over to Miss Teasdale, and I dated it months ago—long before my arrest—so the Crown can't seize it after I'm hanged."

"You're being very shrewd, very wise."

The Crown would confiscate any of his possessions they could locate. Reggie had hidden most of them, and in John's will, what could be salvaged was bequeathed to Raven. But Sarah could have Bramble Bay. She'd be safe there, and her status as a property owner would ensure she'd find a decent husband.

"Tell her..." John had to swallow twice so he could continue. "Tell her to marry well. To be happy."

Charles sighed. "When you attacked Tristan Harcourt, there was a woman on the ship with him."

John's cheeks flushed with shame. He vividly recalled the pretty blond. She'd been so devoted to Harcourt, so fiercely protective. John had envied Harcourt for having such a loyal doxy.

"I remember her."

"Her name is Harriet."

"I heard they survived, that they wed when they got home."

"They did." Charles studied John. "Were you aware that she's your sister?"

John scowled. "She's what?"

"You were so eager to kill your brother, but you almost killed your sister, too."

John shook his head. "You're lying. You have to be."

"I'm not. They're my daughters—she and her twin sister, Helen—along with your sister, Fanny. Is this the legacy you'll leave to them? Is this the memory they'll have of you? That you tried to murder Harriet and you don't even care? That you'll let the King execute you without a whimper of protest? Have you ever considered your sisters and how they might feel about it?"

Charles whipped away and left.

John stood, paralyzed with guilt and remorse, listening as his father's footsteps faded down the hall.

At the last second, John raced over and called, "Charles?"

"What?" his father said again.

"I had no idea. Tell her I'm sorry."

"You can tell her yourself—if you decide you're man enough to fight for your life. Why Miss Teasdale has such faith in you, I'll never know."

Then he disappeared through the barred gate, a guard slammed it shut, and John staggered into his cell and collapsed down on his bed.

CHAPTER NINETEEN

Raven huddled in the dark, watching for Reggie Thompson to emerge from a nearby tavern. There was only a sliver of moon, and no lamp lit on the corner pole, which suited Raven's purposes.

Reggie liked to sit in clean, tidy offices, pouring over ledgers and adding long columns of numbers. He didn't like to get his hands or clothes dirty. But Annalise's treachery had guaranteed they had to carry out duties that weren't normally expected.

Finally, Reggie staggered out, pretending drunkenness in case any of the patrons inside saw him leave. As the door swung shut, he straightened and hurried away.

He passed the spot where Raven lurked like a specter, but didn't glance in his direction.

"He's had her declared a lunatic," Reggie whispered. "He's had her locked away in Bedlam Hospital."

He kept on down the block to their carriage.

Raven listened as Reggie climbed in. Then the narrow street was quiet again.

Another hour dragged by before Archibald Patterson stumbled out of the bar, but Raven hadn't minded the wait. The interval had given him plenty of opportunity for his fury to boil. Not that he'd needed to become any angrier, but an excess of temper focused him.

Patterson swayed to and fro, then unbuttoned his trousers and took a piss on the wall of the building. He shook his cock, shoved it in his pants, and fastened them again.

Once finished, he tottered away, humming an off-key sailor's jig. He walked by Raven without noticing him, and Raven slid from his hiding spot, moving like a ghost, like the Angel of Death.

The past few weeks had been a nightmare of disasters—all caused by Annalise—and there were several loose ends that had to be tied. Starting with Archie Patterson.

Raven had many irons in the fire as he plotted various vengeance for various people. First and foremost, he'd rushed to retrieve Caroline from her brutal husband, only to learn from his servants that the man had never brought her home from Bramble Bay. No one knew where she was, and a terrified housemaid had nervously confided that she was afraid Patterson might have murdered Caroline.

Patterson had been strutting around town, going to work, going to supper, acting as if he'd never had a wife. Raven had finally followed Patterson to his favorite tavern, had sent Reggie in to feign friendship and ply Patterson with liquor until he babbled secrets he hadn't meant to reveal.

The bastard had locked her in an asylum! And not just any asylum, but the most foul, dangerous, squalid one in the land. There were occasions in Raven's life where he regretted his penchant for violence, but this was not one of them.

Patterson approached the entrance to an alley, and Raven swooped in, grabbed him by the waist, and whisked him into the shadows. In a flit of a second, he and Patterson were alone.

"What the hell…?" Patterson drunkenly mumbled.

Raven threw him against a wall. He banged his head very hard and would have collapsed to the ground, but Raven clutched his coat and kept him on his feet.

"If you're hoping to rob me," Patterson muttered, "you're out of luck. I emptied my purse in the tavern."

Raven drew a knife from his boot. The blade was long and sharp, and moonlight reflected off it. Patterson's eyes widened with terror as Raven dug the tip into the soft skin below his chin.

"Where's your wife, Archie?" Raven hissed.

"My wife?"

"Take a look at my face. I realize it's a tad dark in here, but take a good look. Do you remember me?"

Patterson opened his mouth to shout for help, and Raven jammed an elbow into his cheek, breaking the bone. Patterson winced in agony and might have fainted, but Raven slapped him so he'd remain conscious.

"It's pointless to call for help, Archie," Raven whispered. "You can't be rescued from me. Now tell me where you've put your wife."

Patterson smirked. "I have no idea where she is. She ran off months ago."

"Let's review what I told you that day at Bramble Bay."

"Fornicator. Adulterer." The words were slurred, blood gushing from his nose and dripping onto his shirt.

"Those are some of my best traits. Would you try to focus, Archie? You must recollect what I told you. I warned you that if I ever saw you again, I'd kill you. Did you think I wasn't serious?"

"I'm not afraid of you," Patterson blustered. "I'll complain to the authorities that you seduced my wife, then threatened me. A man has rights."

"Yes, he does," Raven amiably agreed, "and *my* right is to protect the woman I love. I know where she is, Archie."

Patterson frowned. "You couldn't possibly."

"Caroline always insisted you drank too much. I guess she was correct." Raven dug the knife in further, deep enough to make Patterson squirm and moan. "Tell me what's become of her. If I hear it from your own stupid lips, I'll let you live."

"Bedlam Hospital," he blurted out. "The whore is in Bedlam, and I'll never free her. She'll die there."

"Didn't you know, Archie? With a big bribe, a fellow can purchase any conclusion, and I'm very, very rich."

Raven moved the knife from Archie's chin, and Archie relaxed, foolishly believing the attack was over. Before he had time to grasp that it wasn't, Raven plunged the blade into his stomach, twisted it, and gutted him like a fish.

Patterson lurched as if he might protest, but it was too late.

"Sorry, Archie, but I'm a renowned liar. I never intended to let you live."

Raven released him, and he fell to the muck on the cobbles, a fitting end for the despicable swine. Raven tarried a minute, then a minute more, until Patterson's heart stopped beating.

He reached into Patterson's coat, sliced through the chain on his purse, and pulled it out. Patterson had claimed he'd spent all his money in the tavern, but some coins clinked together.

During the assault, Raven had noted a street urchin hiding farther down the alley. He tossed the wallet in the boy's direction.

"The nob said he spent his last farthing on liquor," Raven murmured, "but he hasn't. You can have what's left."

The boy scampered out to retrieve the purse, then vanished again. Raven almost reminded him to get rid of it, to pitch it in the Thames where it would never be found, but Raven didn't suppose the lad needed a warning.

Raven, himself, had been an orphan on the streets. A child like that didn't require instructions on how to survive.

He whipped away and calmly proceeded to the carriage parked down the block.

"Take us to Bedlam Hospital," he told the driver.

The man blanched. "This time of night? Are you sure?"

"I have business there that can't wait until morning."

Reggie poked his nose out the window and asked as the driver just had, "Bedlam? Now? It's almost midnight."

"I'm not leaving her there another second. Don't expect me to."

Caroline was lying on a cold floor in a line of twenty other women. They were sleeping, but she wasn't. Since the day she'd first arrived, she hadn't been able to rest.

She was consumed by the worst feelings of dread and shame.

Shame—because she could never have envisioned her life descending to such a low precipice. Dread—because the facility was filthy and dangerous. If she closed her eyes, she was afraid she wouldn't be alive at dawn to open them again.

The woman next to her had a blanket, and she was kind enough to share it with Caroline. On two previous occasions, the woman's husband had committed her, so she'd learned to bring the items she needed.

From the moment Caroline had staggered in, the woman had pitied her, had watched over her and taught her the ropes.

A few of the patients were actually mad, but mostly, they were females like Caroline: a trial to their parents or their husbands, so they'd been locked away.

When Archie had kidnapped her from Bramble Bay, her wrists and ankles bound like a hog being carted to market, she hadn't imagined she'd make it to London. He'd been so angry, she'd thought he would kill her and dump her body in the forest.

But no. He'd driven her straight to town, and she'd been hideously surprised when he'd delivered her to the infamous asylum. The dire event was infuriating, both because she'd been deemed a lunatic, but also because she couldn't escape. Her cordial companion, who'd passed several years in the place, insisted it was impossible, and Caroline suspected she was correct.

As she'd been dragged inside, Archie hissed in her ear that she'd never be released, that she'd die in the putrid spot. It was the ultimate punishment. If he'd taken her home, she could have eventually fled, but he'd guaranteed that he would always know her whereabouts—for the remainder of his days.

Footsteps sounded in the hall, growing nearer and nearer. A guard was approaching, and Caroline shut her eyes and feigned sleep. The guards were all male, and they often sauntered in and left with various patients.

Usually, the women returned beaten or injured in more nefarious ways. Other times, they didn't come back, and there were many rumors: that they were sold to brothels, that they were strangled to death and buried in anonymous graves.

No one ever assumed the women went away to happy endings.

Upon being admitted, they'd cut Caroline's hair very short, and Archie had given her no change of clothes. So she was grimy and grubby, which was good. It was easy to hide her pretty looks, easy to blend in and be invisible.

She was positioned in the very middle of the group. If anyone was removed, it would be a person at the end of the row. Yet to her dismay, the guard strolled down the line, scowling at faces but having difficulty seeing in the dim light.

"Caroline Patterson?" he finally said, and her pulse raced with alarm.

They never called a specific name. They simply grabbed whoever was closest and walked off with her. How had he noticed her? What had she done to stand out?

His voice—masculine and low—in the women's quarters roused everyone. People shifted about, peeking up from blankets.

"Mrs. Patterson?" he said again, and he stopped beside her.

He waited and waited, his impatience clear, and she answered, "Yes?"

"Come with me."

He leaned down and clasped her arm, but she yanked away.

"Why?"

"Don't argue. Just come."

"Not until you tell me what's happening."

Her friend sat up and told the guard, "I'll go with you. You don't need to take her. I'll do it."

Caroline frowned. "Absolutely not."

"Sorry, ma'am, but it has to be Mrs. Patterson."

Women were glaring, but even though there was one of him and twenty of them, none of them would confront him. They wouldn't risk trouble for her.

She glowered at him, determined to save herself, but how?

A wave of fury swamped her. Why was the world so unfair? Fleetingly, she wondered about her dear Raven Hook, but in her current situation, he didn't seem like he'd ever actually existed.

What had he thought when he'd returned to Bramble Bay and she was gone? Had he figured out what occurred? Was he searching for her? Or had she simply vanished, with there not being the slightest clue as to Mildred's perfidy?

She remembered the slip of paper she'd put in his coat, the one with Archie's address printed on it. If Raven found the paper and went to Archie's house, it would be a fruitless trip. She'd disappeared as quickly and completely as if she'd died. The only thing missing was the gravestone and epitaph.

"I haven't got all night," the guard snapped.

He latched on more tightly. He was fat and strong, and with ease, he lifted her to her feet.

They marched out, twenty pairs of stunned eyes watching them depart. She wanted to hear them shouting with offense, demanding he halt, but sadly, the room was quiet.

The hospital was huge, and they walked and walked. Every time they passed a door, she braced, certain he was about to drag her in and commit unspeakable acts without fear of reprisal, yet they kept on.

With each step, she was more reluctant, more frantic. She struggled with him, desperate to pull away, to run back to the other women, but they'd turned so many corners, she wasn't positive she could find the route.

Eventually, they exited out the rear of the building and approached a gate. There were two men on the other side, obviously waiting for her. Was she to be sold to a brothel? Was the rumor true?

Bile rose in her throat, and she began to fight in earnest.

"No, I won't do it," she vehemently said. "You can't make me." She swung a fist at him, but she was off balance and couldn't land a solid blow.

"Hold on, hold on!" the guard griped.

"Caroline..."

Her name whispered by, and at first, she didn't realize it had been spoken. She continued to fight as the guard drew her over to the two men.

"Caroline!" The summons was louder, more firm.

She slowed and peered into the dark, anxious to see who had arrived. It wasn't Archie. So who, then?

"It's me, Caroline," a familiar voice said.

"Raven?" she tentatively murmured.

"Yes, and please hurry. We need to be away."

She assumed she was hallucinating, that her incarceration had left her as mad as the real lunatics in the place. But he seemed to be standing there. Another man—shorter, well-dressed—was there, too. He appeared to be a clerk or accountant.

The guard fumbled with a ring of keys, then unlocked the gate and opened it just a crack. He shoved Caroline toward Raven, and Raven caught her. She could feel him and smell him, so he wasn't a figment of her imagination.

He smoothed a palm across her shorn head. "They cut off your beautiful hair."

"It will grow back."

"Yes, it will." He dropped to a knee and clasped her hand. "Can you forgive me?"

"Forgive...you?" she stammered. "For what?"

"I didn't protect you. I swore I would, but I didn't."

"Of course I forgive you."

She tugged him to his feet, and he stood, towering over her. Instantly, she felt safe again.

"You came for me." She was so amazed. "How did you know where I was?"

"We asked your husband. It only took a bit of coaxing to pry some answers out of him."

The clerk motioned to the guard and gave him a small cloth bag. The contents clinked, and Caroline could tell it was a bribe being tendered.

"Payment in full," the clerk informed the guard.

"I have to count it," the guard mulishly said.

"You doubt the word of the Raven?" the clerk huffed. "How dare you, sir!"

The guard stared at Raven, noting his large size, black clothes, and fierce expression. "Ah...I'm sure it's all here." He carefully closed the gate so it didn't clang. "I'd appreciate it if you could be on your way. The sooner the better."

"We're happy to go," the clerk pompously advised.

He turned and proceeded to a parked carriage. Raven gestured for Caroline to walk to it too, but she was frozen with shock. It had all happened so fast. It was bizarre, like a peculiar dream where she was floating above it all and observing the characters down below.

"It will be all right now," Raven gently urged. "It will always be all right."

"What about Archie? What if he finds out? What if he comes after me?"

"You don't have to worry about Archie ever again. He will *never* come after you."

Raven flashed a look of such calm certainty that, when he gestured to the carriage again, she stumbled over and climbed inside.

CHAPTER TWENTY

"Are you sure about this?"

"Absolutely."

"Would you like me to come in with you?"

Sarah stared at Raven across the carriage seat. It was a cool, blustery day, giving stark indication that summer was over and autumn had arrived. She tamped down a shiver and pulled on her cloak.

In the past few months, so many things had happened, and she'd changed in so many ways. Raven could have saved his own skin, could have sneaked away to France where he'd have been out of danger, but he'd stayed with Sarah at Bramble Bay.

He'd rescued Caroline and brought her home. When they'd learned a short time later that Archie had been slain in an apparent robbery, Raven hadn't seemed surprised in the least.

His only comment had been, *Good. He won't be around to pester us anymore.*

Sarah hadn't questioned him on his lack of concern and hadn't inquired as to whether he'd been involved in Archie's demise. She wasn't sorry that Archie was dead, and however he'd met his end, whoever had orchestrated it, she didn't mourn him.

Caroline was safe, Bramble Bay belonged to Sarah, Hedley was living in town with Miss Dubois, and Mildred had slithered over to Sheldon's and hadn't left.

Sheldon often stopped by to mention that Mildred was ready to return to Bramble Bay, but Sarah ignored his suggestions. Sheldon could deal with Mildred—with Sarah's blessing.

All of her energy was devoted to saving Jean Pierre from the hangman's noose. She didn't have time to fuss over her family or any other issue. She would *not* let him be executed.

She would engage in any ruse to get him released from prison. Barring release, she was determined that he spend his life incarcerated or perhaps be transported to the penal colonies in Australia. If he was transported, he'd have an opportunity to escape, to come back to her.

Through it all, Raven had been her stern ally and staunch friend. If he hadn't been standing by her side, holding her up during the tumult, she didn't know how she'd have weathered her many ordeals.

The trial was approaching, authorities chomping at the bit to apply a harsh dose of British justice. She was growing more and more frantic, her current visit proof that she was as crazed as some of the lunatics Caroline had encountered at Bedlam.

"Were you with Jean Pierre when he boarded Mr. Harcourt's ship?"

"Ah…yes, I was."

"Did you help Jean Pierre try to murder Mr. Harcourt?"

"I believe I might have been the one who lugged Harcourt down the ladder and dumped him into the longboat."

"You *believe* you were? Have you killed so many people that you don't remember?"

"Oh, all right," he groused. "I tossed him in the boat myself."

"Then *no*, you can't come in with me."

"Are you sure?"

"They're not cannibals, Raven. They won't eat me for dinner."

"You can't predict how these rich doffs might behave. I wouldn't want them to upset you more than you already are."

"I'll be fine."

She patted his hand as the driver opened the door and lowered the step. She climbed out.

"I'll be waiting out here," Raven told her.

"That will bolster my confidence, knowing you're close by."

"If they're rude, you leave at once. Don't sit in there and be insulted."

"To save Jean Pierre's life, I can endure a few insults."

He flashed a sad smile. "But only a few."

"Only a few. I promise."

Sarah went to the stoop and gazed up at the imposing house. It was red brick, with black shutters and green flower boxes, the last flowers of the season dried and wilted.

It was an impressive residence, but not a grand mansion by any means. But then, Tristan Harcourt wasn't an aristocrat. He was an earl's brother and ship captain with his own shipping company which, two years earlier, had proved disastrous.

He'd been out on the high seas when his angry, vindictive brother—The French Terror—had attacked. Tristan and Harriet Harcourt were lucky to have survived.

Sarah banged the knocker, and a liveried footman answered. She gave him her card.

"I'd like to call on Mrs. Harcourt. We're not acquainted, but please tell her that her father sent me."

The man took her cloak and bonnet, then showed her into a pretty parlor off the foyer. She sat, tamping down her nerves, studying the furnishings, the paintings on the walls. She and Raven had vehemently debated the visit, thinking it would be impossible to speak with Tristan Harcourt. But his wife…Harriet…

What might her opinion be of Sarah's bald appeal?

Soon, footsteps echoed in the hall, and Harriet Sinclair Harcourt swept in. She was a bit younger than Sarah, slender and vibrant and very fetching, with the typical Sinclair blond hair and green eyes.

She and her twin sister Helen were two of Charles's lost daughters, found by their brother, Phillip, when they were twenty-one and in very dire straits. True love had blossomed when they'd married the Harcourt brothers, James and Tristan.

Sarah didn't understand Fate, but the Harcourts were Florence's sons whom she'd abandoned when she'd fled to Paris. In France, Florence and Charles had collided like a bad carriage accident, and decades later, their children were wed.

What were the odds?

There seemed to be a destiny at work for all of them, but Sarah wouldn't try to figure it out. Her sole concern was Jean Pierre.

"Miss Teasdale," Mrs. Harcourt said, "may I help you? My footman advises that my father asked you to come."

"Yes." Sarah pushed herself to her feet.

"I have to say that I'm surprised. He's never sent me a visitor. I was so curious; I hurried down to see you."

Sarah was gaping like a halfwit, and she murmured, "God, you look so much like him."

"Who? My father Charles? Yes, I hear that a lot."

"No…ah…I was referring to someone else. Forgive me for staring."

"Shall we sit?"

Mrs. Harcourt indicated the sofa, and Sarah eased back down as Mrs. Harcourt settled in the chair across. They waited silently while servants brought refreshments. As they left, Mrs. Harcourt poured the tea.

"Your name is familiar to me," she told Sarah, "but I don't recognize you. Why do I feel as if I should know you from somewhere?"

"Your father may have mentioned me."

"In what capacity?"

Sarah assessed her. Lord Trent claimed Harriet was funny and trusting and would listen to Sarah. He couldn't guarantee she would assist, but she would at least listen.

"I fell in love over the summer," Sarah admitted.

It was a strange way to begin, and Mrs. Harcourt carefully replied, "Well…how wonderful for you."

"He was the last man I would have chosen for myself, but he was very dashing, very intriguing. I'd never met anyone like him, and I couldn't resist."

"He sounds like my husband. When I met Tristan, I thought the very same."

"He won me in a card game."

Mrs. Harcourt considered for a moment, then gasped. "It wasn't Charles, was it? You're not in love with my father?" She groaned with dismay. "You can't be. He has the worst reputation. You're aware that he's married, aren't you?"

"No, no, it's not Lord Trent. I'm sorry. I didn't explain myself very clearly."

"Who is it, then?"

"It's Jean Pierre."

"Oh." Mrs. Harcourt took a deep breath, let it out.

She didn't run screaming from the room, didn't demand Sarah's immediate departure. She simply held very still, her mind working furiously as she tried to devise the appropriate response.

Suddenly, she leapt up and announced, "I think this discussion requires a libation stronger than tea."

She marched to the sideboard, poured two glasses of liquor, and handed one to Sarah. Sarah hadn't ever been much of a drinker, but after living with Jean Pierre, she'd acquired new tastes, new habits. As Mrs. Harcourt sat again, Sarah enjoyed a sip, the warm brandy sliding down easily. It instantly calmed her, instantly halted the shaking of her fingers.

"You should probably call me Harriet," Mrs. Harcourt said.

"I would be honored. And you must call me Sarah."

"I will. So...you're here on Jean Pierre's behalf?"

"No, he doesn't know. He won't allow me to visit him in prison, so I haven't had a chance to talk to him since the arrest."

"Why are you here? What are you hoping to achieve?"

"He's prepared to hang. He won't fight what's occurring."

"Why not?"

"He always expected he'd meet a bad end, so he feels this is his destiny."

"That's an extremely grim outlook."

"Yes, it is, and I can't bear it that he's willing to meekly submit to his own execution. I have to try to save him—especially since he won't save himself."

"Are you certain you should bother? There's an enormous amount of evidence against him. You're definitely waging an uphill battle."

"May I be frank?"

"Of course."

"The evidence is being provided by a former...well...mistress of Jean Pierre's." Sarah blushed bright red. "I apologize for mentioning such a scandalous person."

"I told you to be frank. I can hardly complain when you are."

"This woman is a very jealous individual. Jean Pierre set her aside for me, and she's determined to hurt him because of it."

"She seems to be succeeding. I read about her every time my husband brings home a newspaper."

"But she's very low-born, very disreputable. If I could find some other people—some respectable people—to speak on his behalf, I could counter her allegations."

"Counter them how?"

"Your father has already agreed to help him. He's decided to publically acknowledge Jean Pierre so the world will grasp that he's an aristocrat's son."

"Really? Charles would do that? How did you convince him?"

"It was his own idea. He feels it will make it much more difficult for the Crown to kill Jean Pierre."

Harriet nodded. "I guess he would know."

"And he'll give Jean Pierre an alibi. If Miss Dubois furnishes specific dates as to Jean Pierre's pirating, Lord Trent will testify that Jean Pierre was with him and couldn't have committed any crimes."

"My goodness!" Harriet exclaimed. "I'm sorry, but I just can't picture my father going to such lengths for one of his children." It was Harriet's turn to blush. "I shouldn't have said that."

"It's all right. Once I leave, I'll never reveal what we discussed."

"Thank you. My relationship with Charles is a tad…peculiar."

"I realize that it is."

"I was sixteen when I first learned of him, and I didn't meet him until I was twenty-one. I'm illegitimate and notorious, and what with Tristan and all that transpired, it's so…so…"

Her voice trailed off, and she sipped her brandy and composed herself. The only sound was the ticking of the clock on the mantle. Out in the hall, a maid whisked by, then it was quiet again.

Finally, Harriet said, "You'd like me to do something for Jean Pierre. What is it?"

"I won't deny that he was very cruel to you and your husband."

Harriet flashed a wry smile. "That would be putting it mildly, but then, everything happens for a reason, doesn't it? If Jean Pierre hadn't attacked us, if we hadn't spent months together on that deserted island, we would never have fallen in love."

"Probably not." Sarah smiled, too. "There are a hundred different descriptions of The French Terror, and you're one of the few people who can actually identify him."

"Yes, I can definitely identify him. His face is locked in my memory, but he looks so much like us, too. He's unforgettable to me."

Sarah braced herself, feeling as if she was balanced on a high cliff, as if she was about to jump off.

"I'm asking you to come to the trial as a witness. I'm asking you to tell everyone that you vividly remember The French Terror, and it's not Jean Pierre." Sarah paused, then grimly added, "I'm asking you to lie and save your brother's life."

For a lengthy interval, Harriet was silent. Then she walked to the sideboard and poured herself another brandy. She sipped it and miserably pondered.

"Could you do it, Harriet?" Sarah ultimately inquired.

"I don't know."

"He's not the man you think he is. He's not the man you saw that night out on the ocean."

"I disagree. I think he is *precisely* that man. If I worked to free him, and he continued rampaging, if he hurt others as he hurt Tristan, I'd be partially responsible."

"He had the worst childhood, and he's overcome so many obstacles. After your father left Paris, after he abandoned Florence Harcourt, she and Jean Pierre were so desperately poor. She died when he was ten."

"I'd heard that."

"He was an orphan on the streets, trying to survive. If you could meet him, if you could talk to him and learn what he's really like."

Harriet shook her head. "I can't listen to this right now."

"I understand." Sarah realized she was about at the end of the appointment, and she hurried on. "If I can get him released, he'll marry me, and we'll retire to his home in France. He'll never harm another person. I swear it to you."

"*You* swear. What about him?"

"I swear for him, too. He loves me. In this, he'll do as I ask." Sarah rose, went over to Harriet, and dropped to her knees. "I beg you to help my beloved Jean Pierre. Please? Will you?"

Lord Trent had told Sarah that Harriet valued family above all else, that she'd found her siblings later in life, and they meant the world to her. Could she feel the same about Jean Pierre? Could she forgive him? Could she aid him?

Harriet clasped Sarah's hands and drew her up.

"You're asking so much of me," Harriet said.

"But you'll think about it?"

"Yes, but I'll have to speak with my husband."

"Will you let me know what you decide?"

"I will."

"Thank you."

Harriet escorted her to the foyer where a footman held out her bonnet and cloak. Sarah put them on, then walked to the door.

"Goodbye," she said.

"Goodbye."

"I hope we meet again someday—under better circumstances."

"I hope so, too."

Sarah whirled away, rushed to the carriage, and climbed in

without glancing back.

"How did it go?" Raven inquired as she settled on the seat.

"She was very polite."

"Were you allowed to present your case?"

"As best I could. She'll consider my request, but she has to talk to her husband."

"Oh."

"Yes, oh."

"So perhaps it was a wasted trip."

"Let's envision a positive result."

Raven barked out a despairing laugh. "I will be a veritable fount of optimism. Just for you, Sarah."

"No, for Jean Pierre."

"Yes. For Jean Pierre."

Raven tapped on the roof to signal the driver. The man clicked the reins, and they rumbled away.

"I had a visitor today."

"You always have visitors, Harriet. You're the most fascinating woman in London. Everyone wants to be your friend."

"Very funny." Harriet glowered at Helen.

Fanny piped in with, "They're all waiting for you to slip up and reveal a new salacious detail that hasn't been previously disclosed."

"I'll never confess *all* that happened," Harriet haughtily declared. "I'm respectably married now. There are many things the citizens of London don't need to know about me."

"Especially how you look without your clothes!"

Helen and Fanny whooped with glee, and Harriet rolled her eyes. They were in the parlor at Fanny's town house. They'd finished supper, and their husbands were still in the dining room, having a brandy, so Harriet couldn't prevent her sisters' teasing.

After Jean Pierre had set Harriet and Tristan adrift on the ocean, they'd washed up on a deserted island. They'd lived off the land, like prehistoric natives, like Adam and Eve in the Garden of Eden.

Tristan was an earl's brother, so a huge search had been launched, and when he was located, tales quickly spread about the mysterious maiden who'd been trapped on the island with him. The rumors had been vulgar and obscene.

Man. Woman. Tropical island. Months spent alone, frolicking in the warm waves. The story had catered to every male's most wicked fantasies, and the gossip that circulated about her was lurid and disgusting.

Harriet would never live it down.

"Would you two be serious?" Harriet griped. "I have to tell you something important. I need your advice."

"About what?" Fanny asked once they stopped chortling.

"About my visitor. Charles sent her."

The mention of their father was always riveting. Phillip was the only one who had a meaningful connection with Charles. Fanny, Helen, and Harriet were still learning their way with him.

He was not easy to know or like, and because of his immoral character and disregard for their mothers, they had suffered enormously. Yet they were trying to create a family, and Charles was front and center.

"Charles sent you a visitor?" Helen inquired. "How very odd."

"Yes—a Miss Sarah Teasdale."

Fanny frowned. "Where have I heard that name?"

Helen answered for Harriet. "Didn't Phillip travel to their home over the summer? Didn't they lose their estate to Jean Pierre?"

"Yes," Harriet said, "and Miss Teasdale is in love with him."

"Oh, no," Helen groaned. "What did she want?"

"She wants me to save his life."

Helen gasped as Fanny murmured, "Well, that's certainly a fine burden to dump on you."

"Save his life...how?" Helen said.

"I'm one of the few people in the world who can accurately identify him."

"*Can* you identify him?"

"Absolutely. He looks just like Tristan, but like all of us, too."

Fanny scowled. "How does Miss Teasdale think *you* could save him? He's incarcerated under maximum guard, and he'll hang immediately after he's convicted. The scaffold is already built."

"She begged me to lie at his trial and swear he's not the man who attacked us."

There was a shocked silence. Then Helen asked, "What did you tell her?"

"I can't decide. I had to hear your thoughts before I talk to Tristan. I don't have to speculate as to what his opinion will be."

"To let Jean Pierre die?"

"Yes," Harriet said, "but it seems so wrong. He's our brother."

"Our dangerous, violent, murdering brother," Fanny countered.

"He had a hard life, Fanny."

"We all did."

"You grew up in a vicarage, with kindly, adoptive parents. Helen and I grew up at a boarding school. *He* grew up an orphan on the streets of Paris. Our histories aren't comparable."

"No, I suppose they're not."

"What would have become of the three of us if Phillip hadn't found us? I, for one, would probably have wound up a felon myself and transported to Australia."

Before she'd met Tristan, Harriet had nearly been ravished by her employer. She'd bashed him over the head with a frying pan and, for a long while, had believed she'd killed him. The evil man would have been happy to have her prosecuted and jailed, but Tristan had rescued her.

"So what are you saying, Harriet?" Fanny asked. "You'd like to help Jean Pierre?"

"No, I'm saying I feel sorry for him. What should I do about it?"

Helen and Fanny stared at each other, then Fanny said, "I couldn't let him perish."

But Helen warned, "What if he was released and started another crime spree after he was freed? Any blood he spilled would be on your hands."

"I worried about that," Harriet replied, "but Miss Teasdale claims she could make him stop."

"She assumes she could *change* him?" Fanny asked.

"Yes."

"That's boastfully naïve of her."

"And very humorous," Helen added. "We're closely acquainted with a few Harcourt and Sinclair males. It's not possible to change them."

"Don't forget," Fanny said, "that Jean Pierre is related to both families, so he's doubly cursed with stubbornness. Miss Teasdale is doomed to fail."

"Should I refuse her?" Harriet tentatively inquired.

"Not necessarily. You should consider this carefully. If you don't aid him, and he's hanged, you'll be second-guessing for the rest of your days."

"I couldn't bear it."

"You'd drive yourself mad."

The dining room door opened, and the men joined them. Fanny and her husband Michael went upstairs to check on their children.

James and Tristan settled in, and Tristan noted the tension in the air.

"You two look as if you're fighting. Are you?"

"No."

"They're too much alike," James pointed out. "They can read each other's minds, so they don't have to quarrel."

"If you're not fighting," Tristan said, "why are you scowling?"

"I have to ask you something," Harriet told him.

"When you hear what it is"—Helen glared at both brothers—"there's to be no shouting."

"I never shout," James huffed.

"Neither do I," Tristan insisted.

Helen and Harriet shared a knowing look. The brothers were excitable and volatile. A discussion of Jean Pierre was definitely a topic that would encourage tempers to flare.

Tristan teased, "Tell me what has you glowering like a pair of fussy Puritans."

"If James was dying," Harriet cautiously started, "and you could commit a shady and immoral act to save his life, would you?"

"Of course," Tristan responded.

"You wouldn't hesitate?"

"Not for a moment."

"How about you, James?" Harriet pressed.

"You saw my reaction when Tristan was missing after the pirate attack. I spent every penny I had to mount a search."

"If I could do the same for my brother," Harriet said, "if he was dying and I could save him, should I?"

"If Phillip was dying?" Tristan frowned, not understanding.

"No, if Jean Pierre was dying," Harriet quietly stated.

Suddenly, the brothers looked as if they were eager to punch someone, and Tristan vehemently snapped, "Absolutely not."

"The man is a murdering thug," James agreed. "No, you shouldn't help him."

"But if I could save his life, James!"

"He nearly killed Tristan!" James hotly retorted.

"I know that. I was there, remember?"

"How could you even consider it?"

"I was just wondering."

"Who spoke to you about this?" Tristan inquired. "Why is this vexing you?"

"Miss Sarah Teasdale visited me today. I guess she's Jean Pierre's fiancée. Charles sent her. He doesn't want Jean Pierre to hang, and he's going to publicly claim him and give him an alibi."

"The wretch!" James muttered. "Is there any despicable behavior your father won't attempt?"

Charles was a difficult subject for the Harcourts. Their bitter, drunken father had always told them that Charles seduced their mother, then convinced her to flee to Paris with him. But it wasn't the truth.

Charles had already been in Paris when Florence arrived, and he hadn't known her in London. Their affair had commenced months after Florence left her husband, but James and Tristan had trouble being civil to Charles. They tried, but such intense animosity was hard to put aside.

"James, please," Helen scolded. "Let's not argue about Charles. Let's focus on Harriet's problem."

"Harriet's problem? What problem? This is none of her business. Jean Pierre's doxy can provide the testimony needed to convict him, so we have no reason to be involved." He paused, then pompously announced, "We *shouldn't* be involved."

"He's your brother, too," Harriet insisted.

"No, he's not," James said.

"He is, James."

"He almost killed me, Harriet," Tristan complained. "He deliberately chased me down so he could murder me. He stabbed me! The sword went through my body. You watched it happen."

"I haven't forgotten," Harriet mumbled.

"What are you actually asking, Harriet?" James said.

"What if I testified on Jean Pierre's behalf?"

"To say what?" Tristan fumed.

"To say he's not the man who attacked us. My word would hold more sway than that of his mistress. I could save his life."

"Is it worth saving?" James asked.

"I don't know."

"This is a disgraceful mess, Harriet," Tristan said, "and I don't want you in the middle of it."

"I'm already in the middle."

"Well, you don't have to step in any farther."

Fanny and Michael returned, and as they seated themselves on a sofa, Michael glanced around. On seeing their dour expressions, he said, "Are you quarreling?"

"No," everyone replied even though they were.

Fanny asked Harriet, "Did you tell them?"

"Tell them what?" Michael asked.

Fanny answered him. "Charles is hatching a plot to save Jean Pierre, and he's hoping Harriet will help him."

"Help him how?"

"She'd attend the trial and say that Jean Pierre is not The French Terror."

Michael's brows rose. "What have you decided, Harriet?"

"I *haven't* decided."

She felt young and lost and wished she hadn't mentioned the painful topic. She'd never been particularly smart—she was more prone to rash conduct and wild outbursts—and she'd need the wisdom of Solomon to stumble on a solution.

No matter what she chose to do, it would be wrong and would hurt others. It would take tremendous courage to testify for Jean Pierre, and she'd never viewed herself as a brave person. She'd never viewed herself as being especially clever.

She looked over at Tristan and James and told them, "I keep thinking about your mother."

"What about her?" James churlishly said.

"I've always heard that she loved Charles and cherished Jean Pierre as no mother ever could. If she's watching us from Heaven, what would her opinion be if we could save him, but we don't try?"

"Don't drag my poor mother into it," James seethed, and Tristan added, "She's not the villain in this depressing story."

"Then who is?" Harriet asked. "When Jean Pierre is related to all of us, how can there be a villain?"

"Jean Pierre is the villain, Harriet," Tristan said. "He could have walked any path, but he picked the worst one of all."

Harriet didn't imagine Jean Pierre had *picked* his life. She remembered being on the run herself, hiding from authorities, having nowhere to turn. She'd have done anything to be safe, to survive. She hadn't chosen what had occurred. Circumstances had pitched her down a dangerous road, and she'd simply headed in the direction she'd been tossed.

Granted, she hadn't murdered anyone, but she'd fought violently when she'd been attacked. How could she condemn Jean Pierre for behaving as she'd behaved?

She must have looked woeful, because Tristan pulled her onto his lap.

"Don't fret over him, Harriet."

"I can't help it."

"His fate was sealed long ago, the day he committed his first crime."

"Jean Pierre says the very same. He feels it's his destiny to die this way, so he won't dispute the charges."

"He's correct and much smarter than I gave him credit for being. A man can't engage in a life of crime but expect there will be no consequences."

"I hate to think of him being alone in this. I have all of you, and he has no one."

"He's not a pet stray that you can rescue."

Harriet disagreed. She thought he absolutely could be rescued, and she was being offered the chance to do it.

If she didn't, she'd disappoint her father, the prospect of which was extremely distressing. And despite James's and Tristan's protestations to the contrary, Harriet was positive their mother was gazing down from Heaven, waiting to see how they would act. Yet Harriet couldn't bear to upset her dear husband and brother-in-law.

Finally, she smiled, but it was a sad, resigned smile.

"I'm sure you're right," she told Tristan. "It would be a waste of time. If I assisted him, he probably wouldn't even be grateful."

But even as she voiced the words, they weighed so heavily, and she wondered how she'd ever manage with such a difficult burden balanced on her slender shoulders.

CHAPTER TWENTY-ONE

"I didn't know if you'd come."

"Me? Not come? Are you mad?"

John walked over to his cell door and clasped Raven's hand. For the past week, he'd spoken to no one, but as the trial date approached, as his execution loomed, he'd yearned for a friendly face.

While John had many half-siblings, Raven had always been his true brother. No man had ever loved another as John loved Raven. No man had ever owed more to another.

"I shouldn't have asked you to visit."

"Of course you should have."

"It's dangerous for you to be here."

Raven scoffed. "No more dangerous than anything else I've done by your side."

They shared a soft chuckle.

"These guards are so easy to bribe," Raven said. "We won't be disturbed, and we won't have any trouble."

John gestured to the chairs by the stove. "Let's have a last whiskey together while we talk."

Raven sat as John poured them both a full glass, then he went over and sat, too. He brought the decanter with him. It was his favorite Scottish brew, and it wouldn't go to waste.

They clinked their glasses in a toast to all they'd had, to all that was over.

"Tomorrow, eh?" Raven mused.

"Yes, tomorrow."

The trial was a charade, a spectacle for the masses. There was no question as to the outcome. John had tried to simply plead guilty, to skip the trial and accompanying brouhaha, but the authorities were determined to put on a show.

It would be swiftly completed, with no jury at John's request, and the hanging carried out directly after so the citizenry could cheer and preen. He felt as the Christians must have felt in ancient Rome while waiting for the lion to burst into the arena: weary, on display, anxious for the entire affair to be over.

In about twenty hours, he'd be dead, and he'd come to grips with
that fact. There were some loose ends to tidy before his burial, and
Raven would make sure his final wishes were followed.

"How is Sarah?"   At his speaking her name aloud, his heart
skipped a beat.

"Distraught. Worried—as we all are."

"She tried to see me."

"You should have let her."

"I want her to remember me at my castle in France. I *don't* want
her to remember me here. She shouldn't ever have that vision in her
head."

"Probably wise."

"I gave her Bramble Bay. Has she been informed?"

"Yes, we received the deed from Lord Trent. It's official."

"You'll watch over her for me?"

"'Til my dying day."

"I just...hate that I can't handle things myself."

"I know that about you."

John supposed others would view him as selfish or foolish. Why
wouldn't he fight the charges? Why wouldn't he accept Charles
Sinclair's assistance? Why wouldn't John confer with Charles's
lawyer? Why wouldn't he save himself?

He and Raven had always recognized the consequences of their
behavior, had understood that their lives would be violent and short.
John's end had arrived first, and there was no reason to rail against
fate.

It was Sarah who vexed him. She'd take his demise very hard,
would mourn and lament, which bothered him very much.

She was too kind, a typical female who'd believed they could wed
and have an ordinary life. But such a normal existence had never been
available to him. Already, she seemed as if she was someone he'd
never actually met.

"What of Hedley and Mildred?" Raven asked. "What should I do
with them?"

Now that John was facing his own abrupt conclusion, he'd lost his
thirst for vengeance. If he ordered their deaths, he didn't imagine
Sarah would like it.

"I don't care what you choose," he said.

"Should I kill them? Hedley especially has harmed you. Mildred
allowed the soldiers into the house, but Hedley persuaded her. He
arranged it with Annalise, and he's been running around town,
boasting of his role in your capture. Let me kill him."

"Sarah would grieve."

"She'll get over it."

"He needs to grow up. Maybe he'd benefit from a stint in the
army."

"I could hogtie him and have him conscripted into the navy. If he spent a few years working the sails, it might make a man out of him."

"I doubt it."

"We can always hope."

John nodded, deeming it a fitting punishment for the offensive, spoiled boy.

"Just don't permit them to pester Sarah ever again. If they return to Bramble Bay, they'll take over and harass her in her ownership. She's too polite to tell them to stuff it."

"I'll keep them away," Raven vowed. "What of Annalise? How can she think to evade my wrath?"

"The authorities have probably sworn to protect her."

"Could be. They won't be able to, though. I'm killing her, and your opinion doesn't matter. She gets no mercy from me."

"All right."

John simply didn't care about Annalise anymore. It truly seemed as if he was no longer alive and walking on the Earth. He was exhausted, ready for it to be over.

When he met the Lord, what would he say? How would he explain and justify his many, many sins?

"As to tomorrow..." John murmured. "I have several requests."

"Whatever you ask, I will do."

"I don't want Sarah at the trial or the hanging."

Raven shrugged. "I'll try to prevent her, but I don't know if I can. She's more stubborn by the day."

"I must have rubbed off on her."

John couldn't bear to stare out from the gallows and see her. He felt numb and invisible, and the sight of her might make him rue and regret. And he had no regrets. Not really.

"Once the trial is over," John said, "and they take me outside, there shouldn't be any heroics."

"Reggie told us as much."

Raven and John's crew were eager to attempt a rescue, to rush in with pistols blazing and swords slashing to kidnap him away. But John didn't want anyone harmed. He wasn't worth it.

"I refuse to let you rescue me, but if you have a chance..."

"Yes?"

"Could you shoot me before the King hangs me? I'd love to foil him."

"I can try."

"Don't endanger yourself, though. Only proceed if you can get safely away."

They'd always hated the notion of hanging by the neck, of the horrid spasms the body endured as it swung on the rope. A bullet through the heart was so much quicker and cleaner.

"If I can kill you, I will," Raven promised.

"Thank you, *mon ami.*"

"For you, Jean Pierre. Anything for you."

After that, there wasn't much else to say.

They finished their drinks, and a guard came by, quietly motioning to Raven that it was time to go.

They stood, and John escorted Raven to the door of his cell. They stared and stared, then enjoyed a long and final hug.

"We had a wild ride, didn't we?" Raven said.

"We certainly did. Grow old and fat. Be happy."

"I wouldn't have done anything different."

"Neither would I," John concurred.

"My friend…my brother…how I will miss you."

"It's been my honor and privilege, Raven."

"And mine, as well."

"Goodbye."

"Goodbye forever."

Raven left, and John went over and sat on his bunk, listening as Raven's footsteps faded away.

Sarah was squeezed into the top row of the balcony of the theater that had been rented for use as a courtroom. The trial of Jean Pierre, *Le Terreur Français,* was a public spectacle. There wasn't space to hold it in a regular courthouse. Too many people had wanted to watch.

The streets outside were jammed with thousands surging into the neighborhood, hoping for a glimpse of the notorious pirate. For the prior three days, Sarah had paid a boy to save her a seat.

The gallows had been constructed several blocks away. Once the death sentence was imposed, Jean Pierre would be transported in an open cart. Ghoulish spectators lined the route, eager to observe as he passed by, eager to see him on the scaffold, to hear his last words, to maliciously cheer as the hatch dropped.

Caroline had stayed at Bramble Bay with some of Jean Pierre's armed sailors. Sarah had been afraid Mildred might sneak home while Sarah was in London. Caroline's animosity toward Mildred was potent and glaring, and she would definitely keep Mildred out.

Raven was wandering in the crowd, too unnerved to remain in one place, so Sarah was all alone.

Raven had tried to convince her not to attend the trial, had bluntly apprised her that Jean Pierre didn't want her there, but she'd scoffed at the edicts of both men. As if Jean Pierre could tell her what to do! As if she'd heed him!

The proceedings were swiftly winding to a close. In another hour or so, he'd be executed. She wasn't about to cower in an anonymous hotel, wondering if it was over.

He was standing down in the dock, ignoring everyone. Freshly barbered, his blond hair gleaming, he'd attired himself in his finest clothes—the beautiful lavender coat with the silver stitching—so he appeared rich and bored and nothing like the desperate pirate he was accused of being.

When he'd been brought in—in chains—earlier that morning, the audience had furiously gossiped. He didn't look like a criminal, didn't look like the violent bandit they were expecting. People almost felt cheated.

She didn't know if he'd seen her. If he had, he hadn't given the slightest indication, but she suspected he'd spotted her. He might pretend to be indifferent, but his keen gaze would be taking in every detail.

Sarah was hardly an expert on legal matters, but it didn't seem as if the Crown had much of a case. The two main witnesses had been Hedley and Miss Dubois. Hedley's testimony had been quite irrelevant and full of attorneys' interruptions as he repeated hearsay from Miss Dubois.

The guards from the prison had testified too, but they'd only been able to say that Jean Pierre spoke fluent French and had had few visitors, mostly Reggie Thompson who also spoke French when they chatted.

The soldiers who'd captured him at Bramble Bay had testified that he'd had a knife and a pistol when they'd trapped him, that he'd fought like a madman and was very skilled with fists, sword, and gun. But so what? Many men were accomplished at fencing and pugilism. The world was a dangerous place and a fellow had to be prepared to defend himself.

Miss Dubois had inflicted the most damage, but even her testimony was a bit trifling.

She'd talked about Jean Pierre's castle in France, his ships, his frequent trips out to sea. Her most precise information dealt with his wagering, where she'd often accompanied him to high-stakes games, but gambling wasn't illegal. So it was pointless to discuss it.

As to her allegations of piracy, they rested on the fact that she'd heard him boast of his misdeeds and had seen some of the goods retrieved during his pillaging forays. Yet she wasn't accurate with her dates and didn't have any physical proof except her word that Jean Pierre was who she said he was.

It didn't seem like strong evidence to Sarah. If Jean Pierre would have contested the charges, she was sure he could have explained it all away. But no. The insane oaf would rather die than fight.

For a man who'd spent his life raging, it made no sense, but then, maybe he was simply weary of the struggle. Maybe he was ready to let it all go.

Miss Dubois's lengthy testimony finally wrapped up, and Jean

Pierre's attorney rose to cross-examine her.

He was an older, stately gentleman, Mr. Thumberton, who had been hired by Lord Trent. Mr. Thumberton was greatly respected and only served the best families. His presence on Jean Pierre's behalf indicated that Jean Pierre was a person of means and substance who shouldn't be discounted.

But as far as Sarah was aware, Jean Pierre had refused to meet with Mr. Thumberton. She wished she could march down to the main floor. She'd grab Jean Pierre by the lapels of his beautiful coat and shake him until his teeth rattled.

"Miss Dubois"—Mr. Thumberton's voice was ponderous and weighty—"I realize you're French, but you must have heard the phrase, 'hell hath no fury like a woman scorned'. Have you heard that phrase, Mademoiselle?"

"*Mais oui.*"

"How long did you say you've known Mr. Sinclair?"

"Two years."

"In what capacity did you know him?"

There was a very pregnant pause. People shifted to the edges of their seats. There had been scandalous stories about Miss Dubois in the newspapers, but the prosecutor had skirted over her background and history.

She was modestly dressed in a dark blue gown, her lustrous hair pulled into a tidy chignon, but her beauty couldn't be completely concealed. She was too voluptuous, and everyone was eager to learn if the rumors were true.

She hadn't answered Mr. Thumberton's question, and he repeated it.

"In what capacity did you know Mr. Sinclair? Surely you can tell us," he sarcastically said. "What was your relationship? I don't believe it was ever made clear."

"I was his very good friend," she breathily claimed.

"Is that what they're calling it these days?" Thumberton muttered. "Isn't it a fact, Miss Dubois, that you're an expensive prostitute?"

The term was so shocking that people gabbled over it like hens in a henhouse. The judge banged his gavel, shouting for order.

"Mr. Thumberton, I don't allow that sort of low talk. Watch your language."

"My apologies. Let me rephrase." Thumberton glared at Miss Dubois, and his expression was so contemptuous that she squirmed, her cocky smugness vanishing.

"Isn't it true, Miss Dubois, that your mother was a French courtesan?"

"No!" Miss Dubois huffed, but from her irate glower, it was obvious she was lying.

"Isn't it true that Mr. Sinclair purchased you in a French brothel?"

The spectators began to whoop and gasp, and Thumberton spoke over them. "He saved you from the dreaded establishment, and *this* is how you repay him? With treachery and false statements?"

"Rude dog!" Miss Dubois spat.

"Mr. Sinclair became engaged over the summer," Thumberton fibbed. "You were notified that he was setting you aside."

"He would never set me aside!" She tossed her head imperiously, showing a hint of temper.

"You weren't jealous and furious? Isn't it true that you told acquaintances you would do anything to get even?"

"*Non!* It is not true."

Mr. Thumberton smirked. "You have spread vicious tales about Mr. Sinclair. That would definitely qualify as *anything,* wouldn't it?"

He turned and sat down, observing her as she writhed and fumed. The attitude of the audience was fickle. Suddenly, they weren't quite so enamored of her.

The prosecutor asked her a few more questions, but he wasn't able to dislodge the impression Mr. Thumberton had created that she was a scorned woman seeking revenge.

As she left the stand and swept to her seat, people studied her with disdain. She was no longer their darling, and her back was ramrod straight, as if she could feel their angry frowns pelting her.

Thumberton called his first witness, causing a titter of curiosity as he announced that it would be Charles Sinclair, Earl of Trent.

Lord Trent made a quiet entrance, but it was very grand all the same. He was a notorious character. Londoners were fascinated by him and didn't mind his reputation as a cad. Women loved him because he was handsome and charming. Men thought he was lucky to spend his time gambling and having salacious affairs. They all secretly wished they could behave just like him.

He strolled down the center aisle, walked over to Jean Pierre and whispered in his ear. Their conversation continued unabated until the court officers started to glance at each other, wondering if they should stop him. But Trent was an earl, and no one could tell him how to act. If he wanted to whisper to Jean Pierre he could.

The crowd was beginning to whisper, too. And point at them. With Lord Trent and Jean Pierre side by side, the resemblance was obvious. There could be no denying of kinship, and there was an exciting sense that testimony was about to swerve in an unexpected direction.

When Lord Trent was good and ready, he proceeded to the witness stand. He was dressed in an expensive velvet coat, a lush green shade that highlighted the emerald of his eyes. His fingers were covered with heavy diamond rings, every aspect of his attire specifically selected to underscore his elevated rank and position.

Mr. Thumberton led him through a long recitation of his lineage and many titles, then posed the query that had the audience rippling with shock.

"You're on friendly terms with John Sinclair," Thumberton said.

"I am."

"How do you know him?"

"He's my son."

At the admission, there was a stunned pause, then people shouted and exclaimed. The judge was banging his gavel again. The prosecutor protested, carefully suggesting that Lord Trent was a liar when any fool could see the truth.

The courtroom calmed, and Lord Trent grinned and confessed, "I've sired a few…children in my day. John is one of them."

With a less infamous personage, an embarrassing review of the statement might have been required, but Lord Trent's status as a libertine was common knowledge. There was no need to hash out the details.

A lengthy discussion then ensued of Lord Trent's relationship with Jean Pierre. Trent offered an exacting account of Jean Pierre's whereabouts in prior years. His dates contradicted Miss Dubois's version of events.

Words were like honey in Trent's mouth. It wasn't possible to consider him a fraud.

As he finished, Mr. Thumberton asked, "Is there anything you'd like to add?"

Looking rich and regal, Lord Trent gazed at the judge. "I'm fond of all my children. If one of them—my son John for instance—suffered a misfortune, I'd be very unhappy. I'm a powerful man. I wouldn't think anyone should forget that I am."

The silence was deafening. He hadn't overtly threatened the judge, but his warning was unmistakable. If John was convicted, there would be consequences.

Lord Trent was excused, and Mr. Thumberton advised that he was done presenting evidence.

Sarah's heart sank.

Lord Trent had been extremely credible. He'd made Annalise Dubois seem like a deceitful shrew, but Jean Pierre's life was at stake. Shouldn't there be more? Where were the Sinclair siblings? Couldn't they have helped? Would they let him hang? It was distressing to realize that they would.

The lawyers stood to begin their closing arguments when a ruckus erupted down on the floor. Heads spun toward the rear doors, and the murmuring grew frantic again.

A woman walked down the center aisle. She was short and slender and wearing a cloak, the hood raised, so Sarah could discern her identity.

She reached Mr. Thumberton and lowered her hood, and everyone could see that it was Harriet. She was another notorious Londoner and was recognized immediately.

A general buzz of, "It's Harriet! It's Harriet!" raced around the room.

Jean Pierre recognized her, too. In the first sign of emotion he'd displayed, he muttered, "Thumberton!"

He was still in chains, so he couldn't leave the box, but the guards yanked him back anyway.

"Thumberton!" Jean Pierre tried again. "Absolutely not. I forbid it!"

"Be quiet, you!" a guard threatened, and Thumberton ignored Jean Pierre.

Harriet and Thumberton hurriedly talked, then Thumberton peered up at the judge.

"I have another witness, Your Honor. I didn't think she was coming, but she's arrived at the last minute."

Harriet removed her cloak, and Thumberton escorted her to the witness chair. On the way, they passed by Jean Pierre. She stopped, letting him take a good look, while she looked, too. Then she proceeded on, took the oath on the Bible, and sat. She appeared pretty and young and very composed.

Thumberton didn't waste any time. He quickly established her credentials, her relationship to Lord Trent, to her brother-in-law, James Harcourt, Lord Westwood, her marriage to Tristan Harcourt.

And she was half-sister to John Sinclair.

"Mrs. Harcourt," Thumberton said, "have you heard of a dangerous pirate known far and wide as The French Terror?"

"I have."

"You are one of the few people on Earth who has seen him and lived to tell about it, are you not?"

"I am. I definitely am."

"Tell us about your encounter."

"I was sailing on a ship with my husband off the coast of Spain. We were attacked in the middle of the night. When the mêlée started, I was down in our cabin, but as it progressed, I grew afraid, and I went up on deck."

"What was transpiring?"

"There were pirates everywhere, and my husband was engaged in a fierce sword fight with the lead brigand."

"You approached this brigand?"

"Yes. He stabbed my husband, and my husband collapsed. I thought he was dead."

"How close were you to The French Terror?"

She extended her arm. "Close enough to touch him."

"You saw his face, his hair, his eyes?"

"Yes."

"I daresay, you'll never forget him."

"I never will."

"Look carefully at the man on your right, the man in chains, the man you've identified as your brother."

Harriet shifted in her chair. For an eternity, she studied Jean Pierre.

"Is this the man who attacked you? Is this the man who stabbed your husband? Is this the man who threw you overboard to die?"

Harriet frowned, keeping her focus on Jean Pierre as she spoke. "Of course it isn't. This is my brother, John. It's ludicrous to accuse him."

"Describe The French Terror for us."

"He had very black hair, a bushy beard, rotten teeth. He was short and stout and not very clean. I could smell him from clear across the deck."

She paused, waiting for something, and finally it arrived. Jean Pierre dipped his head—in acknowledgement, in thanks, in shame.

Harriet nodded and yanked her gaze to Thumberton. "Will that be all you need? I am very distressed. May I be excused?"

The prosecutor was flummoxed, the judge aggravated that the trial had unraveled so thoroughly.

Harriet retrieved her cloak and started out as another ruckus erupted down below. People were craning their necks and whispering again as a man came into view. He was tall, dark-haired, fit and handsome.

He clasped Harriet's hands and murmured in her ear. Together, they went to Thumberton and had a brief conversation.

Thumberton turned to the judge. "Your Honor, Mrs. Harcourt's husband, Tristan Harcourt, is here. He would like to testify about The French Terror."

The judge scowled. "Let me guess: He saw the pirate, and it is not the defendant."

"That's correct, and I would point out that Mr. Harcourt is also half-sibling to John Sinclair. If his brother was The French Terror and had attacked him that night out on the water, he would certainly know."

Sarah stared down at Tristan Harcourt, at Jean Pierre. Their angry glances caught for a moment, held, then Mr. Harcourt whipped away. He rested a palm on Harriet's shoulder, as if saying to Jean Pierre, *I'm doing this for my wife, not for you.*

"May I speak, Judge?" Mr. Thumberton asked.

"Can I stop you?"

The audience laughed.

"The Harcourts and Sinclairs are reputable, respectable British families. Lord Trent is a peer of the realm. John Sinclair is his natural son. He is half-sibling to Mr. and Mrs. Harcourt as well as to Mr.

Harcourt's brother, Lord Westwood. You have their assertions stacked against those of a renowned French har..." Mr. Thumberton bit down the term *harlot*. "... renowned French trollop, with an ax to grind."

Miss Dubois leapt to her feet. "I am no trollop. I have told only the truth."

"Be seated and be quiet," the judge warned, "or I will have you forcibly removed by the bailiffs."

Thumberton continued, "I ask the court to consider the source of her testimony. I ask the court to weigh her word against the word of the Sinclairs and Harcourts. I'm sure the court will find there is no comparison."

The prosecutor jumped up. "May I reply, Your Honor?"

"No, you may not," the judge said. "We'll be in recess for half an hour while I deliberate a verdict."

He banged his gavel and left in a swirl of black robes. Jean Pierre was dragged out after him. There was a minute of silence, the spectators too shocked to react, then pandemonium erupted. Most people rushed for the exits. Others rushed to the bar, reaching out with beseeching hands to Harriet as if she was a famous actress or princess.

"Harriet! Harriet!" they cried.

Her husband pulled her away, and Thumberton guided them to the door by which the judge had just escaped. They raced through and disappeared.

CHAPTER TWENTY-TWO

"Where do you suppose they are?"

"I have no idea. They could be halfway to China by now."

Sarah peered out the window, staring down the long lane that led from Bramble Bay Manor and out to the road. She'd been home for several days, but the road remained just as empty as it had been when she'd arrived.

"Will we ever see them again?" Caroline asked.

"I wouldn't try to guess."

"If Raven doesn't come back for me, I'll kill him."

"You'll have to find him first," Sarah acidly said.

"He swore we'd always be together. How could he abandon me?"

"Be glad you were able to wring a vow out of him. All I received were a bunch of empty promises that turned out to be lies."

"Did Jean Pierre tell you he'd always stay? That you'd always be together, too?"

"Yes, and it's obvious how sincere he was."

They were in the front parlor, squawking like a pair of jilted spinsters. They'd spent the summer immersed in passionate affairs, but that season was over, and the world was so quiet and boring.

She wasn't the person she'd been the previous spring, and the tedium was driving her mad. Where once her tranquil country existence had been a soothing balm, it currently provided no solace. She was chafing at the monotony and anxious to get away.

When she'd been in love with Jean Pierre, life had seemed so bright and merry, colors vivid, the sounds and smells riveting. Now everything was painted in shades of gray. She felt deflated too, as if some of her vitality had leaked away.

"Could they be at his castle in France?" Caroline pondered.

"Perhaps."

"What if we booked passage and went there ourselves? Wouldn't it be better to find out than to sit here day after day wondering?"

"I couldn't locate the spot, Caro. I haven't a clue where it was."

The Sinclairs had succeeded in their effort to help Jean Pierre. A week earlier, the heralded trial of The French Terror had ended, having fizzled to a ridiculously pointless conclusion.

After the judge had left the bench, there was a lengthy delay. Then suddenly, he'd hurried in, banged his gavel, and announced that Jean Pierre was *not* The French Terror and was *not* guilty. He'd ordered Miss Dubois placed under arrest for perjuring herself, then he'd banged his gavel again and fled.

There was a shocked silence, then a group of guards surrounded Miss Dubois, tied her hands, and whisked her away. She'd spit and hissed and cursed, but they'd wrestled her out without too much difficulty.

As the doors had shut behind her, the crowd erupted. They'd heard the evidence that indicated Jean Pierre's innocence, but they were indignant that there wouldn't be a hanging.

Quarrels started, then brawls broke out, and chairs were smashed. Bailiffs hustled people out, urging them on with whips and clubs. In the street, a mêlée had ensued, with windows shattered and shops ransacked.

Through it all, Sarah had sat in the theater, waiting in vain for something to transpire. She'd assumed Jean Pierre would reappear or that Raven would come to fetch her. Or that Mr. Thumberton might emerge so she could inquire as to Jean Pierre's whereabouts.

She'd tarried on her bench at the top row of the balcony. Afternoon had faded to evening, then to night, and a cleaning crew arrived to repair the mess the spectators had made. A man told Sarah she had to leave.

She'd gathered her belongings and walked out. By that hour, the mayhem had eased. She'd hailed a hackney cab and was delivered to her hotel.

Where she waited again, for three more days.

Ultimately, she'd written a note of thanks to Harriet and Lord Trent—hadn't received a reply from either—packed her bags, and headed to Bramble Bay.

News of Jean Pierre's acquittal had reached even their isolated corner of the kingdom. Caroline had been frantic for information as to what had become of everyone. She'd expected Raven to send for her or—at the very least—for him to mail a letter that would apprise her of where he was or what would occur next.

But the two men had vanished, and gradually, Sarah's and Caroline's hopes were vanishing, too.

After all, what did they know about the wily duo? Not much.

Why would they stay in England? Why would they risk more trouble?

They were a pair of cunning liars and libertines who didn't deserve what they'd been given by Sarah and Caroline. Sarah kept telling herself to get over Jean Pierre. During his incarceration, he'd been extremely clear as to his feelings about Sarah.

He'd been far down the road to being executed, yet he'd refused to see or speak with her. She couldn't figure out why she persisted, but her liaison with him was the only truly remarkable event that had ever happened to her.

He'd made her so happy, and she couldn't return to being the woman she'd been before she met him.

"I wouldn't have done anything differently," Sarah muttered. "Not a single blasted thing."

"Neither would I."

They sighed over their fond memories, but with regret, too.

Motion out on the lane caught her attention. She pulled her gaze from Caroline and stared out the window.

A horse and rider were passing by, which wasn't odd. But when the rider turned and trotted up the drive, her pulse began to race.

She rose halfway, barely able to keep from dashing outside like a fool.

"What is it?" Caroline asked.

"There's a rider approaching."

Caroline lurched up and ran over to the window. She studied him as he neared, as his size and features grew more distinct. Then she looked over her shoulder.

"It's Jean Pierre."

Sarah was glad she was seated. If she hadn't been, she might have swooned. She took a deep breath, forcing herself to remain calm.

"Are you sure?"

"Very sure."

"Is he alone?"

Caroline sniffed with offense. "Quite alone."

Sarah pushed herself to her feet, then started out. She'd planned to maintain her dignity, to stroll slowly with grace and composure, but after three short strides, she realized poise was impossible.

She flew from the room, down the hall, and out the door, her feet scarcely touching the steps as she sprinted down them. As he reined in, she was waiting for him, awhirl with emotion: fury, relief, dread, elation.

He peered down at her, his expression enigmatic, the corner of his lovely mouth hinting at a smile. He was French again and dressed for traveling. Flowing white shirt, tan trousers, black boots, a sword on one hip, a pistol on the other. The pirate was on full display, the gold earring in his ear.

"Ah, *chérie*," he murmured, "you are just as beautiful as I remembered."

"Where have you been!" she practically shouted.

"I take it you have missed me."

"I've been mad with worry."

"And why would you be? Haven't I always told you not to fret? I am Jean Pierre. Nothing bad will ever happen to me."

"You lout! You cad! You boor! Have you any idea how frightened I've been?"

"We've been parted for so long, *chérie*. I could have sworn you'd be happier to see me."

"I will wring your neck, Jean Pierre! I will wring your lying, deceitful neck!"

With the elegance of a ballet dancer, he jumped to the ground as she leapt into his arms. Then he was kissing her and kissing her and kissing her, right there in the front drive where anyone could observe them.

"Where have you been...what have you been doing...why wouldn't you talk to me...."

She bit out the words between kisses, trying to speak, trying to tell him how upset she'd been, how aggrieved and hurt. Yet she didn't want him pausing to justify or explain. He was home, and he was with her, and they could hash it out later.

He climbed the steps, carrying her, her legs wrapped around his waist. Caroline held the door, the servants hovering behind her in the foyer. Some of his sailors were still in residence, and they eagerly watched him enter, clapping and merrily hailing him in various foreign tongues.

"Where is Raven?" Caroline asked as Jean Pierre marched by her.

"Coming in a day or two," he responded and kept on up the stairs.

They proceeded directly to Sarah's room, not caring what the servants thought or what stories might circulate in the village. He kicked the door shut with his heel, dropped his belt of weapons on the floor, then continued on to the bedchamber. He toppled onto the mattress with her, and he still hadn't stopped kissing her.

Obviously, he'd missed her and was delighted to be with her again. What did it mean? There were a thousand questions plaguing her: Was he planning to stay? Was he *free* to stay? Could they marry now? Would he like to marry her?

But she knew him well. If he didn't wish to reply, he wouldn't.

She rolled them so she was on top, so she could stare down at him. She was desperate for him to understand how distressed she'd been, how infuriating he was, but when he viewed himself as wonderful and always in the right, how could she ever make him feel any genuine remorse?

"You wouldn't let me visit you in prison," she complained.

"No."

"You would have been lowered into your grave without a goodbye."

He shrugged, unrepentant and unapologetic. "It was better that way."

"You scared the life out of me. Have you the slightest notion how afraid I was?"

"With no reason, *chérie*. Everything is fine now."

"It's *not* fine. I didn't think you were coming back."

"I considered it, but then, I decided I should grace you with my marvelous presence."

She bent down so they were nose to nose. "You arrogant ass!"

He laughed and laughed. "Oh, it's so good to be with you again."

He reached for the front of her dress, tugging at the bodice to bare her breasts, but she slapped his fingers away.

"Before this goes any further, we have to get a few things straight."

"Like what?"

"I need to hear a marriage proposal from you."

A surprised brow rose. "You want to marry me?"

"Yes, you oaf. Civilized people wed when they behave as they shouldn't."

"You want to marry *me*?" He said it again, as if it was the strangest prospect ever voiced.

"Yes. I realize you're your father's son, and he's the greatest libertine in the land, but don't imagine for a second that I'll allow you to act as he would. I'm not some green girl with stars in her eyes, and you're not shirking your responsibility. You ruined me, and you're stuck with me."

"But...marriage." He shuddered. "Isn't that a bit drastic?"

"If I keep trifling with you, I'll end up with child. I'm lucky it hasn't already occurred."

"You don't have to worry over it."

"Why wouldn't I? Women who wantonly fornicate have babies."

"Not with me. I can't sire any children."

"What makes you believe that?"

"I never have."

"What if I'm the first?"

The comment stopped him in his tracks. He pondered and stewed, then nodded. "As you wish, *chérie*. Let us wed, and you shall have me for your very own. You poor thing."

She scowled. "Was there a question in there somewhere? You have to *ask* me, Jean Pierre. You can't order me as if I'm one of your sailors."

He nodded again, actually looking contrite. "Will you marry me, my dearest Sarah?"

"That's more like it." She beamed with affection. "Yes, John, Jean Pierre Sinclair. I will, and the sooner the better, you wretch."

"Must we do it immediately?"

"I suppose I could wait until tomorrow," she churlishly agreed.

"Then can you please cease your scolding so I might have a few minutes to be welcomed back?"

"I could probably be persuaded."

She raised her arms and plucked the combs from her hair, the auburn mass swinging down to float across her shoulders. He watched like a connoisseur, like a man who'd just espied the very item he'd always wanted, and she was reminded of the person she became when she was with him. With a hot, searing glance, he made her feel wicked and happy and so very, very decadent.

He drew her down to him, and he began kissing her again, and there was such wonderment at being with him. She felt as if it had been years rather than months, as if she'd been wandering, lost and alone, and had finally been found.

He rolled them so he could be in charge and in control, and she was delighted to let him take the lead. Slowly, he stripped her of her clothes, of her undergarments, stockings, and shoes.

He dawdled, nibbling, tasting, feasting. If disaster had struck at that very moment and she never had the chance to take another breath, she'd go to Heaven as the most contented woman who'd ever lived.

She set to work too, removing his shirt and boots, his trousers. As she tugged them down and off, they were joyous, laughing, with him seeming relaxed and comfortable as he'd never previously been with her.

They couldn't delay for long. Their separation had been too trying, their reunion too precious. And he was a very lusty man. His passion sparked, the physical tension of their bodies quickly increasing.

"I missed you," he murmured.

"I missed you, too."

"Are you still glad you're mine?"

"Are you mad? Why would you have to ask?"

"When I was in prison, I dreamed of you every second."

"You liar. You did not."

"I did, *chérie*. I thought of you lying beneath me like this. I thought of how pretty you are, how you smile and sigh just for me."

"You're such a flatterer. You realize, don't you, that it's impossible for me to be angry with you?"

"Of course it's impossible. I am Jean Pierre, remember?"

"I haven't forgotten. I never will."

He widened her thighs, his torso dropping between her legs. His ministrations had been very thorough, and he entered her with ease, gliding in, buried to her womb.

He rocked his hips, taking her, possessing her. All the while, he was whispering words of love and praise in French, in Italian, in other languages she couldn't identify.

He dipped to her breast and suckled her nipple.

"Come with me, *chérie*," he coaxed. "Come with me to the end."

"I will, Jean Pierre."

"Tell me that I am the one, Sarah. Tell me that I will always be the only one."

"Always you. Always you forever."

She let go, her entire being flying to the heavens. He joined her with a deep thrust, spilling his seed far inside. The pleasure went on and on, never seeming to stop. Then finally, blissfully, they reached the top and tumbled down. Together.

He turned onto his back and pulled her across him so she was draped over his chest, her ear directly over his heart. She could hear its steady beating.

He was quiet, pensive, a calloused hand lazily stroking her skin. She caressed him too, touching his various scars. A stab from a knife. A slash from a sword. A hole from a bullet. A gash from a whip.

So many injuries to his beautiful physique. So much fighting and danger. Oh, how she hoped it was over!

"I wasn't coming back," he eventually admitted.

"I was afraid you weren't."

"I was in Dover, ready to sail away, but I couldn't. I had to see you."

"What now? Please promise me that you're finished with rampaging."

He sighed. "I suppose I must be. When my father and sister have gone to so much trouble on my behalf, it would be a bit ill-mannered to ignore their kindness."

"Yes, it would." Tentatively, she asked, "So...you're done? No more raids?"

"I don't know how I can keep on. My father boasted to the world that I'm an honorable man. He staked his reputation on my good behavior, so how can I not be the person he described me to be?"

She wanted to jump up and raise a fist of triumph in the air, but she tamped down her inclination to gloat and preen. *She* had arranged his family's assistance. *She* had given him this amazing gift.

Instead, she whispered a prayer of gratitude that he was safe, that he would be safe from this moment on.

"You nearly let them kill you without a fight," she petulantly said. "I nearly killed you myself for you being such an idiot."

"It would have been silly to protest my execution. My life was hardly worth saving."

"That's where you're wrong, Jean Pierre. Your life was worth saving because you get me as the prize at the end."

"My fierce little champion," he said, and there was such warmth in his voice that she felt very proud.

He was quiet again for so long that she assumed he'd fallen asleep, but suddenly, he spoke. "You once claimed you'd travel to London with me if I wished to meet my family. Were you serious?"

"Absolutely."

"I've been invited for a visit—by my brother Phillip."

"Oh, Jean Pierre, that is marvelous." She rose up to look him in the eye. "We're going, yes?"

"It appears that we are."

"Will your father be there?"

"I don't think so."

"You owe him your thanks."

His smile was wry. "Don't remind me. It's too galling."

"You can have a relationship with him now and shed this anger that's been driving you."

"Perhaps."

"And Harriet? Will she be there?"

"Yes."

"How about her husband Tristan?"

He shrugged. "I don't know about James and Tristan."

"But the others?"

"Yes."

She grinned. "I'll need a new gown."

"You definitely will."

He snuggled her down as she inquired, "When will we leave?"

"Tomorrow."

"Which means you'll get to avoid your leg shackle for a few more days."

"Look at it this way: We can obtain a Special License while we're in town."

She peeked up at him. "It's the first thing we'll do once we arrive."

CHAPTER TWENTY-THREE

"What time is it?"

"Seven o'clock, which is precisely five minutes later than the last time you asked."

"I'm just so nervous. Aren't you nervous?"

Phillip smiled at his wife, Anne. "If I admit to being on the verge of panic, will you feel better?"

"Yes. I hate that you're so cool and composed. The French Terror is about to walk into my front parlor, and you act as if we're having the neighbors over for tea."

They were gathered in Phillip's town house, and so far, his sister Fanny and her husband Michael were the only ones who'd joined them.

Charles might come—or not. Phillip could never predict what his father might do.

As to Harriet and Helen, Phillip was still crossing his fingers. But as to their husbands, James and Tristan, he wasn't counting on them. There were too many issues separating James, Tristan, and John, but none of them were caused by the three brothers. Their parents were the culprits, but the weight of their parents' indiscretions had landed on their children.

Phillip didn't suppose the three of them would ever be cordial, but then, he probably shouldn't use the word *ever* in his convoluted family.

"What is John like?" Fanny inquired. "Did Charles say?"

"He looks like us," Phillip replied, "and Charles thought, as to his personality, he was very much like me."

Michael scoffed. "Meaning he's stubborn and intractable?"

"Yes. He's stubborn and intractable."

"Was he..." Fanny paused. "I realize I'll sound like a snob, so how can I politely raise this subject? Has he been educated? Is he well-mannered? What sort of individual is coming to supper?"

Michael teased, "Are you afraid we'll have to show him how to use a fork?"

Fanny's cheeks flushed. "When you put it that way, my concerns seem so haughtily arrogant."

"I guess he's quite learned," Phillip said. "His mother had him intensely schooled by the best Parisian tutors until she fell on rough times. Charles found him to be brilliant and articulate, and of course, the ladies all claim he's very dashing."

Michael snorted. "So he takes after Charles more than you, Phillip."

Anne said, "Let's all make a vow to be courteous and get along. No matter what happens or what kind of person he is, I don't want any quarreling."

"Agreed," Fanny said.

"The past is the past," Anne insisted.

Phillip added, "The trouble is *old* trouble, between the parents, not any of us. I—for one—am very fascinated by the notion of who he is, what he's accomplished, and that we're related to him. I can't wait to meet him."

"Neither can I," Fanny concurred. "And if he knows he has siblings who care about him, maybe he'll stop being so angry and behave better."

"If you can pull that off," Michael told her, "if you can persuade the mighty French Terror to cease his rampaging, the entire kingdom will be grateful."

Fanny laughed. "Perhaps they'll crown me Queen for a day."

"I hope not," Michael retorted. "You'd be insufferable as royalty."

A knock on the front door halted their banter. They exchanged frantic glances, as if they'd been caught doing something they shouldn't.

"Just remember," Fanny murmured, "he's probably as nervous about us as we are about him."

"You're correct," Phillip advised, "and remember this, too: Charles *really* liked him, and Charles typically doesn't like anybody. I'm sure we'll all be pleasantly surprised."

The butler entered the parlor and announced, "Master Phillip, may I present Mr. John Sinclair and his fiancée, Miss Sarah Teasdale."

Michael, Fanny, and Anne stood, as Phillip went over to greet them, finally coming face to face with his only brother. They were the same height, with the same blond hair and green eyes, so it was easy to deduce the kinship. But there were differences, too. There was a hardness to John that Phillip had never had to develop.

Although Phillip had been born a bastard, his grandparents had reared him with every advantage, so he hadn't had to learn any difficult life lessons. He'd grown up rich and entitled and happy.

Adversity had weathered John, had given him a wary countenance, as if he was constantly expecting an attack. He reminded Phillip of a hawk out hunting, relentlessly searching the area for trouble and missing no detail.

If Fanny had been worried as to how he'd act during the visit, there was no need. His wealth obvious, he was attired like a damn king, wearing the finest clothes, most particularly a green velvet coat that had gold stitching on the bottom that Phillip suspected was sewn from genuine gold thread.

He was dripping with expensive jewelry, including numerous rings laden with diamonds, and even a gold loop in his ear that Phillip was certain the ladies would find fascinating and exotic.

If he'd been promenading into a grand ballroom, he'd have been the most elegantly dressed man in the place.

He and Miss Teasdale were definitely a committed couple, and John seemed very smitten by her. Their strident connection emanated out in a blatant wave, and Phillip could see why John would be fond. She was beautifully striking, petite and slender, with unusual auburn hair and merry blue eyes.

By all accounts, she'd gone to great lengths to save John, and they all owed her a debt of gratitude.

"Mr. Sinclair," Phillip started, then he stopped. "John, hello. I am Phillip. I am your brother."

"Hello, Phillip," John replied, a slight hint of a French accent in his voice.

Phillip pointed behind him. "This is my wife, Anne, and her brother, Michael Wainwright, Viscount Henley."

"Hello," John said again.

Phillip gestured to Fanny, and she walked over.

"This is Fanny," Phillip said. "She's Michael's wife and one of your sisters."

"Hello, Fanny." John's expression was cool, giving nothing away.

"Oh, John," Fanny gushed, "it's so wonderful to finally meet you."

John didn't respond to Fanny's warm salutation, and Miss Teasdale elbowed him in the ribs, which jolted him into a reaction.

"Thank you for having me."

Miss Teasdale grinned up at John, looking mischievous and pleased. "That wasn't so hard, was it?"

"No"—John smiled, appearing embarrassed—"that wasn't so hard."

"He was afraid to come," Miss Teasdale brazenly explained.

"Sarah..." he scolded. "This is awkward enough. Don't make it worse by telling our secrets."

"He didn't think you really wanted to know him."

"Not *know* him?" Fanny scowled. "Are you mad?" She stepped to John so they were toe to toe. "I am the first of Charles's children that Phillip managed to locate. I'm the first to discover how marvelous it is to belong. Welcome home, my long-lost brother. Welcome to our family. You'll never be alone again. I swear it to you."

Without waiting to be asked, without questioning whether an embrace would be allowed, she wrapped her arms around John's waist and hugged him as tightly as she could.

For a moment, he hesitated, his consternation evident, then he draped his arms across her shoulders and hugged her back.

Miss Teasdale beamed with delight. "I knew everything would be all right. I just knew it."

John stood on the verandah at the rear of Phillip's house. It was nearing midnight, supper over, the evening winding to an end.

He felt as if he was in the middle of a strange dream, where he was confronted by people who looked just like him, and there was an important message being presented, but he couldn't figure out what it was.

Phillip and Fanny had shared the tale of how they'd met, the damage Charles had caused to their mothers, the lives they'd led after their mothers perished. John hadn't supplied many details about his own sorry history, about Florence, how mad she'd been or how terribly she'd suffered because of it.

But Sarah had provided them with other facts that he, himself, wouldn't have mentioned. John never revealed information about himself to anyone. He'd been engaged in criminal activity for two decades so furtiveness was ingrained in his nature. It was odd to have Sarah openly discuss him, to hear her view of who he was.

She'd told many anecdotes about him, and the world hadn't stopped spinning, so maybe there was hope for some normalcy in his future.

Or maybe not.

Since he'd been set free, he couldn't come to grips with who he was supposed to be. He'd been ready to be executed, but hadn't been. As a result of the trial, his identity as The French Terror had been wiped away as if it had never been. Who was he now? If The French Terror no longer existed, who was to take his place?

He was aimless and adrift, as if he was out on the ocean with no sail or paddle and no ability to maneuver to shore.

Sarah stepped outside and walked over to him. The evening had given him an interesting glimpse of her. In their previous acquaintance, they'd spent most of their time alone or wallowing in indecent conduct. It was intriguing to see her chat and mingle, to make friends and win people over with her sunny disposition.

He'd watched the others to deduce what they thought of Sarah, and it was clear she'd surprised them. They must have assumed he'd bring a doxy like Annalise into their midst, and it had been humorous to peek around the table and find that they were charmed by her.

While they were wealthier than she was, her background was similar to theirs. Very British. Very traditional. She'd easily fit in and been accepted as one of them. *He* was the one who had been uncomfortable and out of his element, but then, he'd always felt that way. As if he didn't belong. As if he was the outcast looking in.

"I like your family," she said, snuggling herself to him.

"I like them, too."

"Phillip is just like you."

"I'll take that as a compliment."

"You should." She rose on tiptoe and kissed him on the cheek. "I'm proud of you."

"Proud? Why?"

"This was very difficult for you."

"I expected it would be, but it turned out fine."

"I'm so glad you mustered the courage to come."

"And I'm glad you accompanied me. If you'd refused, I probably wouldn't have bothered."

"So what now? You'll keep in touch with them, won't you?"

"I suppose," but he didn't know if he would.

It was all too much to absorb. The happy siblings. The married couples. The children—nieces and nephews with more on the way over the years. He had no idea how to be part of a family and had always disparaged that sort of bond.

"I have a question," Sarah said. "I've been dying with curiosity."

"About what?"

"At the trial, your father whispered something to you. What was it?"

"He said he was going to save my damn life and that I'd better shut my mouth and let him."

She laughed and laughed, her merriment washing over him like cool rain.

"I went to him," she said. "I found out where he lived, and I shamelessly knocked on his door and begged him to intervene on your behalf. You knew that, didn't you?"

"Yes. I knew."

"I like him."

"You shouldn't."

"He helped you, so he's my favorite person in the world. Besides you, that is."

He snorted and draped an arm over her shoulder, nestling her close. Anymore, it didn't seem as if he was actually tethered to the earth. She kept him attached, and if he wasn't holding on to her, he suspected he might simply float off into the sky.

"I wish he'd stopped by," she wistfully mused.

"Gad, I don't. The man is a menace."

"He's just like you."

"There you go. We hardly need two of *me* in attendance at any event."

"You should spend some time with him. You have to come to terms."

"I've had plenty of bonding for one evening. This should last me for awhile."

He glanced over to the French windows as a woman emerged from the parlor. At first, he thought it was his sister Fanny, but quickly, he saw that it was Harriet. She and her twin sister Helen had been invited, but hadn't appeared. Until now.

John understood their reluctance and wasn't upset by their absence. He was still amazed that Harriet had testified for him and wasn't sure why she had. She'd done more than enough and further interaction wasn't necessary.

As to Tristan and James, he wasn't in the mood for any posturing, so he was relieved they'd stayed away. The waters of a relationship with them weren't ready to be tested.

What would they talk about? How crazed Florence had been? How many bad decisions she'd made?

John wouldn't discuss her with them. His opinion about her many flaws and weaknesses were his own business and no one else's. Especially not James and Tristan Harcourt who had always assumed the worst of her.

Sarah saw Harriet too, and Harriet's nervousness was abundantly clear. Sarah slipped out of John's arms and went over to her.

"Harriet!" she exclaimed. "You're here."

"Hello, Sarah."

They clasped hands and hugged as if they were old friends.

"I can't believe you came," Sarah said.

"I hadn't planned on it." There was an awkward moment, then Harriet asked, "Could I...ah...speak to Mr. Sinclair for a minute?"

"Of course, of course." Sarah escorted Harriet over. "And you must call him John. *Mr. Sinclair* is ridiculously formal." Sarah turned to him. "John, you remember Harriet, don't you?"

How could I forget? he wanted to say, but didn't.

Without a second of remorse, he'd tried to kill her and her husband. Fate and a good deal of luck had saved them. Was he forgiven? Did he wish to be forgiven?

He hadn't had sufficient tutoring in this type of social situation. Could a brother become cordial with a sister he'd almost murdered? At being thrust into her company, he felt ashamed and baffled as to how he should act.

"I'll leave you two alone." Sarah flashed him a telling glare, as if warning him to be kind, to behave, then she hurried inside.

"Hello, Harriet," he murmured once the quiet had settled. "Or should I call you Mrs. Harcourt?"

"Harriet is fine, Mr. Sinclair."

"Please call me John—as Sarah suggested. Or Jean Pierre. Either will work."

"I'll stick with John. The name Jean Pierre conjures up some awful memories."

He was bewildered as to how he should converse with her, so he dawdled like an imbecile, staring, wondering at the strength of Charles's bloodlines. How could there be people in the world who were so similar to himself, but John had lived thirty years without crossing paths with any of them? It boggled the mind.

She took his wrist and spun him toward a nearby lamp, illuminating his features. She studied him as keenly as he was studying her.

"Considering the circumstances of our prior encounter," she finally said, "you seem…different."

"It was perhaps not one of my best nights."

"Did you know I was your sister?"

"No"—he shook his head—"and I wasn't trying to kill you. I was trying to kill your husband."

"Well, that doesn't make it any better."

"I suppose not."

"Are you sorry?"

He could have given a quick and flippant answer, but she appeared genuinely curious, and he felt he owed her an honest reply.

He thought and thought, struggling to recall that dark, long-ago night. He'd been trailing Harcourt's ship for days, having watched for him when he'd first sailed out of the Thames and into the Channel.

John's crew perpetrated swift and violent assaults that rapidly disabled their opponents. Tristan Harcourt had been asleep in his cabin, taken off guard and completely overwhelmed, his initial indication of trouble being the canon blast that had knocked down his main mast.

But after the preliminary foray, after John had boarded the vessel, Tristan had turned out to be one of John's fiercest adversaries ever. He'd battled like a berserker to save his men and his cargo and—John presumed—to save Harriet, the true jewel hidden below decks.

Tristan and John had been of equal size and dexterity, of equal skill with a sword. It had been a fight to the death, with John getting lucky at the end, but of course, Tristan could never have won it. Had he gained any ground against John, Raven would have slain him. But still, Tristan had been brave and loyal and devoted to Harriet and his crew.

John respected him for that. He didn't like him any more than he ever had, but he greatly respected him. As a sailor. As a brawler.

Ultimately, he shrugged. "I don't think I'm sorry."

She sighed. "I had to ask."

"I was very angry."

"You certainly were."

It had all occurred so far in the past, and there had been so many raids. It almost seemed as if someone else had attacked Tristan Harcourt. If John was suddenly apprised that some other dastardly fellow had tried to murder Tristan, he wouldn't have been surprised.

"Thank you for testifying," he said.

"Sarah convinced me. And Charles. I never can say *no* to him."

"It was very bold of you to come—and very kind."

"I couldn't let you hang." She appeared mystified over her willingness to help. "Have you met Charles?"

"Yes."

"It's odd, isn't it? Realizing he's your father?"

"Yes, it's very odd."

They shared a sad smile.

"I'm still learning my way with him," Harriet admitted. "How about you?"

"I've become as closely acquainted as I'd like to be."

"You don't wish to know him better? You don't hope to gain his approval or win his understanding?"

He probably did. When he was around Charles, he was like that ten-year-old orphan who'd kept waiting for Charles to ride to the rescue. Yet he said, "I needed him to supply things when I was a boy and my mother died. There's not much he could give me at this late date that I would appreciate."

"What now, John? You're not interested in having a relationship with Charles. What about the rest of us? Will you stay in England? Will we be friends?"

"I don't know. It's all a bit much for me to take in."

"Yes, I suppose it would be. Are you finished with pirating? I'd hate to have gone out on a limb for you only to have you attack some other poor female out on the high seas."

"I believe I'm done," he carefully stated.

He wasn't positive he meant it, but it felt grand to tell her he'd stopped. Except that he'd been The French Terror for so long. The criminal identity was part and parcel of who he was. If he wasn't a dangerous pirate, who was he and how would he carry on? Would he marry a girl from a rural village in the country and be a husband and farmer?

The notion didn't bear contemplating, and he could scarcely tamp down a shudder of dread.

"I heard that you're engaged to Sarah," she said.

"I am."

"I'm glad. I like her."

"So do I."

"She'll be good for you."

"More than I deserve, that's for certain."

"Yes, much more than you deserve," she baldly agreed. She stared, as if checking for flaws and finding many.

"You're watching me so intently," he said. "What are you hoping to discover?"

"I'm trying to figure out why I keep bothering with you."

"I can't figure it out myself."

"When Sarah asked me to testify, I couldn't imagine why I would. My husband and I—well, let's just say he had a fit when we discussed it."

"I'm not surprised."

"And then there's this supper. Phillip and Fanny invited me, but I couldn't see any reason to attend."

"But you came anyway."

"Yes, which precipitated another quarrel with my husband. Are you worth it?"

"I'm sure I wasn't."

"I couldn't abide that you were in prison all alone. I didn't want you to climb to the gallows without a friendly face in the crowd."

"I was ready for that end. I've always been on my own, so I wouldn't have fretted."

"That's the saddest thing I've ever heard."

He shrugged off her concern. "My life wasn't easy, but I've gotten on all right."

"I feel sorry for you."

"You shouldn't."

"Now that I've met you again, in calmer circumstances, you remind me of my husband. You're very much alike."

What reply could he make to such a statement? He and Tristan were brothers, but John wished they weren't, and the worst aspect of socializing with his siblings was having to constantly recall his blood relationship with the Harcourts.

"I'm positive he and I are nothing alike," he insisted. "I'm certain he's a very fine man, and you shouldn't worry that he possesses any of my bad traits."

"He doesn't—except for your stubbornness. If Florence passed on any common characteristic to her three sons, it was the obstinacy."

"It served me well and kept me alive when times were dire."

"I want to ask a favor of you, John. You owe me, don't you think?"

He sighed. "Yes, I suppose I do."

"I'd like you to meet Tristan and James." He must have looked horrified, because she hastily added, "Not tonight but in the future. Promise me you will." He didn't respond, and she sharply repeated, "You owe me."

"Ah, *chérie,* you drive a hard bargain."

"My husband's resolve is rubbing off on me."

He pulled his gaze from hers and peered up at the stars, wondering if he could honor her request.

He'd spent so much of his life loathing Tristan and James for their safe, entitled existence, detesting their drunken father for his cold disavowal of Florence as she lay defenseless and dying.

Did it matter anymore?

He stared at Harriet again. "If I agree, what will you have achieved?"

"Maybe nothing?"

He chuckled. "I don't know if we can be friends."

"But could you be brothers?" She laid a comforting hand on his arm. "I can't guess why your mother left her family to engage in her affair with Charles, but isn't it the sins of the fathers? Isn't it her sin? Must you and Tristan and James continue to pay the price for their foolishness?"

"Perhaps not," he ultimately murmured.

"So…someday, you'll let me introduce you? You won't fight and bicker? You'll at least *try* to talk like sensible, adult men?"

"For you, Harriet, I will. Because I owe you, and I am grateful."

He made the vow, but it was another promise that might be false. He couldn't predict what path he would choose, if he would marry Sarah, or stay in England, or have any further contact with his siblings.

It was very possible he might ride to his ship that was still docked in Dover and sail away forever.

"Come inside with me," she said.

"Why?"

"My twin sister Helen is here. She wants to meet you, too."

"As always, I am at your service."

She scoffed. "Don't pretend to be meek and compliant. It doesn't become you."

"All right, I won't."

"Please come inside—because I asked. And remember what I said: If you can't be our friend, then be our brother."

"I will try, Harriet. I will try my best."

She tugged him toward the door, and he walked with her, arm in arm, as if he'd known her all his life.

CHAPTER TWENTY-FOUR

"What am I to do?"

"How would I know, Hedley?"

"You said he was The French Terror. You said we would receive the reward."

"I thought we would. How could I guess that his family would step forward and lie for him?"

Annalise shrugged with resignation, wishing the irksome boy would go away and leave her alone.

She'd written to him, pleading with him to visit and being surprised when he'd agreed. It was a prison, for goodness sake, and she hadn't imagined he'd lower himself, but she had no other friends in England. She'd had to ask him for help, but he was so selfish. He wanted to discuss his own troubles rather than hers.

"I bought a new wardrobe and a new carriage and everything," he complained. "I told everyone that I had funds coming and now I don't." He scowled, trying to look ferocious. "They already repossessed my carriage."

"You poor dear," she sarcastically cooed. "How will you survive the loss?"

"This isn't fair, Annalise."

"No, it's not, Hedley."

"You swore we would get the reward, but we didn't. You owe me."

"*Mon Dieu,* you dolt. I am in jail, and you are walking around free. What precisely might I *owe* you?"

"Money. It's only fitting that you reimburse me for what I've lost."

"How can you lose what you never had?"

"But I expected to have it! You've harmed me in so many ways. My stellar reputation is absolutely in tatters."

He was dressed like the dandy he deemed himself to be, wearing a fancy coat, a lacy cravat, his boots blackened to a shine. He'd been primped and barbered and manicured, his perfume filling up the room where she'd been brought so they could chat.

In comparison, she was slowly falling apart. She was still attired in the gown in which she'd been arrested. She hadn't been allowed to bathe, so her hair was filthy and uncombed, and she was starting to smell.

"Hedley, listen to me," she snapped.

"Why should I? You've delivered me to the edge of ruin."

"You must get me out of here."

"How would I?"

"You have to bribe the guards."

"Bribe the guards? Are you mad?"

"It won't cost much. My charge is simple perjury, and it's a petty offense. Who will care if I slip out the back gate?"

He scoffed. "I take it you haven't seen the newspapers."

"How would I have?"

"They're not reporting anything kind about you, Annalise. The authorities are quite vexed that you wasted everyone's time. Were I you, I wouldn't plan on leniency."

"I've wasted no one's time!" she hissed. "He is Jean Pierre! He is The French Terror! Is it my fault if his exalted father said he wasn't? I had no chance against him."

"Do you know what I think?" His expression was sly and condemning.

"What?"

"He wasn't The French Terror at all. His family was correct, and you're a liar."

"Shut up!"

"You were livid because he seduced my sister, and you wanted to get even. Mother warned me about you, but I refused to heed her."

He was quivering with righteous indignation, and she should have slapped him silly. She was larger than he was and violently enraged. She could have lashed out and landed a blow before he realized her intent, but why bother?

She sighed with regret.

Her temper had always been her undoing. Her jealousy, too.

She'd been angry at Jean Pierre, upset over his affection for Sarah Teasdale, and eager to pay him back for his betrayal. Yet he hadn't betrayed her.

He'd offered her a house in Paris, servants, a stipend. It was more than she'd ever dreamed of obtaining, more than she'd deserved. She was a courtesan, and he had honored her for her excellent service with a gracious retirement. After only two years of employment!

She'd never have had to work again, would never have had to welcome another man to her bed. And after Jean Pierre, why would she fornicate with another?

She shouldn't have fought his decision. She should have profusely thanked him and parted on good terms. If she had, he'd have been a friend for life.

Mais non! She'd had to pitch a fit, and wasn't that the most ridiculous choice ever? Who could best Jean Pierre? She knew it was impossible, but she'd tried anyway.

Now look at her. Incarcerated. Abandoned and alone. No pennies in her purse. She had no one to rely on except stupid, arrogant Hedley.

She was very afraid of being transported to Australia. She was very afraid of *not* being transported, of having to spend the winter at Newgate where lung fevers would run rampant. She probably wouldn't survive.

Most of all, she was very afraid of Jean Pierre and Raven. She didn't think Jean Pierre would retaliate, but Raven…

He wouldn't forget the trouble she'd caused for Jean Pierre, wouldn't let her get away with what she'd done. Raven could ask Jean Pierre's permission to murder her, and Jean Pierre could say *no,* and Raven would proceed regardless of Jean Pierre's opinion.

It wasn't likely that Raven would move against her in the locked facility, but the man was so bloody resourceful. She was desperate to sneak out of the prison, to vanish into London's crowded streets.

Her only hope had been Hedley, but she had to accept that she was on her own.

"Go away, Hedley," she muttered.

"You haven't told me how you'll repay me," he sullenly whined.

"Go. Away."

"I can't have creditors chasing me. Mother is beside herself."

"I don't care."

"But, Annalise, you must see how you have—"

She slapped her palms on the table, the sound ringing off the ceiling. "I said I don't care, Hedley. Slither home to your mother, you pathetic mama's boy. Sit on her lap and cry on her shoulder. She will put up with you, but I don't have to."

She rose so quickly that her chair topped over. Then she swept out, yearning to appear regal and magnificent, but in light of her current difficulties, aplomb was hard to manage.

A guard was waiting to escort her to her cell. He gestured down the hall, indicating the route, and she stomped off.

Hedley was sniping, "Annalise! Annalise! Don't you dare walk away from me!"

"Sod off, you rich toad," she mumbled, and the guard snickered.

"We're not finished, Annalise!" Hedley nagged. "Get back here!"

They turned a corner, and his voice faded away.

She was hurrying along, not really focused on her surroundings. After a bit, she glanced around, and she didn't recognize their location. Her cell was on an upper floor, in the women's wing, but they hadn't climbed the stairs, had they? Hadn't they descended? She seemed to be in the cellar.

Gradually, it dawned on her that it was very quiet. She peeked behind her, but the guard had deserted her. Rude dog! When she saw him again, he'd definitely get a scolding he would never forget.

She frowned and nervously called, "*Halo*? Is anyone there?"

Her words echoed and echoed as if the corridor went on forever. It was very dark in both directions, a single lamp burning near the spot where she stood. She thought she should retrace her steps and return to her cell on her own, but she wasn't sure she could find the way.

A shiver of unease whispered down her spine.

Suddenly, a man emerged from the shadows, giving her the fright of her life. He wasn't a guard, but was dressed in a workingman's attire, a brown coat and trousers, muddy boots, a hat pulled low over his face.

She lurched away, a hand over her racing heart, but when he spoke to her in French, she immediately calmed.

"Mademoiselle Dubois?"

"*Oui.*" She spoke in French, too. "You scared me to death."

"I apologize." He came closer, and she could smell the sea, as if he was a sailor. He studied her, his eyes steely as he said, "Jean Pierre sends his regards."

She brightened. Was she forgiven? Was she being rescued?

Perhaps he'd quarreled with Miss Teasdale. Perhaps he was sorry he'd been so horrid to Annalise. Perhaps he wanted her back!

"Is Jean Pierre here? Has he come for me?"

"No. He has not come."

"What is it then? Are you taking me to him?" Excited, she grabbed his arm. "We can go at once. I don't need to fetch my things."

"We are not going." He pressed himself to her, forcing her against the dank prison wall, and murmured, "Raven sends his regards, too."

She gasped with dismay. "Raven! No!"

"I am to tell you exactly this, Mademoiselle: 'If you betray Jean Pierre, you betray me. Did you imagine you would not have to pay a steep price'?"

She'd intended to protest, to defend herself, but he was a skilled assassin, and she'd already uttered her last words.

Quick as a snake, he withdrew a knife and sliced her through her belly. As she collapsed, he moved away so no blood would soak into his clothes. He watched dispassionately, waiting for her final breath to be exhaled.

Off in the distance, her beautiful mother was standing in a field of blue flowers. She was waving to Annalise, beckoning to her, and Annalise was anxious to rise and run to her, but the vision faded and she couldn't see the path.

It grew very dark and very cold, and there was no beauty, no flowered field, no vision of her mother. There was only an eternal quiet and a recognition that there would never be anything else but this.

"Hello, Hedley."

"Halt!" Hedley snapped. "Who goes there?"

He was a bit drunk, swaying slightly, his head pounding.

Earlier in the evening, he'd received a mysterious message from a newspaper reporter who'd been interested in interviewing him about Jean Pierre and Annalise Dubois. The man had offered to pay for the privilege of speaking with Hedley, and Hedley had jumped at the chance.

He was so desperately short of funds.

The tavern where the meeting was to take place was located in a seedy neighborhood down by the docks. At first, Hedley had been reluctant to attend, but vanity and poverty had driven him.

Of course the reporter had never arrived, and Hedley had dawdled for hours, had imbibed too much cheap whiskey. He'd just exited the tavern and was wondering how he'd return to his rented room. He had no money to hire a cab, and it was too far and too dangerous to walk.

Two men had slipped from the shadows. They were very large, dressed in black, pistols blatantly hanging from their belts.

Were they brigands? Was he about to be robbed?

Ha! He'd show them! His purse was empty—thanks to that trollop, Annalise Dubois. They could rob him all night, but wouldn't get a penny. He didn't *have* a penny.

They approached, the lamp on a nearby pole illuminating their features, and he blanched.

"You remember me, don't you, Hedley?"

"Jean Pierre!"

He should have screamed for help, but before he could, Raven Hook had a pistol pressed to his temple.

"If you utter a peep," the bloodthirsty Mr. Hook warned, "I will blow your stinking head off."

Jean Pierre stepped in so Hedley was stuck between him and Mr. Hook. They were tall and tough and menacing. He was shaking, certain Mr. Hook would follow through on any threat.

"At my trial, Hedley"—Jean Pierre's voice was low and severe—"people claimed I wasn't The French Terror. But guess what?"

"Miss Dubois told me everything!" Hedley spat.

"Well, she's been adjudged a liar, so I wouldn't necessarily accept her version. But are you positive you should keep talking about me?"

"If you repeat your opinion ever again," Mr. Hook grumbled, "it would definitely qualify as a death wish. Are you ready to meet your Maker, you pathetic little worm?"

"I'm not afraid of you," Hedley contended, but he was trembling so fiercely that if Mr. Hook hadn't been holding him, he'd have collapsed to the cobbles.

"You're not afraid of me?" Mr. Hook snarled. "You should be."

Mr. Hook lifted and turned him so they were directly beneath the streetlamp.

"Look at my face, Hedley," Jean Pierre said.

"What of it?"

"See any resemblance?"

"No."

"He wouldn't," Mr. Hook scoffed. "He's too stupid to notice what's right before his eyes."

"Guess what I hate the most, Hedley," Jean Pierre groused.

"What?"

"I hate being betrayed."

"You deserved it! You're a criminal! You're a menace to society!"

Mr. Hook whacked him on the temple with the butt of the pistol, hard enough that Hedley saw stars.

"Do you know who Florence is, Hedley?" Jean Pierre inquired.

"Florence? Florence?" His mind raced as he tried to place the name. "My aunt? My mother's sister? That Florence?"

"Yes, that Florence." Jean Pierre grinned an evil grin. "There is one fact you have heard these last months that is absolutely true. My mother was Florence Harcourt, so you and I are cousins."

"I don't believe you."

"I don't care. I'm openly claiming kinship, which means I'm the elder male in the family."

"Never."

"From now on, I'm making all the important decisions."

"You are not!"

"My initial act was to buy up all your debt."

"You what?"

Hedley struggled to sort through the ramifications. His debt was enormous. What was the benefit to Jean Pierre? What was the benefit to Hedley? He was quite sure there was no benefit and could only be great detriment.

"I refuse to have you own it!"

Mr. Hook sneered, "You should be a tad more grateful, Hedley."

"Give it back to my creditors."

"I'd rather not," Jean Pierre said, "and besides, they're glad to be shed of you. You're a bad risk."

"I'll tell my mother," Hedley declared. "She won't let you get away with this."

"How will she stop me? She's poor as a church mouse—all because of you. As a favor to your sister, I will support Mildred to rescue her from your recurring folly."

Hedley's reasoning was muddled, so he couldn't accurately assess the situation. Why would Jean Pierre assist Mildred? She'd participated in his arrest. Why wasn't he angry about that duplicity? His generosity to her made no sense.

"I don't want you involved with my mother."

"I doubt she'd agree with you. I hear she's desperate."

"She's not desperate," Hedley blustered. "I'm taking care of her."

Mr. Hook snickered. "You live in such a world of fantasy, Hedley."

"Since she'll be totally dependent on me," Jean Pierre continued, "she'll never be able to aid you in any fashion unless she first gains my permission."

"What are you saying?"

"Your days of mooching off her, of deceiving and using her, are over."

"You can't come between a son and his mother. It's not right."

"It's time for you to grow up, Hedley."

"I'm plenty grown, thank you very much."

"No. You're a sniveling, annoying child. How old are you?"

"Twenty."

"You have to abandon your juvenile ways and learn to be a man."

"You're talking in riddles."

"Jean Pierre usually kills people who betray him," Mr. Hook said, "so you're lucky. He's giving you a second chance. Because of his blood relationship with you. Because of your sister."

"I should murder you," Jean Pierre added, "and put you out of your misery. But your death would distress Sarah, so I won't."

"How very magnanimous!" Hedley sarcastically oozed.

"Shut up," Mr. Hook ordered, "and mind your manners when speaking to Jean Pierre."

"I won't be silent!" Hedley fumed. "You can't—"

Mr. Hook clobbered him with the pistol again, and Hedley's meager protest was ended. He gaped up at Jean Pierre, yearning to see a glimmer of compassion, but his eyes were cold and blank, no emotion visible.

Hedley didn't understand Jean Pierre's dislike. Everyone had always loved Hedley, so he was able to convince them to let him act however he pleased. Only Jean Pierre couldn't be seduced by Hedley's many charms. His aversion was palpable, and Hedley was extremely confused by it.

His dizziness was increasing, his headache pounding more relentlessly. He peeked up at the streetlamp, and there was an odd blue glow around it. For a frantic moment, he worried that he was going blind.

"How are you feeling, Hedley?" Mr. Hook asked.

"Not very well."

"It will get worse shortly, but you'll live through it."

"What do you mean?"

"A fop like you," Jean Pierre advised, "shouldn't drink alone down by the docks."

"Why not?"

"Disreputable tavern owners drug your whiskey."

Hedley was horrified. "Why would they?"

"So you pass out. So they can hand you over to an unscrupulous ship captain who is looking for warm bodies to man the sails."

"I don't wish...to...to...man the sails." His words were beginning to slur. He was losing his ability to speak, to stay on his feet.

"It doesn't matter what you wish. The captain will have paid a bribe to the tavern owner, and you'll be delivered, bound and gagged."

"The captains have difficulty," Mr. Hook added, "mustering a full crew. The work isn't very...pleasant. There's a high turnover, a high death rate. They'll take anyone. Even a rude, obnoxious dolt like you."

Hedley would have complained, but his lethargy was escalating.

He was about to say something, but what was it? Before he could recall, a gag was stuffed between his lips.

"You shouldn't have hurt Sarah," Jean Pierre said. "You don't deserve to be her brother, and you'll never have another chance to harm her." Quietly, he vowed, "I swear to you, Hedley. I swear it on my life."

I never hurt Sarah, Hedley insisted behind the gag, but he had. He'd squandered her dowry. He'd gambled away her home. He'd given her to a violent stranger.

"I've indentured you to an acquaintance," Jean Pierre explained. "He's not bad for a captain, so you'll probably survive. Just keep your mouth shut, learn a few lessons, and you should be all right."

"Five years, Hedley," Mr. Hook murmured in Hedley's ear. "He'll bring you back in five years—if you're still alive."

"Use the time wisely, my little cousin." Jean Pierre looked more evil, more menacing than ever. "Grow up and become a man. For if you return in the same condition as you left, I will be happy to rid the world of your sorry presence."

Hedley felt his wrists and ankles being tied, felt himself being hoisted over Mr. Hook's shoulder. His next conscious thought occurred many hours—or perhaps days—later.

With a great deal of effort, he opened his eyes, and he scowled, anxious to ascertain what had transpired. He was stretched out on a narrow wooden bunk, in a dark, dreary kitchen. A sloppy, disheveled man was chopping vegetables over at a table.

Hedley wanted to sit up, to demand the man's identity, but the floor seemed to be swaying. He was incredibly nauseous, the gentle rocking exacerbating his discomfort.

"Where am I?" he croaked, but his tongue was swollen, his mouth so dry he might have been chewing on sand.

The man didn't glance up, and Hedley tried again.

"You there, sir! Where am I?"

The man frowned and laid down his knife.

"So you're alive, are ya? Figured you was dead, sure enough."

He grunted a comment in a foreign language and went back to his vegetables.

Hedley's focus was improving, and he pushed himself up on an elbow. He studied his surroundings, seeing numerous hammocks hanging from the rafters, barrels and crates and ropes neatly coiled.

He blanched with shock. "Am I...am I...on a ship?"

"You're a real genius, ain't ya?" the man answered.

Hedley pondered furiously, struggling to recall his last cogent memory. He'd been in a tavern in London. The bartender had plied him with drinks even after he'd run out of money. He'd grown too intoxicated and...and...

Jean Pierre! Raven Hook!

Hedley lurched up, but the bunk above him was very close, and he banged his head on it so hard that he nearly knocked himself unconscious.

For a few minutes, he lay very still, letting his pulse slow, then he rose more carefully. His beautiful coat was gone. His jewelry. His purse. His boots. He was wearing only his trousers.

"Where are my clothes?"

"Sold."

"They must be returned to me at once!"

"Won't happen. You won't be needing them anyways. The captain has clothes for you." He pointed with his knife. "There on the floor. Best put them on and get yourself up on deck."

"To do what?"

"Work. What do you think?"

"I don't wish to work."

"You have to if you intend to be fed." The man grinned maliciously. "No work, no eat."

Hedley shook his throbbing head. "There's been some mistake. I demand to speak with the captain."

"He's busy."

"But I must inform him that I've been robbed."

"Kidnapped, too."

"Kidnapped! But...that's a crime."

"Not where you're going."

"Listen to me: Have you heard of a vicious pirate named Jean Pierre? He's The French Terror. This is all his fault. He hates me. I had him arrested, and I was supposed to receive a reward for his capture. You have to turn this ship around and take me back to

London."

"Not possible," the man scoffed. "And sonny?"

"Yes."

"Jean Pierre's a hero on this vessel, so you'd better mind your tongue. There's many a fellow who'd be upset to learn that you'd caused him trouble."

"He's a murdering felon!"

"Not in this world, and you're not in London anymore. You'll get your throat slit."

Groaning with dismay, Hedley flopped onto the bunk.

He cursed Jean Pierre and Raven Hook. He cursed Annalise Dubois. He cursed the stupid judge who'd released Jean Pierre. He cursed Sarah who now owned Bramble Bay. He cursed his mother for being so far away, for not saving him.

Then he closed his eyes and wailed like a baby.

"I demand entrance."

"Well, I *deny* entrance."

Mildred glared at Caroline. They were on the front stoop at Bramble Bay, with Mildred assuming she could bluster her way in, but Caroline was blocking the door.

For most of two decades, she had mothered Caroline. Grudgingly, she would probably admit that she hadn't done the best job, but she'd been irritated to have the foolish girl foisted on her.

Bernard had been her father's friend. Bernard had been named her guardian. Not Mildred. Yet Bernard had dragged her home and insisted Mildred raise her, but Mildred had never liked Caroline.

Despite Caroline's flaws, Mildred had found her a husband, and she'd tossed him away in order to roll in the gutter with a criminal. Now, Archie was dead, and Caroline was widowed and merrily carrying on at Bramble Bay as if she'd never been a wife.

Mildred was the one in a jam. She had no husband, home, or money. She'd been living with Sheldon for months but had overstayed her welcome.

She'd tried every trick to get him to propose, but he'd ignored her sly coercion. He constantly asked when she would be returning to Bramble Bay, and she had to accept that he would never marry her and was eager for her to leave—but he was too polite to come right out and say so.

She'd packed her bags and traveled to Bramble Bay in Sheldon's carriage. But before she could sneak in, Caroline had appeared, almost as if she'd been watching for Mildred.

Mildred pulled herself up to her full height, intending to intimidate and bully as she would have in the past, but for once, her confident manner had no effect.

"Let me in," she seethed.

"No."

"I must speak with Sarah. Where is she?"

"She's been in London, frantically working to save your nephew's life."

"I heard she succeeded."

"No thanks to you."

"I heard she was back."

"She left again."

Mildred gnawed on her bottom lip.

They'd received precisely one newspaper that had contained wild accounts of an outrageous trial that had ended with a not guilty verdict. Apparently, Mr. Sinclair had strolled out of the courthouse a free man, and Mildred spent every moment in a frenzy of fear, wondering if he was on his way to Bramble Bay, wondering what he would do to Mildred when he arrived.

She couldn't locate Hedley. Where was he? Annalise Dubois had been jailed on perjury charges. Had he been incarcerated with her? If the deceitful harlot had brought doom to Hedley, Mildred would wring her neck.

"When will Sarah return?" she asked.

"I couldn't guess."

"Is she with Mr. Sinclair? Are they coming to Bramble Bay?"

"I have no idea."

She studied Caroline, disturbed by her cool, steely attitude. Caroline had always been flighty and flippant, easily manipulated and maneuverable. Events had altered her. Their roles had been completely reversed, and Caroline held all the cards.

Mildred dipped her head, trying to look contrite. "I apologize for my sharp tone."

"Apology accepted."

"I'm just very worried about Hedley. Have you heard from him?"

"No."

"And you've had no recent word from Sarah as to her plans?"

"None that I would share with you."

"I feel awful about everything. Miss Dubois told us her tales about Mr. Sinclair, and we believed her. We shouldn't have, but we were taken in by her smooth lies."

"Yes, you were."

"I'm very sorry for the trouble we caused Sarah."

"That's kind of you."

"And I'm aghast over Archie and how he treated you. When I sent for him, I truly thought I was acting in your best interest. I'm aghast over how you were imperiled."

"I appreciate your concern."

Mildred gazed woefully, hoping to exhibit remorse and regret, but not sure if she'd achieved her goal. "It's grown a tad awkward at Sheldon's"—she chuckled, forcing levity—"and I've been there so long. I am afraid he's tired of me, and I really need to get out of his hair."

"He's been a bachelor for decades. I imagine he's chafing at having extended company."

"He is, he is," Mildred enthusiastically agreed. "I'm so relieved that you understand my situation. May I please come in?"

Mildred smiled, and Caroline smiled, too. For a moment, they visually bonded, remembering all that had been between them. Yes, there had been rough patches, but they were family, weren't they?

Yet suddenly, Caroline scowled and said, "Come in? No, you may not."

She slammed the door and spun the key in the lock.

Mildred stood there, fuming, thinking she should shout and pound on the wood, that she should bellow for the servants to help her. But she was a hard taskmaster, and the servants had never liked her. They wouldn't obey her over Caroline, and Mildred wouldn't embarrass herself by scrambling around the property like a beggar.

She trudged to her carriage and ordered the driver to take her to Sheldon's. Then she clambered in, refusing to glance up to see if he was irked by her command.

He clicked the reins, and they rumbled away, and as they rolled past the house, she stared longingly, confused over how she'd lost it and anxious to get it back.

Sarah couldn't stay away forever, and while Caroline might have been callous and cruel, Sarah was malleable and foolish and too respectful for her own good. She'd always been kind to Mildred, and eventually, Mildred would presume on her compassionate nature.

Of that fact, Mildred had no doubt.

"Don't move."

Caroline's eyes flew open with alarm. She was asleep in her bed, and without her being aware, a man had crept in. His large body crushed her into the mattress, a palm clasped over her mouth.

"I'm going to pull my hand away," he whispered. "Promise you won't scream."

Clouds had been covering the moon, and they drifted away, moonlight abruptly flooding the room so she could identify her assailant.

"You oaf! You rat! What are you doing? You scared the life out of me."

"Hello, Caroline." Raven grinned like a halfwit. "How have you been?"

"How have I been? How have I been?"

She wiggled out from under him and jumped to the floor. She was wearing her nightgown, and she grabbed her robe and crammed her arms into the sleeves. She marched to the fireplace and seized the poker, brandishing it like a weapon.

"You have exactly ten seconds to tell me why you'd dare to barge in without being asked."

"Maybe because I knew I'd be welcome?"

"Ha! You might have been welcome before you vanished without a word."

"I'm back now."

"For how long? An hour? A day? A week?"

"I might be here an entire month."

"Ooh, aren't I lucky."

"Yes, you are very, very lucky. You can have me for your very own."

"As if I'd want you, you wretch!"

"Why, Caroline," he murmured, "you seem a bit angry."

"You haven't begun to see angry. Keep talking, keep saying stupid things, and you'll see angry." She waved the poker. "If I whack you with this a few times, I'm sure I'll feel much better."

"I thought you detested violence."

"I've changed my mind."

He patted the mattress. "Come and lie down."

"Not until you tell me where you've been."

He shrugged. "Here and there."

"Doing what?"

"This and that."

"Is that an answer? Should I be calmed by it? Should I be reassured?"

"Why are you *not* calm?"

"Because I've been waiting for you! Because I've been worried sick."

"About what?"

"About you, you miserable snake in the grass."

"Why would you worry about me? I'm too smart to get myself in a jam and too tough to die."

"Spoken like a clueless idiot who will fall off a cliff when he's not looking."

"Come here," he said again.

The poker was heavy, but she couldn't bring herself to drop it. She felt stronger with it, as if she was making a point, when she couldn't figure out what her point was supposed to be.

She was so glad he was back. She was so relieved.

"Your husband is dead," he stated, "and I'm not sorry. Are you?"

She scoffed. "Are you joking? No, I'm not sorry."

"You're a widow."

"I am."

"So you're free to marry again. Or to engage in a wild, illicit affair." His eyes twinkled with merriment, his slow, sexy smile melting her spurt of temper.

"What are you asking? Are you asking me to marry you? Or are you asking me to engage in an illicit affair?"

"How about the illicit affair until we're shackled good and proper?"

"You want to marry me? Really?"

"Of course I want to marry you. I was just wondering if *you* wanted to marry me. Would you consider it?"

"Would I consider it?" she repeated like a dunce.

"Life is too short, Caro. I can't keep thinking I don't deserve things. I have to grab for what I want."

"What things don't you feel you deserve?"

"You. I'm so unworthy of a woman like you, but I thought I'd take a chance. Will you have me?"

He sat up, his legs dangling over the edge of the bed. For the first time in their acquaintance, he appeared flustered and lost, and it occurred to her that he'd been extremely courageous in tendering his brisk proposal.

He didn't think he deserved her? He didn't think he was worthy? Was he mad?

"Raven, I'm an orphan."

"I know. So am I."

"I don't have any dowry or prospects."

"I'm rich, though, so I don't care about any of that. We'd be all right."

"My only possession was my house with Archie, but his family swooped in and claimed it. I don't even have any clothes."

"I can retrieve your stinking house for you—if that's what you want."

"I don't want it. I mention it merely because you should understand that I'm not quite the marvelous catch you imagine me to be."

"I disagree, Caro. From where I'm sitting, you're pretty damn fine."

"I'm a ninny who's scared of her own shadow."

"Well, I've never been afraid of anything. You'll always be safe with me, and your silliness doesn't bother me. I kind of like it."

"What sort of life would we have together?"

"The same as all couples, I guess. Jean Pierre would have to be my top priority, though. You'd have to recognize that. I might have to travel occasionally or be away for extended periods."

"Could I travel with you?"

"No, but I swear I'd always come back."

"Where would we live?"

"Wherever you like. Here at Bramble Bay. Or France. Or China if that would make you happy."

"It would have to be forever, Raven."

"It better be. I don't go around proposing everyday."

"No, you're definitely not the type."

"Is that a *yes*? Are we getting hitched or what?"

She paused, letting the moment last just another few seconds, wanting to be certain she never forgot a single detail.

"Can we proceed immediately?" she asked.

"Sure, but you Brits have some fussy rules that might delay us. I figured we could ride to Dover, pay some ship's captain to take us out on the water. He could marry us in a snap."

"We'd wed on a ship?"

"Why not? A ship's captain is authorized to perform the ceremony. We wouldn't have to apply for a license or any of that foolishness."

"Could Mr. Sinclair do it for us?"

"I don't know his plans. I don't know if he'll be back this way."

"What about Sarah? She's not leaving with him again, is she?"

"No, she's not leaving."

Caroline frowned, flummoxed by his comment. Sarah was in London with Mr. Sinclair, meeting his family and obtaining a Special License so they could wed right away, too. They weren't marrying? What had happened?

"Has Mr. Sinclair broken her heart?" she inquired.

"Not yet."

"But he might?"

"With Jean Pierre and his women, I wouldn't try to predict what will occur."

"But it's *Sarah*."

"Yes, it is, but I wouldn't expect he'd rush to the altar. He wouldn't view himself as a good candidate for matrimony. He'd probably figure Sarah was better off without him."

"Did he tell you that?"

"No."

She studied him, wishing she could read his mind. She was positive Mr. Sinclair would have confided in Raven, but where the two men were concerned, Caroline would always be on the outside of their relationship.

She wondered if she'd ever grow weary of it, but as long as they didn't drink to excess or carouse with loose doxies, she supposed she could put up with anything.

"I'd like the wedding to be here," she said, "at the chapel in the village, after Sarah is home so she can attend."

"Then Bramble Bay church it is, Mrs. Patterson."

"Don't call me that."

"What should I call you?"

"How about Mrs. Raven Hook, who is madly and passionately in love with her husband?"

She tossed the poker on the floor, raced over, and leapt into his arms.

CHAPTER TWENTY-FIVE

"Will you take me back to your castle someday?"

"If you wish."

"It was a real place, wasn't it? I didn't dream it?"

"No, you didn't dream it."

Sarah smiled across the table at Jean Pierre.

They were heading to Bramble Bay and had stopped at a coaching inn for the night. Shortly, they'd reach the coast, would turn north and complete their journey. Before riding out, they were enjoying a leisurely breakfast in the dining room.

She sighed with contentment. She was so happy!

"Why are you smiling?" he asked.

"Because you're with me, and we're on our way to Bramble Bay."

"It doesn't take much to gladden you."

"No, it doesn't. I'm a simple woman with simple tastes. Bramble Bay is my home, and you are my one true love. I'm lucky to have you both."

She knew him well enough now to understand that he wouldn't voice a similar statement of heightened affection, but still, she waited for it. She was such a romantic person and wouldn't believe he didn't love her. He just didn't realize it yet and would probably never be able to tell her.

"I like your family," she said.

"You would."

"You liked them, too. Don't be surly. Admit it."

"They were all right."

"Who was your favorite?"

"Must I pick a favorite?"

"Yes. I liked Harriet. How about you?"

"I liked Harriet."

"What did you two talk about when you were out on Phillip's verandah?"

"She told me how awful I was."

Sarah rolled her eyes. "She did not."

"She wanted to know if I was sorry for how I behaved toward her and her husband. I said I wasn't."

"Oh, you are the most exasperating man. You *are* sorry. Why must you deny it?"

He grinned a self-deprecating grin. "I suppose I might be sorry, but it happened such a long time ago. It doesn't seem as if I was actually the culprit."

"Trust me: You were," Sarah scolded. "Now tell me the truth. What did you discuss?"

"She demanded that I stop pirating."

"Of course you'll stop. Your life of crime is over."

"And she wants me to meet Tristan and James."

"Will you?"

"I haven't decided. She claims I owe her and my meeting them was the boon she requested so we'd be even. But you're aware of how stubborn I am."

"You'll likely refuse just on general principles."

"It's entirely possible."

Sarah didn't think he and Harriet would ever be even, but she didn't say so. She was delighted to imagine he would eventually meet his Harcourt brothers.

"Perhaps we should invite them to our wedding," she suggested merely to needle him. He was so horrified that she laughed and laughed.

They had obtained a Special License so they could marry immediately. The ceremony would be held at the church in Bramble Bay village where she'd always attended services. Once they were home, she would spend a few days making arrangements, then they'd proceed.

He was the consummate bachelor and still chafing at the notion of being shackled, and she received incredible amusement from watching him squirm and fret.

"James and Tristan Harcourt?" he practically gasped. "At my wedding?"

"You'd survive it."

His scowl was ferocious. "No, we're not inviting them."

She laughed again. "I doubt Harriet realizes the obstacle she's created with her demand. You'll be a hundred years old before you've calmed enough to speak civilly with them."

"I might be a hundred and fifty."

"You might be two-hundred and fifty."

"I might."

She abandoned all manners and placed an elbow on the table, her chin resting in her hand. She never grew tired of looking at him and wondered if she ever would. He was studying her too, as if committing her features to memory.

Ever since the party with his siblings, he'd been observing her intently. She sensed that he was extremely distressed, as if he was dying to confide a secret, but couldn't spit it out.

The past few months had been very difficult for him, even though he pretended he wasn't affected. He'd been in prison, certain to be executed. But then, he hadn't been. That sort of experience could definitely warp a person. How did a man come out the other side with any equilibrium? She suspected it would be a long while before he was completely recovered from his ordeal.

She was taking him to Bramble Bay so he could relax and regroup, so she could gradually get him to ponder the future and how he would carry on. She was eager for him to pick a new path where he could feel relevant and useful in an endeavor that interested him.

She still owned Bramble Bay, and she'd tried to give it back to him so he'd have a connection to the property, so he could start to plant roots and learn what it meant to belong. But the oaf wouldn't accept it.

"I need to explain several things," he said, and his tone was so serious that she was greatly unnerved. For days, he'd seemed on the verge of confessions. Would they finally be voiced?

"What things?"

"First, I bought a house for Mildred in London, and I've set up a small trust fund for her so she'll have an income."

"You did that for Mildred? After all the trouble she caused you?"

"I did it for you. I'm turning over a new leaf, remember?"

"Yes, I remember."

"My mother wouldn't want me to punish her."

"You're being very kind—when I know you don't think Mildred deserves it. Thank you. I hope it will bring about a reconciliation between you."

He didn't agree or disagree, but pulled an envelope from his coat and slid it across the table.

"This contains all the information for her."

"Can't you give it to her yourself?"

He shook his head. "I have made many concessions for you, *chérie,* but there are limits."

She sighed, recognizing that she'd be walking a long road with him, but she was an optimist, and any conclusion might occur. Mildred was his aunt, and they should resolve their differences. Sarah would always expect it to transpire.

"All right," she said.

"Mildred may have these gifts from me—with my blessing—only if she leaves Bramble Bay. She can't ever come back."

"I wouldn't mind."

"I would. If she tries to return, it will all be revoked, and she'll have nothing. I need to be sure you're safe from her."

"I have you to protect me now."

He nodded, but didn't reply. "Please also apprise her that Hedley has left England. She'll worry, and she shouldn't."

Sarah frowned. "Left England? Where did he go?"

"He's joined the merchant marines."

"He's on a sailing ship?"

"Yes."

His expression was completely blank, the one he was so good at displaying when he didn't want her to guess his mischief. She hated seeing it.

"What have you done to him?"

"I'm giving him a chance to grow up. That's all."

"So you forced him to work on a ship?"

"It seemed better than killing him. If I'd murdered him, I thought you'd be upset."

Her temper sparked. "You can't just kidnap someone off the street and toss him in with a crew of sailors. Hedley has never worked a day in his life! He'll likely perish from the pressure of it. What were you thinking?"

"You have to be safe from him, too."

"Oh, for heaven's sake, I'm not afraid of Hedley. You should have asked me to—"

He laid his hand over hers, the gesture quieting her complaint. He looked so grave, so somber.

"Reggie Thompson has been reviewing the estate ledgers at Bramble Bay."

"What has he found?"

"Your father bequeathed you an inheritance and a very fine dowry."

"No, he didn't."

"He did, Sarah."

"Mildred and I discussed it on numerous occasions. There was no mention of me in the will."

More firmly, he insisted, "Your father provided for you. He was very generous."

"Then what happened to the money?"

"Hedley squandered it."

There was a lengthy, excruciating silence as she digested the news, the ramifications.

"Did Mildred know?" she eventually asked.

"Yes. She spent quite a bit of it, too."

"I see…" His hand still covered hers, and she glanced down at it, liking how it seemed to shelter and bolster her. She gave a futile laugh and tears filled her eyes. "She told me my father didn't care about me."

"She lied, *chérie*."

"She said I was a disappointment to him, that he hadn't been proud."

"She's a hard woman, Sarah."

"Yes, she is."

"So this is why you must swear to me that you won't let her prevail on you. Even if I'm around to protect you, she might go behind my back to pressure you, and I wouldn't know. I've made arrangements for her specifically so there's no reason for you to bother with her."

"I understand."

"Do you?"

His sharp question had her fuming.

"Yes, I understand."

"Promise me that you won't ever permit her to live at Bramble Bay and that you'll allow me to support her—so you never have to."

"I promise. I won't let her back."

"Good."

He studied her for another long while, the tense moment festering, and she hated that they were quarreling. Over Mildred again! It was so exhausting, and Sarah loathed how family issues bubbled up to plague them.

She smiled, desperate to ease over the awkwardness. After the previous stressful weeks, she only wanted him calm and content.

"How many children do you think we'll have?" she asked.

"Me? A father? Are you mad?"

"Children are usually the end result after a marriage. Didn't anyone tell you?"

"But *children*. Gad." He shuddered. "Besides, I can't sire any; you know that. Why you'd wed a man who can't fill a nursery is a mystery to me."

She ignored the comment. "If our first is a girl, shall I name her after your mother?"

"And curse her? No. Give her a pretty name that will notify everyone she is beautiful like her mother."

At the compliment, she preened with delight. "You can be so charming when you wish to be. What if it's a boy? Should I name him after your father?"

"Absolutely not."

"How about after you."

"Again, why would you curse him? Give him a name that will warn the world he is a force with which to be reckoned."

"I'll make a list, shall I? Or shall I surprise you with my choices?"

"Surprise me, *chérie*."

"I will." She assessed him, afraid for their future, but excited for it, too. "Will you be happy at Bramble Bay? I want you to love it there—as I have always loved it."

His thoughts unreadable, he said, "I don't know if I've ever been happy."

"Then you'll be very happy with me, for I intend to spend my life spoiling you."

"You're kind to me, Sarah. Kinder than I deserve. I'm lucky to have met you."

"Yes, you are."

He gazed at her, brimming with affection, then he rose and stepped around the table.

"I must settle our bill. Finish your breakfast. I'll be back in a few minutes."

"I can't bear to be parted from you even for a short time."

"I'm sure you'll manage."

He leaned nearer, as if he might kiss her, right there in the inn's dining room while they were surrounded by other customers. But in the end, he didn't.

He drew away, and she watched him go, gaping like a smitten ninny. She pulled her eyes away from the door and began eating again. With her recent tribulations, she was constantly hungry. She gorged like a field hand, cleaned her plate, then cleaned Jean Pierre's, too.

He hadn't returned, and she figured he was out in the yard, having the horses saddled. She drank a cup of tea. Drank another. Still, there was no sign of him.

She'd just decided not to wait any longer, to join him in the yard, when she heard booted strides out in the foyer. She glanced up, expecting Jean Pierre, but to her consternation, Raven was there instead.

She stared and stared, not comprehending what she was witnessing. Why was Raven at the coaching inn?

"Hello, Sarah." He came over and sat in the chair Jean Pierre had vacated.

"How did you know we were here? Did you see Jean Pierre out at the stable?"

"No, I didn't see him."

His expression was odd, as if he was regretful or embarrassed.

"Where is he?"

"He's gone, Sarah."

"Gone...where?"

"To France."

"He...what?"

"He left."

She cocked her head, confused, as if Raven was speaking in a foreign language.

"We're on our way to Bramble Bay." Pointlessly, she added, "We're getting married."

"He didn't want to get married."

"What? Of course he wanted to. The celebration is all planned. We applied for a Special License and everything."

Her comments sounded plaintive and naïve, as if she was the stupidest woman who'd ever lived, as if she'd been seduced by a rogue and was only now learning the true extent of her folly.

"He loved you, Sarah. Never think he didn't. That's why he went."

"Because he loved me?"

"Yes."

"You're not making any sense."

Raven stood and held out his hand. "Let's go."

"To where?"

"To Bramble Bay. I'm here to take you home."

"But…but…Jean Pierre was taking me. Don't tell me he isn't."

Raven was quiet for a lengthy interval, then he murmured, "When enough time has passed, you'll realize this is for the best."

"It's not for the best. I have to see him! I have to talk to him!"

"He doesn't wish to talk to you. I'm sorry."

He gestured to the door, and she studied him, the door, him again. She yearned to jump up and rush outside, to climb onto her horse and race after Jean Pierre. How many minutes had elapsed? How far had he traveled? Which direction had he ridden?

But with a heavy heart, she grasped that if he didn't want to be found, he never would be.

The strength had gone out of her legs, and she couldn't catch her breath. She couldn't push back her chair, couldn't stand.

He left…he left…he left…

The words kept ringing in her mind.

How long ago had he decided?

If Raven had been informed of where they would be and when— he'd come to fetch her as if she was a stray dog on the side of the road—then Jean Pierre had never intended to marry her. He'd ruined her with impunity, then fled. Apparently, he was his father's son in every way.

Every detail about him had been a lie. She'd imbued him with character traits he didn't possess, had convinced herself that he could change, that he could become the man she'd dreamed he could be rather than the man he was.

Though she'd temporarily believed differently, she wasn't unique or special, wasn't able to entice and hold a man like John Sinclair. Not at all. Hadn't Mildred always said as much? Her nephew was simply reconfirming her low opinion.

What now? What was Sarah to do with herself?

For so many months, her entire world had revolved around him. She'd assumed they would be together. Yet a connection was the very last thing he'd envisioned. All this time, what had he thought? What had *he* planned?

While she'd been weaving a grand scheme for the future where they would be blissfully content at Bramble Bay, he'd been watching the rear door, wondering if it would be a good moment to sneak off.

His ability to walk away as if she'd meant nothing, as if she'd given him nothing, was cruel and malicious. How could he treat her so badly?

A wave of fury swept through her. It was so virulent that she was glad she was sitting down when it hit. If she'd been standing, the force of it might have knocked her over.

"Yes, let's go home," she mumbled more to herself than to Raven. "And swear to me that you won't mention his name to me ever again."

"Sarah, he didn't feel he was worthy of you. You're so fine, and he—"

"Swear to me!"

He sighed. "All right, I won't."

She lurched to her feet and staggered out.

CHAPTER TWENTY-SIX

"I suppose I would consider it."

"You're too kind, Sheldon. I can't tell you how grateful I am."

Mildred was in the hall outside Sheldon's front parlor. He was sequestered with a female, the door ajar, and she frowned, wondering to whom he was speaking.

He'd been gone for several days and was finally home. She'd had a maid fix her hair, had put on her best dress, then hurried down to greet him as if they were married, as if she was his wife.

She kept trying to solidify their friendship, eager for him to recognize that she was helpful and competent, but he ignored her every attempt to ingratiate herself.

Quietly, she stepped nearer and peeked in. To her dismay, Sarah was with him, sitting in the exact spot where Mildred sat in the evenings when it was late and she and Sheldon were alone.

"There are many issues to contemplate," Sheldon was saying. "I'll have to meet with my solicitor."

"I don't have a lot of time for delay. Very soon, there will be no hiding it."

"I could probably have an answer for you in two weeks. This situation has been worsening for months. Another week or two won't make a difference."

"I feel so disgraced. I wouldn't want to add to the gossip, and I wouldn't want any shame to attach to you."

"We're the largest landowners in the neighborhood. Who would dare to spread stories?"

"With the way my luck's been running, just about anyone."

Suddenly, Sheldon appeared very sly, and he said, "If I decide to assist you, I should get Bramble Bay for my trouble. Wouldn't you agree? You'd have to sign it over to me."

Sarah seemed taken aback. "You'd expect to have it?"

"I'd be giving up an awful lot. Think of all you're asking me to do."

"It hadn't occurred to me," Sarah murmured. "I thought I'd keep it."

He scoffed. "I always forget how young you are, how inexperienced in business matters. There's a price for everything."

"But Bramble Bay."

"I'm afraid it would have to be part of any deal we struck. I couldn't move forward in any other fashion."

Mildred scowled. Sheldon was demanding Bramble Bay and Sarah might give it to him? What were they discussing?

Mildred had few options remaining, but if Sarah relinquished the estate to Sheldon, Mildred had no options at all. Sarah couldn't surrender Bramble Bay. Mildred absolutely would not let her.

She braced and breezed into the room, pretending she'd just arrived, pretending she hadn't eavesdropped.

"Sheldon," she cheerfully said, "I heard you were home."

"Hello, Mildred." On seeing her, his annoyance was clear, but he quickly masked it, exuding his typical courtesy.

Mildred blustered through the awkward moment. "Sarah, I didn't realize you were visiting."

"Mildred." Sarah tipped her head in acknowledgement, but offered no other greeting.

She and Sarah hadn't spoken since the day of John Sinclair's arrest, but Sarah had always been kindhearted, willing to forgive and forget. Mildred prayed this occasion was no different.

Mildred had to reaffirm her relationship with Sarah, had to set Sarah to rights so she remembered her family, her responsibility to Mildred. Sheldon had to be put in his place. He wasn't getting his greedy paws on Bramble Bay.

"You two certainly look glum," Mildred said. "What's happened?"

"Mildred"—Sheldon's exasperation bubbled up—"this is a private chat. I'll have to ask you to leave."

"Leave? Don't be silly. Sarah is my stepdaughter, and there have never been any secrets between us." She flashed a warm smile at Sarah. "You don't mind if I listen in, do you, Sarah?"

She didn't know what reply she'd expected from Sarah, but it wasn't the one she received.

"How much money was bequeathed to me in my father's will?"

Mildred sucked in a sharp breath, then glanced away. Her cheeks reddened; she couldn't stop a shameful blush from spreading.

"I've told you numerous times: You weren't named as a beneficiary."

"What was to be in my dowry? Was it property? What had Father arranged?"

"Sarah, he left you *nothing*, and I hate it that you persist in inquiring."

Sheldon butted in. "Why are you asking, Sarah?"

"Before Mr. Sinclair returned to France, his accountant audited the estate ledgers."

"Obviously, he found a discrepancy," Sheldon said.

"Father provided me with a very fine inheritance and dowry. Mildred lied to me and—"

"I did not!" Mildred indignantly huffed.

Sarah ignored her and kept talking to Sheldon. "Hedley squandered it in London. Mildred wasted a good portion of it, too."

"Mildred, is this true?" Sheldon's disdain was aggravating to witness.

"No, it's not true. Why would you accept the word of a notorious pirate over mine? Of course we didn't take what wasn't ours, because there wasn't anything to take. There was no dowry for Sarah."

"Despite what you claim," Sheldon pompously intoned, "Mr. Sinclair is *not* a pirate. The court adjudged that he's the natural-born son of the Earl of Trent and a very rich gentleman in his own right. I hardly suppose he'd fabricate an audit."

"Sheldon," Sarah said, "did you ever discuss the issue with my father?"

"No, and now I'm regretting it. If I'd known about this, I'd never have let them steal from you."

"We stole nothing!" Mildred insisted, but she couldn't hold their condemning stares.

"Did Mr. Sinclair leave the ledgers at the estate?" Sheldon asked Sarah.

"Yes."

"Then we'll get to the bottom of it." He sat back, looking pretentious and irritating. "If Bramble Bay is to be mine, I might have a case to recover some of what they pilfered."

"Bramble Bay might be *yours*?" Mildred feigned innocence, as if it was the first time she'd heard the news. "Why would it pass to you?"

"Sarah and I are considering marriage."

Mildred shook her head to clear her ears. "You're what?"

"We're thinking of marrying. Mr. Sinclair has left England, and before he went, he gave the property to Sarah. If we proceed, it will come to me as her bride price."

"But...but..." Mildred stammered.

She wanted to say, *I thought you and I would wed! I thought I would be your wife! It can't be Sarah! Anyone but Sarah!*

Yet if she dared to comment, she'd embarrass herself.

He had never evinced by the slightest word or deed that he would propose, but she'd worked so intently to win him. Sarah couldn't just waltz in and take him. Where was the fairness in that?

"Are you certain you should, Sheldon?" she blandly inquired. "Have you forgotten all the months I urged her to have you, and she constantly refused and delayed? Surely you should ponder a little more carefully."

Sheldon focused his gaze on Sarah, and he studied her, appearing a tad aggrieved with her, but only a tad. After all, if they married, he'd get Bramble Bay.

Sarah didn't shrink from his assessment, but was stoically silent, as if she deserved his rude appraisal and much more.

"Circumstances change," Sheldon ultimately mused, "and I believe Sarah has come to her senses."

"Well, I wouldn't trust her," Mildred churlishly snapped.

"You're not the one marrying her. It's between Sarah and myself. You shouldn't vex yourself over it."

"John Sinclair has a message for you, Mildred," Sarah said.

"A message from that brigand? I don't wish to hear it."

Sarah continued as if Mildred hadn't spoken. "He had Hedley kidnapped and conscripted into the merchant marines."

Mildred gasped. "He what?"

Sarah retrieved a satchel from the floor and pulled out some papers. She handed them to Mildred.

"It's all explained in these documents. He's proclaimed himself the male head of your family."

"The what? The man is insane!"

"He really is Florence's son, Mildred. I'm sorry for you that you were so cruel to him. Perhaps you should rethink the level of your dislike."

Mildred paled, growing so dizzy she thought she might faint. She staggered over to a chair and eased herself down.

"He can't be Florence's son," she muttered. "He can't be."

"He is. He sent Hedley away, and he's arranged for you to move to town."

"I don't want to move to town."

"He bought you a house."

"I don't want his blasted house!"

"Then I can't help you, and as Sheldon requested, you must leave us alone so we can finish our discussion. I'm a bit distraught, and there's nothing else for you and I to say to one another."

"I want to return to Bramble Bay!" Mildred fumed. "I want my home back! I want my son back! I want my life back!"

"None of that will happen, Mildred, and you really need to go away."

Sheldon—always the calm port in any storm—stood and clasped Mildred by the elbow. He tugged her to her feet.

"Let's get you up to your room."

"I won't be shuttled off like a recalcitrant toddler."

"After Sarah departs, you and I can review the paperwork Mr. Sinclair prepared. I'll bet we can have you packed and ready to travel to London tomorrow morning." He grinned condescendingly. "I'm happy to let you use my carriage."

He pushed her into the hall and closed the door. The key spun in the lock, and she lurched to the stairs and trudged up to her bedchamber. She flopped down on the bed, wailing in misery, a veritable cauldron of fury and woe.

She'd lost everything. Because of Florence. Because of her rebellious, indecent, immoral sister.

She'd had to wed Bernard because of Florence. She'd had to settle in the country in the middle of nowhere, had had to live quietly and futilely at the rural farm. Decade after decade, the excitement of town had sped by.

Now, because of Florence, she'd also lost her home and her son. And Sarah, too. Sarah was the only person who might have aided Mildred, who might have allowed Mildred to come home where she belonged.

When she arrived in the city, her first act would be to purchase a pistol. She'd keep it loaded and would carry it with her at all times. If she ever saw John Sinclair again, she'd shoot him right between the eyes.

"Sarah, there you are. Where have you been?"

"I went to talk to Sheldon."

Sarah was standing at the rear windows of the parlor, gazing down the sloping lawn to the ocean off in the distance. It was a cold autumn day, the water stormy with whitecaps.

Was John Sinclair on the other shore, in France, staring at the same roiling waves? Or had he sailed off to warmer climes, to sunny beaches and tropical foliage where he could drink and loaf and pretend he had no responsibilities? Was the impertinent ass enjoying himself? Did he ever wonder about her—as she wondered about him?

Stop it! she scolded. *Stop moping over him! Stop obsessing!*

There was no point anymore, was there?

She glanced over her shoulder to where Caroline hovered in the doorway. She was no longer Caroline Patterson, but Mrs. Caroline Hook, having married her beloved Raven at the earliest opportunity.

While John Sinclair had flitted off to parts unknown, having no ties to bind him, Raven had proved himself to be absurdly devoted. He'd stayed with Caroline. He'd wed her, and they were ridiculously happy.

Sarah wanted to be glad for them, wanted to celebrate Caroline's marvelous turn of fortune. But apparently, Sarah was a very petty person. She couldn't bear to watch them cuddle and coo.

Fate was so cruel. Why had they ended up with everything while Sarah was to have nothing? She was sick at heart, feeling wretched and betrayed and more alone than she'd ever been.

"You went to see Sheldon?" Caroline said. "You poor dear. Are you ill? Are you deranged?"

"Come in, would you? And sit down? I need to tell you some distressing news."

"My goodness. This sounds serious."

"It is."

Caroline plopped down on a sofa, and as Sarah seated herself in the chair across, Caroline scowled.

"Sarah, you look awful. I was joking about your being ill. Are you?"

"I'm not ill."

"Then what's wrong? You're pale as a ghost."

There wasn't any reason to dither or delay. Wasn't it best to get it out in the open? To be blunt and direct?

"Sheldon and I have decided to marry."

Caroline gasped with astonishment. "You what? No, no, no, you can't mean it."

"He has to resolve some issues with his solicitor, but once all the contracts are drawn up, we'll wed."

"Oh, Sarah, I can't let you. This is madness. What are you thinking?"

"I'm increasing," she brusquely stated.

"You're...having a baby?"

"Yes."

"And Sheldon agreed to marry you?"

"Yes."

"The child couldn't possibly be his. Who is the father?" Caroline stopped herself. "Well, obviously, it's Jean Pierre."

Sarah merely shrugged.

"Did you tell Sheldon about your affair?"

"I was very frank, and he was very kind."

Caroline scoffed. "Sheldon is many things, but he's *not* kind. Don't pretend that he was."

"Under the circumstances, he was a veritable knight in shining armor."

"Does Jean Pierre know?"

"I don't see how he would. Sheldon is the only one I've told besides you."

"We have to get word to him immediately. Raven has a secret method for contacting him. We'll send a letter."

"We're not sending any letter."

"Yes, we are. He has to haul his sorry behind back to England and marry you himself."

"No." Sarah shook her head. "I don't want that."

"Don't be daft. Of course he has to come back."

"John Sinclair doesn't care about me, Caroline. He doesn't care about anyone but himself. He never has."

"This doesn't have to do with *caring*. This has to do with the fact that he sired a child on you, and he has to pay the price. Matrimony is the price."

"He wouldn't think so."

"He doesn't get to have an opinion. That's how the world works. A man misbehaves, and shortly after, he finds his butt at the altar, with a leg shackle being hammered onto his ankle."

"Not John Sinclair. He's his father's son in every way, and I won't humiliate myself by begging him to assist me."

"Don't say that."

Sarah sighed, hating the entire conversation.

From the moment she'd realized her condition, she'd known what she had to do.

John had been very clear as to his feelings about Sarah. While she'd been merrily planning their future, he'd been furtively plotting to abandon her at a coaching inn. He'd ridden away without a goodbye or backward glance.

It remained the most mortifying episode of her life, and if she lived to be a hundred, she didn't imagine she'd ever recover from the shame of how he'd treated her.

Still though, all these weeks later, she kept stupidly assuming he'd change his mind. She kept watching the road, expecting to see him galloping in on his white stallion. She kept watching the mail, assuming he would write to tell her he hadn't meant it, that he was coming back to her.

Yet from the day they'd met, he'd played her for a fool, and she had to cease her fantastical dreaming that she could have a different ending with him. He was who he was: a cold, hard man who didn't bond or attach himself. She didn't think he *could* attach himself.

She could have Raven rush to France, could wait and pray that Raven could persuade him. But he wouldn't return, and she didn't dare deceive herself, because she didn't have time to waste. If Raven chased after him, it might be months before Raven staggered in with the degrading news that she'd been rebuffed.

What then?

She'd leapt into their affair without pausing to worry about the ramifications. She'd been so idiotically enamored, so unsophisticated at amour, that the prospect of a pregnancy or the fact that she had no ring on her finger had never occurred to her.

As she'd grown more wary and had fretted, John had sworn he couldn't sire a child. She'd believed him! And she had to accept that—like his reprehensible father—he probably had offspring scattered across the globe.

A single woman couldn't blithely fornicate without consequences arising. There were laws and moral teachings that prohibited decadent acts. No person in the neighborhood would tolerate her disgraceful ruination. No person would be civil or forgive her sins. She couldn't stay at Bramble Bay and be a mother with no husband.

The only other option was to leave and give birth elsewhere, to have the baby adopted. But she truly thought it would be the sole child she would ever have, and she simply couldn't force herself to hand it over to strangers.

She had frantically ruminated, had chastised and searched for solutions—but there was only one solution. That being marriage as rapidly as it could be accomplished.

Sheldon was the only man available to her. She didn't know any other candidate whom she could possibly ask to take such a shocking step, to wed her when she was carrying the babe of another.

He'd been her father's friend. He'd been Sarah's friend, and she'd gone to him because she could confide in him, because he would listen and help. She'd prevailed on him horridly, and he'd agreed to aid her. It was over. It was done, and she wouldn't renege or second guess.

Once in her life, she'd deemed him fussy and pedantic and much too old for her. But now, he was the perfect choice: wise, mature, prudent. He would see her through the coming debacle, and in return, she would be a good wife to him.

Previously, she'd viewed herself as a hopeless romantic who would only wed for love and passion. Well, she'd had all the love and passion a female could ever imagine, and where had it landed her?

Abandoned at a roadside coaching inn, that's where.

She needed constancy. She needed stability. She needed a savior who would proceed quickly and quietly prior to anyone being aware of how she'd shamed herself.

"I'm marrying Sheldon," she said again. "It's already settled."

"Even after you told him everything?"

"Yes."

"He's willing to raise another man's child as his own? Why would he? It makes no sense. What has he to gain by granting you this enormous favor?"

"I offered him a large dowry. When he learned the amount, he was more than happy to have me."

"A dowry? You don't have two pennies to rub together."

"No, but I have Bramble Bay."

Caroline frowned, confused. Then understanding dawned, and she blanched. "You're giving him your family's home? The Teasdales have owned Bramble Bay for hundreds of years. How could you consider it?"

"What else can I do, Caroline? I must have a husband." She gestured toward the door. "Is there a row of suitors lined up in the hall? It's not as if I can court and woo. I have to move forward right away—before the scandal leaks out."

"But Bramble Bay, Sarah! Think what you're doing!"

"Believe me. I've thought plenty."

"Jean Pierre gave the estate to you so you'd always be safe."

"Yes, and I'm using it to save myself. It seems a fitting conclusion, doesn't it?"

"You can't do this, Sarah. I'm telling Raven. There has to be a better way."

"There is no other way, Caroline. Just let it go."

Sarah was weary and afraid and exhausted. She pushed herself to her feet and staggered from the room before Caroline uttered other painful comments she couldn't bear to hear.

CHAPTER TWENTY-SEVEN

John dismounted and tossed the reins to his stable boy.

He'd been riding for hours out in the countryside, the brisk winter wind whipping at his hair and clothes. He felt dead inside, so he was trying to animate himself, desperate to learn if anything—cold temperatures, exhausting fatigue—could make a dent.

Weeks earlier, he'd returned to his castle where he was anxious to recuperate after all the drama in England. Yet to his surprise, he'd found no solace.

His prior visit, he'd brought Sarah with him, and he'd believed he could come back without her. But nothing was the same, and she seemed to be haunting the halls.

He gazed to the small harbor. Out in the Channel, the ocean was angry and gray, whitecaps roiling the water. Sarah was on the other shore, safe at Bramble Bay.

After being freed from prison, they'd spent a few contented days together. She'd assumed he would stay in England with her, but he'd never yearned for any of the pleasures she enjoyed. He'd never craved a home or family or wife. Had he?

He constantly posed that question, and he was so confused by the answers he received.

He'd left her because he was the worst wretch in the world, and he'd only hurt her in the end. But he ceaselessly obsessed over what might have been. She'd dangled a life in front of him that he'd never expected to have. He hadn't wanted what she was offering, so why couldn't he let it go? Why couldn't he forget about her?

Did she ever stand on the verandah at Bramble Bay and stare out across the Channel? Did she ever think of him and wonder how he was faring?

He snorted with disgust. Of course she didn't. She'd hate him now, having realized it had all been lies, that it had been physical seduction and naught else. He wasn't capable of giving a woman more than that, and she'd dreamed of so much more.

"Stop it!" he muttered to himself. He had to stop pining and fretting over her.

"Have I upset you, sir?" the stable boy asked.

"No, no." John shook his head, feeling stupid and worried that some of his mother's madness was finally taking hold.

He was loitering in the yard, talking to himself, and consumed with memories of a female he'd harmed terribly and would never see again. If that wasn't a sign of pending lunacy, he didn't know what was.

He pointed to the harbor where an unidentified ship had dropped anchor.

"Have you heard who's arrived?"

"No," the boy replied, and he kept on with John's horse.

John went into the castle, and as usual, a bevy of servants flitted up. Everyone was eager to help, to serve.

"You have guests," the butler said.

"Guests?"

"Yes. From England."

His heart literally skipped a beat as he figured it had to be Sarah. But as quickly as the ridiculous notion arose, he pushed it away. Sarah wouldn't have any idea how to find his tiny village, and even if she could, she'd never waste her time.

"Master Hook is here," the butler advised. "They traveled with him."

"Raven is back?" John grinned with delight, but there was concern beneath the surface. Raven was supposed to be at Bramble Bay watching over Sarah. Had something happened?

Dread flooding him, he asked, "Where are they?"

"In the main hall. I invited them to stay and dine with us. Master Hook will, but the others declined."

"Their loss." John's chef prepared fine suppers, and John was happy he wouldn't have to share his meal with any stuffy Brits.

"Will you see them?"

"Yes." John started off, the butler dogging his heels. "What are their names?"

"Master Hook wishes to make the introductions."

John raised a curious brow, then marched in. It was Raven and two men, and John bit down a wave of disappointment that Sarah wasn't with them—even though he hadn't expected her to be.

Raven lived with John, so he was lounged on a sofa, enjoying a brandy and a warm fire. The other two were standing over by the window, staring out, their backs to John. They were dressed in expensive clothes, which meant they were rich snobs who would annoy John enormously.

They were tall, dark-haired, broad-shouldered, their legs spread as if they were soldiers ready for inspection by their commanding officer.

Typical Englishmen! he fumed, his habitual dislike bubbling up like soup in a pot. Fussy. Pompous. Irksome and vain. They thought they owned the bloody world, and he'd always been thrilled to prove that they didn't.

"There you are," Raven said in French. "I didn't think you'd ever get here."

The visitors spun to face John, and one of them said, "Speak English, Mr. Hook. I've been out of the schoolroom for a long while, and my French isn't that fluent anymore. I want to be sure I understand every word you two scoundrels say."

Raven rolled his eyes as John studied the pair. There was a familiar aspect to them, but he couldn't quite place it.

"You're guests in my castle," John snapped, "so you have an incredible amount of gall to hurl insults the moment I walk in. If you can't mind your manners, you don't have to remain. I'm big enough and bad enough to throw your asses out. Shall we see if I can manage it?"

"This is going to go as poorly as I suspected," Raven mumbled. "Sorry, Jean Pierre, but they insisted I escort them, and I let them persuade me." He flicked a thumb at the glowering oafs. "The fellow on the right is your brother, James Harcourt, the exalted Earl of Westwood. The fellow on your left is your brother, Tristan."

"The one we tried our best to kill?" John snidely taunted.

"Yes, and unfortunately, we didn't succeed."

John was so stunned that he could barely stay on his feet. He couldn't show any weakness and should have tossed them out as he'd threatened he would, but he was too bewildered to storm over and do it.

They'd crossed the Channel to find him? Why would they have? During all the months he'd been in England, they hadn't bothered. When he'd been sitting in the execution cell at Newgate, they hadn't bothered. When he'd had supper at Phillip's, they hadn't bothered.

Yet suddenly, they were dying to make his acquaintance. Suddenly, they'd braved the winter ocean in order to meet him. Raven had dared bring them—when he'd known how John would resent the intrusion.

"Obviously a peculiar event has transpired, and you can't wait to tell me about it."

"Obviously," Lord Westwood sneered.

The butler was hovering, and John gestured to him. "It looks as if this will be a lengthy discussion. Pour whiskey all around, would you?"

The man nodded and hurried to comply. Swiftly, he had the sideboard opened, the drinks served. As he slipped out, Raven peered over his shoulder and said to the Harcourts, "You demanded to speak with him. Get on with it."

"If you'll excuse us, Mr. Hook?" the earl said. "This is a private chat."

"If it concerns Jean Pierre," Raven replied, "it concerns me. I guard his back and always have. If he asks me to knock your foolish heads together and drown you in the harbor, I will."

Tristan Harcourt bristled as if he might stomp over to see if Raven was tough enough to carry out his threat, but Lord Westwood stopped him.

"We're here about Sarah Teasdale," the earl haughtily announced.

It was the last comment John had anticipated, and he carefully shielded his reaction. Was she sick? Was she injured?

"What about her?" John coolly inquired.

"It's come to our attention," Tristan said, "that you ruined her, then abandoned her without following through on the marriage you promised."

"And your point is...?"

"We have a few issues with cads who seduce innocent maidens and leave them in the lurch."

Tristan appeared too incensed to continue, and the earl was happy to jump in.

"We especially have issues with Charles Sinclair ruining maidens and walking away. We're not about to let his son do the same."

"Miss Teasdale is fine," John bit out. "I won her home from her brother, but I returned it to her. Raven is there to watch over her, and my clerk—Mr. Thompson—is there too, to assist her in getting the accounts back in the black. So if you're here to complain about her situation, it was a wasted trip."

Westwood glanced at his brother and murmured, "He doesn't know. I figured he didn't."

"I figured he did," Tristan seethed. "I figured he knew and didn't give a damn. Just like his father."

"What the hell are you talking about?" John snapped.

Raven supplied the answer. "You planted a babe in Sarah's belly, Jean Pierre."

"I...what?"

"She's having a baby. You've left her in a terrible jam."

"She didn't mention it to me."

"When you headed to France, I doubt she knew."

"She definitely knows now," Lord Westwood muttered. He ordered Raven, "Tell him what she's planned."

But Raven didn't take orders from anyone but John.

"Tell him yourself," Raven spat.

"I can't. I'm so disgusted to see another Sinclair male acting this way that I'd probably choke on the words."

John looked at Raven. "What is she doing?"

"She's arranged to wed her neighbor."

"Which one?"

"Some asshole who's thirty years older than she is. He was a friend of her father's."

"She told me about him once," John said.

"Tell him the rest," Westwood insisted. "Let him hear the worst of it."

"He's demanded a dowry."

John frowned. "She doesn't have a dowry."

"She has Bramble Bay," Raven explained, "and he wants it as his bride price. She's agreed to give it to him."

"She wouldn't have," John said.

"She has," Westwood confirmed. "He'll marry her and raise her child as his own, but at a steep cost. I don't believe she should have to pay it. Do you?"

The question hung in the air between them as John furiously assessed the catastrophe he'd set in motion. The news was so surprising and disconcerting.

He'd never previously sired a child, was convinced he *couldn't* sire a child, so he hadn't worried about any carnal consequences for Sarah. If she'd lived in Paris, she might have been able to brazen it out, might have been able to birth a bastard and flaunt it to the neighbors. But she couldn't get away with such brash conduct in stuffy, rural England.

Yet, what was the best way to assist her?

She was better off without him. He wasn't the man she assumed him to be, and he would never be that man. Nothing had changed to alter that fact, so why would he inflict himself on her?

He didn't know how to be a father, didn't *want* to be a father, but he couldn't allow another man to rear his child. It wasn't an ending he could tolerate.

For a moment, he could practically see the baby they had created. It would be a little girl with his blond hair and her mother's pretty blue eyes. He could visualize his daughter skipping through the foyer at Bramble Bay Manor, her starched petticoat swishing with each step. She'd be smart and sassy and merry in a manner John had never dreamed of being as a boy.

But as quickly as the vision arose, he shoved it away. He was never ruled by sentiment. He never let emotion push him to recklessness. He thought carefully, then acted.

What did he want? What should he do?

"My wife," Tristan Harcourt stated, "is very fond of Miss Teasdale."

"Mine, too," Westwood added. "They are affronted that you— their brother—would behave this way. You suffered so dreadfully because of Charles's illicit affairs, yet you're behaving in the same dastardly fashion."

Tristan said, "Miss Teasdale saved your life and this is how you thank her?"

John downed his whiskey, poured himself another and downed that, too. He went over to a chair and eased himself into it. He studied the floor, trying to decide the best path.

Finally, he looked over at his brothers and admitted, "I left her because I knew she'd be better off without me."

"I'm sure she would be," the earl concurred, "but that ship has sailed, Mr. Sinclair. My wife will not sit idly by and have her niece or nephew born a bastard."

"And *my* wife," Tristan fumed, "reminds you that you owe her. She demands you wed Miss Teasdale."

John sighed, having long since accepted that he and Harriet would never be even.

"I can't deny Harriet any request," he grumbled.

"You shouldn't even think about it," Tristan warned.

"What is it you're asking of me?"

"Travel to England with us."

"Tonight?"

"Yes, on the next tide."

"Why so fast?"

"The wedding is in three days, and we intend that you arrive before it's held."

"To do what?"

"To marry her yourself, you thick oaf," Tristan snarled. "Now pack a bag so we can get going.

Tristan stared out at the starry sky, enjoying the roll of the waves beneath his feet. He didn't sail much anymore and hadn't realized how much he missed it.

He still owned a fleet of ships, but ever since he'd come face to face with The French Terror, he let others captain them. The vessels were heavily fortified, the sailors trained and armed. No pirating brigand would ever take a Harcourt ship by surprise again.

He'd always considered himself to be very brave and probably still was, except that he had occasional nightmares where he was in the deadly swordfight with Jean Pierre. So why was he fussing with the wretched criminal? Why had he listened to Harriet? Why had he shown up at Jean Pierre's trial? Why had he agreed to drag Jean Pierre to the altar when he clearly didn't wish to be dragged?

Tristan adored his wife and would do anything for her. It was the sole answer that made any sense.

It was very late, and he'd thought he was the only one who couldn't sleep. But as he glanced toward the stern, he was irked to see Jean Pierre leaned on the rail and gazing out at the stars as Tristan was doing.

As Tristan noticed him, he noticed Tristan. Their dislike was blatant, but there was keen interest, too. How could there not be?

Tristan couldn't help but be curious. What drove a man like Jean Pierre? How could he sustain so much animosity? Had he calmed? Was he finished raging against the Sinclairs and Harcourts and their London friends?

Tristan had imagined he and his half-brother would hover in an awkward silence, but Jean Pierre astonished him by speaking.

"You love being out on the water."

"I do."

Tristan's response provided an opening. Jean Pierre strolled over, stopping next to Tristan.

"My courteous reply," Tristan rudely said, "wasn't an indication that we should be cordial. I'd rather not converse. I can't think of a single thing we need to say to one another."

"It's a free damn boat. Go to your cabin if you don't like the company out here on the deck."

"Aren't you afraid I might toss you overboard when no one is looking?"

"You can try, but you won't succeed. I'm always armed. I'll kill you before you can move." Jean Pierre tugged on his coat so Tristan glimpsed the butt of a small pistol.

"Maybe I'll risk it. Maybe I'd feel it was worth it."

"Raven Hook is sitting on a bench in the shadows behind us. If you get lucky and kill me, he'll kill you. He won't bat an eye."

Tristan peeked over, wondering if Hook was really hiding and watching them. He couldn't see Hook, but that didn't mean he wasn't there.

"Do you always have a nanny guarding your back?" Tristan snidely inquired, intending to needle Jean Pierre, but his half-brother shrugged.

"Always. You should consider it yourself. It beats being attacked in the dead of night and being set adrift on the ocean."

"Are you sorry for trying to murder me?"

"No."

"Harriet said you weren't, but I had to ask. Will you *ever* be sorry?"

"Perhaps if Sarah makes me into a better man, but I wouldn't count on it. I'm awfully incorrigible."

"Poor girl—having to marry you."

"Yes, a very poor girl indeed."

Jean Pierre turned to the water, and he peered out, ignoring Tristan, but Tristan couldn't resist studying him.

They were the same height, had the same stature of broad shoulders and long legs. Their feet were braced exactly the same way against the swaying of the ship. Only their hair and eyes were different. Tristan had the dark hair and blue eyes of the Harcourts, while Jean Pierre resembled his scoundrel father, Charles.

"You look just like me," he muttered.

"I noticed."

"I hate that."

"So do I."

Jean Pierre pulled out a flask and enjoyed a gulp of liquor. He offered the flask to Tristan, and Tristan hesitated, then grabbed it and took a swallow.

"You drank out of it first," Tristan said when he finished, "so it's probably not poisoned."

"No, it's not poisoned." Jean Pierre snorted with amusement. "Haven't you heard? I can't hurt you. I promised Charles and your wife. My pillaging days are over."

"I had heard you swore, but are you a man of your word? I wouldn't suppose so."

"I'm usually a liar, but Harriet and Charles went to so much trouble on my behalf. It would be churlish to repay them with deceit."

"I agree."

"I must pick a new path."

"What appeals to you?"

"Nothing, really. I relished my prior occupation."

"I imagine so. I'm told you have a criminal's heart."

"I do. I admit it. In comparison to piracy, every other profession seems terribly tepid."

"There are worse things in the world than tedium and monotony."

"I can't think of any."

"Didn't you get tired of the constant danger and risk?"

"No, never."

Jean Pierre gazed out again, and Tristan thought he actually looked sad and a bit lost as if—now that he'd vowed to improve himself—he couldn't figure out how.

Tristan felt a quiver of sympathy, and when he recognized it for what it was, he shook it away. He wouldn't empathize with Jean Pierre, wouldn't pity or commiserate. The man was a crazed killer, and no amount of cordial conversation would change that fact.

"You don't captain your own ships anymore," Jean Pierre said.

"Where did you hear that?"

"You'd be amazed at how much I know about you." He focused on Tristan again. "How can you bear it? Don't you miss having the waves under your feet?"

"Each and every second."

"You can take command again. I won't bother you."

"Harriet would wring my neck."

"It's difficult to go against her, isn't it? She's a tiny sprite, but she's a tyrant."

"You have no idea," Tristan mused. "If I'm in the mood to unfurl a sail, she'll only permit me pleasure jaunts up and down the Thames."

They both smiled, an exact curving of cheeks and lips that fully clarified their close kinship. They were quiet, sipping from Jean Pierre's flask, staring out at the stars.

Tristan was perplexed to find himself sharing a companionable moment, and he was awhirl with questions. Why not ask them? What was preventing him? He didn't expect to see Jean Pierre ever again, so he might not have another chance.

James had been two when their mother deserted them, and Tristan just a baby. They didn't remember her, and she'd been exorcised from the family history. There'd been no pictures of her in the house, no humorous anecdotes about her quirks and habits.

James always claimed he didn't care about their mother, why she'd left, why she'd stayed away. But her forsaking them had never rested easily with Tristan. Could Jean Pierre provide beneficial details? Should Tristan seek them?

"I must tell you, John"—Tristan called him by his English name—"that you speak very well, and you're purportedly a brilliant businessman, yet you were raised on the streets of Paris. How have you thrived? Were you educated?"

"Of course I was educated." He was incredibly irked by the uncouth query. "My mother was a British countess and my father a British earl. I wasn't some urchin, begging for bread."

"Not until you were ten anyway."

"You're correct: not until I was ten. Things fell apart that year, but prior to that, I had quite a grand life. We lived with my mother's various friends, and she was popular with a certain group of people. Writers and composers and the like. I had all sorts of tutors."

The most important question of all was on the tip of Tristan's tongue. Yet a voice in his head was crying, *Let it go! After all this time, how can it matter?*

Before he could talk himself out of it, he asked, "What was she like?"

"Our mother?"

"Yes. I was a baby when she ran away, so I have no memories of her. I've never even seen a picture of her, and I haven't heard any stories except that she was wickedly immoral."

John reached into his coat and retrieved a small gold locket. He gave it to Tristan.

"What's this?" Tristan inquired.

"Open it. There's a portrait of her inside."

Tristan stared and stared, the locket feeling hot and heavy, as if it was burning a hole in his skin. For some silly reason, his heart was pounding, and he couldn't bring himself to look. He tried to hand it back, but John wouldn't take it.

"You can have it," he said. "I have a few others as well as a full painting of her in one of the bedrooms at the castle. I can have a copy made and shipped to you if you'd like."

Tristan was trembling, and he frowned and flicked at the clasp on the locket. It was a dark night, but there was a lamp up by the wheel.

His mother was brown-haired, with merry blue eyes and a striking face. Most disturbingly, she was very young, and it had never occurred to him that she'd been little more than a girl during that tumultuous era. He always viewed her as aged and hardened.

"She was pretty," he murmured, stunned.

"She was."

"And young. I never remember that she must have been."

"When she went to Paris, she was only nineteen."

Tristan attempted to return the locket again, and John waved him off again. Tristan stuck it in his pocket, and he was suffering the oddest feeling, as if he possessed a magically sinful talisman, as if he'd betrayed his father and James by keeping it.

"What was she like?" he asked again.

"Foolish, imprudent, extremely unhappy. As I reflect on those days, I've also decided she was a bit mad, too."

"Mad...how?"

"She truly thought she could flee her husband with no consequence."

"Why would she think that?"

"She had a friend who filled her head with wild ideas."

"She shouldn't have listened."

"No, it was her downfall. She met Charles very soon after she arrived in Paris, and she convinced herself that she'd made all the right choices. But you know what he's like."

"The veritable definition of a rogue."

"Charles left her—as he always leaves—but she was a very romantic person. She clung to a deranged notion that he would come back to us. She insisted he would until it became an obsession. When I was a boy, I waited for him—especially after she passed away. I was positive he would rescue me."

"He never would have."

"I understand that now, but it was a tad difficult to accept when I was ten."

"She died loving him?"

"Yes, she went to her grave, whispering his name."

"Mad..." Tristan snorted.

"Probably."

Tristan felt as if the world had suddenly tipped off its axis.

He'd spent his life hating his mother, obediently touting his father's version of her as being cold-blooded and callous. But John's account was very different.

She'd been stupidly irresponsible, pushed to rash conduct by negligent acquaintances. If she was crazed too, then she'd been unable to make good decisions or pick a wiser path.

What was he to think? The tenets upon which his past was constructed had been plucked away.

"Did she ever tell you why she left us?"

"Because your father was a drunken brute."

"He was not," Tristan loyally huffed.

John shrugged. "Believe what you will."

"He wasn't!" Tristan declared.

John arched a caustic brow, appearing so confidently certain that Tristan was rattled. Another foundation of his life dropped away.

His father *had* been a drunkard, but Tristan recollected that he'd started in after Florence ran off. Had he tippled heavily all along? Had he been violent toward her?

His father had been a hard man, prone to grabbing his belt when he was angry, and James and Tristan had received their share of whippings. Had their mother received them, too? Tristan and James had been too young to recall.

What was the truth? Who should Tristan believe? His father who'd been so horridly wronged? Or Jean Pierre—a notorious brigand and liar?

"Are you aware that my father was John Peter Harcourt?" Tristan said.

"Yes, I'm aware of that."

"And you're John Peter too, although you use the French adaptation. If Florence loathed my father so much, why would she name you after him?"

John was surprised, and he chuckled. "Who told you I was?"

"No one. We just assumed."

"I'm named after Charles. His actual name is John Peter Charles Frederick Sinclair."

"Oh."

Tristan turned to watch the moon sparkle on the rolling waves. He'd been crammed full of unwanted information and couldn't wait to go below and wake James. His brother would absolutely have a fit when he heard what Tristan had learned.

He sighed and glanced over at John again.

"You're my brother," he groused. "My wife constantly tells me that I can't pretend you're not."

"Sarah kept saying the same to me. That's why she dragged me to London to meet Phillip and Fanny."

"I can't fight with you. Harriet won't let me."

"And I can't kill you. Sarah won't let me, and if I tried, Harriet would make me feel too guilty. I couldn't bear it."

"I guess we'll have to find a way to muddle through."

"I guess we will."

Tristan nodded as if sealing a deal.

"Thank you for giving me the picture of our mother."

"You're welcome. Let me know if you want a copy of the portrait I have of her in France."

Tristan pondered, then said, "I would like a copy."

He spun and walked away, John's curious eyes following him until he vanished down the ladder into the hold.

CHAPTER TWENTY-EIGHT

"We're here."

"We certainly are."

Caroline pulled back the carriage curtain, and Sarah stared out at the church. Neither of them moved, and Sarah in particular was frozen in her seat.

Sheldon had invited his servants, and she'd invited hers, so people would have walked, and there would be a crowd inside. But the place looked deserted. It seemed ominous, as if no one cared that it was her wedding day, as if the chapel was empty.

A horse was tethered out behind, and it belonged to Sheldon. He wouldn't have deemed the occasion special enough to hitch his carriage. After all, he'd been married three times already. He'd be perfectly happy to ride home in Sarah's vehicle, and shortly, the carriage and everything else would be Sheldon's. There was no need to quibble over whose coach would take them to their wedding breakfast.

It was a cold, blustery morning in late November. The clouds were angry and gray, rain squalls blowing in. She yearned to be in a cozy parlor at Bramble Bay and sitting in front of a warm fire. She couldn't shake the perception that she'd arrived to attend a funeral.

Her own.

While she was resigned to her fate, shouldn't she have felt a bit of joy? If she couldn't feel any joy, couldn't she at least feel relieved?

"Tell me I'm doing the right thing," she murmured to Caroline.

"I won't tell you that. You're *not* doing the right thing."

"Caroline, please. We've been through this. I need you to be on my side."

"There has to be a better way. We just have to come up with a different plan."

"What plan? I'm out of options."

"You are not."

"We've discussed this. I can wed Sheldon to protect myself and my child. Or I can flee Bramble Bay, check myself into a convent, and have the baby there. I'd have to allow them to give it away to strangers."

"Then give it away."

"Are you mad?"

"Women do it all the time. You wouldn't be the first. Save yourself. Don't let Sheldon manipulate you like this."

"Manipulate me? Is that what you think is happening?"

"Yes, it's absolutely what is happening."

"I asked him to marry me."

"You shouldn't have."

The footman was lowering the step, preparing to open the door, and Sarah reached for the latch, wanting to be inside, to get it over with so she'd quit debating. Once the vows were spoken, there would be no going back, and her nerves would calm.

She rose to climb out, but Caroline clasped her wrist and yanked her to her seat.

"Don't do it, Sarah," Caroline pleaded.

"Sheldon is waiting for me."

"So let him wait. Let's leave. Let's just take off."

"To where?"

"To wherever you like. We'll rush to Dover and book passage on the first ship we encounter that's sailing right away. We'll travel to Spain or Italy and rent a villa in the sun. We'll find an old midwife to tend you, and we'll lounge on the beach while you grow fat and happy. We'll forget all this trouble. We'll refuse the sensible marriage and the pragmatic choice; we'll beat the odds."

For a moment, Sarah closed her eyes and wallowed in the vision Caroline had painted.

She could practically see the spot they'd select, tucked on a hillside overlooking the ocean. They'd have a shaded porch and hammocks strung between the palm trees in the yard. Like a pair of native girls, they'd bronze their skin and go barefoot. They'd loaf and eat and dicker over baby names.

It was a pretty picture, and she supposed there were women in the world who could behave so outrageously. Caroline probably could, but Sarah couldn't.

She was who she was: Bernard Teasdale's daughter. She'd been raised on a quiet rural estate and had never committed any wild or bizarre acts until John Sinclair had crossed her path.

The past few months had given her a hint of the adventure that lurked on the horizon. But there was a reason a female remained at home, guarded her reputation, and obeyed moral strictures.

Temptations abounded, but they only brought shame and ruin.

Sarah would spend the rest of her life picking up the pieces from her pointless dance with pleasure and excitement. She was doing the best she could, making the choices she assumed were the correct ones. A braver female might have walked another road. Caroline might have flitted off to Spain. But Sarah was going into the church to wed Sheldon.

The ceremony was a new beginning for her where she would leave scandal and dishonor behind. From here on out, she would be an exemplary person, would perform good deeds, would be helpful and kind. Surely there was some redemption to be had.

"I can't go to Spain," she said.

"You *can* go. I'll stay with you every second."

Sarah patted Caroline's hand. "It's a fool's dream, Caro. This is reality. Let's head inside."

"But...but..." Caroline gnawed on her cheek.

"What?"

"Couldn't you delay a few more days?"

"To what end?"

"I have to tell you something. Promise you won't be angry."

"Well, that depends on what you're about to say."

"Raven went to France."

At the mention of France, Sarah's heart raced, and she scowled. "You told me he was in London."

"No, he's in France."

"What for?"

"To inform Jean Pierre that you're increasing and marrying Sheldon."

A wave of hope swept through Sarah, but it was swiftly followed by a wave of exasperation.

"What exactly is it that he expects John Sinclair might do?"

"We thought...that is...it might make a difference if he knew there was a babe. He might return and wed you himself."

"You thought a *babe* might make a difference to John Sinclair?"

"Yes." Caroline glanced away. "It was worth a try, don't you think?"

"No, I don't *think*."

"What if you marry Sheldon today, and Jean Pierre rides up in a week or two? What then?"

"Then I'll already have a husband, that being Sheldon—my neighbor who agreed to assist me in my time of great difficulty."

"Jean Pierre might come, Sarah," Caroline pressed. "It could happen."

"He is his father's son in every way. He won't come, and I can't believe you'd hurt me by suggesting it. Now I'm late, and this discussion is ridiculous."

Sarah banged on the door, and the footman pulled it open. He guided her down, and she spun to wait for Caroline, but Caroline didn't move.

"I can't attend, Sarah."

"Please?"

"I can't watch. It seems so wrong."

"Do it for me. Do it because I've always been your friend, and now, I need you to be mine."

Caroline moaned in misery and nestled against the squab. Sarah tarried in the muddy drive, feeling like the last person on earth, with no family or place or future. Behind her, she could hear the organist playing a quiet hymn.

She sighed and muttered, "Fine. Be that way. I'll go through it on my own."

She whipped away and went in. The vicar's wife was anxiously hovering in the vestibule as if she'd worried Sarah might jilt Sheldon. There was no one else to greet her, though. Not her parents who were deceased. Not Hedley who should have been present to escort her down the aisle.

At that moment, she was so forlorn that she'd have welcomed Mildred, but Sheldon had taken Mildred to London. She'd cursed and fumed and refused, but he'd taken her anyway and left her there in the new house she hadn't wanted.

"Are you all set, dear?" the vicar's wife asked.

"Yes."

"You look lovely."

Sarah knew it was a lie. She looked wan and exhausted and distraught, and there'd been no time to have a new gown sewn. Still, she appreciated the sentiment, and she forced a smile.

"Thank you."

"I'll tell my husband you're ready." She shoved a bouquet of wilted flowers at Sarah. "He'll step out with Sheldon, then the organist will begin the entry march. Come in when the music blares."

"I will."

Then she was gone, and Sarah was alone again.

The woman hurried down the aisle and slipped in a side door by the altar. The church was full, and people peered back at her. They grinned encouragingly, but Sarah pretended not to notice as the vicar and Sheldon emerged and stood together. Sheldon stared and glowered.

The door opened behind her, and she peeked over to see Caroline hasten in. Tears of gratitude flooded Sarah's eyes.

"I'm sorry, I'm sorry," Caroline whispered as she rushed in.

"It's all right."

"Of course I'll stand with you, and it will be over before you know it."

"Yes, it will."

The organ rang out, the loud chords urging her to proceed, but the altar seemed miles away, as if it was a mirage and she could never reach it. For a frantic instant, she was terribly dizzy, as if she might swoon, but Caroline squeezed her hand.

"I'll go first," Caroline said, "and you can follow me. Or would you like me to walk you down?"

"No, I'm fine. I'll follow you."

Caroline started off, and Sarah had a minute to reflect on all she'd lost, all she was giving away, all she was gaining. She'd lost the love of her life and was giving away her home. She was gaining a father for her child, security and companionship and her reputation protected and restored.

Was it an even trade?

It had to be, and she wouldn't consider that it wasn't.

She wondered what Raven had said to John Sinclair, what John had said in reply.

Did it matter? No, it did not.

In the lonely months and years ahead, would he ever think fondly of her? Would he ever regret his decision to abandon her? Would he ever be sorry?

No, he would not.

He'd left her at a roadside coaching inn and rode away. There was no other fact she ever needed to understand about the man.

Caroline slid into the seat reserved for her in the front pew. She glanced back, her calm expression pushing Sarah to take the first step. After the first one, it wasn't that difficult. Before she realized it, she was next to Sheldon.

The vicar nodded solemnly and recited the familiar words. "Dearly beloved, we are gathered here in the sight of God…"

She tried to focus, but her mind kept wandering to her wedding night. She'd deliberately ignored the whole idea of lying down with Sheldon, of removing her clothes and permitting him to touch her as John Sinclair had touched her, but the prospect finally crashed down on her. She couldn't breathe, and a swoon became more and more likely.

Do you take this man as your lawfully wedded husband? Yes. Will you love honor and obey? Yes. In sickness and in health, 'til death do you part? Yes.

"If there be a man present," the vicar intoned, "who knows any reason these two should not be joined together in holy matrimony, let him speak now or forever hold his peace."

Suddenly, the door slammed open at the rear of the church, a cold blast of wind racing in, making her shiver. There was muttering and stamping of feet that interrupted the ceremony.

Who had so rudely arrived? Couldn't they see that a wedding was in progress?

Sarah and Sheldon peered back. The guests were looking, too. Whispers commenced, and they grew and grew until the congregants were overtly exclaiming.

Several men were in the vestibule, but it was dimly lit, and she couldn't identify them. They were dripping wet, shaking rain off their hats and cloaks.

"Excuse me"—the vicar blandly addressed the group—"but would you please take your seats? We're about finished."

"You had better not be," a man retorted. "Not after I've traveled all this way to stop her."

He sauntered in, and Sarah blinked and blinked as Sheldon blanched with shock. It seemed as if John Sinclair was smiling at her, but that couldn't be right.

John Sinclair didn't care about her. John Sinclair was in France.

He was attired much as he'd been when they'd originally met: flowing white shirt, tan trousers, black boots. Since it was nearly winter, he'd added a wool coat over top. He was armed with his usual pistol and sword, and he brazenly marched in with the weapons strapped to his belt.

He spoke to the vicar. "Sir, what was the question you just posed?"

"I asked if anyone objected to this union."

"I am John Sinclair, and I object."

The response brought gasps and mumblings of *I've never heard the likes! Not in all my days!*

The vicar's query was rhetorical, an ancient formality that was still included in the vows, but no one ever protested. No one demanded a ceremony be halted. It simply wasn't done.

"You object?" the vicar wheezed. "On what grounds?"

"On the grounds that she's mine, and Mr. Fishburn can't have her."

Appearing dashing and aggrieved, John stomped toward her. His entourage followed. Raven came in, then—to Sarah's enormous surprise—Tristan Harcourt entered, too. He was accompanied by another man of similar size and features, and Sarah could only surmise that it was James Harcourt, the Earl of Westwood.

There were excited cries from people in the pews: It's the pirate! It's The French Terror!

John ignored them and approached until he was directly in front of Sheldon. His brash advance yanked Sheldon out of his stupor.

"I can't *have* her," Sheldon scoffed. "You're a fine one to talk, you bounder."

"I am a bounder," John proclaimed. "I admit it."

"You have no place here. Be gone, or I'll have my guests throw you out." Sheldon turned to the vicar and said, "Keep going. This scoundrel has no right to interrupt."

The vicar stammered, "Ah…I've never actually had an objection before. Once a protest is voiced, I don't believe I can continue."

"Oh, for pity's sake," Sheldon grumbled. "I am the largest landowner in the neighborhood. My donations pay your salary and buy the candles for this decrepit building. I'm ordering you to continue."

Yet the vicar didn't proceed. He was flipping through his prayer book, searching for instructions on how to handle the situation.

Sarah began to tremble, emotions pummeling her: fury, elation, dismay, shame, gladness. She'd never been happier in her entire life. She'd never been more angry.

How dare he show up! How dare he barge in and ruin everything! Hadn't he caused enough trouble?

She'd found a way to save herself, yet for the tiniest second, she considered hurling herself into his arms and weeping with joy. Was she mad?

She'd cast her lot with him once before, and she wouldn't succumb to such lunacy ever again.

"Get out," she scolded. "I'm busy, and I don't have time for your nonsense."

"Ah, *chérie,*" he murmured, "I wish I could oblige you, but don't you remember? I never listen to women."

He wedged himself between her and Sheldon, clearly demonstrating that a separation was occurring.

"Now see here," Sheldon blustered, "I don't know what you think is—"

"Don't you? I *think* I'm stopping your wedding."

"And I am refusing to step aside. The contracts have been signed, the dowry accepted. You have no right to interfere."

"You can't have Bramble Bay," John insisted. "I gave it to her so she'd always be safe. She's not turning it over to you. I don't care what you promised her. She's not doing it."

"Bramble Bay is mine," Sheldon huffed.

"Over my dead body," John seethed.

He gestured to Raven, and Raven pulled Sheldon away.

"Sorry, Mr. Fishburn," Raven said, "but your presence is no longer required."

"Unhand me, you fiend!" Sheldon commanded, but of course, Raven ignored him.

They started away, Sheldon vociferously complaining, but he couldn't halt Raven's steady progress toward the door. Everyone watched—agog—as they reached the vestibule, and Raven pushed him outside. A phalanx of John's sailors was guarding the entrance, a determined wall to prevent him from rushing back in.

Raven returned to the front, and Sheldon was shouting, demanding to be readmitted, but they all pretended no ruckus was transpiring.

Raven drew Caroline to her feet.

"You stand with Sarah," he told his wife, "and I'll stand with John."

"Yes, that's perfect."

Caroline moved next to Sarah and Raven next to John. The Harcourt brothers eased in and stood behind them. Sarah felt hemmed in, trapped so she couldn't escape.

John linked their fingers and grinned up at the vicar. "Hurry up, preacher. My wedding banquet is waiting at the house. The food's getting cold."

Sarah was reeling, events speeding by much too rapidly. She didn't know what was best, but she wouldn't be bullied into marrying John Sinclair. It didn't matter what the Harcourt brothers wanted, didn't matter what Caroline and Raven had plotted out. It wasn't any of their business.

Since she'd met John the previous spring, she'd been bombarded by one catastrophe after another. She'd been bankrupted and kidnapped and seduced and abandoned. He'd proved himself disloyal, deceitful, and dangerous. He couldn't be trusted, couldn't be relied on, and at the first hint of trouble, he was out the door without a peek behind him to see what type of chaos he'd left in his wake.

They all believed she should wed him? Were they insane? She'd already suffered too much of love's peril and had barely survived.

"Stop it, John." She yanked away and scuttled out of his grasp. "I don't care what you've planned. After how you treated me, I'm not about to marry you."

He didn't bother to glance at her, but kept his focus locked on the vicar. "Go ahead, preacher. My friend, Mr. Hook, can answer for her."

The vicar was flummoxed, and he slammed his prayer book shut. "I really must have a few minutes to sort through the technicalities."

"It has to be now," John said.

"Sir, the lady doesn't wish to marry you."

"She'll get over it."

"You pompous ass," Sarah seethed.

The vicar was stammering again. "I…I…have a Special License that authorizes me to wed her to Mr. Fishburn."

James Harcourt, Lord Westwood, said, "And I have one that authorizes you to marry her to John Sinclair. I insist you comply immediately."

Lord Westwood approached and handed the license to the vicar.

"Do you know who I am?" Westwood asked him.

"No, but I assume you view yourself to be a gentleman of some renown."

"You're correct. I am James Harcourt, Earl of Westwood. I am a peer of the realm, and I am ordering you to marry them. We won't leave until this bounder—as Mr. Fishburn fittingly called him—is leg shackled and can't flee her marital noose."

"See?" John gazed at Sarah. "They're quite adamant, and you hate to have me fight with my family. They won't be satisfied until you say *yes*. We have to proceed."

"We do not," she snapped.

The vicar scowled at her and inquired, "Would you like to wed Mr. Sinclair? It seems that you're opposed."

"I am mortally opposed," she declared.

The vicar sighed and advised Lord Westwood, "Then I can't possibly continue. This isn't the Middle Ages. I can't force her against her will." There was a loud rapping at the door, Sheldon's bellow drifting in. "And there's the situation with Mr. Fishburn. I must postpone any ceremony so I can seek guidance from my bishop as to how this should be resolved."

Lord Westwood shook his head. "You're not listening to me, Vicar. We're *not* leaving until this Sinclair scoundrel is married."

Tristan Harcourt added, "If we have to remain here for the next ten years, we will."

John glared at Sarah, his exasperation clear. He never brooked insubordination, and his poor ego had to be crying out with dismay.

"Let me handle this," he said to his brothers.

He walked over to her, and she felt like a rabbit watching the hawk swoop down. She'd never been able to resist him, had never been able to stay strong or behave as she should. When she was around him, her common sense flew out the window, and she couldn't make good decisions. If he was kind and sweet and charming, how might she act? The prospect was too frightening to ponder.

He faced her, looking smug and cocky and confident, and she braced for the onslaught. But just as she expected he'd speak to her, he turned to the guests instead.

"Every bad rumor you've heard about me is true," he told them. "Last winter, I gambled with her brother, Hedley, and I won Bramble Bay from him. When I came to take possession of the estate, I didn't know he had a sister. I was instantly smitten."

"You were not," she huffed.

"I was," he asserted. "I seduced her and ruined her."

"Mr. Sinclair!" the vicar chided. "Mind your tongue. This is a house of worship."

John ignored the warning. "I enjoyed myself, too."

"Be silent!" she fumed.

"I'm a cad; I admit it"—he shot her a hot, searing look—"so I didn't suppose I should wed her. I'm not much of a catch—"

"No, you're not," she agreed.

"—and I decided she'd be better off without me. I signed over the deed to Bramble Bay so she'd own it and could keep it safe from her brother. All of you know what a wastrel he is." There were nods all around. "Then I went to France."

"You left me at a coaching inn! You rode off without a goodbye."

He grinned out at the guests. "Has it been mentioned that I'm a scoundrel? I believe it has." Everyone was nodding again. "A few days ago, my brothers arrived to inform me that I'd created more havoc than I realized. For you see, Sarah Teasdale is increasing with my child."

"You wretch!" Sarah wailed. "Is there any humiliating thing you won't say?"

"Some of you may have heard that my father is Charles Sinclair, Lord Trent." At the news, numerous women gasped. "So you're aware of my inherited penchant for low behavior. My brothers thought I should turn over a new leaf."

Sarah glowered. "You're not turning over any leaves with me, you despicable rogue."

He shrugged to his audience. "Once I learned of her condition, I couldn't let her marry Mr. Fishburn, could I?" The congregants shook their heads. "I had to stop the wedding to keep her from making a ghastly mistake—and to do this."

Sarah was wary, terrified of what he planned, and stunned when he dropped to a knee. He took her hand and smiled up at her.

"I love you, Sarah Teasdale. Will you marry me?"

"What?"

"Will you marry me?"

"No, I won't!" she hissed.

"And why not? The entire town knows you're disgraced, and I'm begging you to wed. How can you refuse me? What will your neighbors say?"

"They'll say I dodged a bullet!"

"Perhaps, but what if they're wrong? What if I'm precisely what you need most in the whole world?"

"You're embarrassing me. Get up."

"Not until I have my answer."

"My answer is *no*. Now get up."

She grabbed his arm and tried to raise him to his feet, but he was the most obstinate man who'd ever lived. He wouldn't oblige her.

"Tell me you never loved me," he murmured. "Tell me you don't love me now."

To her horror, tears welled into her eyes. She had worshipped him, had thought he walked on water, that he was amazing and charismatic and dynamic and she could have him for her own.

But he never let anyone be close, and she wouldn't tether herself to someone who didn't want her, who would never need her. With Mildred and Hedley, her life had been a tedious slog of not belonging, not fitting in.

She was making her own choices, building her own family, and she could pick any arrangement she wished. She chose companionship and permanence and commitment. What she *didn't* choose was turmoil and disloyalty and disregard.

He brought every awful thing in spades, and she couldn't imagine carrying on a day to day existence in the midst of so much drama and upheaval. With him, there would never be a moment of peace or tranquility or even a bit of calm.

He thrived on violence and lies and deception. If he promised himself to her, how could she believe him? Would he even stay? He'd likely speak vows, then stroll out the door and never come back. Where was the benefit in that?

"Don't you dare start crying," he said. "You know I can't bear it when you're sad."

"Then don't do this to me."

"What should I do instead? Should I leave you to that old reprobate who would steal your property from you? *Non, chérie,* I cannot allow it to happen."

"You're asking too much of me."

"Am I? I don't think I'm asking nearly enough."

"I'm so confused," she moaned. "I don't understand why you're here."

"I want you to marry me—right here, right now. I want you to love me forever so I will always be yours. I want to sail my ship into the bay outside Bramble Bay Manor, to look up at the parlor and see a candle burning in the window just for me. I want to know you are waiting. I want to know that I am welcomed home."

The pretty speech rattled her. A few of the tears that had threatened slid down her cheeks. What woman could remain unaffected by such endearing words? Could she?

"Have me, Sarah." He kissed the center of her palm. "Let me be your husband. Let me be a father to this child we've created. I'll spend the rest of my life making you happy."

Her uncertainty increased, and she took a deep breath, then slowly exhaled. He was adept at manipulating her, at bending her to his will, and he was professing sentiment she'd been yearning to hear. Yet how could she trust him?

"You can't mean it," she muttered. "You can't possibly."

"Why would you say so? In France, I would stand on the ramparts of my castle and stare out toward England. I would picture you on the other side of the water. It seemed as if you were calling to me."

She frowned. "I did that, too."

"While I was there, guess what I realized?"

"What?"

"Without you, I'm nothing at all."

"Please get up," she said again. She pulled on his wrist, and this time, he obeyed.

He towered over her, looking wonderful and magnificent and just as dashing as he'd been that very first day out on the road.

She was deluged by happy memories. When she was with him,

she felt vibrant and electrically alive. She would have killed for him. She would have died for him. How had she forgotten his potent effect? How had that joy slipped away?

The church door opened again, and three women entered. As they stepped from the dark vestibule, Sarah was stunned to see it was Fanny, Helen, and Harriet. There were two men with them, Fanny's husband Michael and their brother Phillip. His wife Anne had accompanied them, too.

The group halted, taking in the odd scene, and Fanny asked, "We're not too late, are we?"

"No," Lord Westwood said. "You haven't missed it. In fact, we're still trying to determine whether it will occur or not."

"Don't be ridiculous," Fanny scoffed. "Of course it's going to occur. We won't accept any other ending." She scowled at her sisters. "Will we?"

"No," the twins replied together.

Lord Westwood explained, "Miss Teasdale isn't too keen on having him as a husband."

"I can hardly blame her," Fanny retorted. "He *is* Charles's son after all, but he's changing his ways." She glared at John. "Aren't you?"

The three sisters marched up the aisle, the others trailing after them. They stopped and stood with Raven and Caroline, all except for Harriet who walked to John.

"You promised to behave better," she scolded.

"I went to France because I thought it was best for her."

"You left her alone and in trouble."

He shrugged, actually looking abashed. "I hadn't been informed of her condition, and I came as soon as your husband notified me."

"I'm glad to hear it. You're improving already. I knew there was hope for you." She stared at Sarah. "Has he proposed?"

"Yes."

"Down on one knee, humbled and contrite?"

"Well...down on one knee. I don't suppose he's ever been humble or contrite."

"No, I don't suppose he has," Harriet agreed. "If he's proposed, what is the problem?"

"I'm afraid he won't stay with me, that he won't love me, that he doesn't mean it."

"I can't force him to love you," Harriet firmly stated, "but he'll stay. Won't you, John? I'm demanding it of you. What is your answer?"

"I can't refuse you, Harriet."

"No, you can't." Harriet smiled at Sarah. "He'll stay, Sarah. Always. I swear it to you."

"Until my dying day, *chérie,*" John vowed. "I will love you 'til I draw my last breath."

His siblings approached—Fanny, Helen, Phillip—so they were behind him. Tristan and James Harcourt—his other siblings—came, too. John peered over his shoulder at them, then at Sarah.

"My family is here, Sarah. They have given me their blessing, so I ask you in front of them. How will you reply? Will you have me?"

Sarah gazed at John, surrounded by the siblings he'd never wanted and had declined to claim. He was one of them now, their bond blossoming, and over the years, it would continue to grow.

She looked over at Caroline, snuggled with her darling Raven Hook.

She remembered the prior summer when she'd been so happy, so filled with elation she could have burst.

John, Jean Pierre could make a woman feel that sort of joy. He could make a woman feel special and unique. He'd offered himself to her, with his family looking on. How could she say *no*?

"Ask me again," she told him.

He dropped to a knee and clasped her hand. "My dearest, Sarah, will you marry me. Will you have me?"

"Yes, my dearest, Jean Pierre. I will have you forever. I will have you 'til my dying day."

He paused for a moment, then pushed to his feet. He grinned his devil's grin.

"I knew I could convince you."

She snorted with disgust. "Oh, you're the worst."

"Yes, I am, but you're very, very lucky."

"Why is that?"

"Because I'm yours, and you'll never be shed of me."

"You're mine," she murmured. "I like the sound of it."

"So…can we get married? How many more times must I ask?"

"No more times." Sarah nodded, satisfied and contented and finally at the spot where she'd always belonged. "Yes, Jean Pierre, we can get married. Right here. Right now."

He led her to the altar, as the guests in the pews began to cheer.

EPILOGUE

"You didn't attend Fanny's anniversary party."

"No, I didn't."

Charles stared across his desk at Phillip. They were in Charles's library, having a companionable brandy. He'd been out of town, and upon arriving back in the city, his initial act had been to invite Phillip to visit.

He sipped his drink and studied his oldest child, being constantly surprised by how they could be so similar but so different.

Phillip was kind and generous and noble. He possessed a sense of duty and loyalty that mystified Charles, that exasperated him but that made him proud, too. He was glad he'd sired such a fine man, but he attributed Phillip's stellar characteristics to the grandparents who'd raised him. Charles had had naught to do with it.

He knew he should feel more of a bond with his children, but he didn't. He and Phillip had a relationship because Phillip pursued it, because Phillip insisted on it. If the situation had been left to Charles, no connection would have been considered.

"I was going to come and fetch you," Phillip complained. "I'd have dragged you over to Fanny's whether you agreed to attend or not."

"I was in Scotland."

"On purpose? So you wouldn't have to socialize?"

"Perhaps," Charles admitted. He'd deliberately traveled so as to miss the event.

"You're a wretch, Charles."

"I'm cognizant of my faults. I don't need you enumerating them."

"Fanny took it as an insult. She said she didn't, but it was obvious she was hurt."

"I'll send her a gift to smooth over her upset."

"She doesn't want...*things* from you. She wanted you at her party—in the flesh. Though why she bothers—why any of us bothers—is beyond me."

Charles narrowed his gaze. "Are we quarreling?"

"I know better. It's a waste of energy to quarrel with you."

"Yes, it is. And to scold. Please don't."

If he was in the mood to be scolded, he'd dine in and have supper with his wife.

"Helen and Harriet were aggravated, too," Phillip said.

"I guess I'll be buying more than one gift."

Phillip rolled his eyes. "Would you stop it? They're fascinated by you. Be nicer to them."

"I'll try."

"Not that you deserve to be apprised, but they're both increasing. They spent the entire evening waiting for you to arrive so they could tell you."

"Is this your method of informing me that I'm about to be a grandfather again? You're aware of how I hate the news. It makes me feel so old."

"Everyone gets old, Charles. Even you."

"Unfortunately." He sighed. "I wish I was still twenty-five. That was a good year for me. I really enjoyed myself."

"Ha!" Phillip scoffed. "You caused too much mischief. The world is a better place, having age and reason slow you down. We're all grateful that you're not young anymore."

"When are the babies due?"

"Late summer or early fall."

He was pensive, pondering his daughters and the children they were having.

He wasn't a *family* man, had never aspired to being a father. It was so strange to be nearing fifty, to suddenly have offspring popping into his life.

He was perplexed by the changes and couldn't figure out what role he should play in their lives. Most times, he didn't think he wanted to have a role. But other times, he was delighted to be claimed by them.

If he was honest with himself, he was lonely. He owned several dozen homes, was rich as Croesus, could go anywhere and do anything. Yet he was always alone, and all those houses were so bloody empty.

"How was Jean Pierre's wedding?" he asked.

"As peculiar as I could have predicted. Nothing with Jean Pierre is easy or normal. He's like you that way."

"But he married our Miss Teasdale?"

"Oh, yes. He married her. I'm not sure if he came to the altar willingly. He said he was happy to proceed, but I wouldn't be surprised to learn that James and Tristan forced him with a pistol aimed at his back."

"Still though, he did the right thing."

"Unlike some other Sinclair males I could mention."

Phillip had tried to convince Charles to ride with him to Bramble

Bay for the ceremony. Charles had actually considered it, but in the end, he hadn't gone. Oddly, he regretted it and wished Phillip had been a little more adamant.

"I was wed when I was seventeen," Charles explained. "I could hardly have attached myself to any of my paramours."

"Don't remind me," Phillip huffed. "My mother was one of your first conquests, remember?"

"I've always loved women—and there are so many of them. They're all so pretty and too eager to accommodate a wealthy man like me."

"No, you love the chase, the pursuit and the temptation. Once you succeed in getting what you're after, you grow bored and leave."

"I suppose you could describe it like that."

Occasionally, he thought of those impetuous days when he'd been wild and carefree and negligent. He'd perpetrated untold misery, but he'd relished every minute of that era and wouldn't apologize for his behavior.

Age had mellowed his worst habits. He kept mistresses now. They were experienced trollops who were paid for their services and had no reputations that could be ruined. He was more discreet and determined not to sire more children. He hadn't in years.

"What is your opinion of Jean Pierre?" he asked. "He's quite amazing, isn't he?"

"He's exactly like you, which I wouldn't view as *amazing.*"

"When you realize what he endured as a boy, he turned out remarkably well."

"He did," Phillip agreed. "Sarah will have her baby just before Helen and Harriet have theirs. How many grandchildren will that be for you? Seven? Eight? Two from Fanny. Two from me. One each from the twins—unless they stay true to form and bear twins themselves."

Charles snorted with disgust. "You're cruel to twist the knife, Phillip."

"I simply like you to recall that you're mortal."

"Trust me. I always recall."

He frequently wondered—if his father hadn't made him wed so young, if his father had picked someone other than Susan—would Charles have been happy? Would he have tamped down his conduct?

Might he instead have married for love and had a fine life with a sweet-tempered wife? Or would he still have walked the scoundrel's road?

He was fairly sure he'd have been an awful husband to any bride thrown into his path. He was fairly sure he'd have been a libertine no matter what.

"I have something for you." He opened a desk drawer, pulled out a letter and slid it across. "It arrived while I was away."

"Susan didn't burn it?"

"You know my butler collects the mail and hides my correspondence."

Phillip studied the handwriting on the front. "Need I ask what it's about?"

"No."

Phillip flicked at the seal and read the words that had been penned. "Another daughter? Named Mary?"

"It could be."

"Do you remember the mother or the town? Can you give me a clue about her?"

"I was in York that summer. I had several dalliances."

"Why am I not shocked to hear it?" Phillip said. "Would you like me to find her for you?"

"No, you should find her for *you*—and for Fanny and Helen and Harriet. They'll want to be certain she's all right."

"Yes, they will." Phillip downed the last of his drink and stood to go. "I'll make some inquiries. I'll let you know what I discover."

"Thank you."

"Jean Pierre and Sarah will be in London next month. Harriet is hosting a supper for them. Will you come?"

"Perhaps. Or perhaps not."

"It wouldn't kill you."

Charles smiled. "It might."

Phillip departed, and Charles remained in his seat, listening as the butler escorted Phillip down the hall, as the butler helped him with his coat. The door shut behind him, and an annoying silence settled.

He went to the window and watched Phillip mount his horse, watched him ride away. Long after he'd vanished from sight, Charles continued to stare at the spot where he'd been.

Phillip was a devoted son and a good friend. And there might be a new daughter to join them. Mary. It was a pretty name he'd always liked.

He walked to the sideboard and poured himself another brandy. He swallowed it down as he contemplated his children in their various homes around the city.

Briefly, he debated whether to have the carriage prepared so he could go visiting. He'd intentionally missed Fanny's party, but that didn't mean he couldn't stop by now. He could take baby gifts for Helen and Harriet.

If Harriet opened her door and found him on her stoop, what would she think? The notion humored him immensely, but he couldn't imagine doing it.

Sometimes, he yearned to be closer to all of them. But on further reflection, it seemed too difficult to pull it off with any aplomb. Was it worth the bother of trying? Maybe not.

He returned to his desk and sat. The shadows lengthened and the evening faded away. The house was very quiet, and he was all alone. As he'd always been. As he probably always would be.

THE END

CHERYL HOLT is a *New York Times, USA Today,* and Amazon bestselling author of over thirty novels.

She's also a lawyer and mom, and at age forty, with two babies at home, she started a new career as a commercial fiction writer. She'd hoped to be a suspense novelist, but couldn't sell any of her manuscripts, so she ended up taking a detour into romance where she was stunned to discover that she has a knack for writing some of the world's greatest love stories.

Her books have been released to wide acclaim, and she has won or been nominated for many national awards. She is particularly proud to have been named "Best Storyteller of the Year" by the trade magazine Romantic Times BOOK Reviews.

She lives and writes in Hollywood, California, and she loves to hear from fans. Visit her website at www.cherylholt.com.

Made in the USA
Coppell, TX
11 January 2020

14384435R00177